Terry burst out of the church, hearing feet pounding up the aisle in pursuit. The limousine had departed, its place taken by a parked ambulance with open rear doors. Standing beside it was Dr. Zimmerman. Because he wore normal clothes—and had been so sympathetic yesterday—she almost started to him for help. Then she realized he, too, must be a Nazi—he and Lloyd and Nora and everyone else at Warlord's Hill.

She cut away from the ambulance and ran toward the nearest side street, afraid to look back. Within seconds, the first pair of hands—Catherine Schall's—clutched at her shoulders. She tumbled to the rough pavement, felt the upper half of her dress rip away, and managed to kick Catherine off and rise once more before a half a dozen black-garbed women again pushed her to the ground, tearing at her delicate skin with their nails and teeth, like crows competing for the flesh of a dead rabbit.

"What have I done to you?" Terry cried. "What have I done?"

Another Fawcett Crest Book
by George Fox:

AMOK

WARLORD'S HILL

GEORGE FOX

FAWCETT CREST • NEW YORK

A Fawcett Crest Book
Published by Ballantine Books

Copyright © 1982 by George Fox

Library of Congress Catalog Card Number: 82-50042

ISBN 0-449-20421-9

This edition published by arrangement with Times Books, a division of
Quadrangle/The New York Times Book Co., Inc.

Printed in Canada

First Ballantine Books Edition: January 1984

For my mother and father,
who know the territory

※ ONE ※

Drumbeats always hung on the edge of his memory after nightfall. Whenever he was certain the Nazis were watching him again, the phantom rhythms grew louder.

In less than twenty minutes of play at the craps table, the man who now called himself John Rawls had won nearly three thousand dollars, his first run of luck since coming to Coeur d'Alene. It would have been enough, along with what he'd saved from the road building job, to buy him passage to a refuge even farther from his tormentors. But as soon as he passed through the archway linking the gaming room and the lounge, he sensed that they had found him—or, more likely, had been lurking nearby, waiting until he achieved some kind of victory before they moved in to snatch it away.

I won't run from them, he decided. Not this time.

He sat at the end of the bar, next to a man sipping a half-and-half mixture of beer and tomato juice, the color of blood. It was a popular local drink. He looked away in distaste, signaled to the bartender, and ordered a double shot of rye.

"Heard you got lucky, Johnny," said the bartender, a broad smile of congratulations breaking out on his plump, youthful face.

John Rawls nodded, gulped down the shot, gestured for another. During the next hour, he drank with grim relentlessness, as if the whiskey were the antidote to a poison and had to be consumed in vast, steady quantities to ward off agonizing death. The beer-and-tomato-juice drinker went to the rest room; when he returned, he moved to a stool farther down the bar. Afraid of me, Rawls guessed bitterly. He had long known that he frightened people whenever he realized the Nazis had found him again. It isn't *me*, he wanted to explain. *They* are your enemy!

It had been eight years since he discovered the bastards were after him again. He had no idea why they had tracked him down. But, starting from the day of his escape from the VA hospital, he had sensed their presence. Perhaps they had been there from the beginning, nearly thirty-five years ago.

Where did it happen? Rawls wondered, silently cursing the head injury that had fragmented his past.

He remembered the yellow farmhouse where he and his sister, Rosemary, and brother, Vincent, stayed that summer, the first time any of them had been away from their parents for more than a night or two. But the farmer himself was a distant, overalled, faceless figure walking through fields of ripening corn. Better defined were the shy, pinched features of the little boy, no older than six, who was already at the farmhouse when they arrived. Had he been the farmer's son or, like themselves, a summer boarder? More important, who was the other kid—the slender, blond-haired boy who led them to the pit? Where had he come from? Why had he always refused to cross the loose, three-strand barbed-wire fence that marked the borders of the forest surrounding the farm, making the others promise not to tell the farmer or his wife that they had met and become friends? Rawls must have known once, but the truth had been cut out by the bony splinters that had penetrated his brain, further obscured by the agony that wracked his body for years after the beating.

Only the final night was fully intact. Even the pungent smell of those ugly, humpbacked pine trees tingled in his nostrils when he recalled that long-ago journey through the woods. . . .

Except for the soft, far-off drumming, the forest was silent. The blond boy led the way, his white sweater glowing like a beacon as he casually followed rutted trails that Rawls could barely see in the dim moonlight. Twice they crossed fast-running streams, using natural bridges of toppled, rotting tree trunks. Rawls, at twelve, had been as heavily muscled as most grown men, but he had had to push himself to keep up with the boy's swift form. He was grateful whenever Rosemary, leading the six-year-old boy by the hand, insisted on a rest.

"We have to keep going or we'll miss everything," the blond boy grumbled during a break. Only the day before had he finally agreed to guide his playmates to the source of the mysterious music they had heard while lying in their beds at night.

After they moved on, a faint chorus of male voices rose in song, but Rawls could make no sense of the words. Soon both the drumming and the singing ceased, but the blond boy continued to hurry forward. The drumming resumed, much louder now. Moments later they came to a broad, deep recess in the earth; light rose from it in flickering, pale-orange waves. At a gesture from their leader, Rawls, Vincent, and Rosemary went on their hands and knees, crawled to the edge of the pit, and cautiously peered over. The six year old, his lips slack with exhaustion, stayed behind, huddled against the trunk of a spindly pine.

Row after row of brown-uniformed figures were gathered below. Backs straight, the heels of their gleaming boots touching, most of them faced a white altar. Behind it, a scarlet banner rose almost as high as the pit wall. Atop the framework supporting the folds of rich velvet perched a giant steel eagle with outspread wings, its talons directly above a pattern of black, straight lines joined like the hub of a wheel. The symbol, frighteningly familiar to Rawls from movies, was centered in the flags carried on spear-tipped staffs by every other man flanking an open corridor ending at the altar. Between each flag-bearer stood a rigid drummer, staring expressionlessly across the corridor, as if oblivious to the motions of his own hands pounding sticks against the taut-skinned drums hanging from his neck. On the fringes of the formation, torches burned in holders driven into the pit floor.

"They're Nazis," Rosemary whispered to Rawls, her

3

smooth, olive-skinned face contorted with shock. "Like the ones who killed Benny."

"I guess," he replied uncertainly. Their cousin Benny had died in Italy, during a war that ended when Rawls was in the fifth grade. But why would enemy soldiers be *here*, years after their defeat? It didn't make sense.

A roar erupted from the throats of the uniformed figures. Rawls watched in fascination as an immensely tall man with wide, bony shoulders strode up the corridor and mounted a low platform before the altar. He turned to speak to the crowd but uttered only a few incomprehensible words before the blond boy yelled, "You're lying! They're *huntsmen*! They *help* people!"

Rawls abruptly realized that he and Vincent were alone on the edge of the pit. Rosemary and the blond boy had moved away, were quarreling; enraged, he was pummeling her with his fists. Blood gushing from a split lower lip, she covered her face with both hands and ran shrieking toward the trees. Before Rawls scrambled erect and hurried to his sister's rescue, he saw dozens of white faces flash upward.

He caught the boy, tried to pinion his upper arms, and found himself in a wild struggle. His slender opponent, far stronger than he looked, broke free, throwing swinging punches. Rawls again grabbed him and they staggered backward. Their locked, thrashing bodies tumbled over the pit rim, rolled together down the steep slope, separated at the instant of jarring impact when they hit level ground.

Just had the wind knocked out of me, Rawls thought. Then he tried to sit up and felt a stab of pain through his right side. He heard rapid footsteps, saw someone standing over him. He caught only a glimpse of the man's face—young, blunt-featured, skin so pale that it seemed almost gray—before the toe of a jackboot crashed into his left temple. . . .

Which are they? Rawls brooded, anger and recollected pain wrenching his thoughts back to the present. He peered at the cocktail lounge patrons, the few whose faces could be distinguished by the dim, red, indirect lights. They all fit into the club's regular Friday night crowd: men in Western-style shirts and jeans; women in the puffy-sleeved, garish blouses that

4

never seemed to go out of style in towns like this. A few couples shuffled over a tiny dance floor, moving to the twanging rhythms of an old Charlie Pride record. But, naturally, they would take care to look and behave like normal people, he realized, the fury within him suddenly bursting its bonds.

"Which of you are the Nazis?" he shouted in rage.

Except for the jukebox, the room fell silent, every face turning in his direction. A hulking bouncer from the gaming room appeared and headed toward him, but halted when the bartender shook his head. "Cutting you off, John," he announced softly.

"They *are* here," Rawls pleaded, raising his calloused hands in a gesture of helplessness.

"If you say so. You need any help getting home?"

"No, thanks, Vic," he muttered.

Seated on the bar stool, because of his powerful shoulders and arms, he would have looked over six feet tall to a casual observer. Erect, however, he proved to be below average height, the shortness of his legs lending his body an almost apelike appearance as he headed toward the street door. His meek acceptance of the bartender's order had shown the crowd that he wasn't likely to go berserk after all. But he could still feel curious or pitying or scornful gazes on him. They figure I'm drunk, he told himself with satisfaction, exaggerating his slight limp. So must the Nazis. They may not be as careful as usual when they follow me.

The beer-and-tomato-juice drinker waited more than a full minute before leaving the lounge by a side door. He had seen Frank, seated alone in a rear booth, follow almost on the heels of the man in the bright orange Pendleton shirt. It would look suspicious if they both went out the same way, especially after the attention their quarry had drawn to himself with his crazed howl.

He emerged in the parking lot, hurried toward the street facing the main entrance, and found his partner waiting at the next corner. "Hurry on up, Duane," the second man urged, his pale, almost chinless face knotted with annoyance. "He's moving fast."

"Maybe we should get the car."

Frank shook his head. "Parked too far away. We're liable to lose him as it is."

The gambling club was located in the hilly area between the business district and the city's small skid row, a low-lying collection of flophouse hotels, cheap bars, and brothels catering to zinc miners and seasonal farm workers. The area had few streetlights but, luckily, the man's orange shirt was so glaring he was still visible hundreds of feet away.

"Where in the hell is he headed?" Duane complained as they set out on foot, keeping in the shadow of storefronts whenever possible.

"A place where the bartender doesn't cut off a guy's drinks until two weeks after he's dead." Frank guessed. "Makes it easier. Down there, you hardly see anybody this late at night."

They had closed the gap to only a few yards when the orange shirt was abruptly swallowed up by blackness. Seconds later, they reached the narrow side street where the man must have turned. The street was even darker than the one they had left, the only light coming from two widely separated Hamms' beer signs.

"Chances are he hit the closest bar," Frank muttered. "I'll go on in and look. He might remember you from the club. You were sitting right next to him."

Duane shrugged nervously. "He's not acting . . . *right*, somehow. You know what I mean?"

"Neither would you if you'd put away that much booze in under an hour. Only surprise is that he can walk at all. Now let's get on with it."

But there was no need to search the bars. When they soon came upon a debris-choked alley, Duane glanced into it and put a cautioning hand on Frank's sleeve. Halfway up the alley, just past a battered cardboard packing case, a man wearing a bright orange shirt lay sprawled on his face, the toes of his worn shoes pointed together. Bubbling, alcoholic snores echoed off the alley's cinderblock walls.

"Tuckered out," Duane said contemptuously.

Frank waited until they entered the alley before he took the switchblade knife from his plaid jacket, just in case someone was watching them from a window overlooking the deserted

6

street. "Finish it quick," he ordered, flicking the weapon open.

Duane nodded, knelt by the man, and realized that the orange shirt was merely draped across his shoulders; the empty sleeves dangled over naked arms. He bent closer, almost gagging on the stench of cheap wine—and saw the sagging, white-bearded, grime-encrusted profile of an ancient derelict.

"Frank, it's not him!" he gasped, turning just in time to see his friend die. . . .

Rawls had left the gambling club intending to go straight to his rooming house, three blocks away. Then, despite their precautions, he spotted the two men following him. I was right, he exulted. They think I'm helpless, so they've gotten careless. Since anger still surged inside him, his first impulse was to turn and confront the pair, demanding to be told why they had dogged him all these years. That would be foolish, he decided. They'll pretend not to understand what I'm talking about, just like the others. How could I prove they were lying?

The answer was to maneuver them into a position where denials would be useless, their guilt certain. On this wide hillside street, setting such a trap would be impossible. But only a few blocks away lay the twisted alleys of Coeur d'Alene's skid row. The night was warm for Idaho in early June, so plenty of decoys would be available for his rapidly forming plan. He limped past the turnoff to the rooming house, unbuttoned the sleeves of his orange Pendleton shirt. He didn't glance back again, sure the Nazis were still there.

He found what he needed in the second alley he checked—an old wino sleeping on the ground amid slopping-over trash cans and stacks of empty cartons. The vagrant's knees were drawn to his chest, his upper body covered only by a ragged, sleeveless denim shirt. With just seconds to work, he hauled the limp figure into the center of the alley, where he would be plainly visible from the street. He tore off his new shirt, placed it over the unconscious man's shoulders, and glanced around for a hiding place. The best cover was provided by a large plank-and-cardboard case, the kind used to ship refrigerators and other heavy appliances. Only two of its sides were intact but, by shifting the frame closer to the alley mouth and crouching down, he was sure he couldn't be seen until the Nazis were past his position, not with their attention riveted on the inert body in the orange shirt.

As a kid, he had learned to recognize the opening click of a switchblade; he had no need to see the weapon. "Finish it quick," a man's voice growled, only inches from his hiding place. The order—and the simultaneous release of the knife spring—revealed that the Nazis were no longer satisfied to spy on him, spread lies that cost him jobs, force him to move on again and again. This time they meant to murder him.

Both pursuers' backs were to him when he emerged from behind the packing case. The taller man held his knife at waist level, pointed horizontally away from his body. Rawls would have no time to capture the weapon without warning the second Nazi kneeling beside the vagrant. So he lashed out, clutched the would-be killer's knife hand just above the wrist, squeezed the man's fingers around the handle, and thrust the hand and forearm upward by slamming the heel of his own left hand into the crook of the Nazi's arm, simultaneously kicking his feet out from under him. The man's head was flung downward to meet the ascending knife. Razor-sharp steel ripped through the fleshy underside of his jaw, scraped his teeth, pinned his tongue to the roof of his mouth, and finally plunged through the nasal cavity into his brain; death came so quickly that the only sound he uttered was a faint squeak.

"Frank, it's not him!" exclaimed the other Nazi, swiveling.

Rawls released his first victim, lifeless fingers still gripping the black handle of the switchblade, seized the kneeling man by the back of the surprisingly frail neck, dragged him to the alley wall, and slammed his forehead into the rough cinderblock with brutal impact. Like a patient housewife using a worn-out piece of steel wool to scour a stubborn spot of grease from the bottom of a skillet, he continued to scrub the wall with the Nazi's face until he was sure the unpleasant job was done.

Afterward, fury spent, he briefly peered down at his fallen pursuers. The one with an intact face looked to be in his early thirties, probably had not been born the night he had watched

8

the secret ceremony. Of course, the uniformed men in the pit would be old or middle-aged now; they must have recruited younger followers over the years.

Fear returned as he began to foresee the repercussions of what he had done tonight. He *could* tell the police he had killed in self-defense, that the dead men were Nazis with orders to destroy him. But they wouldn't believe it, no more than Vic the bartender had. They would put him in prison or, even worse, send him back to the VA hospital. So he would have to run again, find yet another place to hide from his persecutors.

He bent to retrieve his new shirt, but halted before his fingers touched the garment. The shirt must already be infested with lice and foul odors from the bum's months-unwashed body; the notion of wearing it again repelled him. He turned quickly and left the alley, taking care not to step in the two streams of dark blood inching side-by-side along the cement paving.

At a few minutes past three A.M., Victor Schall, the assistant bartender at the gambling club, closed up the lounge for the night. He was walking toward his car, the last in the parking lot, when an ambulance raced by with siren blaring, headed down the hillside. A little earlier, he had heard police sirens going in the same direction.

He suddenly envisioned the hurt and rage on the face of John Rawls, the wildness in his eyes as he stumbled out of the club. Probably has nothing to do with him, Vic thought, again rebuking himself for letting the little maniac go home alone. Still, it could do no harm to make sure.

The stocky young bartender drove off the lot, followed the route the ambulance had taken, and was soon stopped by two city police cars parked nose-to-nose to barricade the street. The ambulance had halted beyond the cars, and attendants were easing a motionless body—too lanky to be Rawls—onto a wheeled stretcher. More than a dozen cops were visible in the glare of patrol car headlights, concentrated on the mouth of an alleyway.

A patrolman waved a flashlight at Vic's car, indicating a detour. The bartender nodded, started to turn to the right.

9

Then he saw two more cops come out of the alley, supporting a man too injured—or too drunk—to stand unaided. The limp figure wore a bright orange Pendleton shirt. Vic slammed on the brakes so hard that he stalled the car. He pretended to have trouble restarting the engine until the straining cops hauled their burden closer to the lights, revealing a glassy-eyed, beard-stubbled, totally unfamiliar face. But where, he wondered, had the derelict got his hands on a brand-new fifty-dollar wool shirt?

"Move it or I'll call a wrecker!" yelled the cop with the flashlight. Behind him, the ambulance attendants were rushing another stretcher into the alley.

Vic Schall made the turn, circled the block, and drove up the hill to the rooming house where John Rawls had lived since coming to Coeur d'Alene seven months ago. His room was at the back of the first-floor hall. As soon as Vic saw that the door was ajar, he knew that the man was involved in whatever had happened in the alley, so seriously involved that he had run away. Despite his enormous physical strength, his attitude toward self-protection rivaled that of a ninety-year-old widow living alone in a crime-ridden slum. Whenever Vic had visited the place, he had waited impatiently in the hall after identifying himself, while bolts, chains, and double locks were unfastened. Rawls wouldn't have left the door open if he planned to return.

Vic entered the room. A glance into the closet, empty of clothes and luggage, confirmed his suspicions. The standing orders, if the man who called himself John Rawls left town without telling Vic his destination, were to report the news to the sanctuary, then immediately attempt to pick up his trail. But the circumstances of the disappearance were so confused that Vic wasn't sure how to proceed. Better get all the facts first, he decided, grateful that, in a few hours, decision-making would be out of his hands. Yesterday afternoon he had learned that the Master Huntsman was coming west again.

Harry Krug's plane, delayed by headwinds, landed in Albuquerque more than two hours late, so he was already irritated when he checked into the Hilton Inn and the desk clerk

10

handed him a message. It was from Vic Schall, asking him to call Coeur d'Alene as soon as possible. He crumpled the pink rectangle of paper and put it in his jacket pocket. Schall had violated one of the primary rules of security: Never use an outsider as an intermediary, especially if, as in this case, it produced a record. Krug had little fear of listening devices or phone taps or other electronic gadgets; the greatest danger to the sanctuary lay in the written word, even in so inoffensive a form as a half-sentence scrawled on a hotel message slip.

After going up to his room, he unpacked before telephoning Vic Schall, allowing his anger to subside. If Schall had risked contacting him, instead of waiting to be called, a serious problem might have arisen. He preferred to approach it with a controlled mind.

Nevertheless, he was unprepared for the message blurted through the receiver: "He killed two guys and ran away."

Under Harry Krug's icily exact questions, Schall told how the morning TV news had reported a passerby's discovery of the bodies in the alley. Photographs of the victims had appeared on the screen. Although the shots were several years old, Vic recognized both men; they had been in the lounge when John Rawls screamed out at the imaginary Nazis. He knew it wouldn't be long before another employee or club patron made the same connection and reported it to the police. He was right. Just before noon, a plainclothesman came to his apartment, showed him the photos he had already glimpsed on television, asked if he had seen the subjects before—and if he knew the name of the man in the orange shirt who had caused a scene in the club.

"You told the truth?" Krug asked.

"I had to. He spent so much time in the bar that—"

Krug cut him off. "You acted correctly. Just take it easy until I fly up there tomorrow. I'll contact you after I arrive."

He hung up the phone and began to pace the hotel room floor. The decades-old problem of the man who called himself John Rawls had taken a turn he had never anticipated. If he were sentenced to prison or a hospital for the criminally insane, the threat he presented to the sanctuary could be prolonged for years. The only hope lay in the man's history of violent behavior. Krug longingly envisioned him fighting

11

back when the police caught up with him, dying in a hail of gunfire.

A manila folder, propped against a stack of shirts on the bed, caught his eye. He picked it up, glancing at the single typed sheet inside. Tomorrow was Sunday, so government offices, libraries, and other sources of further information would be closed. Possibly, he could accomplish part of his mission before catching a flight north, but he disliked doing a hurried job even in so routine a matter, so he decided to settle the vital business in Coeur d'Alene before resuming his background investigation of Roy Hammil's wife.

⚒ TWO ⚒

Terry Hammil again glanced around the bare living room of their two-and-a-half room Greenwich Village apartment, checking for at least the dozenth time to make certain she had overlooked nothing. A single cardboard packing case remained, filled by her husband before he went for the car.

A lone black man from the storage company entered through the open door, taped the packing case, and presented Terry with a ballpoint pen and an invoice. A few seconds after signing the paper, she was alone with the half dozen suitcases they would take to Warlord's Hill.

The name of the vast estate—strangely inappropriate, she thought, considering its function as a sanctuary—had long been familiar to Terry, but she had never imagined that she would actually visit the place. Until six months ago, she had been the New York publications director of the Society for Environmental Action. For decades SEA had tried to get permission to photograph Warlord's Hill, the largest privately owned wildlife and botanical preserve in the northeast. Inevitably, the annual request was turned down, although the letter of refusal was often followed by a large contribution. "Ah, the guilty conscience of the rich," the local director had once grumbled to Terry.

The prospect of spending the summer exploring the almost legendary acres excited her—but neither she nor Roy fully understood why they were going to Warlord's Hill. Three weeks earlier, her husband had come home from the public relations agency where he held a junior partnership and told her that the president of the firm had asked him to perform an unspecified project for a New Jersey congressman named Lloyd Bauer.

Naturally, Roy Hammil had heard of Bauer. Although he didn't recall meeting the representative during his twelve years as a reporter in Washington, the man had lately been the subject of heavy press coverage; less than month ago, *The New York Times* Sunday magazine had run a lengthy profile on him. The only son of Paul Bauer, the retired industrialist who owned Warlord's Hill, he was considered the front-running Republican candidate for the U.S. Senate in next year's elections.

The proposal had been delivered by William Freytag, a Bauer family attorney, in the office of Merle Huggins, the president of Roy's PR firm. Since the Bauer Foundation for Geriatric Research was a major client, Roy's superior had cleared the assignment before speaking to him. "I suppose this has come as a surprise," said Freytag, a sixtyish, balding man with a genial smile. "We've been looking for a campaign media consultant—if, of course, Lloyd decides to make the run. You were his first choice."

Roy stared at the attorney in bafflement. "Why?" he asked. "I quit the newspaper business more than three years ago. And I was an investigative reporter. I'm not even sure what a media consultant is."

"Neither am I," Freytag admitted. "But Lloyd has decided you're the right man to handle preliminary research."

Roy shook his head. "In politics, 'research' always means travel."

"Unacceptable?"

"At least for the summer," Roy replied, explaining that his apartment building had gone condominium and that he and Terry would have to vacate by the end of July. "My wife has been ill. She's in no shape to go hunting for a new place on her own."

"I'm sure that's an easy problem to solve," Freytag said. He picked up the phone on Huggins' desk, put in a call to

Lloyd Bauer in Washington, and got through immediately. Freytag explained the situation, then listened in silence to the representative's reply. After hanging up, he told Roy that Bauer had offered the Hammils the unrestricted use of a guest house on the family estate until they found a new apartment. "He must *really* want you, young man. I've been a Bauer attorney for twenty-seven years and I've never once been invited to Warlord's Hill."

Roy held off a decision, telling Terry of the offer that night. "Merle didn't twist my arm after the lawyer left," he said, "but I could tell he wants me to do it. The Bauer Foundation account pays a lot of the bills, and it's the kind of easy, institutional stuff he always handles personally."

Terry listened to him with suppressed amusement, realizing perfectly well that pleasing Huggins would have no bearing on her husband's decision. Although he had never complained to her, she had long sensed that he regretted his decision to quit newspaper work. The move had been made impulsively after the head of his syndicate's Washington bureau had reneged on a long-standing promise to give him his own column. Now—even if in the once-despised role of a congressional campaign aide—he had an opportunity to temporarily immerse himself in politics, an opportunity she couldn't deny him.

"It'll be like when we were first married—apart for days at a time, all that crap," he said. "And you'll have to put off going back to work until fall. So just give me the word and I'll tell Merle and the congressman to shove it."

"Warlord's Hill, it will be," she said, laughing. "A change of scene might be good for both of us. And we have to move anyway."

Terry went to a curtainless front window, gazed down onto Waverly Place, and watched the van pull away from the curb, taking most of their possessions to a Manhattan warehouse. The sense of loss she had fought against for days finally began to penetrate. Another home was slipping away from her.

She heard a familiar, lightly insistent knock and turned to see Leah Golding—a small, dark, plumply pretty woman

15

with chronically agitated hands—standing in the hall doorway. Their upstairs neighbors, Leah and her husband, Walter, a theatrical lighting director, were the only friends the Hammils had made in the building.

"Just want to see if you needed any last-minute help," Leah said, coming in.

"Nothing left to do. Roy went for the car early so we could get started as soon as the movers were finished. I don't know what's taking him so long."

"Walter said that place you're going to in South Jersey is famous."

"In a way, I suppose it is."

"Funny," Leah said with a nostalgic shrug. "I've spent my whole life right across the river but I don't think I've set foot in Jersey since I was a kid. Every year in February, back in the forties, my father would take us to a resort called Lakewood. In those days, if you were a Jew with more than five hundred dollars in the bank, you were supposed to freeze your ass off in Lakewood for at least a week. Most of the big old hotels are kosher retirement homes now, and no wonder. Some winter resort—absolutely flat, the whole town. The only sports were ice skating and playing Ping-Pong in the solarium."

Terry's laughter sounded strained even to her own ears. "I'm sorry, Leah," she murmured, "but moving always gets me down. If I could, all I'd do until it's over is find a room with heavy drapes, pull them shut, and sit in the dark with my knees drawn under my chin."

Leah reached out, gently touching the sleeve of her friend's tailored khaki blouse. "Hasn't there already been too much sitting in dark rooms?"

"Yes," she said—and again her mind was flooded by the memory of that horrifying morning last December when she had picked up the phone and been told by a captain in the New Mexico State Police that her mother, father, and younger brother, Philip, had been killed in a head-on car crash.

Roy Hammil rushed through the door, and Terry realized that, as usual, they would start their trip at a dead run. "Garage elevator got stuck again," he explained with an apologetic shrug. "I'm double-parked, and the kid I handed a buck to watch the car looks like he might jump-start it and be off in thirty seconds."

He lifted the two heaviest suitcases, hurried back toward the door, and halted when Terry bent to pick up a third valise.

"I'll help," she said.

"No." His tone verged on sharpness. "I'll be back for the others in a minute. You take it easy."

"Such consideration," Leah remarked when Roy Hammil had departed. "If Walter and I played that scene he'd be strapping a steamer trunk to my back with rawhide thongs."

Terry forced a slight smile. Leah didn't know that she longed for the day when Roy would not lunge when he saw her taking out the garbage, or ask if she were tired after a walk of a few blocks. Only when he provided her with a normal ration of neglect could she be certain that, at last, she had totally emerged from the grief-induced depression that had held her fast throughout the winter and spring.

"Was hoping we'd get to talk a little before you left," Leah said. "This is like seeing Bonnie and Clyde off."

"We'll only be a couple hours' drive from the city. First time we can make it in, I'll call ahead."

To Terry's surprise, Leah threw both arms around her shoulders. "Anyway, you'll always be my favorite *shiksa*," she proclaimed.

Her laughter genuine this time, Terry returned Leah's embrace. She could already hear her husband pounding up the hall stairs.

Leah Golding stood alone at a window, watching the Hammils load the trunk of their 1973 Jaguar XJ6. Roy crammed in the last bag, and then gestured to Terry, who handed him the narrow black case she had carried out of the apartment. Even after shifting the larger pieces of luggage, he wasn't able to fit it in. He shrugged in defeat, opened a rear door, and put the case on the floor.

I shouldn't have come down, Leah told herself. People trying to move have enough trouble without entertaining last-minute guests, Walter had warned. But she had wanted to make sure her friend was all right. Only in recent weeks had Terry's delicately beautiful features lost the expression of furtive pain that had haunted them for months. Leah had been relieved to see that she showed only the normal tensions most women feel about breaking up a home.

She watched the Jaguar turn onto Sixth Avenue before going upstairs to her own apartment. "They get off okay?" Walter asked casually.

"Terry looked fine."

"Told you not to worry so much," Walter said. "I guarantee it—two or three weekends from now they'll be back with suntans, expecting to be put up overnight."

"No," Leah replied slowly, surprised at the deep, instinctive certainty of her own feelings. "We'll never see either of them again."

Soon after they left the Holland Tunnel, Terry was reminded of her first months with SEA. Fresh from Smith College, she had imagined herself composing thunderous pronouncements against the senseless ravaging of water, land, and air. Instead, with two other recent graduates, she had ended up in a windowless back room of the lobby's Washington headquarters, cataloguing and filing thousands of photos of mass fish kills, oil-soaked otters, insecticide-poisoned birds, and other victims of industrial pollution. This part of Jersey—a region of huge, anonymous oil refineries and chemical plants encircled by rancid marshes—had been a favorite source of material.

Roy was one of those men who fell into a state of silent, brooding introspection during long drives. For a while, as the Jaguar purred down the Garden State Parkway, Terry studied his profile. When they first met, she had considered his features ordinary, almost bland. But she had soon discovered that this surface impassivity was an illusion, like the motionlessness of a hawk perched in the highest branches of a tree, waiting patiently for a mild stirring in the brush below to signal quarry. Whenever something excited his interest, his heavy-lidded blue-gray eyes would take on a gleam of fixed concentration that she still found a little frightening; his facial muscles would grow tighter and harder. She had once remarked on the contrast to Langston Fellows, the syndicated political columnist who had then employed Roy as his chief aide. "It's a talent all first-rate reporters have," the elderly

18

newspaperman had replied with a reminiscent smile. "They can make themselves invisible when necessary. But the moving-in-for-the-kill look is closer to reality."

"Always those sick-looking bushes," Terry mused. "Does the view ever change?"

Roy wrenched himself away from his private thoughts. "Your guess is as good as mine, honey. I've never been down this way before."

His statement surprised Terry. From his earlier manner, she had assumed he was familiar with the area where they would be staying. She often thought about how little she really knew about the personal background of the man she had married. To Terry—so steeped in family history that before age five she had memorized the name of the ship that had brought her ancestors to America in 1654—Roy's disinterest in his past was unsettling. During their first few evenings together, she had learned that he was an only child who had grown up in St. Louis, and that both his parents had died years before. At the time, she had been amused at how reluctantly he doled out these sparse facts, unaware that further information would be even more unwillingly divulged.

They had been on the parkway less than ninety minutes when Roy passed her a folded road map. "Our exit has to be coming up soon," he said, "but I've forgotten the number. It's ringed in red marker."

Terry spread the map across her knees. The Pine Barrens—the forested region surrounding Warlord's Hill—stood out vividly. To the north, south, and west lay networks of state, county, and federal highways, but, with the exception of Route 72, only hairline indications of local roads marred the blank paper. Roy's markings showed that he planned to follow 72 most of the way to their first destination, the town of Chatsworth. To maintain the preserve's ecological purity, he had explained, the Bauer family refused to allow even guests' vehicles on its roads. They would have to garage the car, then finish the journey in an estate limousine.

"Exit sixty-three," she said.

He winced. "Passed it five minutes ago."

She again glanced at the map. "About twelve miles to the

19

next one but we won't have to double back. There are other roads into Chatsworth. They look easy to follow."

They were supposed to meet the Bauer limousine at three o'clock. Judging from the road map, their destination couldn't be more than half an hour's drive from the parkway exit. However the sun was below the treetops when, after being lost most of the afternoon, they rounded a sharp turn and saw a community of small, peak-roofed bungalows ahead. "This *has* to be it," Roy muttered.

Unlike her husband, Terry had been fascinated by the hours spent wandering through the Pine Barrens. She had read about the wilderness lying on the edge of the nation's most congested urban area but, having herself written so much environmental hype, she had considered the descriptions exaggerated. For a few seconds after Roy guided the Jaguar down an exit ramp onto a narrow, blacktopped road, she could still hear the parkway traffic. Then, with the rush of a descending guillotine blade, silence enveloped the car. Although they were almost at sea level, the air tasted as cool and pure as that of the New Mexico highlands where she had grown up.

The visual transformation was just as startling. Terry had expected a buffer zone of surburban homes or farmland between the parkway and the forest, but all she could see was endless walls of tall, dark green pines, extending to the shoulders of the road, their trunks growing so close together that only a child could pass among them. The trees' gaunt upper branches were clustered on one side of the trunks, positioned like antennas to soak up the powerful rays of the morning sun; the massed, arcing tops gave the entire forest a hunched, crippled look.

"I've never seen anything like this, Roy!" she gasped. "Pines aren't *supposed* to grow that way. Not so densely."

"Since Vietnam, I've never trusted a tree that's less than twenty feet away from every other tree," he replied wryly. "Incidentally, the road is about to disappear."

The blacktop had already given way to a scraped sand surface, which now abruptly narrowed to a rutted, two-track trail. Obviously, their map was inaccurate. They U-turned, tried without success to get back on the parkway, and then settled for another paved road heading northwest. It too ended in the middle of the woods. "Roads are supposed to *go* someplace, not string themselves out between abstract points," Roy complained, after three more baffling detours. A moment later Chatsworth appeared ahead.

The Bauer family's New York attorney had told Roy that the limousine would be waiting in front of a combination grocery, gas station, and lunchroom. Even in the unlikely event they missed the store—the only one in town—they couldn't possibly have overlooked the limousine—a long, flowing expanse of polished silver-gray steel, simultaneously out of date and bewilderingly modern, its top-of-the-fender headlights clashing with the aerodynamically perfect sweep of the engine hood. The chauffeur standing beside it wore a uniform that exactly matched the paint.

"What is that?" Terry asked as Roy pulled in behind the gigantic automobile."

"One of those twelve-cylinder monster Packards from the thirties."

"And I thought you did a great job of keeping up this poor old Jag," she said with feigned lightness, fighting the fatigue that, for months, had settled in on her body at dusk, no matter how hard she tried to fend it off.

The chauffeur, a tall, ruddy man in his late fifties, walked over to the Jaguar. "Mr. and Mrs. Hammil?" he asked.

"Sorry we're so late," Roy said. "We got lost."

"Everyone does, sir, the first time they come into the Pines. I'm Gerald."

"Where should I park our car?"

"We have an arrangement with a local family."

They followed the Packard to a nondescript house on the edge of town and drove the Jaguar into a large, detached garage. Already parked inside was a sleek, cream-colored convertible with front-end chrome grill-work so ornate that it reminded Terry of the marquee of Radio City Music Hall. "A Cord speedster," Roy told her.

Gerald had already transferred their luggage to the limousine's cavernous trunk when Terry remembered the small black case on the rear floor of their car. By the time she retrieved it, the chauffeur had already closed the trunk. "I'll just carry this," she said. "Doesn't weigh anything."

Terry couldn't be sure how long it took them to reach Warlord's Hill.

Sinking into the plush rear seat of the Packard, lulled by the limousine's uncannily smooth ride, she soon semidozed, her head pillowed on her husband's shoulder.

The sun had set, transforming the world beyond the car windows into a vast expanse of darkness. In the beginning, she half-listened to the conversation between Roy and the driver.

"The congressman has been unexpectedly delayed in Washington until tomorrow," the chauffeur said. "I was told to give you his apologies. Of course, we'll all do our best to help you and Mrs. Hammil feel at home."

"Thank you," Roy said. "Why do you call the place Warlord's Hill?"

He's doing it again, Terry thought with drowsy amusement. When moving into unfamiliar territory, she had noticed years ago, Roy always asked dumb questions of the first person he met, as if he were still a muckraking reporter setting up an interview subject for the *real* questions he would spring when the victim's guard had been lowered.

"The name dates back to the American Revolution," the chauffeur said in the over-rehearsed monotone of a tour guide. "The mansion served as headquarters for the Continental Army forces stationed in the Pines. From the roof, in those days, a man with a pocket telescope could often see as far as the Hudson River. So the commanding officer, perhaps as a joke, dubbed the building 'Warlord's Hill,' an old artillery term for high ground overlooking strategically valuable targets. Even today, when a storm off the ocean has cleared the air, we can occasionally make out the beacon lights on the Empire State Building."

"And the World Trade Center," Terry murmured.

"I imagine so, ma'am," the chauffeur said after an uncertain pause, as if he had never heard of the World Trade Center but didn't want to admit it. "In any event, Colonel Seth Bassing, who settled the land in 1761, continued to call the tract Warlord's Hill after the British were defeated. It was an apt phrase in another way, since Colonel Bassing ran the biggest bog iron works in the Pines and forged most of the guns and cannonballs used by Washington's armies. When Congressman Bauer's father bought the tract from the Bassing family in the thirties, he promised to preserve the buildings and the land exactly as he first saw them. He kept his word.''

"So I've been told."

"Except for historic restorations, nothing about Warlord's Hill has changed since nineteen thirty-nine," the chauffeur assured them. "Nothing at all."

Terry had almost fallen asleep when bright light suddenly roused her. She sat up quickly and saw that the limousine had halted at a floodlit gate in a high, chain-link fence. The forest had been cleared of trees and undergrowth for at least fifteen feet on both sides of the barrier, which was topped by thick coils of barbed wire strung between Y-shaped steel yokes.

"Almost there, honey," Roy said, putting his arm around her shoulders. "We're at the main gate."

A brawny, stolid-faced young man stood by Gerald's window. He nodded when the chauffeur told him, "Phone the guest house and tell Wilma the Hammils have arrived."

When they started off again, Roy glanced through the rear window, watching the man swing the heavy gates closed before returning to a wooden guard shack.

"Who's Wilma?" he asked the chauffeur.

"Your housekeeper, sir."

"Hell of a fence you've got there."

"Species of deer and other animals extinct everywhere else in the country live in the preserve. And the Pineys—that's what the people around here call themselves—are incorrigible poachers."

The area past the fence looked no different from the rest of the forest until, nearly fifteen minutes later, the road gradually began to wind upward. At the top of the rise, the limousine broke out of the trees and the main house came into view. Terry had never seen a late-eighteenth-century American home of such immense size. Even though, in the pale moonlight, she couldn't make out architectural details, she sensed that the shadowed, four-story structure was starkly plain, as if the builder had started to erect an ordinary colonial farm-house and lost his composure along the way, adding room after room and wing after wing before his family had the sense to stop him.

Gerald speeded up when the house was behind them. The road curved downward again; at the bottom of the hill, the limousine rumbled across a plank bridge and she could hear the roar of water rushing over a nearby spillway.

"Home at last," the chauffeur announced.

The guest house—a two-story miniature version of the Bauer mansion—must have originally been the quarters of an overseer or foundry supervisor. It was also the first building with lighted windows they had seen since entering the gates. Equally welcome was the smoke rising from its chimneys; even back in Chatsworth, an unexpected chill had penetrated Terry's light cotton jacket. Waiting on the narrow wooden porch was a stout, white-aproned woman in her sixties.

"Wilma will have already prepared supper, I'm sure," the chauffeur said, gently braking the limousine. "With your permission, I will bring your luggage to the master bedroom."

As Gerald predicted, Wilma had set out platters of cold cuts, bread, and salads. They had missed lunch but Terry had not felt hungry until she entered the small dining room; to her surprise, she not only finished the meal but had a second helping of potato salad. After coffee, she and Roy went into the living room. They sat on a couch facing the wood-framed fieldstone fireplace. The warmth cast by the blazing logs soothed Terry's tired muscles like a miraculous, healing balm.

"When the driver told us nothing had changed here since thirty-nine," Roy said, looking around the room, "I figured he meant the landscape."

Terry abruptly understood. All of the room's furnishings—from the art deco ashtray on the coffee table to the black, dial-less telephone on the open secretary desk—dated from the thirties or earlier. There was even a glossily polished, floor model Philco radio in the far corner.

"It's as if *we're* out of place," she mused wearily. "They had showers in nineteen thirty-nine, didn't they?"

"Of course."

24

"Good," she said, brushing her lips across his cheek. "Because I'm going to take a hot one and head straight to bed."

"Been a rough day," he agreed. "I'll be up in a little while."

Terry suddenly released a burst of husky laughter.

"What's funny?"

"Something Leah said to me this morning, just before we gave her the apartment keys: 'You'll always be my favorite *shiksa*.' We were out the door before the meaning sank in. Is it possible, after living in the same building for three years, she doesn't know I'm Jewish?"

Terry awoke shivering with cold. Instantly she realized that the quilted down-filled coverlet had slipped off her body. She reached out for Roy but discovered that he had not yet joined her. Since only a few coals still glowed sullenly in the bedroom fireplace, she knew that she must have slept for hours.

Leaving the bed reluctantly, she traced the draft to a window that had been left open about six inches. She tried to lower it and realized it had lodged at an awkward angle in its crooked frame. All day, while she and Roy drove through the Pine Barrens, the air had been still. But as she struggled to push down the window, a strong wind eddied through the gap, penetrated the lace bodice of her nightgown, chilled her breasts.

She shoved hard with the heels of both hands and finally felt the window work free. It had started to descend before she heard the massed drumbeats, so faint and far away that, for an instant, she mistook the sound for the flutter of moths' wings against the panes of the next window.

※ THREE ※

His first view of the living room of Vic Schall's cramped furnished apartment told Krug that the man's corruption had begun. The nineteen-inch color television in the corner was the most overwhelming piece of evidence; it hadn't been there when he had installed Schall in the place. Equally damning were the copies of *Time* and *Playboy* on the cheap pine coffee table. Of course, Krug wasn't surprised. Schall had left the sanctuary for the first time less than five months ago and had been exposed to a complex, frightening world he had never known existed. In addition to picking up the trail of the man who called himself John Rawls, Krug would have to reevaluate the young huntsman's performance, decide whether he could still be trusted to function outside the wire.

But the John Rawls matter would have to take precedence. Harry Krug already knew the problem was even more difficult than it had seemed yesterday in Albuquerque. That morning, he had flown to Spokane, Washington. While waiting for the Hertz car he would drive to Coeur d'Alene, he had checked a local paper for the latest news on the double killing just across the state line. The story, shorter than half a column, identified the victims as Duane Cole, 26, and Frank Ruggles, 32, both of Butte, Montana. Few facts were added to what Schall told him over the phone, except that both dead men were ex-convicts, with long arrest records on armed robbery and assault charges. The Coeur d'Alene police, despite the brutality of the attacks, were using the term "homicide" instead of "murder." Although a construction worker named John Rawls was sought for questioning, he still had not been officially pronounced a suspect.

Krug's first words to Vic Schall, spoken as soon as the apartment door closed behind him, was the terse question: "What did you fail to tell me yesterday?"

For a few silent seconds, beads of sweat breaking out on his forehead, the pudgy bartender stared at the Master Huntsman's blunt-featured face. In a frailer man, Krug's weathered skin—so pale that it virtually merged with his close-cropped gray hair—would have looked unhealthy; in his case, it added to the aura of strength generated by his height and the thickness of his neck and shoulders and upper arms, as if his flesh had somehow metamorphosed into a layer of protective armor.

"The money," Vic Schall said in a barely audible voice. "He won about three thousand dollars in the back room."

"And had it on him when he left the bar?"

"Yes, sir."

Harry Krug shook his head in disgust. "He killed those hoodlums in self-defense."

Harry Krug had already figured out the answer—and realized that John Rawls could not be allowed to fall into the hands of the authorities. " 'Which of you are the Nazis?' That's what he shouted in the bar?"

"Yes."

"Did he ever use the word 'Nazi' before?"

"I'm not certain," Vic declared. "When he had too much to drink, he would babble nonsense about secret plots, people out to destroy him. But dozens of customers did the same thing. He sounded no madder than the rest."

"Less mad, actually," Krug said with an ironic smile. "He must realize that he's been under surveillance for years—and who has been watching."

"Impossible," Vic Schall stammered. "I followed orders to the letter. I made friends with him, won his confidence. But I asked no personal questions, did nothing to arouse his suspicions."

"I'm sure of it. Otherwise he would have killed you, not those poor wretches in the alley." Harry Krug looked at his watch. It was a few minutes past nine P.M. back East, time for him to find a telephone he had never before used and make his daily report to the Old Man. "I'll be back soon, Victor. Wait for me."

He had started toward the door when, in an urgent, almost throttled voice, Vic Schall asked, "Have you been to the sanctuary?"

"Only last week."

"My wife and my mother—are they all right?"

"Of course. Catherine is working in the mansion again, by the way. I'll give you all the news later."

"Thank you."

Krug's gaze flicked to the nineteen-inch color television. "I suppose you will have other questions."

"I don't understand."

Krug smiled paternally. "Don't be ashamed, Victor. I experienced the same shocks you did when I left the sanctuary for the first time—and, unlike yourself and most of the huntsmen, I spent the early years of my life outside the wire, had a better notion of what to expect."

Victor had noticed the other man's study of the television. "I mainly watch old movies," he said, a guilty flush rising in his round cheeks, "the ones they show in the afternoon and early morning. Did you know that Errol Flynn and Gary Cooper are dead?"

"I'd heard, Victor."

"And Ginger Rogers is *fat*?"

"It's the sort of thing we all learn to live with," replied the Master Huntsman, wondering with astonishment why the Old Man had authorized training Vic for duty outside the wire. As long as he had had the simple job of keeping track of John Rawls, his inadequacies had not mattered. Now that Rawls would have to be executed three weeks ahead of the timetable, they might constitute a serious handicap. That, even though unarmed, he had so easily trapped and killed two professional criminals showed him to be a wily and dangerous opponent.

* * *

Less than eighty miles north, in an isolated fishing shack on the wooded Priest River, John Rawls wondered if he might be insane after all.

He had rented the shack, using yet another name, a few weeks after he found work in Coeur d'Alene, had stocked it with a month's supply of canned goods. Always, when he came to a new area, he provided himself with an emergency hiding place, a place to run if the enemy found him again, giving him time to plan future moves. After earlier crises— like the night he threw the Nazi off the wrought-iron balcony in Key West or the afternoon in Iowa he outmaneuvered a carload of pursuers so skillfully that their convertible left the road and overturned in a flooded irrigation ditch—he had gone underground immediately, never learning his tormentors' names or even whether they had lived or died.

But this time there was a difference: the money in his wallet. Sensing that the Nazis were after him, he had forgotten about his craps winnings. Only after he had killed the attackers and fled Coeur d'Alene did it occur to him that they might have simply wanted his money. He had been only a few miles from the dirt road that led to the shack before the full effect of last night's whiskey had worn off; his brain was flooded with the awesome clarity that occasionally bridges a binge and a hangover.

That afternoon he had taken a chance and driven to a nearby logging town, bought the *Coeur d'Alene Press*, and hurried back to the shack. The front-page story included police mug shots and detailed arrest records of the dead men. Frank Ruggles, the elder of the pair, had beaten a murder rap in Butte before his twentieth birthday and later served a sentence for armed robbery. Duane Cole had done time for assaulting and robbing drunks. Ruggles and Cole had first met in Montana State Prison and had intermittently worked as a team ever since. Two years ago they had been arrested in Las Vegas on suspicion of mugging more than a dozen men and women who had won big in the casinos.

All that afternoon and most of the night, Rawls had struggled to sort out these apparently documented facts, reconcile them with what he had perceived as reality for so many years. If he accepted the newspaper story—that the two men *were*

29

ordinary thugs—it opened the possibility that the man in Key West had not been a disguised Nazi, just an unusually persistent fag. And the men in the convertible in Iowa might have chased him down the highway because he had shouted an obscenity after their convertible ran a stop sign and nearly broadsided his new Pinto. What evidence did he possess to the contrary—except for his emotional certainty that the Nazis were out to get him. *Paranoid schizophrenia* had been the damning words he glimpsed on the ward attendant's clipboard in the VA hospital. What if he *had* been mad—and, even more frightening, still was mad?

It had been nearly three A.M. before he had managed to doze restlessly in the sleeping bag he had spread on the fishing shack's raw board floor. After awaking, past noon, he still felt the same doubts. He tried to keep busy, arranging his supplies; sweeping out the shack; stripping, cleaning, and oiling his Sturm-Ruger .44 Magnum carbine; adjusting the weapon's Weaver V9 telescopic sight. But soon all the necessary work was done and he was again left with his tormented thoughts.

The sun was low on the horizon when he walked down to the rocky fast-rushing river and gazed out over the tall firs on the opposite bank. The trees around the pit had been a deeper, darker green, he recalled—unless the experience had been imaginary, a childhood nightmare. But how could that be? He remembered every terrifying detail perfectly, from the scarlet folds of the swastika-marked banner to the torchlit faces of the uniformed men massed in front of the white altar. Could he possibly have imagined a scene so vivid that it had shaped his life? In the jungles of Vietnam, he had used these memories to reinforce his will to fight, imposing the pale features of the Nazis over the brown faces of the real enemy that appeared again and again in his gunsights; it had made the killings easier, more comprehensible. He had told the doctors in the VA hospital about this trick but they hadn't understood; they simply stared at him with that fake solicitude he had come to recognize within a week of admittance.

He looked down at the burnished stock of the carbine, which he had carried with him from the shack. He had selected it, years ago, because no other model so perfectly combined long range accuracy, fast fire, and high muzzle velocity. But of what use was even the greatest weapon in the world if the demons opposing him were imaginary?

How often, Harry Krug wondered idly, had he checked into a cheap motel room like this one, just to make a telephone call and then wait hours or occasionally days for a return message? As far back as 1948, when Krug had gone on his first mission outside the wire, he had realized that the security measures demanded by the Old Man were too rigid and cumbersome. He had complained the night he returned to the sanctuary. "You are absolutely right, Harry," had been the quiet reply of his predecessor as Master Huntsman. "The regulations make no sense at all." And then the Master Huntsman—who also happened to be Harry Krug's father—had savagely smashed him across the mouth with the back of a thick-knuckled hand.

Only when the new fence was complete had Harry Krug fully understood the cause of his father's anger—and the real reason for the Old Man's seemingly excessive caution.

He placed a long distance call to the house in Chatsworth. An aged, uncertain female voice said, "Hello?"

"It's Harry, Grandma Miller," he replied. "Please turn on the machine."

He heard the usual whirring click and knew that his words were being recorded. For the next quarter hour, often speaking in the euphemistic code phrases he had learned as a child, he delivered his report. He declared his certainty that John Rawls fully remembered what he had witnessed in the pit so many years ago. Therefore, every effort should be made to find and assassinate him before June 28, the rapidly approaching target date for the purge of the last human threats to the success of the Old Man's master plan. If the police should find him first and he was held on homicide charges, he might tell them everything. Even if no one believed the story, the authorities might pursue the matter long enough to learn Rawls' real identity—or, he might reveal it himself under pressure. Either way, for reasons the Old Man well knew, the results could be disastrous.

Harry Krug ended the report by stating that Vic Schall was incapable of completing the assignment on his own. If the

Old Man approved the change in tactics, he suggested that a team of more experienced huntsmen be detached from their present duties and sent immediately to Coeur d'Alene. He realized that the June 28 plan had already put a strain on the elite force empowered to operate outside the wire, but, in this unexpected emergency, he had no alternative to making the request.

Krug hung up the phone and began the inevitable wait. Grandma Miller would immediately give the tape to one of the younger family members, who would rush it to the sanctuary. He mentally pictured the Old Man listening to his words on a cassette player, the only piece of modern electronic equipment allowed within the fenced perimeter.

Even if the Old Man recorded his decision immediately, Krug knew it would be at least two hours before the motel room phone would ring. Travel time between Chatsworth and the sanctuary made a faster response physically impossible. Nevertheless, in normal circumstances, he would have remained at the motel. But he had been disturbed by Vic Schall's manner; the man was obviously frightened by the occurrences of the past weekend, so frightened that he might prove unreliable in the difficult days ahead. He should be morally reinforced immediately—or at least debriefed of the information he had accumulated during the past six months.

The young bartender's apartment was less than a five-minute drive from the motel. Krug would have plenty of time to question Schall fully or—in the unlikely event it proved necessary—to kill him before he next heard the Old Man's recorded voice.

When the Master Huntsman had not returned by six forty-five, Victor Schall phoned the gambling club, told the manager that he had suddenly been taken ill, and said he wouldn't be able to report for work.

He started to turn on the television, but hesitated. Failing to hide the set from Harry Krug had been a serious enough mistake. Having it on when Krug came back would be even more stupid. So he went into the kitchen, opened a beer, sat on the living room couch, and waited, wondering edgily what punishment the Master Huntsman had in mind for him. He hadn't been deceived by the I-too-have-been-young benevolence in Krug's voice; beneath it had lain an undercurrent of icy anger. He mentally framed replies to Krug's inevitable questions, realizing that his best course was to sound a little dumb, honestly puzzled—but thoroughly loyal.

Not for an instant in the first twenty-seven years and three months of his life had Victor Schall doubted the teachings of the sanctuary's leaders. From the age of four, in the Bremen nursery school, he had heard over and over again the story of the eight families. They had all lived in the old Bremen, a town far beyond the woods, where they had worked for a great crusade to bring peace and order and justice to the entire world. Then an evil force—led by Jews, Communists, and other diabolical, subhuman cults—had gained control of America, plotted immediately to exterminate everybody who had opposed them in the past. Named on the first death list in 1941 had been most of the older men and women now inside the wire. Agents of the corrupted national government were only minutes away from making the arrests when the Old Man had warned the heads of the eight families, led them to a sanctuary deep in the Pine Barrens, and fed and clothed and sheltered them through all the years that followed.

Vic's first exposure to the strange, perverted society described in the training course for huntsmen selected to go outside the wire had not seriously disturbed his faith. For the first few days, he had been too swallowed up in confusion to even consider his assumptions—the bewildering number of sleek, bizarrely shaped cars on the highway on which he and the Master Huntsman drove north; the hundreds of people, more than he had ever seen together in his life, milling about the vast interior of Newark Airport's main terminal; his queasiness on entering the giant airliner, stunned to discover that all the inhabitants of the sanctuary could have fit into the center section alone; seeing the skyscrapers of Manhattan loom up in the window after takeoff, even more awesome than the photograph in the 1939–40 New York World's Fair guidebook he had once checked out of the Bremen Public Library.

But after the Master Huntsman set him up in Coeur d'Alene—turned over the garden apartment, bribed the manager of John Rawls' favorite hangout to hire Vic as an assistant bartender—the doubts began to seep into his consciousness. In the beginning he had followed instructions perfectly—refused to read current books or magazines or to attend films, though he had always loved movies. He already knew about television, having read an article on the phenomenon in the April 1938 issue of *Popular Mechanics,* illustrated by a photo of a bulky wooden cabinet with a hinged mirror atop it. Reflected in the mirror had been a tiny picture of Lyle Talbot kissing Iris Adrian on the neck. Usually the club set was tuned to football or basketball games, but occasionally a patron would ask Vic's boss to switch on the eleven o'clock news or Johnny Carson or a movie, usually a picture made after 1940. Even the last had yielded bits of disturbing information. As the weeks went by, the totality of his belief began to erode subtly, like little chips of tile falling off the surface of an ancient mosaic.

In the second month of his mission, he rented a TV set for his apartment, primarily to kill the hours of aching loneliness. He had been married less than a year when the Master Huntsman told him he was to be sent outside the wire. Lying alone in bed—without the warmth of Catherine's sleek, pillowing flesh against his body or the sweet smell of her thick auburn hair tingling in his nostrils—might have been tolerable if the assignment permitted compensating diversions, however innocent. But the Master Huntsman's orders had been firm: "Except for the enemy you have been assigned to befriend, you will avoid prolonged contacts with men and women you meet. Be polite, amiable—you were chosen because you *are* naturally amiable—but never put yourself in a position where you can reveal more about yourself than necessary."

And so, deprived of companionship except for a sullen, suspicious brute of a roadworker who, initially, reacted contemptuously to his friendly overtures, Victor Schall had settled for television. The same afternoon the set was hooked up, he chanced on the next to the last installment of a British-produced series about the Second World War in Europe. Narrating and appearing in the brief introduction was Laurence Olivier, a personal favorite. He had last seen *Wuthering*

34

Heights in the Bremen theater only a week before he left the sanctuary. Vic winced in pity at his first glimpse of the frail, sick figure on the screen. "The Rhine now lay behind them," the unexpectedly old actor had proclaimed, "and the Allied forces had begun to smell victory, unaware that the stench of history's most unspeakable horror lay ahead." Olivier's color image dissolved into a piece of gray, splotched newsreel film, showing a mesh fence topped by masses of tightly coiled barbed wire. Instantly, he had been reminded of the fence around the sanctuary. . . .

Vic's thoughts were interrupted by the ringing of the doorbell. The Master Huntsman had returned.

"There were so many things I just didn't understand," Victor said shamefacedly a few minutes after Harry Krug, carrying an attaché case, entered the living room. They were sitting across from each other—Vic in a corner of the couch, Krug on a straight-backed chair from the kitchen. Although Vic had asked most of the questions, he soon realized that Krug was conducting an interrogation.

"For instance?"

"The Old Man taught us that Americans who openly supported Germany in the late thirties and early forties were imprisoned or executed, that their descendants—like ourselves—are still outcasts. But no one I've spoken to here has ever mentioned this. I bought books on the war and found nothing in them about such persecution."

Krug's cold-eyed gaze, contradicting the understanding smile on his thin lips, had never left Vic's perspiring face. "The hatred has slackened over the years," he admitted, "but the Old Man felt that the safety of the sanctuary—and the maintenance of a defiant spirit—justified suppressing a few superficial, misleading facts. And you mustn't forget that murder warrants are still outstanding against many of us—including both our fathers, if they still lived."

"After more than forty years?"

Krug nodded. "You have heard of the Federal Bureau of Investigation?"

"Of course—the Zionist-controlled secret police."

"At least two of the traitors executed by the men of the old

35

Bremen were FBI informers, planted in the movement. In such cases, they put no time limit on vengeance. Members of the German National Socialist Party—some of them in their eighties—are still tried in Europe on trumped-up war-time atrocity charges. Why would the government here treat us any differently?''

''I suppose they wouldn't.''

''And other, much more recent acts would be regarded as murder—if the sanctuary is penetrated. The last such act was carried out by yourself, only seven months ago.''

The reminder had to come, Vic Schall thought, fighting nausea. He would never forget the stunned, sagging face of the ancient Jew in the faded blue hospital bathrobe, several sizes too large for his shrunken body, his eyes so clouded by drugs that he seemed unaware of the surrounding ring of torches and the brown-uniformed men holding them. At a gentle command from Dr. Zimmerman, he had sunk to his knees on the pit floor. And then the Master Huntsman had pressed the automatic pistol into Vic Schall's numb hand, gesturing toward the kneeling figure. Until he actually felt cold steel against his palm, he had not fully accepted the reality of the fact that, this time, the Ceremony of Passage would be performed by himself, proving to the others that he was capable of facing the perils that lay in wait beyond the wire. If he backed down now, he would spend the rest of his life disgraced in the eyes of his mother and his cousins and his wife and everyone else in the sanctuary. The Old Man, standing before the altar, had spoked the order. Vic Schall had then placed the muzzle of the pistol against the back of the Jew's wrinkled neck and squeezed the trigger. A set of dentures had shot from his victim's mouth with such force that they disappeared into the sand, like a frightened rodent trying to claw its way to the safety of its burrow. A triumphant shout had erupted from the throats of the assembled huntsmen, so loud that it drowned out the drums.

''May I go back home?'' Vic Schall pleaded. ''I just want to run the tavern again, like I used to. I swear I will never say a word—not even to Catherine—about the things I saw out here.''

Harry Krug decided he could risk letting Vic Schall live

until the end of the Rawls mission. Unlike the three huntsmen who, in the past, had defied his authority when they discovered the discrepancies between the Old Man's vision and the reality beyond the wire, the bartender seemed incapable of rebellion or even deep anger. However, he must not allow Vic to return to the sanctuary; this contemptibly weak man couldn't be trusted to keep a vow of silence. And another martyr's name on the Heroes Park monument always stiffened the resolve of the citizens.

Krug abruptly bent over, opened the attaché case on the coffee table in front of him, and took out a cassette recorder. "You will be home soon, Vic," he promised. "But you'll have to stay here until your replacements arrive. To help them in the hunt, I want you to repeat everything you have learned about the man we are after."

"I telephoned full weekly reports to the house in Chatsworth."

"I am not interested in the last few days," Krug said, switching on the recorder. "Can you recall him mentioning places he might like to visit? Even casually?"

"New Zealand," Victor Schall said into the microphone Krug held out to him. "He talked about New Zealand sometimes . . ."

It was nearly eight o'clock before the Master Huntsman departed. "I'll probably leave Coeur d'Alene this evening," he said, putting the recorder back in his attaché case. "Do not return to work—or even go out for more than a few moments. I don't want valuable time lost because the new men can't locate you."

"I understand, sir."

When he was alone again, Vic Schall gave way to the tension that had built inside him, clutching the back of Krug's chair to still the trembling in his hands. Muttering aimless recollections about Rawl's behavior, his thoughts had actually been riveted on Krug's smooth explanations of why the full truth about the world outside the sanctuary had been withheld. All lies, he realized with dawning horror. He had begged to return home, remembering the peace and happiness he had known there until the night he shot the old Jew; on reflection, he saw that, by going back, he was committing himself and Catherine and their unborn children not to paradise but to a prison.

He considered running away. But what good would that do? John Rawls, far tougher and more resourceful than himself, a man who once calmly mentioned that he had killed at least forty-six people during the war in that peculiar Asian country whose name Vic could never recall, had been running away from the hutsmen for years. And each time he fled they had picked up his trail as easily as a pack of hounds might pursue a fox whose hind legs had been crushed in a trap. Besides, his mother and Catherine would remain helpless pawns of the Master Hutsman's vengeance. The only remaining possibility—to go to the federal police, tell them about the sanctuary—was equally impossible, even if he were willing to betray the community that had been his entire world until six months ago. "By purging us of this vile parasite," the Old Man had intoned just before the Master Huntsman handed Vic Schall the pistol, "you join the purest, most exalted order of our movement, the men who will spearhead the way to our inevitable triumph." He had not added that, by blowing out a helpless prisoner's brains, Vic Schall and every other man who underwent the Ceremony of Passage now shared guilt for crimes committed before most of them were born.

Crimes. He realized it was the first time that he had consciously thought of the huntsmen's actions in such terms. Feeling a sudden weakness in his bladder, he started toward the bathroom, but halted when the doorbell rang again. Oh, God, he forgot something, Vic thought, glancing about the living room; he saw no unfamiliar objects. He hurried to the door, remembering as he swung it open that he had already heard the Master Huntsman's car drive away.

Vic Schall recognized his caller, involuntarily cringed as he back away from the threshold.

"It was you, wasn't it?" asked John Rawls, his lined, swarthy face rigid with fury. "All these years. You and others like you. Men who pretended to be my friends. *You* were the Nazis."

Vic, too frightened to run, released a single cry before Rawls' huge, powerful hands closed around his pudgy throat.

*   *   *

The phone rang less than five minutes after Harry Krug entered the motel room. "You have a message for me?" he asked when he heard Grandma Miller's brittle, quivering tones.

The tape player clicked on, and the Old Man's deep, precise voice echoed in his ear. As Krug anticipated, he approved the early execution of "John Rawls," then reminded Krug that he was scheduled to report to the sanctuary by tomorrow night.

"Your East Coast duties must take priority," the Old Man said. "I have detached one man each from our Port Jefferson and Washington forces. The Washington agent will come here to receive your detailed orders. The other man will first complete your aborted mission in Albuquerque, then proceed to Coeur d'Alene."

Forget about the damned Hammil girl, Krug wanted to shout into the phone. *She isn't important!* But no one ever questioned the Old Man—and, even if he dared, what was the point of protesting commands given by a machine?

※ FOUR ※

That morning, Terry Hammil had been jolted awake by a hoarse, frightened cry.

She sat up, momentarily confused by the unfamiliar surroundings; then her memory of the trip to Warlord's Hill returned with a sort of instant, splintered clarity, like the crash of a fine crystal wineglass on a black slate floor. Roy, lying beside her, uttered another cry, lower than the first, filled more with sadness and regret than fear. "Everything's all right," she said, gently shaking his naked shoulder. His eyes blinked open, stared up at her unseeingly, then closed again. The muscles in the shoulder lost their cable-tautness.

It was a strange switch in their usual roles, Terry reflected. She had lost count of the number of times she had awakened drenched in perspiration from a nightmare to find Roy's arms around her. But never before had she comforted him in the same way. He had always told her that he never dreamed and, until this moment, she had believed him.

She tried, without success, to go back to sleep, listening to Roy's now-regular breathing. The squeal of brakes outside dashed her last hope. She got up, pulled on a robe, and went to a front window. A boxlike green school bus—another relic of the thirties—had pulled into the graveled horseshoe drive. Wilma stood by the bus door, taking a suitcase from a voluptuous, full-breasted girl with milk-white skin and masses of auburn hair spilling over her shoulders. The girl stepped back on the bus, which headed toward the main house.

Terry glanced at her wristwatch, saw that it was a few minutes before seven. Considering the strain of the previous day—packing for the movers in New York, driving four hours along the aimless roads of the Pine Barrens—she was astonished at how fresh she felt. In Manhattan, she usually slept past ten on Sundays, managed to overcome lethargy only after her third cup of coffee.

She went downstairs and met Wilma carrying the suitcase in from the tiny entrance hall. "I'm sorry, ma'am," the housekeeper said. "Did I wake you?"

Terry shook her head. "That was a beautiful girl you were talking to outside."

"My daughter-in-law, Catherine. She works at the mansion." Wilma glanced down at the suitcase. "A few items I forgot yesterday."

"You don't live here ordinarily?"

"No, ma'am. With my son and his wife. I only move in when Mr. Bauer has company."

"I'm sure my husband wouldn't mind if you slept in your own home. We don't need much looking after, especially at night."

"No, thank you," Wilma said. "I like getting off by myself once in a while."

"Do you and your family live in Chatsworth?"

For a few seconds, the round-faced housekeeper looked at her without comprehension, as if Terry has asked if she commuted daily from Khartoum. "Oh, no ma'am," she finally said with a vague half-smile. "We all live here at Warlord's Hill. Would you care for breakfast now?"

"When my husband comes down. But coffee would be nice."

Nodding, Wilma carried her suitcase toward the servant's quarters, beyond the kitchen.

Terry opened the front door and went out onto the small porch, gathering the lapels of her robe closer against the damp morning chill. Her first daylight view of Warlord's Hill pulled together all the vague impressions of the night before, revealing that nothing was quite as it had seemed. The plank

41

bridge the limousine had crossed spanned a narrow, fast-running stream, a few yards from a small dam. What she hadn't realized was that the water pouring over the dam's steel-gated spillway fed into a wide lake. Tall pines on the far shore were barely visible through mists crawling over water so impenetrably dark that it might be covering a three-mile-deep trough in the North Atlantic.

Her gaze lifted, following the road to the top of the rise, not nearly as steep as it appeared at night. The mansion, though only on a slightly higher elevation than the guest house, dominated the landscape. The building was even more peculiar than she had guessed. Its towering outer walls were gray, scaling masonry, like the loose, about-to-be-shed skin of an aged reptile. Weathered chimneys jutted perilously high above the green, corroded iron roof; even supported by heavy steel rods, the spindly columns of crooked brick looked capable of collapsing at the first strong gust of wind.

Below the mansion, the bus had halted again, dropping off half a dozen men at a complex of perfectly preserved colonial barns and stables adjoining split-rail-fenced pastures running all the way to the pine woods. Except for the bus and the bib overalls worn by the workers, the scene could be taking place hundreds of years ago, when the surrounding forest marked the border of the secure world of the land's original settlers. Somewhere a horse whinnied, impatient to leave its stall for the false freedom of the pasture.

Terry turned and re-entered the house. After a cup of coffee in the kitchen, she went upstairs to dress, not expecting Roy to be awake. However, the four poster was unoccupied and she could hear water splashing in the shower. It took only a moment or two to locate the drawer in a massive oak bureau where Wilma had placed her undergarments. She removed her robe and nightgown, was pulling a pair of cotton panties up over her firm, flat belly when Roy, a towel around his waist, emerged from the bathroom. His sandy hair, just starting to be flecked with gray at the temples, was plastered damply against his forehead. Clothed, Roy Hammil appeared slim, almost slight in build; actually, he was as hard-muscled as a decathalon champion, a condition maintained by countless hours of merciless handball play or equally grueling workouts on the parallel bars he had mastered as a college gymnast. Terry had always been puzzled by the intensity with which he approached exercise, driving himself like a middle-weight boxer training for a title shot that, through supernatural intervention, kept being postponed year after frustrating year.

Roy's gaze fixed briefly on her small but exquisitely formed breasts, then veered to the unmade bed. He let the towel drop to the floor. Usually, she didn't feel passionate in the early morning. But—in this unfamiliar, anachronistic room, so distant from her normal surroundings—her own excitement grew as he walked toward her.

"It's a good thing I told Wilma to hold breakfast," she said, removing her panties and climbing into bed.

With the past several wearying evenings given over to packing cartons for the warehouse, they had not made love in days. Terry expected Roy to enter her with the driving force he usually displayed after a long abstinence. Instead, to her surprise, he took his time, gently roused her with his lips and hands before easing his body between her smooth, delicately fleshed thighs. Even then, bracing his muscular torso on outstretched arms to keep his weight off her, his thrusts were teasingly slow and exploratory, almost goading, for long minutes. Cool water fell from his sopping hair and broke like tiny raindrops on her body. One large bead enveloped her taut, pink right nipple. His head swooped down like an enormous bird, the tip of his tongue flicking up the moisture. Such unexpected gestures often pushed Terry to the peak of response. A warm, tingling wave surged downward from the nipple and spread across her lower belly. She clutched Roy to her with both hands, held his hard rigidity motionless within her, let her own body control the final throbbing seconds of the act. . . .

After they had lain side by side for minutes, Terry's head on his shoulder, she asked: "Did you hear drums?"

"That's a new way to put it," he replied. "Erica Jong will go crazy with envy."

"Seriously," she chided. "I heard drums last night. Way off in the woods. You hadn't come to bed yet."

"I fell asleep on the couch."

During breakfast, she grew increasingly aware of his restlessness. He had barely touched his over-easy eggs, obviously waiting for her to finish so that he could light a cigarette. "You know what it is?" he asked defensively, noticing her suppressed amusement. "It's not having the Sunday *Times*. I'd even settle for *The Philadelphia Inquirer*."

"You *are* desperate."

Roy summoned Wilma, asked if newspapers were delivered to the mansion. Her reply, as Terry had anticipated, was cheerfully negative. "Just as well," he said when the woman left the room. "If it's like everything else around here, the headline would probably read: LOUIS KO'S SCHMELING."

Terry shook her head. "It's not the paper, you hypocrite. You simply hate being in the country and always have. You even had a nightmare. Carried on like you'd been locked up in hell itself."

"I don't dream."

"You did this morning."

The phone rang in the living room—a loud, insistent, almost aggressive ring. Wilma answered it, then announced the call was for Roy. "Bauer got in," he said when he came back to the table. "We've been asked to dinner tonight. And he wants me to drop over at eleven. I'm afraid it's time to go to work."

Climbing the road toward the mansion, Roy Hammil again wondered why Representative Lloyd Bauer had gone to such trouble to obtain his services—and what those services might prove to be.

The recent *New York Times* profile on the congressman had offered few clues. It had been the standard piece newspapers ran whenever a still fairly young and extremely rich man mounted a grab for national attention in politics, focusing on the why-in-the-hell-would-he-want-to-be-bothered angle that was supposed to fascinate readers. With minor changes in period and ideology, the article could just as well have been about a Rockefeller or a Kennedy or a Heinz. The American offshoot of a German family that, before the Second World War, held vast international shipping, chemical, and mining interests, they had ignored politics until Lloyd Bauer ran successfully for the House. In fact, the representative's father had retired in the late forties, devoting all of his energies to developing the wildlife preserve at Warlord's Hill. The congressman himself appeared to be a stock upper class New Jersey Republican, complete with Princeton education and a voting record just conservative enough to please his largely rural and small-town constituency without alienating enclaves of labor union members in the northern part of his district. Naturally, *The Times* speculated that his eventual goal was the White House, but Roy Hammil had already taken that for granted, presidential ambition being to independently wealthy politicians what black lung is to coal miners.

As he passed the open doors of the sprawling barn that served as the estate garage, Roy spotted the cream-colored Cord speedster he had noticed earlier in Chatsworth. Half a dozen other classic vehicles were lined up inside, ranging from a black Model A to a glaring yellow Hupmobile touring car. Gerald, the chauffeur, was waxing the limousine they had used the night before. "Good morning, sir," he called out cheerfully. Roy returned the greeting with a wave.

He was admitted to the mansion by a lush-bodied maid with a mane of tumbling red hair. The sight of her lace-aproned uniform and clear white skin was as jarring to his sense of time as the furniture in the guest house and the cars in the garage; like them, a young, lovely Caucasian domestic seemed as out of place in present-day New Jersey as an abacus in the accounting department at IBM. She led him down a long, dark-paneled central hall toward a pair of sliding double doors. Before they reached it, two small boys— the elder not more than ten—whipped out of a side doorway and ran past on bare feet, laughing shrilly. They slammed the front door so hard that the stained glass upper panel—almost certainly an original Tiffany—rattled in its frame.

"The congressman's kids?" he asked the maid.

She sighed tolerantly. "Yes, sir. They take a while to settle down when they first get home for the summer."

"I guess you've noticed we're a shade out of date here," Lloyd Bauer said with an easy grin, rising from behind a massive oak desk, when the maid ushered Roy into a book-lined study. He was taller—well over six feet—than he appeared in photographs, with the assured but not overtly domineering manner politicians cultivated for TV talk show appearances; Roy had a hunch it came to Bauer naturally. Although he knew that Bauer was older than he was, Roy had difficulty accepting the fact at first. There was something essentially youthful about the man's tanned, handsome, unlined face and light blond hair. Even his choice of clothing—beige designer jeans and a white cashmere sweater—had the same quality of frozen post-adolescence.

"Just a bit."

"Always unnerves first-time visitors. And then, two or three days later, they start to wonder why this week's *Colliers* is late." Bauer waved him toward a chair, then sat down behind his desk again. "Seriously, my father's decision to live in a period of his own choosing isn't that uncommon. Henry Ford put millions of people in cars, but he ended his life on a Michigan estate that reproduced the era of his childhood so faithfully that automobiles were banned. And who's to say that sort of thing is wrong? Dad is very frail now, rarely leaves his bedroom. But when he looks out the window he sees the world that existed when he was young and vital, a world of promise instead of decay."

The world of the Great Depression at home and the first Nazi conquests in Europe, Roy Hammil silently reflected.

"I was astonished when you didn't succeed Langston Fellows," Bauer said. "Common knowledge on the Hill that you'd done all the work for years."

Here we go, Ray thought with dry amusement, the what-really-happened questions. Every new acquaintance with even superficial knowledge of his self-aborted journalism career asked them. However, he was unprepared for Bauer's insistence on keeping to the subject for nearly ten minutes. Reluctantly, Roy told how Langston Fellows had hired him after his return from reporting the Vietnam war; how, under the old columnist's tutelage, he had developed his skills, researched and wrote the series of columns that triggered more than thirty trials of corrupt federal officials, earning him and Fellows a shared Pulitzer.

"Nothing terribly complicated about why I switched to

PR," Roy concluded. "Three years ago, when Lang retired, I was supposed to take over the column. Instead, Jim Blum, the bureau chief, decided to discontinue it. Claimed that my name wasn't well-known enough to the small city dailies."

"But surely you got offers from the New York and Washington papers when the word got out?" Bauer said.

Roy shrugged. "A couple of weeks before Blum axed the column, Merle Huggins had asked me to join his outfit. I was a thirty-nine-year-old legman whose only real prospect in the newspaper business was to become a forty-year-old legman. So I took Merle's offer."

"Any regrets?"

"None," he lied.

"Well, I'm glad you made the move—and that Merle was willing to loan you to us for a while," said Bauer, wrenching the conversation back to the present. "I suppose you're curious about why I want you aboard?"

Roy nodded. "I'm registered Independent, have no experience on your side of a campaign—and, frankly, even honest politicians try to avoid the kind of reporter I used to be."

"And will be again," Bauer said, gazing intently at Roy's face. "At least for the rest of the year. You'll have an unlimited expense account, all the legal and research help you'll need. However, no one but myself will see your reports. I want a thorough study of the subject, everything you can learn between now and the filing deadline for next year's primary. Family history, childhood, education, sexual kinks, any piece of information, no matter how seeming farfetched, that could be used in a really rough campaign."

"Kind of overkill, isn't it?" Roy asked. The next Democratic senator up for re-election currently faced indictment for diverting campaign funds into a personal bank account. "Even in New Jersey, the odds are he won't run again."

Lloyd Bauer smiled without humor, his features no longer as youthful as they had seemed only moments earlier. "I'm afraid you don't understand, Mr. Hammil. You're going to investigate *me*."

After Roy left for his meeting with Lloyd Bauer, Terry finally resolved to telephone Leah Golding. Yesterday she had been amused to discover that her friend didn't realize they shared the same religion. Now she found the situation awkward. What, after all, could she say except: *Guess what, Leah? I'm a Jew, too. Just never mentioned it.* No matter how she rephrased the statement in her mind—more seriously, more flippantly—it sounded foolish. How long had it been since a member of the Hedricks family had really practiced his faith, been part of a Jewish community except in the most abstract and token way? More than a hundred and fifty years, she guessed.

Even as children, she and her brother, Philip, had viewed the past as an historic not a religious heritage. Their Sephardic ancestors had been in the first group of Jewish immigrants to set foot on the North American continent, disembarking from the *St. Charles* at New Amsterdam in 1654. Centuries before that, Hedrickses had been among the few court-favored Jews permitted large personal landholdings in Spain—until forced to flee the Inquisition, first to Holland, then Brazil, and finally America. Generation after generation they had prospered as bankers and merchants—but, as Terry's father had told her again and again, hidden deep in the family's nature had been a desire to return to the land. In 1846, only weeks after the Treaty of Guadalupe Hidalgo ceded most of New Mexico to the United States, Terry's great-great-grandfather, Raphael Hedricks, had purchased vast grazing areas from a war-impoverished Spanish aristocrat. A full-length portrait of her ancestor had hung above the fireplace at Two Moons Ranch; the expression on his lean, side-whiskered face had reflected a kind of benign, triumphant arrogance. *I have brought our family full circle,* the look seemed to say, *banished the descendants of those who once banished us. No man will steal our home again.* But, of course, it had been stolen—by time and mismanagement and, finally, by death. She thought again of that last dazed afternoon at the cemetery in Albuquerque, standing over the fresh graves of her parents and Philip, listening to a rabbi intone Hebrew prayers that made no more sense to her than they did to Roy and the dozens of other Gentiles who made up all but a handful of the mourners. As his voice droned on, all she had been able to think, over and over again, was: *Now Roy and I are both orphans.*

Well, to hell with it, she decided, striding to the black phone on the living room secretary. She picked up the receiver, heard a female voice say: "Extension, please."

"I'd like an outside line."

The request was followed by seconds of silence then the baffling statement: "I'm sorry, ma'am, but I can't do that."

"Why not?"

"We don't *have* any outside lines."

"Thank you," Terry said, hanging up the phone. She noticed Wilma standing in the arched entrance to the dining room, watching her with crinkled, pleasant, and, Terry suspected, secretly amused eyes. "There's really no way to place a telephone call off the estate?"

Wilma shook her head. "One of Mr. Paul Bauer's oldest rules, ma'am. If you want to make a call, Gerald will drive you into Chatsworth."

"It was nothing vital," Terry said, actually relieved that she could postpone her confession.

When Roy returned from the meeting with Lloyd Bauer, he was toting the black case which, Terry abruptly realized, she had left in the limousine last night. "Oh, Lord," she sighed, "I went and forgot it again."

He explained that he had recalled the case while passing the estate garage. Gerald had gone off for lunch, so he had simply opened the rear door of the freshly waxed Packard and found it wedged behind a folded jump seat. "Careful," he whispered theatrically. "It's contraband."

"What are you talking about?" she asked. Then she remembered, from *The Times'* article, that television was among the excessively modern gadgets Paul Bauer had banned from the preserve. The case held Roy's last birthday present to her—a miniature electronic entertainment unit including a cassette player, AM and FM radio, and a three-inch TV screen, all battery powered. "I guess you've heard about the phones, too?"

"When the congressman's father abandoned the contemporary world, he went all the way." Roy hesitated. "If you'd rather not spend the summer in the Twilight Zone, there's still time to find a place back in the city. Or we could rent at the beach here in Jersey.''

She knew that his words had nothing to do with a strange, probably senile old man imposing an obsolescent life-style on his family and employees. Roy must be worried about being unable to contact her directly while on the road, leaving her in the care of strangers who, however kind, were unaware that she was recovering from an emotional breakdown. ''The real world hasn't been all that great lately,'' she said, stroking his cheek with her fingertips. ''Maybe the Twilight Zone is what I really need, darling.''

Wilma came into the living room, announced that lunch was on the table.

Roy, probably to avoid being overheard by the bustling servant, didn't describe his meeting with Lloyd Bauer during the meal. Afterward—when Terry had stored the black case in a bedroom closet—they took a walk along the lake shore, climbing a meadowed rise south of the mansion. From it they could look out over a stretch of the Pine Barrens so thickly wooded that the only signs of civilization were a widely spaced chain of old-fashioned wooden fire watchtowers.

''Reminds me of the gun towers at the fortified hamlets in Vietnam,'' Roy remarked. ''The ARVN troops who were supposed to man them usually sneaked off when an officer wasn't around. Couldn't blame them. The Vietcong liked to zero in their mortars on the damned things.''

Terry realized that she and Roy were viewing the silent forest from different perspectives. What she found calming and beautiful he found faintly disturbing. ''Right from the minute we turned off the parkway, all this reminded me of Two Moons Ranch,'' she said. ''Not physically. The woods are too heavy and I miss the mountains beyond the trees. But the feel is the same somehow. It's as though I've come home.''

His wife seldom spoke of it, but Roy knew how deeply she had felt the loss of her family's land. The triggering events had been familiar. Her father, apparently a man without any business sense, had sold off parcel after parcel of the once-giant ranch to accommodate a grandiose life-style he could no longer afford. A prolonged drought, a steep fall in cattle prices, and back taxes had forced the sale of what little remained of her inheritance.

"Then this is the place for you, Terry," he said, although he had intended to suggest one last time they seek more conventional lodgings for the summer. He decided not to mention the baffling nature of the "research project" he was to conduct for Lloyd Bauer. Under the circumstances, she would be more comfortable believing his duties were routine.

"Is something the matter?"

"I have my marching orders. Bauer is only here to get his wife and kids settled in for their vacation. Tomorrow he's off for a local speech or two and then it's back to Washington until Congress recesses. I'll be going with him."

For nearly an hour after Roy left the mansion's ground-floor study, Lloyd Bauer remained seated, his troubled eyes focused on his large, clasped hands, interlocked fingers clenching and unclenching on the desktop, as if he were in the middle of an angry, silent prayer. It was a nervous mannerism he had continually to fight against, especially when delivering a speech to an unresponsive audience.

At last, knowing it was expected, he rose and went into the hall, climbing the maid stairway to report to the Old Man. His journey ended at the door of a fourth-floor bedroom overlooking the lake. He knocked once, then heard the Old Man's deep, still-powerful voice giving him permission to enter. As usual, though it was a pleasant afternoon, the heavy window blinds were drawn.

The Old Man, who had been reading a book by a dim table lamp, looked up slowly. "The interview went well?"

"I don't think he believed me. Not all of it, anyway."

"Is it important that he should?"

"Yes," Lloyd Bauer said. "You don't seem to understand. He's a dangerous man. When he was in Washington, many of the highest figures in the government feared him."

"He is no longer in Washington, however. And we are paying his salary, not a newspaper."

Lloyd Bauer shook his head wearily. "Why not use Harry Krug?"

51

"He already has the answers to the riddles Hammil will try to solve. Success would prove nothing."

"At least be more careful," Bauer pleaded. "Gerald told me they held a rally in the pit last night. Why take the chance with Hammil and his wife living here?"

"Inviting them to stay in the guest house was entirely your idea," the Old Man replied.

"It was the only way to make certain he'd accept my offer."

The Old Man shrugged his wide shoulders. "Hammil will be gone most of the time, and the girl will see nothing out of the ordinary. Nothing out of the ordinary ever happens at Warlord's Hill—unless I wish it to happen."

For as long as he could remember, Lloyd Bauer had tried to break through the cold, invisible shield of power that surrounded the Old Man, provoke him to a display of anger or doubt or any other human weakness, diminish his fear of him. Once again he had failed. "We'll be leaving early tomorrow."

The Old Man nodded and turned his attention back to his worn leatherbound copy of Hegel's *Logic*.

The next morning Terry Hammil watched from the doorway of the guest house as her husband drove off in the gigantic cream-colored convertible he had admired in Chatsworth. Lloyd Bauer was behind the wheel.

Last night's dinner at the mansion with Bauer and his wife, Nora, had convinced Terry that, thankfully, few attempts would be made to further integrate her into the social life at Warlord's Hill. "It'll be nice for Nora to have another woman besides the servants to talk to," Bauer said, mixing cocktails in the living room of the mansion. "This can be a maddeningly quiet place in the summer, especially after Washington." Nora Bauer's reaction—a faint half smile—indicated that, in fact, she didn't have the slightest desire for extra company. Like many politicians' wives, she was far less physically striking than her husband—a thin, pretty-enough brunette with slightly sallow skin and a habit of picking at her right palm with her ring finger. Except for a few stock pleasantries, she didn't speak all evening, her eyes remaining firmly fixed on her husband's actor-handsome features. Lloyd Bauer struck Terry as a too-studiedly charming but amiable man determined to put her at ease. "We're not nearly as isolated as we seem," he declared as the red-haired maid served the *chateaubriand*. "If Roy wants to reach you, all he has to do is call the Millers in Chatsworth. They own the house where you left your Jaguar. They'll send someone over with a message at any hour of the day or night. And Gerald will drive you into New York or Philadelphia—or Baltimore, for that matter—any time you feel like shopping or visiting friends." She realized that Bauer, like her husband, probably wouldn't believe that all she wanted was to immerse herself in this "maddeningly quiet place."

When the Cord speedster disappeared around a curve in the road, Terry started back into the house, pausing when she heard shrill cries. Two little boys in bathing suits ran past the front porch, heading toward a narrow strip of lakeshore that must serve the Bauer family at a beach. Hurrying into the kitchen, she told Wilma about the children.

The housekeeper, shelling a bowl of peas, nodded calmly. "The congressman's boys, Roger and little Paul."

"Shouldn't someone be watching them?"

"Someone is, I'm sure."

Despite Wilma's vague assurances, Terry left the house, following a narrow footpath that led to the lake. By now, both boys were in chest-deep water. The taller wheeled about, clamped both hands on his brother's head, forced him beneath the surface, and laughed as his victim's frail arms flailed the air. Terry walked faster toward the shore—then realized that Wilma had spoken the truth. About fifty feet past the beach lay a clump of the white birches that occasionally broke up the solid green of the pines, like wisps of pale hair growing out of a mole. A black, just-vaguely-human outline began rippling through the slanted, close-spaced trees at the same instant Terry quickened her pace; it slowed down when the smaller child reared up out of the lake, furiously spitting water. "You dumb creep!" he yelled at his brother as he splashed toward shore.

She waved at the other would-be rescuer, who had already

53

retreated back into the trees, although she doubted that the half-seen guardian had noticed her presence.

"You were right," Terry said when she returned to the kitchen.

Wilma snapped the last peapod. "Don't you worry, Mrs. Hammil," she said reassuringly. "No one is ever really alone at Warlord's Hill."

❋ FIVE ❋

A sense of solitude settled in on Terry Hammil a few hours after Roy drove off with Lloyd Bauer—but not the wracking loneliness she usually felt when he departed on a long assignment. The difference, she soon came to understand, was that they were separated as much by time as physical distance. He had left not only a place called Warlord's Hill but the long-past period in which its inhabitants still lived, moving on to a chaotic, uncharted decade called the 1980s. And, right now, she had no desire to follow him.

I can get well here, she decided on the first afternoon without her husband. I can get well because none of the bad things have happened yet. I haven't even been born.

All day her unexpected enchantment with Warlord's Hill deepened. Just before noon, she swam in the lake that lay only a few yards from the guest house door; like the clarity of the air and crisp, dark-green needles on the pine trees, the tingling, exquisitely cool water had no natural right to exist this close to sea level, as if a concealed pipeline had carried it down from a distant mountain range. Wilma had a lunch of vichyssoise, thin-sliced prosciutto, and a cucumber salad ready for her when she got back to the house. After the meal, she sat at the desk in the living room and began a letter to Leah Golding. But somehow the right words wouldn't come.

Finally, she gave up, crumpled the sheet of stationery, and

jammed it into the slash pocket of her denim skirt. She would try again tomorrow, she decided. She went over to the Philco radio and turned it on, moving the dial to a station she occasionally listened to in the early afternoon. Instead of the soft-rock music she expected, she heard a mid-thirties dance number, complete with violins and sibilant clarinets and a whispering snare drum. No matter how far she turned the dial, the same tune played.

For an instant she considered summoning Wilma, asking her why the set picked up a single station—but, of course, she already knew the answer. Somewhere on the estate, a Bauer employee was busy playing ancient radio transcriptions, channeled to this and all other local receivers by a Muzak-style system—yet another strategem to preserve the illusion that time had halted. Lloyd Bauer had remarked at dinner that failing health virtually confined his father to his room. She pictured a wispy figure lying in bed, listening to this outdated tune. She wondered if the old man actually believed that it was 1939. Or was he in full possession of his mental faculties, playing an elaborate game, amused at his power to compel his relatives and servants to act out a whimsical fantasy?

That night, alone in her bedroom, Terry removed her miniature TV-radio-recorder from its hiding place in the closet, feeling the same conspiratorial thrill she had experienced as a little girl, listening to her portable radio under the blankets at an hour when she was supposed to be sound asleep. She put the unit at the foot of the bed, inserted the earplug attachment to prevent Wilma from hearing, and switched on the eleven o'clock news. The screen, brightening to off-gray life, showed a row of plastic-wrapped corpses lying in the exercise yard of a Michigan state prison. On Saturday morning she had read that rioting convicts had seized the institution, holding more than twenty guards hostage. Apparently, she thought with a shudder, the crisis had ended in the usual way. She turned off the set and returned it to the closet, deciding to stick with 1939 a while longer.

During Sunday's dinner, Lloyd Bauer had invited Terry to make use of the estate stables. Except on unsatisfactory city park bridle paths, she had rarely had a chance to ride since her marriage. On Tuesday morning, following another night of deep, healing sleep, she decided to take up the congressman's offer.

After breakfast, she donned a pair of bluejeans, pulled on the handmade Mexican boots she packed on every move and so seldom used, and walked to the stable. Inside a young, overalled worker lethargically pushed a wide broom down a narrow concrete walkway between the rows of empty stalls. He looked at her with startled eyes when she asked for a mount, clutching the broom-handle so hard his knuckles whitened.

"I don't know you," he gasped.

"I'm Terry Hammil. My husband and I are staying at the guest house."

"Nobody told *me* anything. And I'm responsible."

"Call Mrs. Bauer. She'll explain."

"Yeah, I guess so," he muttered.

The stablehand hurried into the tackroom, shut the door behind him. Deciding the youth might be a little retarded, Terry went outside, propped her crossed forearms on a top fence rail, and studied the horses grazing in a broad green pasture. I guess I should have made a bigger fuss with the kid, she thought. However, Terry realized that her position at Warlord's Hill was too ambiguous to permit bullying of the help. No matter how graceful a face Lloyd Bauer put on the situation, Terry was actually the wife of an employee, not a true guest—a fact communicated at dinner by the faintly patronizing smile on Nora Bauer's thin little mouth.

However, when nearly twenty minutes passed and the stablehand still had not come after her, she surrendered to growing irritation and started back toward the stable. She had taken only a few steps when an old Buick station wagon—its wooden body so dark and oiled that it might have been fashioned from the frames on the British Museum's Rembrandt collection—came down the hill from the mansion, halting near the open stable doors. Nora Bauer emerged from the front passenger seat and gave Terry what was supposed to be a cheerful wave, her thin right arm rising and falling with the jerkiness of a badly strung puppet. The driver—an elderly,

balding, narrow-shouldered man in a tweed sports jacket—
followed Nora as she quickly walked toward Terry.

"Poor Jake just called the house," Nora Bauer said, right
ring finger nervously digging her palm. "Your really want to
go riding?"

"Is there any reason why I shouldn't?"

"Of course not." Nora's gaze took in Terry's checked
cotton blouse and Mexican boots. "We only have English
saddles."

"I think I can manage."

"To tell the truth, I'd feel better if you'd wait until I find
someone to go out with you. It's so ridiculously easy to get
lost in those woods. I never ride alone myself."

The man in the tweed jacket caught up with the congressman's wife, his lips forming so uncannily exact a duplicate of
Nora's condescending smile that Terry realized instantly they
must be related. In twenty years, Nora's already slightly
sallow skin would take on the same yellow cast, like that of an
old white linen envelope left for years in a closed desk
drawer.

"Won't you introduce me, Nora?" the man said.

"Terry, I'd like you to meet my father. Terry Hammil, Dr.
Roger Zimmerman."

Dr. Zimmerman shook Terry's proferred hand a little
clinically, as if taking a pulse. "My daughter is the worrier in
the family," he said. "However, she has a point. Until you
become more used to Warlord's Hill, I would advise staying
close to the paved roads. There are no marked bridle paths,
and the tracks through the forest would have confused Daniel
Boone. Most of them go nowhere."

"And please avoid the woods south of the lake," Nora
added. "The forestry staff just finished reseeding two hundred acres we lost in a fire last month. The whole area is
off-limits until the new plants take root."

"I'll be careful, Nora," Terry promised.

As Terry walked back to the station wagon with Nora
Bauer and her father, Dr. Zimmerman volunteered that, besides running a clinic for the estate workers, he was a director
of the Bauer Foundation for Geriatric Research and had returned only last night from a symposium on the subject held

in New Orleans. As she listened to his flat, professional voice, Terry idly wondered why he and his daughter had bothered driving down to the stables. Everything they had to say could just as easily have been conveyed over the tackroom telephone.

The peculiarities of the Bauer and Zimmerman families soon left Terry Hammil's thoughts. After Nora and her father drove off, the suddenly affable Jake helped her select a horse. As she expected, he tried to steer her toward the most docile animal in the pasture. Instead she chose a spirited young bay mare and insisted on saddling and bridling the horse herself, knowing it was the fastest way to gain the trust of an unfamiliar mount.

Even before hearing Dr. Zimmerman's warning, Terry had no intention of taking off into the forest her first time out on horseback. The way Roy had gotten confused during the drive to Chatsworth had shown her that the Pine Barrens was an uncannily easy place in which to lose your bearings. She decided that the simplest way to avoid becoming the object of an embarrassing after-dark search was to always keep the estate's utility poles in sight. It meant staying on major roads—and the monotonous view of massed pines that had already started to pall—but with the entire summer ahead of her, she saw no reason to become foolishly adventurous.

For the next hour, she rode along the shoulder of the same tarred road Gerald had driven from the estate's gate to the main building compound. Then, to her surprise, she noticed a line that inexplicably ran off into the woods, paralleling a trail that, although unpaved, was deeply rutted with tire tracks.

On impulse, Terry cut onto the trail. Less than twenty minutes later, she passed between two immense elms and reined up the slightly skittish mare at the top of a bluff. Below, in a bowl-shaped hollow, lay a town. Because of the multitude of trees, she thought she had stumbled upon a cluster of, at most, a dozen houses. Like the elms, the trees around the structures were high and heavily foliaged—black-trunked wild cherries, huge oaks, broad-topped willows, all growing so close together that their upper branches touched to form a natural canopy. The pilot of a small plane flying more than a hundred feet above treetop level probably would be unaware of the buildings' existence.

Terry gently nudged the bay to a canter. Not until they reached the bottom of the winding grade and hard-packed sand gave way to a tarred surface did she see that a real town lay ahead, that she was on its main street. Every time she changed the direction of her gaze, the shapes of new buildings emerged from the foliage, the way outlined figures would materialize on those find-the-ten-animals puzzle drawings that used to be printed on the backs of cereal boxes. Wilma had implied that most of the Bauer employees lived on the estate; obviously, this must be where they were quartered. Doubting that even so isolated a community had hitching posts, she dismounted, tied the bay's reins to a birch, and continued on foot.

Although the early afternoon sun was high, the sheltering trees cast an unbroken veil of shade over the street. A few yards past the spot where she left the horse, a sidewalk began. She paused at the edge of the first cement square, staring thoughtfully at the small, brightly painted buildings ahead. They ranged from rickety nineteenth-century falsefronts to featureless, utilitarian brick or cinderblock boxes, all as consistently pre-1940 as everything else at Warlord's Hill. Dirt side streets intersected the paved road. Extending no more than two or three blocks, each harbored a handful of modest, shingle-roofed bungalows. At the end of the main street sat a plain white church, vaguely New England in style except for its truncated steeple. The church crouched beneath the limbs of the thickest, most gnarled oak Terry had ever seen.

Curious as she was about the little town, Terry Hammil hesitated to proceed any farther. On their first night in the guest house, she had jokingly suggested to Roy that *they* might be out of place. The feeling returned with greater force as she studied the street ahead. The sidewalks were empty of pedestrians and the sole visible automobile, parked in front of a tiny movie house, was the green school bus that had brought the farm workers to Warlord's Hill yesterday morning. The block letters on the theater's jutting V-shaped marquee read: CLAIRE TREVOR AND JOHN WAYNE IN STAGECOACH. The only break in the silence was the just-faintly-audible voice of Bing Crosby, singing "Blue Skies." She suddenly felt like mounting the bay and riding back the way she had come, fearing that, by revealing her presence, she might forever shatter the tranquility of the scene.

You're being silly, Terry told herself. If the prince in her favorite fairy tale had thought that way, poor Sleeping Beauty would still be lying there with bed sores. She stepped onto the cement and walked down the sidewalk. Whoever was playing "Blue Skies" must have tired of the record and lifted the phonograph arm too hastily. In the middle of a note, Bing Crosby's comforting baritone skidded off into a high, startled squawk.

The illusion of being displaced in time deepened as she proceeded, the heels of her Mexican boots clicking loudly on the cement. She reached the movie theater, pausing to examine the poster advertising the next attraction—*Each Dawn I Die* with James Cagney and George Raft. A sandwich board near the ticket booth proclaimed the Saturday kiddie matinee lineup—Bruce Cabot and Constance Bennett in *Wild Bill Hickok Rides;* Chapter 11 of *The Green Archer* with Victor Jory; and six animated cartoons. A sign above the cashier's window read: ADULTS, 75¢; CHILDREN 25¢. Other anachronistic prices soon materialized. Two buildings down from the theater she glanced through the broad window of a barber shop. HAIRCUT, 50¢ read the cardboard sign mounted on the mirror facing two leather-and-ironwork chairs; a little man in a white tunic was carefully arranging a row of scissors and open straight razors on a towel-covered countertop. Directly across the street, a poster in a confectionery store window showed a gigantic ice cream cone beneath the improbable words: DOUBLE DIP—FIVE CENTS.

The barber was the first human being Terry had glimpsed. But soon she had evidence of other inhabitants. On the next block she passed the open doors of a firehouse, by far the largest structure in the community. Six gleaming red trucks were lined up inside and she faintly heard male voices, one of which released a harsh, raucous laugh just as she went by. Other municipal buildings came into view—a one-story brick schoolhouse, its front door padlocked for the summer; a house with a small PUBLIC LIBRARY sign fastened to a porch railing; a cinderblock police station with barred windows.

At the end of the street, next to the squat-steepled church, was a tiny, triangular park area, where two green wooden benches flanked a marble memorial. Behind the stone slab, a forty-eight-star American flag hung from a short white pole. Terry sat on a bench, examining the rows of brass nameplates affixed to the gray marble. Although the memorial lacked a dedicatory plaque, she assumed that the names on the plates were of local men killed in war time. The earlier metal rectangles, despite obvious care over the years, had darkened to a lustrous gray-green, and bore names like SAMUEL WEBBER . . . MAURICE DORN . . .ROBERT KRUG . . . THOMAS SCHALL . . . However, the last three plates still shone so brightly that they must date from the Vietnam war.

Terry heard the soft clopping of hooves. She rose from the bench to see a slightly built boy—sixteen years old, at most—in faded denim work clothes; he was leading the bay mare along the street toward her. As the boy came closer, she noticed that his features were almost beautiful, his lightly tanned, high-cheekboned face dominated by huge, somber, green-flecked hazel eyes. His hair was so pale a blond that it approached total whiteness.

"Shouldn't have tied Iolanthe to a skinny little birch," the boy said, handing her the reins. "She bit right through the branch, was wandering back to the main road when I caught her."

"Thank you," Terry said, laughing with delight.

"I didn't say anything funny," the boy murmured accusingly.

"Of course you didn't," Terry said. "It's just that this is the first time I ever borrowed a tree-eating horse named after a Gilbert and Sullivan opera."

Her own words sounded so absurd that she laughed again. This time the boy smiled, hesitantly and with effort.

"That didn't make a bit of sense, did it?" Terry asked.

"No, ma'am."

"Who named her Iolanthe?"

"Somebody at the big house, I guess."

"What's *your* name, by the way?"

"Eric."

62

"*Just* Eric?" Terry asked, mounting the mare. She hoped that someone from an estate workers' family would at last volunteer a surname. Until coming to Warlord's Hill, she had assumed that the era of semianonymous servants had gone out with the Edwardians. However, before the boy could answer—if he had intended to—the mare pulled at the bit, nervously edging sideways. It took Terry only a few seconds to regain control of the animal. But when she switched her attention back to the boy, he was gone. Only a slight rustling in a cluster of small pines beyond the memorial indicated the direction of his flight.

Terry started to call out after him, then hesitated, again reminding herself that she was a guest here, with no right to tamper with the Bauer rules, no matter how antiquated. She rode back down the main street, abruptly aware that the town was even quieter than when she had entered. The doors of the fire station were now closed, and she could no longer hear the voices of the unseen firemen. Blinds had been lowered in the barber shop window.

"I think they're scared of us, Iolanthe," she whispered, patting the mare beneath her right ear. "I wonder why?"

The end of the paved section of road lay just ahead. She urged Iolanthe to a trot as soon as her hooves touched dirt. As Terry had half-expected, the birch where she had tied the horse was intact; unlike his fellow citizens, Eric must be curious about strangers. Just past the two giant elms, she glanced over her shoulder; the nameless town was again lost in the forest.

"Mrs. Hammil found Bremen this morning," the Old Man said calmly as Harry Krug crossed the threshold of the fourth floor bedroom.

Krug didn't have to be told. Before reporting to the mansion, he had stopped off at his house to shower and change his clothes. Everyone he encountered on Elm Street, their voices taut with fear and confusion, had told of the strange woman visitor, the first outsider ever to penetrate the community. "Couldn't you have stopped her?"

"How? We can hardly confine her to the guest house for the rest of the summer."

"It does not matter, Harry," Dr. Zimmerman added. The room—illuminated, as usual, by a single table lamp—was so dark that Krug hadn't noticed the physician sitting in a shadowed corner. "What did she see, after all, but a country town? Exactly like thousands of others except for a few anachronisms."

"The real danger isn't what people say to *her*," Krug pointed out. "It's what she can tell *them*. Why were the Hammils allowed to come here, anyway? We have never taken such chances before."

"Lloyd invited them," the Old Man replied. "Under the circumstances, I had to go along with his decision."

Krug shook his head in dismay. "None of this would have happened if you had only told him the truth years ago."

"*Which* truth, Harry?" The Old Man smiled thinly. "Put it out of your mind. You have too much work between now and June twenty-eighth to worry about matters of such little consequence."

"If the girl is unimportant, why are we bothering to check her background so thoroughly?"

"It may become necessary to keep her at Warlord's Hill. I want to know who, among her friends and relatives, is likely to investigate her disappearance."

Caution, Harry Krug thought. The only flaw in the Old Man's implacable will was his occasional reluctance to move decisively until he had considered all possible repercussions of an order. Krug again recalled the night, more than thirty years ago, when they had discovered a group of children spying on a rally in the pit and the Old Man had failed to give the command that would have made unnecessary that approaching blood purge of June 28.

Krug's rebellious brooding—which, he knew, he would never dare articulate in the Old Man's presence—was interrupted by a knock on the bedroom door. "That must be Lew Dorn," the Old Man said. "I've selected him to take over the mission in Coeur d'Alene."

"A good choice," Harry Krug said, relieved. Dorn was one of the most senior huntsmen—ruthless, dedicated to the sanctuary, unquestioningly obedient.

"I am sorry for what Eric did today," Dorn apologized

after he entered the bedroom. "His mother didn't even know he had left the house until she saw him leading that stupid horse to the woman. It must have got free of its tether."

The Old Man shrugged. "He behaved sensibly. What could look more suspicious than a town full of people cowering behind windowblinds when a perfectly harmless girl wanders down the street? In fact, your son showed me how to deal with her in the future."

"I want you to take the first available flight west, Lew," Krug said. "We have less than three weeks to locate our man again, and Vic Schall won't be much help. Still, we have no one else on the scene at the moment—and he gave me a piece of information that may tell us where to start looking."

Krug went to the Old Man's rolltop mahogany desk, opened it to expose a tape recorder, and slipped in the cassette carrying his interrogation of Vic Schall. "You can listen to the rest later," he told Dorn, pressing the fast-forward button until he reached the section that had intrigued him.

Vic Schall's strained, uncertain voice emerged from the speaker. "*I did notice one peculiar thing. Months ago, I went to his room for a drink. There was a new, very expensive fishing outfit on the table. A flycasting rod and a tackle box, all sorts of gear, still wrapped. 'You like fishing, John?' I asked him, and he gave me a funny smile and said, 'Not a hell of a lot, to tell the truth.' I'd thought about asking him on a weekend trip—you know how I love to fish—but I dropped the idea, naturally.*"

"*He had bought a gift for someone, perhaps?*" Krug's voice asked.

"*For who? He never spoke of relatives, and he has no friends except me. Anyway, the gear was still there—and still unopened—whenever I visited him. I didn't really think about it again until the night I searched his room after he killed the two men in the alley. He had packed very hurriedly, took only clothes. All sorts of things were left behind—an electric razor, valuable-looking cufflinks, even his TV set. But the fishing gear was gone.*"

"Why would a man on the run bother to pack tackle?" Dr. Zimmerman asked when Krug switched off the machine. "Especially if he doesn't like to fish."

"It was part of a disguise," the Old Man said.

Harry Krug nodded agreement. "Three times in the years we have followed him he has vanished. In Key West and Madison, Wisconsin, and Dubuque, Iowa. We gave him no reason to fear—never revealed our presence—but he simply disappeared, without a word to anyone. It took months to make contact again, after he had established himself in another town hundreds of miles away, assuming a new identity. Now we know that, all along, he sensed that we were watching him. The only possible answer is that he mistook complete strangers for huntsmen—as he did three months ago when those thugs attacked him."

"And went to ground in a hideout prepared long in advance," Lew Dorn guessed.

"Of course," Krug said. "Someplace where he would be out of sight for weeks or months—and someplace close to the area from which he had fled. A long plane or bus or even car trip would mean dangerous, unnecessary exposure. The rivers and lakes around Coeur d'Alene contain many isolated cabins and fishing camps. I'll give you odds he's holed up in one of them now."

John Rawls gazed down at the only person he had trusted in nearly a decade. Vic Schall—his face a puffy mass of blackened bruises, lips and mouth and eyes so crusted with caked blood that he could barely see or breathe—lay sprawled in a corner of the fishing shack. "Why didn't you kill me?" he moaned.

John Rawls did not reply, continuing to study Schall with the detachment of a biologist who has chanced upon a loathsome, but pricelessly rare, form of primeval life. Last night, finally deciding that his persecutors *had* been phantoms, he had driven back to Coeur d'Alene, planning to recruit Schall as intermediary in a surrender to the police. He parked on the street outside the complex of small, cheap garden apartments where Schall lived and was less than fifty feet from the building when Schall's front door opened and a tall pale-faced man stepped out onto the illuminated stoop. Instinctively, Rawls moved into the shadow of a clump of bushes, intending to hide until the stranger departed.

Then he realized that he had seen the man before; the rugged features had been permanently seared into his memory, the way a hot iron burns flesh. He tried to tell himself that he was mistaken, that too many years had passed for him to recall the face of the Nazi who had nearly stomped him to death in the forest pit. Nevertheless, as his imagination overlaid the face with the lines and sags of decades, he grew certain. Childhood fear—deeper, more powerful than any fear he had experienced as an adult—momentarily paralyzed him. By the time he forced his body into motion, the man had rounded the corner of Schall's building and entered a tenants' parking lot. John Rawls reached the lot just in time to see his car drive away.

The faint hope that Vic wasn't part of the plot against him vanished after the door opened and Schall, his plump face instantly contorting with terror and guilt, backed into the living room. So enraged his vision had become a swirling red blur, he clamped his outsized hands around Vic's throat and dug his thumbs into the writhing bartender's windpipe. He heard the hiss of Schall's voiding bladder, felt liquid splatter on his left shoe. His anger gave way to contempt and he released his strangling grip, drove his fists into his victim's face and body until Schall lay at his feet like a mound of bloodstained laundry.

I'm going to let him live, John Rawls decided, unwilling to destroy a link to the men of the pit. For a moment, he considered remaining in the apartment, on the chance that the gray-faced man would return. But that would be too dangerous. He had no idea how many other Nazis had joined Vic Schall in Coeur d'Alene—or might have been here all along. And if he waited until morning to return to the Priest River fishing shack, he would increase the chance of being spotted by the police or someone who knew him. Better to go now, take Vic along, wrest the truth from him before striking back at his enemies.

After binding and gagging Schall with neckties, he had driven his Pinto to the deserted tenants' parking lot, stowed the bartender's limp body in the rear cargo area, and covered it with a blanket ripped from Schall's bed. The moon had not yet set behind the tall fir trees when he again reached the shack.

Now, more than twenty hours later, he still lacked the answers to the questions that had long tormented him. For most of the day, Schall had lain unconscious on the plank floor, defying every attempt at revival. At one point his frustrated captor, convinced that the bartender was faking, hauled him down to the river and held his head under the water for nearly a minute—but the heavy, slack body hadn't stirred. He couldn't believe that Schall's skull had been fractured, since his only head blows had been to the face and jaw. Still, John Rawls remembered GIs in battle who had remained semicomatose a day or more after suffering moderate concussions.

The sun was again low when, with a shuddering groan, Vic Schall opened the scabbed-over slits of his eyes.

The questioning began—with results that only added to Rawls' now-controlled rage. Although he didn't attempt to deny that he had been spying on his friend, Vic insisted—in a barely audible whine that filtered moistly through his swollen lips—that he didn't know the name of the visitor to his apartment, that the man had hired him to report on Rawls' movements but had never explained his motives for the surveillance. "Paid in cash," Vic moaned. "Didn't see any harm in it. . . . Figured he was a lawyer, something like that. . . ."

"You're lying," his companion snarled. He opened a wallet he had taken off Schall, removed a small card, and threw it at the bartender's feet.

"My Social Security card."

"The paper is almost new—still white, hardly a wrinkle in it. Why would a man your age have a Social Security card that fresh?"

Schall didn't answer.

He tossed down another card, laminated in plastic. "Idaho driver's license, issued January seventeenth of this year. A new license, not a renewal. You always said you'd lived in Idaho for years. If that's so, how come you never had a license until a month and a half after I moved to Coeur d'Alene?"

"Lost my old one."

"Bullshit! What's your real name?"

"Victor Schall."

"Then why aren't you carrying any ID more than six months old?"

Because I'm not real, Vic Schall wanted to reply. My parents never filed a birth certificate. I went to a school with no official existence, that kept no records. Outside the sanctuary *I* didn't exist either. The Master Huntsman paid hundreds of dollars in bribes to get me my Social Security card and driver's license. . . . But Schall did not speak, remembering the newspaper descriptions of how the two muggers had died Sunday morning—one with a knife driven through the length of his skull, the other beaten so horribly that his face looked like raspberry jam spilled on a white tiled kitchen floor. As much as he feared the Master Huntsman, he feared John Rawls more, realizing that once Rawls unearthed the truth about the sanctuary, he would destroy him with the same casual brutality with which he had slain his attackers.

Rawls took a third rectangle of paper from the wallet. "A long time ago, I ran into a bunch of crazy bastards who shouldn't have been around anymore," he said mockingly. "Or even been in this country to start with. But they still *are* around, along with younger crazy bastards. I could tell the cops but what good would that do? I'm crazy myself, the VA doctors say. And what if they ask me where the crazy bastards live? All I can answer is, 'I was just a kid when I ran into them the first time and, to tell the truth, I never knew where I was exactly. A place that looked like *this*.' "

He threw the snapshot between Vic's legs. Even without looking, Vic knew it had to be the photo of Catherine. Her red hair spilling over her shoulders, she had posed sitting on a picnic blanket, gazing up at him adoringly; behind her lay a copse of twisted pines. "Could have been taken anywhere," Vic murmured.

Rawls shook his head. "Only one spot in my life I ever saw pines like that—with branches growing on just one side—and that was in the woods near the pit. You going to tell me where it is?"

"Can't."

"You carry around a woman's picture and you don't even know where she's from?" He took a step closer to Schall, smiling as the bartender released an involuntary whimper. "Ever been beaten up before?"

"No."

"Didn't figure you had. I've been a couple of times. Haven't had but eleven of my own teeth since I was thirty. You know how it is on TV? Hero gets worked over and a couple days later he's got a Band-Aid stuck on his head and he's punching it out with the bad guys again? That's not how it happens. The first time, that white-faced friend of yours broke my legs, stove in eight or nine ribs, put a tear in my scalp so bad it took years for hair to grow back over the scar. For a while, I was the way you are now. Didn't give a damn whether I lived or died, mostly hoped I'd die. I couldn't even feel anything much—not the shots the doctor gave me, nor the pain in my legs."

"Why you telling me this?"

"I wanted to explain why I'm not going to hurt you again tonight. We're going to be stuck on this river for weeks— long enough to be sure the local cops have quit looking for me. You're young and you'll heal quick, start wanting to be in bed with that redhead with the great tits, start wanting all the things guys with a stake in life want." John Rawls' smile vanished. "*That's* when I'm going to hurt you again."

Even in his stunned confusion, Vic knew that John Rawls meant his threat. His dazed, squinting eyes peered past Rawls, focusing on the dismantled casting rod on the room's crude table; the open tackle box, filled with hooks and lures, beside it; the handnet and rubber hipboots in the corner near the door. His captor must have put out the gear to convince chance visitors that he was a vacationing sportsman. Vic remembered the gleam of interest in the Master Huntsman's eyes when he had mentioned the new fishing outfit he had noticed in Rawls' furnished room—and right at this moment, the new team of huntsmen must be starting their search.

Last night, Vic Schall had finally understood that from birth he had served a force dominated by madness and evil. But now only that force offered him a frail hope of survival.

✖ SIX ✖

On Monday, as he and Lloyd Bauer drove away from Warlord's Hill in the cream-colored Cord speedster, Roy Hammil had been baffled about how to proceed with his assignment. *I'm taking your money under false pretenses,* he had felt tempted to say to the man at the wheel. The next primary election was nearly a year away—and despite the impression given by films and popular fiction, he had never heard of a reporter exposing a major scandal except in the heat of a campaign or its bitter aftermath. Anyone with dirt on Bauer—if, in truth, such dirt existed—would hold back his information until he had an opponent of the congressman's with whom to deal, trading facts for power or money or influence.

Bauer barely spoke until the guard at the checkpoint in the barbed wire fence waved them through. As soon as the gates closed behind them, he uttered a gratified sigh, smiled apologetically when he realized that Roy had noticed his reaction. "Do you have any idea what it's like, for a politician, trying to function for days at a stretch without a telephone?" he asked. "Sometimes, after a week at home, I go back to the office and ask if I've gotten any messages from Tom Dewey."

Roy faked a laugh; the congressman's relief, even expressed facetiously, was too heartfelt to provoke a real one. "Must be like living in a huge toy," he remarked.

Bauer glanced at him, surprised. "Exactly the way I've always felt about the place. How did you know?"

"Because, after a single weekend, that's how *I* was starting to feel."

This time Bauer's smile was genuine. "I was eighteen before I learned that cars with automatic transmissions even existed. Thank God my father picked Princeton. By the time my classmates realized I was hopelessly out of date I was two years ahead of them."

As they talked, Roy realized that he had begun to like Lloyd Bauer, which disturbed him; newspapermen who succumbed to a politician's charm were setting themselves up for betrayal. But, he reminded himself, I'm not a reporter anymore. I'm a "media consultant." And I'm not working for Langston Fellows or some hard-assed managing editor. I'm working for the man I'm supposed to investigate. The situation was as hallucinatory as the world Lloyd's aged father had established at Warlord's Hill. He felt as if he were taking part in a perversely complicated game—but without any knowledge of the rules, not even sure he was a player.

As they neared a curve, Roy was surprised to see an ambulance approaching. Since the road ended at the estate, he wondered where an emergency vehicle could be headed in this wilderness. The ambulance passed and he read the words GOLDEN ERA RETIREMENT CENTER, LAKEWOOD, NJ, on its side.

Bauer, who hadn't even glanced at the ambulance, pressed the gas pedal to the floor when they came out of the curve. "We're running a little late," he said as the speedometer needle moved past seventy.

In daylight—and at a much higher speed than Gerald had driven—the trip to Chatsworth took little more than half an hour. Parked inside the Miller garage, next to Roy's burgundy Jaguar XJ6, was a new green Cadillac Seville. On the way, Bauer had informed him that they would meet again that afternoon at his office, located in a small central Jersey city.

Lloyd Bauer had entered the Cadillac and started the engine when Roy approached the sedan's window. "Before I go to work, I'd like to know a bit more," he asked.

Bauer glanced at him quizzically, as if he had no inkling of Roy's meaning. "About what?"

"Obviously, my best souce of facts in this investigation—if that's what we're calling it—is yourself. What limitations are you putting on my questions?"

After a thoughtful pause, Bauer said, "You can ask whatever a regular interviewer or a group of reporters at a press conference might ask. Anything beyond that would defeat our purposes."

"And all your answers will be the truth?"

"Of course not," Bauer said with a grin. "That would be giving you an unfair advantage."

"Unfair advantages are supposed to be taken, not given. Yesterday you said you wanted the services of the kind of reporter I used to be. That kind of reporter would never let the subject of a story set his schedule."

"Listening to me give the same speech, with minor theological variations, to the Cherry Hill Knights of Columbus and the Perth Amboy B'nai B'rith might not prove terribly productive," Bauer agreed.

"Washington seems like a logical place to kick off."

"All right. I'll call my assistant, Sidney Levin, and tell him to reserve you a hotel room. The Hay-Adams okay?"

"Much better than I'm used to."

Bauer backed the Cadillac out of the garage and sped off with a casual parting wave.

Leaving the Pine Barrens—this time taking care to stay on Route 72—Roy tried to plan a course of action for the next few days. However, his thoughts kept returning to Terry. "It's as though I've come home," she had said yesterday as they stood in a high meadow and looked out over the forest. Realizing that it made no sense—that, in fact, he should be gratified—he was disturbed by his wife's enthusiasm over spending the summer at Warlord's Hill, the sudden resurgence of her confidence and vitality. He knew that her feelings weren't entirely due to the prospect of being surrounded by the wooded solitude she had always loved; somehow, she found the anachronistic atmosphere of the place comforting. And Roy had never trusted comfort rooted in illusion.

He reached Newark Airport in time to catch the noon Eastern Airlines shuttle. By two o'clock, he was in his room at the Hay-Adams hotel, placing phone calls. Most of them were to former colleagues on the House beat, setting up appointments throughout the rest of the week. Despite the man's apparent openness, he had sensed a hard, enigmatic core in Lloyd Bauer's personality and wanted evaluations by reporters who saw him on a regular basis.

However, the first call—the one he guessed would be the most important—went to Langston Fellows. The retired columnist had a lecture date the next day, but he agreed to see Roy on Wednesday morning.

Fellows' reaction to Roy's account of his assignment from Representative Lloyd Bauer was a quiet, mildly disbelieving chuckle. "And what do you imagine could create such a bizarre streak of caution in a modern American politician?" he asked, as if he were still the most powerful columnist in Washington asking condescending questions of a young apprentice. "After all, even in New Jersey Republicans must have some memory of their sins."

Nearly three years had passed since Roy had met his former employer but, though he had entered his eighties, little about Langston had changed. The part in his silver-white hair still started slightly off the center of his brow; his old-fashioned diplomatic-service moustache, as neatly trimmed as ever; his slim hands, perfectly manicured. Although it had been barely midmorning when Fellows had greeted Roy in the front parlor of his nineteenth-century Alexandria town house, he wore an immaculately pressed Dunhill suit, a neatly folded handkerchief in his breast pocket. Only the steel-framed walker beside his chair contradicted the old journalist's air of free-floating elegance.

"I have a hunch Bauer isn't afraid of personal scandal," Roy replied, sipping at the coffee brought to him by a young black maid. "I think something happened far in the past, a family disgrace that might come out if he went national in a big way."

Fellows stared at him with piercing blue eyes, amused. "How can you be so sure, Roy? You certainly don't buy that he's-too-rich-to-be-a-crook nonsense? Millionaire politicians have risked jail for taking payoffs of a few thousand dollars."

"Because I can think of just one reason why he'd hire

me—the fact that I spent twelve years as your legman. No one else in the business has your knowledge of political and business corruption stretching back to—"

"Warren Harding?" Fellows chuckled dryly. "You're probably right, my boy, simply because no one I started out with is still alive. However, I doubt that the Bauers are paying you just to riffle through whatever is left of my memory. You're a first-rate reporter."

"Who hasn't worked at his trade for years. Hell, Lloyd Bauer has been in Washington long enough to know that I've lost most of my contacts. And that without a powerful daily or a syndicate behind me, I'm not going to make any new ones."

"I can't tell you much about the Bauers that isn't on the public record."

"A very distant public record. Lang, I'm out of my depth on this. You always said I lacked a proper sense of history. You were right. I could start from square one, hit the libraries, but it'd take me weeks to learn what you have at your fingertips."

Langston Fellows loftily corrected him. "*Months*—if at all."

"I also thought you might be kind of intrigued."

"I *am* intrigued," Fellows said, pushing himself out of his chair with a pained grimace, lurching over to grasp the sides of the walker. "Besides, I'd do almost anything to avoid working on my damned memoirs."

"What happened?" Roy asked, gesturing at the walker.

"Fell downstairs and broke my hip." Fellows maneuvered the frame toward a door which, Roy recalled, led to the narrow central stairway. "Like any sensible man, as soon as I was out of the hospital, I got rid of the stairs."

"Where are we going, by the way?"

"My office. Mind catching the door?"

Roy opened the hall door and halted in astonishment. The hall had disappeared, as had the rooms beyond it—for all five above-ground stories of the town house. Taking their place was a tiered gallery of laden bookshelves, reaching all the way to the building's skylight. Walkways, linked by steel stairs in the rear wall, ran along each level. At the southeast corner of the ground floor was a small, open-caged elevator.

"Remember Gwen, my last wife?" Fellows asked as he edged the walker toward the elevator. "Roaring bitch, like the rest of them?"

"Yes."

"Too many books, she said. No room to move around the place. She insisted I put most of them in storage. Well, they're all back now."

"I can see that, Lang," Roy said, struggling to hide his amusement.

"That's the best thing about being divorced four times with no kids." Fellows gingerly backed into the elevator, lowered himself onto its narrow single seat. "You can forget about ruining the resale value of your home and concentrate on improvements that *count*. Wait here and I'll send her back down."

"I'll walk."

As the elevator ascended toward the top floor, Roy paralleled its course on the rear wall stairs. The cage moved with such excruciating slowness that he had to restrain himself from getting too far ahead, his gaze traveling over the volumes of history and political science and economics—spelled by an occasional murder mystery and what suspiciously resembled paperback pornography—crammed onto the shelves.

"So you and Terry have discovered the Pine Barrens," Fellows called across the thirty-foot space separating them. "Amazing place—probably the biggest unmarked cemetery in the northeast."

"I don't understand."

"During prohibition, bootleggers operated hundreds of stills in those woods—and blew each other's heads off with appalling regularity. Later, the Murder Incorporated people executed and buried most of their victims in the Pines. The police found more than seventy bodies in just one mass grave. And, of course, they provided a suitably barbaric—and secure—setting for the old German-American Bund's rallies. Even a Midwesterner must have heard of *them*."

"A pro-Nazi paramilitary organization back in the thirties."

"Except that the imbecilic word *paramilitary* hadn't been

76

invented yet. It's funny but few people *do* remember the bundists. In nineteen forty-two, the United States government put thousands of innocent Japanese-Americans in concentration camps on the theory, backed by absolutely no evidence, that they were a menace to West Coast war plants. On the other hand, right up until the time of Pearl Harbor, battalions of German-American thugs openly paraded through Yorkville and South Jersey and Suffolk County, wearing brownshirt uniforms and swastika armbands and saluting posters of Adolf Hitler. So far as I know, only three or four of them ever saw the inside of a jail—and that was for looting the Bund's treasury."

Roy laughed sardonically. "Japanese-Americans weren't as big a voting bloc as German-Americans."

"Here we are," Fellows said, halting the elevator at the fifth level.

Roy hurried around the steel walkway, met Fellows at the open cage door, moved back as the columnist rose and edged his walker forward, glancing back at the elevator with distaste. "Always feel like a roast turkey being sent upstairs in a restaurant dumbwaiter," he sighed.

The two men entered the small office where they had hammered out Fellows' column for the last twelve years of its existence. The desk was piled high with books, individual pages marked by inserted file cards. "References to the Bauer family?" Roy guessed.

"When you called the other day and told me about your job, I thought I'd give you a head start."

"Thanks, Lang."

"You won't find much, I'm afraid!" Fellows swung the walker about, started through the open office door. "Yell down when you've gone through all this. And then I'll be back to tell you what the learned gentlemen left out of their books—or never knew in the first place."

Roy sat behind the desk and randomly picked up a massive history of the I.G. Farben chemical cartel. All of the index cards were clustered in the last quarter of the book. He began to read with the peculiar intensity he brought to any task, so immediately absorbed that he didn't hear the clatter of the elevator mechanism as Langston Fellows started his descent.

He needed less than an hour to read the marked references in the stack of books. All scholarly studies of German industry from the thirties through the early postwar period, they contained only brief references to the Bauers. The longest section dealt with Paul Bauer's testimony at a 1947 Securities and Exchange Commission hearing on the disposition of German assets frozen in America during the Second World War. Like most of the other material, the pages were written in nearly incomprehensible economists' jargon.

However, even to Roy's less-than-expert eyes, the material led to an inescapable conclusion: Lloyd Bauer's father had pulled off one of the most brazen—but perfectly legal—ripoffs in financial history.

He went out on the walkway, called down to Fellows. When the ex-columnist rejoined him in the office a few minutes later, his eyes gleamed with the special delight he reserved for the appreciation of monumental scoundrels. "Wonderful, isn't it?" Fellows asked, sinking into a worn leather armchair.

"The old son of a bitch," Roy agreed admiringly.

"Did you get it all?"

"A translation into normal English might help," Roy conceded. "And whatever personal details you can add. I wasn't even born when some of this stuff happened."

"Simple enough, my boy. Paul Bauer—like his father and grandfather before him—was essentially an agent and broker, not only for industries controlled by the German branch of his family but for other European concerns as well. In the First World War, the United States impounded a fortune in German assets—and, what with reparations payments and such after the Kaiser went smash, damned little of it ever got back into the owners' hands. Kraut tycoons were a lot cagier when Hitler began rearming in the thirties. They transferred title to billions of dollars worth of overseas assets to American-controlled dummy corporations, even to individual U.S. citizens, like Bauer, whom they considered totally trustworthy. All the big ones did it—Krupp, I.G. Farben, G.A.F., the lot—guaranteeing themselves a block of protected postwar assets in case the unthinkable happened and the Allies won. Of course, our government got wise, sued to prevent transfer of the titles back to their real owners. The resulting litigation was so complex that it dragged on for decades. The Interhandel case wasn't settled until nineteen sixty-five.''

"In Interhandel's favor," Roy recalled.

"Letting an old man ramble, are you?" Fellows asked.

"Naturally, I'd read about the bigger cases years ago. But the stuff on Bauer is new to me. He kept it *all*?''

"Every bloody *deutschmark*—at least a hundred million dollars. I remember the S.E.C. hearing. All of the other witnesses—major figures in the U.S. chemical and petroleum industries—were surrounded by enough attorneys to staff the Harvard Law School. Big guns like John Foster Dulles. No one would admit anything. Even requests to go to the men's room were challenged for the record. Then Paul Bauer came on—with just one lawyer and cold as ice. We couldn't believe what we were hearing when he testified under oath that title to all stock, bonds, certificates of deposit, and patents bearing his or his firm's name were free and clear. As a result, if he were to sell the properties back to the original German holders at less than current market value, the suspicions raised would open him up for a perjury rap. And the best part was that the Krauts couldn't sue him without publicly admitting they had made the secret transfers in the first place. Bauer had them by the balls!''

Ever since driving through the main gate at Warlord's Hill, Roy Hammil had been puzzled by the estate's heavy security arrangements. Now the precautions made sense. Especially in the beginning, Paul Bauer might have feared for his life. He had betrayed industrialists who had authorized underlings to beat and starve and work to death millions of slave laborers; powerful men who still had contact with hard-core Nazis. Inevitably, blocked from legal retribution, they would have sought a more direct means of vengeance.

"But *why* did Bauer do it, Lang?" Roy asked. "He was already rich, must have realized that he had set himself up for murder. Why else did he turn Warlord's Hill into a fortress? Obviously, all that bullshit about preserving a prewar life-style—at least in the first few years—must have been a cover.''

"Oh, I'm certain I know why," Fellows said with a self-satisfied shrug. "And it had nothing to do with quadrupling his bank account. He was trying to get even—in the only way he could—for what the Nazis did to the von Behnckes. Lloyd Bauer never mentioned his aunt and her husband?"

"He never mentions anything without a fight."

"The Bauers always maintained close ties with relatives and professional acquaintances in Germany. Paul Bauer graduated from Leipzig University, spent as much time in Europe as he did at home. His younger sister Margarethe even married an old-line Prussian nobleman—Horst von Behncke—in the middle thirties, and refused repatriation when the United States came into the war. Von Behncke was a lieutenant general commanding a Panzer division; he ranked as a popular hero just a notch or two below Rommel . . . ."

"Until Hitler hung him," Roy said. The information suddenly surfaced in his mind, unbidden.

"Then you already knew all this?" Fellows asked in surprise.

"Not all of it, no. But it does ring a bell—I must have read or heard about the man at one time or another."

"Even before the war, von Behncke had been a secret anti-Nazi," Fellows continued. "Helped plan the July nineteen forty-four bomb plot on Adolf Hitler's life. Of course, Hitler survived the explosion—and von Behncke, like dozens of other Wehrmacht conspirators, was hung from a meathook with piano wire. I knew him and his wife back in thirty-seven, when he was a military attaché at the German embassy. Amazingly beautiful woman—tall, ash blond, elegant."

"What happened to her after the execution?"

"The Nazis confiscated the von Behncke estate, right down to the family silverware, and threw Margarethe and her children onto the streets with nothing but the clothes they were wearing. Her two older boys were barely in their teens but the army conscripted both, then sent them to the Russian front. Never heard from again. Her daughter was killed a few months later in an air raid. The only other child was a boy, born shortly before von Behncke's death. He and the mother somehow survived, although they were public outcasts, forced to live in bombed-out ruins like diseased, starving animals."

"No one helped them?"

Fellows shook his head in disgust. "Bauer's former associates were the men who kept the Nazi war machine going, a few of them so powerful that even Hitler himself wouldn't dare cross them. Yet none of the swine offered aid, even secretly, to Margarethe von Behncke and her baby. If you were Bauer, would you have given them their money back?"

"What happened to the sister after the war?"

"I understand Paul Bauer got her and the child to the States. That's the last I heard of either of them. You met Bauer?"

"No. Lloyd said he rarely leaves his bedroom. Just sits there pretending it's nineteen thirty-nine."

"You find that strange?"

"Don't you?"

"Not in the least. And if you ever get to be Bauer's age—or, God help you, mine—you won't either," Langston Fellows said with a soft laugh. He pushed himself up on his walker, edged it to a broad window, gazed at the sprawling, decayed public housing project on the other side of the street. A black teen-aged boy, directly across from the town house, was urinating against the door of a parked Volkswagen. "When I bought this house in thirty-three, nothing lay between here and the Potomac except trees and green fields. Do you honestly believe, if I had the money, I wouldn't tear down that rat warren and put back the view?"

Roy realized that, despite his habitually condescending tone, Fellows was lonely. He suddenly wished he hadn't made a lunch appointment with Jack Rudd, a *Washington Post* reporter. "Thanks for all your help, Lang," he said, rising from his chair.

"I doubt that any of it will be of use. Broad public exposure of the fact that, years ago, your candidate's father robbed a bunch of rich Nazis right down to their socks hardly constitutes a major scandal. In fact, it would probably clinch the Jewish vote."

"A start, anyway."

Roy noticed a look of uncertainty on Fellows' finely wrinkled face, as if he were about to add a new piece of information but had abruptly changed his mind. "If I think of anything else, I'll call you at the Hay-Adams or that Jersey number you left. And next time bring Terry. I've missed her."

"I'll be sure to."

"Mind letting yourself out?" Fellows asked. "As long as I'm up here anyway, I might as well get back to those ridiculous memoirs."

After Roy's departure, Langston Fellows moved behind his desk, put on the thick glasses he wore only when alone, and unsuccessfully tried to focus his attention on his manuscript, written on yellow legal pads in a large sweeping hand; failing vision made using a typewriter impossible.

Perhaps I should have told Roy, he thought, recalling the morning, two months earlier, that he had received a phone call from Vera Blum, the wife of his former news syndicate's Washington bureau chief. He had already heard that Jim Blum had suffered a massive coronary the day before and was not expected to live.

"He wants to see you, Lang," Vera said in a quavering voice. "He wouldn't tell me why."

"I took a payoff," had been the faint message emerging from Blum's gray lips; before speaking, he had insisted that his attending nurse leave the hospital room. "Only time in my life, Lang. . . . Had a girl on the side. . . . And college tuitions were busting me. . . . Newspapermen ought to have vasectomies after three kids. . . . Hundred thousand bucks. . . . Couldn't turn it down . . ."

"A payoff for what?"

"Roy Hammil . . . They didn't want him to take over your column. . . ."

"Who didn't, Jim?"

"Doesn't matter now. . . . Just wanted Roy to know. . . . Had nothing to do with him. . . . He did a great job. . . . I felt like a real prick afterward . . ."

Fellows hadn't been able to convince Blum to reveal who had paid him to destroy Roy's career. He was still trying when the agitated nurse had returned and ordered him to leave. Jim Blum had died less than six hours later.

What good would it have done to tell Roy? Fellows asked himself again. Especially without being able to provide the guilty man's name. In the years he had done the legwork for the column, his aide had made hundreds of bitter enemies in Washington. Still, how many of them would have been willing—or possessed the financial means—to pay a hundred-thousand-dollar bribe just to cost a newspaperman his job?

He forced the matter out of his thoughts—but found that he was still unable to read the words on the legal pad.

Half a block east, a young man in coveralls sat behind the wheel of a parked, unmarked panel truck, studying the public housing project so grotesquely juxtaposed to the elegant town houses nearby. After urinating on the Volkswagen, the addict in the ragged sweater and torn, faded jeans had staggered down the street, sat on the curb, and let his head flop forward on his crossed forearms. In the two hours he had been stationed here, the driver had observed four open drug buys and a fight in which a shrieking black whore had ripped open another girl's face with the sharpened point of a beer can opener. Watching such barbarism, the driver liked to think of the day when the Old Man's vision of the future would finally be realized, the day when centers of depravity like the project would be leveled and their subhuman inhabitants removed from civilization, trained to perform simple but socially useful labor.

He was jolted back to the present by the sight of Roy Hammil descending the front steps of Fellows' home, entering his rented car. "He's leaving," the driver said to his companion in the rear of the truck; the second man had been monitoring listening devices planted months ago in the town house. Before starting the truck's engine, the driver waited to make sure that the surveillance team's other vehicle—a nondescript blue Chevette—had pulled away from the curb in time to follow Hammil's car. Then he drove straight to the red brick house on Massachusetts Avenue that had served for thirty-two years as the sanctuary's Washington outpost. The Master Huntsman was waiting in the basement, which was equipped with banks of sophisticated electronic gear. He took the box of recordings from the driver, nodded his thanks.

"Peter Uhl is staying with Hammil," the driver said. "Want us to go back to Alexandria?"

"Not necessary," Harry Krug replied.

When the driver arrived with the tapes, Krug had been studying the log of Roy Hammil's movements the day before. His schedule had been predictable—half a dozen meetings with old friends from the Washington press corps, undoubtedly to obtain their views on Lloyd Bauer's political past and future. Krug had kept track as a matter of routine, aware that only Langston Fellows might possess information dangerous to the sanctuary. If, as he feared, the dying Jim Blum had told Fellows the truth about how Hammil had been maneuvered into quitting his job, the two men were certain to have discussed the matter this morning.

The bugs had been planted in the town house's front parlor, office, and dining room after Krug learned that Fellows had been among the dying Jim Blum's last visitors. Since the surveillance team's notes accompanying the tapes stated that Hammil had entered the house at ten-fourteen that morning, it was unlikely that he had come for breakfast, so Krug played the front parlor reel. The first moments of conversation told him that neither man was aware of the knowledge he possessed. Hammil explained his mission to his former employer, and both expressed puzzlement at Lloyd Bauer's motives before going to the fifth floor office.

Blum didn't tell him about the deal, Krug thought with relief. If he had, Fellows would have brought up the subject immediately.

Krug put the office tape reel on the console, moved it to fast-forward, caught the brief conversation before Fellows left Hammil alone. For nearly an hour afterward, the only sounds were light coughing, bursts of private laughter, the turning of book pages. Then Fellows' voice sounded again: *Wonderful, isn't it?* The discussion that followed assured Krug that both men accepted the web of ingenuous subterfuge the Old Man had started to spin so many years ago. The manipulated record was all there: the retention of the fortune entrusted to the Bauer family by German companies; the theory that Nazi mistreatment of Margarethe von Behncke and her children had provoked an act of financial revenge; the smug assumption that none of these time-faded facts could have an adverse effect on Lloyd Bauer's political career.

It's going to work, Harry Krug told himself with grim satisfaction. If he followed his present line of inquiry, Hammil could not possibly unearth the truth in the brief time remaining before the June 28 purge. That left only John Rawls as a serious threat to the first phase of the master plan. He glanced at the digital clock on the recording console, saw that it was four seventeen. Since the trip involved three flight changes, Lew Dorn would still be en route to Spokane, where he was to link up with Conrad Webber, the huntsman who had taken over the task of checking out Roy Hammil's wife.

After a week of traveling all over the country, Harry Krug was grateful for a chance to get to bed at a decent hour and retired to his room after dinner. However, he had been asleep only minutes when his night table telephone rang. He picked up the receiver, muttered an irritable greeting.

"Vic Schall has disappeared," Lew Dorn said.

The message jarred Krug to full consciousness. He listened intently as Dorn told how he and Webber had driven to Schall's apartment in Coeur d'Alene but got no response from within. Knowing that Schall had orders to leave the building only for brief periods, they had waited a mere half hour before jimmying the simple lock on the front door. The stale, closed-in odor of the living room and kitchen told them that the doors and windows hadn't been opened for days.

"He must have run away as soon as I left him," Krug guessed. "I didn't think he was that frightened." Or, he added mentally, perhaps that brave.

"He didn't skip," Lew Dorn said. "The closet was full of clothes, his car was in its numbered space next to the building—and we found big patches of dried blood on the living room carpet."

John Rawls must have figured out that Vic Schall had been his true nemesis and returned to Coeur d'Alene to confront him. If so, had he killed Vic? Unlikely, Krug decided; Rawls would have had no reason to move the bartender's body. He was probably hiding somewhere, trying to beat the truth out of the captive huntsman. The record of instinctive brutality running through his life had been consistent up to now: blind rage triggering immediate, unthinking retaliation against his enemies, real or imagined. For decades the rulers of the sanctuary had managed to deceive trained government investigators, highly placed political figures, canny journalists like Roy Hammil. That their most dangerous living opponent might prove to be an escapee from a VA mental hospital struck Krug as numbingly ironic.

"Any change in our orders?" Dorn asked.

"No. Find them and kill them."

"I might need more men."

"No one I can spare, Lew. I'm sorry."

"I understand." Dorn hesitated. "Conrad finished his research on the woman. She's a Hedricks."

At first, Krug didn't grasp what Lew Dorn meant. Then he remembered the speech on American history the Old Man gave every year at the Bremen school's eighth-grade graduation ceremony. He had been outside the wire on the day of this year's commencement but, as Master Huntsman, he usually had the duty of handing the children their diplomas. He himself had been a student when he first heard the speech. The Old Man, his voiced filled with righteous loathing, told the assembled graduates how, in 1654, a ship bearing twenty-three Sephardic Jews had landed at New Amsterdam. *From that vessel*, the Old Man thundered, *like rats bearing plague, emerged the first of their abominable cult to set foot in the New World, creatures with forever-cursed names like Cardozo and Baruch and Lombroso and Hedricks, creatures who for centuries have corrupted our system of justice and our commerce and even the rich earth itself . . .*

※ SEVEN ※

Early Friday afternoon, Terry Hammil set out to explore the woods south of the lake. It was the first time in four days—since the morning she found the town—that she had managed to get off by herself. Abandoning her distant manner, Nora Bauer apparently had decided to make friends after all, twice having Terry to lunch at the mansion, accompanying her on morning rides.

Nora insisted that Jake or another stablehand go along, always keeping his mount far enough ahead of the women to be out of earshot. Obviously, it was a routine to which Nora and the guides had long been accustomed. "I really admired the way you galloped off on Iolanthe yesterday," Nora said during their first ride together. "I could never do it."

Why not? Terry wanted to ask. She had already realized that what she had mistaken for hauteur was actually a deep, almost agonized shyness. After the strained encounter at the stables, the woman must have forced herself to assume the role of hostess.

Nora volunteered the answer to Terry's unvoiced question: "I became terribly lost once, when I was seven years old. There used to be a big patch of huckleberries on a rise a little past the old foundry dam. I went to pick them without telling anybody, took a wrong turn. It was nearly midnight when the huntsmen found me, so scared I never forgot what happened."

"Huntsmen?"

"The men who look after the forest areas."

What an inappropriate term for the caretakers of a wildlife preserve, Terry thought. "You've been coming to Warlord's Hill since you were a kid?"

"Actually, until we were married and Lloyd went to Congress, I never lived anyplace else. That I can recall, anyway. Dad dropped all of his outside patients years ago, so he had no reason to maintain a home off the estate."

How isolated Lloyd Bauer and his future wife must have been as children, Terry mused. How out of place they must have felt whenever they left this quiet near-wilderness, literally rooted in a bygone time. And then, on Nora's part, to be plunged into the nerve-wracking social duties of an ambitious young congressman's wife. During her own years in Washington, she had observed the damage to the spirit of political wives with far more conventional backgrounds. No wonder the woman seemed insecure.

"I know how it is," Terry said. "I grew up on a ranch in New Mexico. Had a hell of a time adjusting when I went away to college."

The look of sad amusement flashing across Nora Bauer's face hinted that Terry had absolutely no idea how it had been.

On Friday, Nora called the guest house, asking Terry to accompany her on a shopping trip to Philadelphia. She declined, pleading a mild cold. Actually, she planned to make her first real expedition into the forest. During the horseback rides, she had glimpsed plants like none she had ever seen—ferns twice the size of any supposed to grow in the East; delicate tree orchids that, theoretically, weren't found north of Georgia. Nora Bauer had indicated that the woods past the lake, far from cultivated land and paved roads, were in an almost pure wilderness state. She recalled Nora's warning that, because of extensive reseeding after a fire, the area was off limits. But as long as she stayed on the trails, how could a lone woman on foot possibly do any damage?

Summers spent roaming the high forests of New Mexico with her brother, Philip, had convinced Terry that, with sensible precautions, she could safely find her way about the preserve. Besides her 35 mm camera, she took along a spiral ring sketchpad when, just after lunch, she started off on the dirt road bordering the eastern lakeshore. About a quarter of a mile from the guest house, she encountered a deeply rutted track cutting south. Before taking it, she drew a crude map on the first page of the pad, indicated the direction she was following with an arrow. Every time she came upon a fork or a sidetrail in the hours that followed, she recorded it on a fresh page, charting her exact progress. By reversing the sequence when she decided to turn back, it should be easy to find her way home.

The thick sketchpad was half-filled when, to her surprise, she came upon a paved road, so badly deteriorated that the macadam was reduced to pulpy gray fragments scattered around the roots of high weeds that had long ago burst through the surfacing. Until now nothing at Warlord's Hill had even hinted of decay, heightening the sense of desolation that swept over her.

A few hundred feet north lay a house, the same kind of modest bungalow she had seen in the nameless little town where the estate workers lived. The sun was still well clear of the pines west of the collapsed roadway, so she knew she had plenty of time to get home before dark. She walked toward the structure, which must have been abandoned years ago; its sagging walls and crumbling porch were pale gray. A roofless barn and the overgrown fields on three sides of the house indicated the place had once been a farm.

Terry passed a rusted RFD mailbox, its post leaning at nearly a 45-degree angle. Incongruously, the box's pitted flag was up; she almost expected to see the ragged remnants of an outgoing letter inside. Gingerly, she tested the house's lowest porch step with the tip of her right boot. As she anticipated, the termite-riddled wood collapsed with a groan that sounded like a muffled cry of human pain, amazingly loud in the forest stillness. Soft, scuttling sounds came from the house's crawlspace. She knew they had to be made by rats.

I have no right to be here, she thought, feeling a chilly, sinking sensation in the pit of her stomach, as if she had abruptly realized she had violated a tomb. Amid the perfection of Warlord's Hill, the house seemed cursed, the way feudal barons would let a rebellious serf's burned-out hut stand as a warning to other peasants under their rule.

Terry felt an overpowering impulse to get away. But before retracing her steps along the crumbling macadam, she photographed the bungalow. She wasn't certain why she bothered—perhaps to prove to herself, when she went over the pictures in later years, that not even the most astutely managed Eden lacked a flaw or two.

When, using her sequence of penciled maps as a guide, she started back toward the lake, the hands of her wristwatch stood at a few minutes past four. The sun outside the forest wall shone with almost noontime brightness. But as soon as she left open ground, Terry realized that she had overstayed her time. By now the taller stands of pine and red oak blocked the sun's rays so extensively that sections of the trail were as dark as night.

Terry knew she was lost. One of the intersections she had marked on her chain of maps must have been so shadowed that she missed a turn. Along the way, she had stopped to photograph unusual flowers or trees, had been especially on the lookout for patches of black-green club moss; she had read that large masses of the species were rare outside the Warlord's Hill preserve. Now, in one of the increasingly brief periods of good light, she saw sprawling hummocks of the spongy moss on both sides of the track.

Terry sat at the base of a broad-rooted oak, glancing again at her watch. It was just 5:02 P.M., but already, she was surrounded by darkness. The Pine Barrens had closed in on her and there wasn't a damned thing she could do about it. She wished that she had told Wilma of her plans instead of making sure that the housekeeper was busy in the kitchen before beginning her rash excursion. But if Terry had mentioned where she was heading, Wilma would have immediately telephoned the mansion and had a guide forced upon her. From the moment Roy left, Terry had sensed that here, even without him, she would again be overprotected.

I could use a little overprotection right now, she reflected wryly. She had no fear of the woods. If she stayed put until morning, she was sure that she could at least find her way back to the old macadam road. What really disturbed her was the certainty of becoming the object of a massive search. When Wilma reported that she had not appeared for dinner, parties of estate workers would be recruited to scour the trails.

She ruefully recalled Nora Bauer describing the afternoon she had gotten lost, how the huntsmen had finally found her in the dead of night. Now they'll be after me, too, she thought. Only I can't plead childhood as an excuse. I'm a twenty-eight-year-old fool.

Then she heard a low, threatening growl and rose quickly to her feet. A huge, gray-furred dog moved out of the shrouded pines on the other side of the track. The animal paused, studied her with flat, wary eyes—then continued its advance, baring brownish-yellow fangs. In the trees behind the animal, still more than thirty feet away, a black-garbed human form began to take shape.

In another forest, thousands of miles west, Lew Dorn peered through high-powered binoculars, realizing that he and Conrad Webber had lucked out. One of the men they had been sent to kill was pinpointed—and the second could not be far away.

Dorn had expected the search—if it succeeded—to take at least another week. All they had to go on was Harry Krug's unconfirmed belief that John Rawls had holed up in a hunting or fishing cabin in the mountains near Coeur d'Alene. Obtaining a list of those who had rented such places the previous winter was easy enough, since only three local real estate agencies bothered to handle short-term, low-commission leases. Forged documents identifying Dorn as an operative for a national detective agency—and, far more effective, cash payoffs to the realtors—quickly provided the names and the addresses of everyone who had taken out such rentals last winter.

The hitch was that the cabins were scattered over hundreds of square miles of rugged country with which the two huntsmen were unfamiliar—and each prospect would have to be approached with maximum caution. They spent the first morning in their motel room, checking off local renters with verifiable addresses. Phone calls to long distance information operators eliminated most out-of-town possibilities. They ended up with a list of thirty-two isolated cabins, rented by men whose identities couldn't be firmly established. On a detailed Fish and Game Department map, Dorn marked each location. "We'll start with the outlying places," he told his companion. "He'd want a cabin as far as possible from other people."

That afternoon the search began; hour after hour they had bounced over mountain roads in the four-wheel-drive Cherokee they had rented in Spokane; secretly approaching each site on foot, hiding until they glimpsed the cabin's occupants or were certain the place had not recently been occupied. "This isn't going to work," Webber muttered after a drive to a mountaintop lodge revealed that it was inhabited by a couple with seven or eight noisy children.

"We have no other leads," Dorn said, shaking his head in weary disgust as he turned the vehicle around.

"Why didn't they kill Rawls—or whatever his real name is—years ago? Why have they even bothered to keep track of him for so long?"

Although Dorn had often pondered the same questions himself, he gave Webber a reproving glance. "The Old Man has a good reason for everything he does," he snapped. "Tomorrow we'll try farther west, along the Priest River."

A little past three o'clock on Friday afternoon, they reached the last cabin on the south bank of the river where they found a hidden vantage point on a heavily scrubbed bluff overlooking it. The Cherokee had been left a quarter of a mile away. The only human figure in sight—a man in a waterproof jacket and hipboots—stood with his back to them about twenty feet out in the fast-running stream. As the huntsmen looked on, the line on his rod went taut and he began playing a strike with sure, unhurried skill. Minutes later, he reeled in his exhausted catch—a striped bass nearly two feet long, too large for his creel. He turned, holding the weakly thrashing fish by the gills, and waded toward the river bank. Despite the dark bruises and scabbed cuts on his round face, the fisherman was instantly recognizable.

"It's Vic Schall," Dorn grunted. He reached inside his jacket to open the holster flap on his .38 automatic pistol and heard Webber click off the safety on his sniperscope-equipped rifle.

"Can you see Rawls?" Webber asked.

Dorn swiveled the binoculars toward the shack but was unable to distinguish even vague shapes through the grimy glass of its windows. Beyond the shack, he spotted a car parked in a copse of firs, where it could not be viewed from the road. "No—but he wouldn't let Vic out of his sight for long."

Although it was a cool afternoon, beads of sweat appeared on Webber's upper lip. "If the son of a bitch is holding Vic prisoner, why would he let him go fishing?"

The only answer, Dorn thought, was that Vic Schall had formed some kind of alliance with Rawls, confirming the wisdom of the Old Man's decision to execute him. Schall placed his catch on a grassy bank, next to three smaller fish, and splashed back into the water. A few yards east of the bartender's fishing spot was a patch of cottonwood trees and waist-high brush, running all the way to the river. Dorn studied the area for a moment and decided to make use of the cover.

"We'll wait it out," he said. "Rawls has to show himself eventually. And we'd better set up a second line of fire. This way one of them might be able to slip into the woods when the shooting starts."

Dorn crawled off on belly and elbows, expertly working his way down a side of the bluff invisible from the shack. Five minutes later he reached the cottonwoods and positioned himself in a patch of tall grass affording a view of both Schall and the structure. If Rawls was inside, he would be bracketed by gunfire the instant he stepped through the door.

He was so close to Schall that he could hear him muttering unintelligibly to himself. Even though the apparent collaboration with Rawls marked Vic as a traitor, Dorn wished that Harry Krug had given somebody else this assignment. Vic was his wife's first cousin and Dorn himself had always liked the young tavernkeeper. Dorn remembered his own confusion when, more than fifteen years earlier, he had learned that the country outside the wire differed from the Old Man's teachings. But, like the others, he had soon realized that allegiance to the sanctuary could not be broken without dire consequences to his family and neighbors, that if the regular world ever learned of their existence, he and everyone he loved would be branded falsely as monsters. And, despite the Old Man's subterfuges, Dorn had never lost faith in the future that the huntsmen were helping to create.

Nevertheless, he would be happy when, only days from now, the last of the sanctuary's enemies were destroyed and missions like this would become unnecessary. He thought of his son who, if the Old Man's plan failed, might one day undergo the Ceremony of Passage. He had long suspected that Eric was too gentle to kill without remorse, even when the victims were senile, subhuman trash, of so little value that their own people had abandoned them.

Lew Dorn forced his full attention back to the job at hand. Through June 28, at least, the killing would go on.

Terry had no time to experience real fear when the dog and its shadowy human follower materialized from the trees. Don't run, she told herself, remembering the rules her father had taught her. And keep your hands straight down.

The animal, hackles rippling, continued to pad toward her—until its master snapped a command to halt and it instantly froze in place. The figure came close enough for her to recognize the teen-aged boy who had brought Iolanthe to her in the workers' town. His delicate features clashed oddly with his clothing—dark watch cap, black sweater and pants, black boots.

"Can you please show me the way home?" she sighed gratefully.

"You shouldn't have come out alone," the boy said as he led Terry toward the guest house. "I've spent my whole life here and I still get mixed up sometimes."

"I won't be so silly again," she promised, amused at the sternness in his voice. It was as if Eric were the adult and she the child. In these forests, she realized, that wasn't too far from the truth.

The dog—probably a German shepherd and boxer mix—continued his suspicious appraisal of her for minutes after they set off. "Is he as ferocious as he looks?" she asked.

"Yes," Eric said.

"I figured he might be. Why are you out here, anyway?"

"Had guard duty."

"Guarding against what?"

"Poachers."

"Then you're a huntsman?"

"We're all huntsmen. Boys over fourteen, leastwise."

Terry sensed that finally she had found someone who might give straight answers to her questions. Even for isolated backwoods people, the inhabitants of Warlord's Hill had so far been maddeningly taciturn. "Have you ever caught a poacher?"

"No," he admitted, an embarrassed flush rising in his cheeks.

"What are you supposed to do if you find one?"

"Don't tease me, ma'am," the boy said.

"I'm sorry. It's just that there's so much I don't understand. Why were the people in town afraid of me the other day?"

"They *weren't* afraid."

"Then why did they hide?"

The boy turned on to a track so masked by undergrowth that Terry never would have spotted it in broad daylight. "No one from outside ever came before," Eric explained. "Not that I remember, anyway. The folks were just kind of surprised."

Terry Hammil had dozens of other questions but, judging from the increasingly defensive set of the boy's lips, she knew satisfactory replies would be doubtful. Her brother, Philip, had behaved the same way at that age—straightforward right up to the instant he felt his sister was patronizing him. Then sullen silence.

Dusk had fallen when they entered a meadow north of the old foundry dam. For a few seconds, Terry was disoriented. She had started out south of the dam that afternoon, followed what must have been a horseshoe curved course; that she hadn't at some point encountered the broad stream feeding into the lake seemed impossible.

"Lots of brooks run underground for miles," Eric said, apparently guessing her thoughts. "Just a couple feet beneath the sand. But you can always tell where water is, up top or not."

"How?"

"By the cedar trees."

Terry had noticed the narrow strips of white cedar running like pale, endless ribbons through the forest.

"They have thirsty roots," Eric went on. "If you follow the cedars, chances are you'll be right over a hidden brook. After a while, it'll move above ground again. And they all end up in the lake sooner or later."

"A nice thing to remember the next time I get lost," Terry said, brushing her lips over the startled boy's cheek. "Thank you, Eric. I can make it the rest of the way on my own."

The gray dog, at heel behind Eric Dorn, growled deep in its throat as the woman hurried toward the bridge over the foundry dam. A sharp downward flick of the boy's right hand halted the beast's lunge of pursuit. I wonder what her name is, Eric mused, remembering the alarm that had gone through him when, from the window of his attic bedroom, he saw her dismount on Elm Street four days ago. Townspeople who worked regularly at the mansion had already told of a strange couple that had come to Warlord's Hill—*real* people, not the shambling, half-dead creatures kept in the annex to Dr. Zimmerman's clinic—but no one expected to see either of them in Bremen. He turned off his phonograph, accidentally scratching his favorite Bing Crosby record, and hurried out of the house.

Later, he wasn't sure why he decided to approach her—or how he had gathered up the courage. Long before Eric was born, his father had become a member of the elite force allowed to work outside the wire. However, Lew Dorn refused to discuss—with either his wife or two children—what had happened on his increasingly frequent missions in the chaotic near-hell of a world that the Old Man had described over and over again to Bremen's school children. Abruptly, the boy felt an overpowering urge to speak to someone from that terrifying world. He went to the unpaved section of Elm Street and untethered the bay mare, an animal he had often exercised when assigned to work at the stables. He led it toward Heroes Park, where the woman had halted. Even from yards away, he could tell that she was young and beautiful, with long, tawny hair and clear green eyes.

Later that afternoon his father unexpectedly returned home, learned what had happened from his mother, and furiously rebuked Eric for his foolhardiness before reporting to the mansion. But when he came back to their bungalow that evening, the anger in Lew Dorn's eyes had been replaced by puzzlement. "The Old Man said you did the right thing," he muttered. "He's even given you a job. You'll watch her house, follow her whenever she goes into the pines alone. He wants to know everything she does."

"Is she an enemy?"

"Neither a friend nor an enemy," his father replied. "But she *is* from outside the wire. She knows nothing about the sanctuary, of how we live or what we believe—and she must never know."

Although he realized he had violated orders, Eric felt compelled to help the woman when she got lost today. Otherwise she would wander, cold and frightened, throughout the night. He didn't want that to happen, even if it meant enduring the full force of his father's wrath when Lew Dorn completed yet another unexplained mission outside the wire.

Victor Schall, standing thigh deep in the Priest River, knew that John Rawls would soon appear. The sun was close to the western mountain peaks, throwing an orange glare across the water that made visibility difficult—especially for anyone peering through a gunsight. Every day Rawls had called him in at this hour, doubtless afraid that he would take advantage of the confusing light to make a run for the trees.

Vic had no intention of running—not until he had done his best to drown Rawls. Yesterday afternoon, he had noticed a wide pool of suspiciously still water near the river bank, saw that the graveled bottom fell off sharply to a depth of six or seven feet. Now he had carefully positioned himself on the far side of the pool, reeling in line until the two-barbed lure at the end barely touched the surface; in a split second he could bring the rod into casting position. In hands as skilled as Vic Schall's, a rod could be a crippling weapon. The too-heavy nylon line—strong enough to land marlin—that the inexperienced Rawls had bought added to his desperate captive's chances.

Even after being beaten and held prisoner, bound and gagged every night, Schall had planned his move reluctantly. Rawls had made no further attacks—physical or verbal—but, somehow, this lack of hostility was more frightening than anger, emphasizing that, whenever Rawls chose, the torture would resume. As Rawls had predicted, Vic's injuries, despite the bruises on his face and rib cage, proved to be superficial. After the first day he had felt strength return to his aching body—and recalled his captor's steely promise: *When you start wanting all the things guys with a stake in life want*—that's *when I'm going to hurt you again.*

On Wednesday morning, Rawls ordered him to don hipboots and waterproof jacket. "If anyone should stumble on us, I want things to seem normal," he said. "Who in their right mind would stay in a dump like this if he wasn't really fishing? So you're going fishing, Vic. And don't think about trying to get across the river. I can't swim, so I'll have no choice except to shoot you."

Throughout that first, seemingly endless day of casting, every movement sent waves of pain through his body. For more than half an hour, whenever he glanced over his shoulder, he caught Rawls peering at him with expressionless black eyes, the carbine held loosely at his side, muzzle down. Then he looked again and his captor was gone, without a sound.

Quivering from the river cold, Vic retreated to land at noontime, expecting Rawls to challenge him. When nothing happened, the impulse to flee became overwhelming. But his captor had to be nearby; there was no place else to go in this wilderness. So Vic limped over to the shack, prepared a makeshift lunch of tinned Vienna sausages and warm Coors beer. When he left the cabin, Rawls was still nowhere to be seen.

Again he considered trying to escape—and recalled that the thugs who followed Rawls into that Coeur d'Alene alley on Sunday morning must have had him in view every foot of the way—right up to the instant their unarmed victim slaughtered them. Defeated, Vic went back into the river. The glare of the setting sun was bouncing off the water when Rawls at last called to him from the riverbank. The routine was repeated on Thursday. And probably would be followed again today.

Ironically, after Vic Schall finally decided to act, he made his first decent catch, a large perch. Within an hour, he reeled in three more fish, the last a trophy-sized striped bass. He deposited the fish on the grass and waded out into the river to wait for John Rawls, watching orange brightness spread like fluorescent paint over the water.

Vic involuntarily hunched his shoulders when the gunshot rang out. He turned, his vision blurred by the glare he had hoped to use against John Rawls, and saw a nimbus-ringed black silhouette. With a wrist-snapping motion—like the lash of a bullwhip—he sent the lure hurtling toward its target and was rewarded by a piercing howl. He wound in the line with frantic speed, yanking his still-screaming quarry into the river. Simultaneously he heard a second shot, felt a massive weight slam into his chest, and realized he had been hit. Vic Schall continued to wind in the reel until consciousness faded and he tumbled backward into the river.

Lew Dorn had been as startled as Vic by the gunshot, which came from the bluff where Conrad Webber was stationed. Webber must have sighted Rawls, ignored his instructions, and opened fire. Silently cursing the other huntsman's rashness, Dorn lunged from his hiding place, raising his .38 to pick off Schall.

His hand was tightening around the trigger when he heard a rustling whirr and felt the hook stab into his forehead, joining his right brow to the eyelid below. He got off a single shot then dropped his pistol and grabbed at the taut fishline with both hands, trying to slacken it. The nylon strand snapped free of his fingers and, from then on, nothing mattered except the fiery pain. He'll rip out my eye, Dorn thought, stumbling into the river, desperately trying to run faster than Vic could reel in. With a sound like a zipper bursting open, his brow and eyelid tore away; waves of blood gushed down his cheek and into his gaping mouth. Whimpering, he swam back to shore, crawled toward his discarded weapon, and picked it up. He glimpsed a man with a rifle descending the bluff, yelled: "Conrad, help me!"

But it wasn't Conrad Webber. A short, swarthy man with hulking shoulders and wiry black hair halted just beyond accurate handgun range, studying Dorn contemptuously. "Where is the pit?" he shouted. "Tell me and I'll let you live!"

Lew Dorn raised the .38, put the muzzle in his mouth, angled it upward, and squeezed the trigger.

By the dim light of a kerosene lamp, John Rawls began studying the articles spread out on the shack's crude log table, Minutes earlier, he had buried the two Nazis in the woods. A search of the riverbank for Vic Schall's body had proved unsuccessful; the bartender must have been caught in a strong current, swept miles downstream. Poor Vic, he thought. Too damned dumb to realize he'd been staked out.

Even when he believed he had found a safe hiding place, Rawls never relaxed his guard. During the hours Vic stood exposed in the river, Rawls sat atop a high hill on the other side of the road that afforded a view of the countryside for miles around. Vic could have fled at any time—but Rawls had counted on the bartender's own fear to keep him a prisoner. His precautions justified themselves when he spied the Cherokee pulling onto the roadside east of the shack. Two men—one carrying a rifle—got out of the vehicle and slipped into the brush, eventually reappearing on a bluff near the shack. When the man with the automatic headed toward the riverbank, Rawls left his own vantage point, came up on the rifleman from behind, blew away the top of his skull, and zeroed in his carbine on the patch of cottonwoods into which the other Nazi had moved.

Nothing that happened afterward made sense.

Why had the Nazi with the handgun shot Vic? He had watched him for minutes through binoculars, could not possibly have mistaken him for Rawls. Why, after days of refusing to answer Rawls' questions, had Vic turned on a comrade? And why, given a chance to surrender, had the assassin committed suicide rather than take Vic's place as a potential informer? What kind of fanaticism drove such men?

Immediate answers were not to be found among the objects on the table, taken from the Cherokee and the Nazis' bodies. A rental agreement for the vehicle, charged to the Visa card of Wayne L. Rhue. A Maryland driver's license bearing the same name and a New York state license issued to Lyle Stallings of Port Jefferson. A document identifying Wayne L. Rhue as an employee of a nationally known detective agency, stationed in the company's Washington, D.C., headquarters. A Fish and Game Department map of northwestern Idaho. Close to $20,000 in large bills, stuffed in a moneybelt worn around the suicide's waist.

Whatever group the dead men belonged to sure wasn't poor, Rawls thought as he picked up a sheaf of water-soaked hundred-dollar bills. Added to his craps winnings, the currency might enable him to start over again in New Zealand. But now even that fantasy prospect had been poisoned. Weeks ago, he had told Schall of his plans, which Vic must have dutifully reported to his masters. Even if he hadn't, Rawls knew that continued flight would not help in the long run. This time the Nazis had located him in a few days; they would find his scent again, no matter where he went.

But the bastards would assume he had headed farther west, following his pattern of the past eight years. He decided to fool them, drive back East, follow up the clues provided by the captured papers. His course was now clear: Find the men who had ordered a lifelong campaign against him, wipe them from the face of the earth.

※ EIGHT ※

Roy Hammil returned to Warlord's Hill on Monday morning. Lloyd Bauer had already left Washington; after the usual dramatic flurry of voting on obscure last-minute bills, Congress had begun its summer recess.

For a week of putting in fourteen-hour workdays, Roy realized that he had accomplished damned little. Langston Fellows' revelations about Paul Bauer's postwar financial manipulations had been fascinating but, as Fellows himself had pointed out, what bearing did they have on his son's political future? Buying breakfasts, lunches, dinners, and countless drinks for former colleagues was even less productive. Except for Fellows—whom he trusted completely—Roy didn't tell any of his friends his real purpose in consulting them, saying merely that his firm had been approached about handling television and newspaper publicity for a possible Senate race by Lloyd Bauer and wanted the honest off-the-record views of veteran newsmen on the representative's strong points and weaknesses.

"May be hard for you to believe but I didn't have a single contact with Bauer when I worked for Lang Fellows," he told Jack Rudd of the *Post* during their Wednesday lunch.

Rudd signaled the waiter. "Oh, I believe it," he said. "Bauer didn't get moving until after you left the business. One year he's a backbench nebbish. The next he's on Foreign

Affairs and Ways and Means and a couple other big muscle committees. Never saw a congressman make it so fast. Like somebody had lifted a half-ton concrete block off his back."

"I know his record. I don't know the man himself. Not well enough."

"In other words, what's wrong with him?"

Roy nodded.

Rudd ordered a second Jack Daniel's and water before replying. "Not a hell of a lot, actually. What I said a minute ago pretty well covers it. He's a puzzling guy, contradictory. One of those rich men who go into politics without *really* wanting to go into politics."

"I've met my share of them."

"He's got one of the sharpest minds in the House," Rudd continued. "He's a first-rate speaker. All the plus things. But *outside* Congress he doesn't exist. Not in Washington, anyway. I doubt that Bauer and his wife show at more than five or six parties or dinners a session—the ones you have to attend to keep the party leadership from putting out a contract on your grandmother. He owns a big house in Chevy Chase, but you can't get anybody on the phone there between Friday night and Monday morning. Most weekends it's back to Jersey with the family. For a politician aiming as high as Bauer's supposed to be, that's downright peculiar!"

Especially, Roy mused to himself, in view of the fact that only three days ago, Lloyd Bauer had told him how constricted he had always felt by the enforced isolation at Warlord's Hill.

Before catching the Newark shuttle on Monday morning, Roy paid a duty call at Lloyd Bauer's congressional office. If he actually did become Bauer's "media representative," he decided he might as well meet a few of the people with whom he would be working. The only occupants of the suite were a middle-aged secretary and a skinny, intense young man who introduced himself as Sidney Levin, Bauer's chief aide. For want of a better excuse, Roy asked for samples of literature from the last House campaign.

"You've really been staying at Warlord's Hill?" Levin asked as he shoved pamphlets, fliers, and mimeographed press releases into a large manila envelope.

103

"Yes," Roy replied, anticipating Levin's next words.

"You're the first person I've ever known who's been invited. What's it like?"

"Too many trees."

Levin uttered an uncertain laugh. "Lloyd is sort of apologetic sometimes. 'It's not really my house,' he told me once. 'It's the old man's house.' "

After his plane landed at Newark Airport, Roy telephoned the Miller place in Chatsworth and told the woman who answered that he would require transportation to Warlord's Hill in two hours. Jesus, what an insane system, he thought as he drove his car—retrieved with a large dent in the left rear fender from the terminal parking lot—down the Garden State Parkway. But, if you wanted to block out the world, an incredibly effective system. Last night he had considered telephoning word ahead to Terry that he was leaving Washington the next morning. Because of the complicated logistics involved—especially so late in the day—he decided to forget about it.

In the early afternoon, Gerald dropped Roy off at the front door of the guest house. Refusing the chauffeur's offer to carry his single suitcase, he hurried inside, calling out for Terry.

"Mrs. Hammil isn't here, sir," Wilma announced from the kitchen. "She's off with Eric."

"Who the hell is Eric?" he asked irritably when the housekeeper came into the entrance hall, wiping her flour-covered hands on her apron.

"A boy who helps out at the stables sometimes. He's showing your wife around the Pines. No one knows the wild places like Eric does."

Saturday morning, after the previous afternoon's long and embarrassing trek, Terry Hammil had slept past ten o'clock for the first time since coming to Warlord's Hill. Awakened by shrill, quarreling voices, she knew that the Bauer children must be swimming again. She went to a window overlooking the beach and saw that Nora, wearing a one-piece bathing suit, was watching her chronically belligerent sons from a canvas lawn chair.

Terry dressed quickly, went down to the lake. "Good morning," Nora said, lowering a book. "I phoned to see if you wanted to ride, but Wilma said you were sleeping in."

"How did the Philadelphia trip go?"

Nora shrugged her thin, sallow-skinned shoulders. "Decided to stay home."

"Could I beg a favor?"

"Of course."

"You've been wonderful about keeping me company," Terry said, "but I must be a burden by now. With your family and such a big house to look after."

"Not at all," Nora said, nervously digging at her palm.

"I've been wanting to explore the preserve—*really* see it—but not at the cost of taking up all of your time. I was wondering if you could lend me Eric for a few days."

"Who?"

"He's one of the foresters' children. About fifteen or sixteen. Naturally, if he can't be spared—or doesn't feel like shepherding a klutz like me—I'll understand."

"I'm certain there'd be no problem," Nora said. "What's his last name?"

"He never told me." Terry was surprised that Nora didn't know the boy; in the woods yesterday, Eric had mentioned that he frequently groomed and exercised the estate's saddle horses.

"Where did you meet him, by the way?"

"In the town where the estate workers live."

"How in the world did you end up in that place?" Nora's patronizing smile, absent for days, returned to her narrow lips.

"It was where the trail ended."

"I'd try to avoid it in the future." Nora said. "Our parents didn't allow Lloyd and me to go there when we were children. We still hold to the rule. Once, when I was about eight, I asked to visit the home of a little girl who came to the mansion occasionally. Her mother was the third-floor maid. 'It's *their* town,' my father told me. 'We have no right to intrude on their personal lives.' "

Terry Hammil repressed a slightly appalled smile. Nora was in her early forties, was the wife of a United States congressman—and yet she still adhered to a silly, snobbish edict that must have contributed vastly to her childhood loneliness.

"I don't want to intrude on Eric's personal life," she said. "I just want him to keep me from getting lost more often than absolutely necessary."

"One of the servants will know which boy you're talking about. I'll talk to them when we get back."

"Like a cup of coffee? We can keep an eye on the kids from the back porch."

"No, thank you," Nora said, raising the book from her lap.

Tears of humiliation scalded Nora Bauer's eyes after Terry's departure. Nora hadn't believed a word the girl said, knowing that she had simply been seeking an excuse to avoid her company. She had cultivated Terry's friendship at her father's insistence, after their unsuccessful attempt to dissuade her from riding alone on the forest trails.

"The Old Man wants you to be nicer to Mrs. Hammil," Dr. Zimmerman had told her on Tuesday evening.

Having anticipated the order all day, Nora felt her hands tighten involuntarily. "I can't be around people like her! Why do you make me?"

"Calm yourself."

"I don't *know* anything!" Nora said. "Every time Lloyd and I come home from those awful parties in Washington I go into the bathroom and throw up. Because I've spent hours with people who *know* things and I can't talk to them. Because *I* don't know anything!"

"All you have to do is humor her for a week or two," her father said, ignoring Nora's tirade. "It's all she'll expect."

The next morning, Nora had asked Terry Hammil to go riding. And, to her surprise she gradually found herself enjoying her guest's company, especially after learning that Terry had grown up on a remote southwestern ranch and understood the effect such isolation could have on a young girl. But Terry had escaped, Nora thought bitterly, had attended real schools and a real college. Nora's only place of learning had been the long-unused nursery on the mansion's top floor, where the Old Man had taught her how to read and write and perform basic mathematics—and, the most important subject, how to be Lloyd Bauer's wife. Terry Hammil must have finally seen through the facade of faultless manners and grammar and chilly condescension that Nora used to conceal her ignorance. She suddenly appreciated, all over again, how hurt the third-floor maid's daughter must have felt when Nora refused her invitation to play in Bremen.

I'm getting worked up over nothing at all, she told herself angrily, struggling to redirect her attention to Book Three, Chapter Seven of *Anthony Adverse*.

With Terry unaware of Roy's imminent return to Warlord's Hill, this was the day that Eric served for the first time as her official guide. He had appeared at the guest house the previous afternoon, murmuring self-consciously that Gerald the chauffeur had assigned him his new job.

"If you'd rather stick with your regular duties, Eric, just say so," she had told him.

He had shaken his head. "You want to go somewhere today, ma'am?"

"Tomorrow will be fine. I must have already cut into your Sunday. I'm sorry."

They started out the next morning on horseback, following a trail around the lake's northwest shore. Until this ride, the only wild animals Terry had glimpsed were squirrels or rabbits. Now, as if magically conjured by Eric, a deer bounded across the trail only a few yards ahead, grouse fluttered up from a clump of mixed thornbushes and prickly pear. Thousands of birds—including species she had never seen before—wheeled and darted in the sky or perched in the branches of high oaks, their calls filling the air. The farther they rode from the meadows and cultivated fields around the mansion, the more wildlife seemed to appear.

Throughout the journey, Eric remained silent except to indicate something he believed might interest her, as when they rode past a dead pine and he pointed out a wispy, five-foot-long snakeskin impaled on a gray branch thirty feet above the forest floor. "Female flycatcher does that. Finds the skin of a timber rattlesnake after it's shed, hangs it near her nest. Scares off crows and jays and other egg-stealers. I guess crows and jays are so dumb they think rattlesnakes can climb trees.''

However, unlike the afternoon he brought her out of the forest, Eric failed to respond to even such banal personal questions as: ''What grade will you be in when you go back to high school this fall?'' Every attempt was met by an uncertain smile or an embarrassed shrug. She had hoped that, when he learned to relax with her, he could explain some of the aspects of life at Warlord's Hill that still puzzled her. But his reserve seemed to deepen the more time they spent together.

After a halt to rest the horses and eat a picnic lunch packed by Wilma, Eric asked: ''You like to see the place where the orchids grow? The most kinds?''

''I'd love to,'' she said. ''I minored in botany at college.''

The ride to the low-lying area—on the western border of the preserve—took nearly an hour. At the end of a dirt track, they tethered the horses and continued on a footpath winding among copses of tall trees separated by open fields. Within minutes, Terry noticed several varieties of rare tree orchids—rose pogonias; helleborine; even a cluster of southern yellow fringeless, believed extinct in the northeast. The ground plants were even more incredibly varied. Much of what she saw and photographed didn't even belong in North America, including a form of goldcrest that shouldn't exist outside Australia! No wonder Paul Bauer sealed all this off, she thought, imagining the permanent damage that even limited access would cause.

''What you going to do with the pictures?'' Eric asked.

''You've been watching me all along, haven't you? Even before I got lost on Friday?''

The suddenness of the question—and the calm, gentle certainty of her tone—momentarily confused the boy. A deep flush rose in his cheeks and, when he tried to lie, nothing emerged from his lips but an unintelligible stammer.

''Occurred to me after you led me back to the house,'' she continued. ''You said you and your dog had been patrolling the fence, but, actually, we weren't anywhere near it. And I already knew someone secretly watched the Bauer boys while they were swimming. Was that you, too?''

"No, ma'am. We take turns."

"But why do you have to hide?"

"Gerald told me Mr. Bauer wants them to feel free while they're here. Not like babies who have to be looked after all the time."

"That's how *I'm* regarded? Like a child?"

For the first time since they had met, a totally unforced smile came to Eric's lips. "You *did* get yourself lost awfully easy."

She had to laugh at the truth. I suppose the Bauers meant well, she thought. As a woman temporarily alone—and a professional environmentalist—she must have seemed a sure bet to get in trouble. Nonetheless, the idea that Nora or her husband had ordered Eric to spy on her—no matter how benign their intentions—was infuriating.

Eric's hazel eyes widened with fear. Seconds later, Terry heard the faint flapping of rotor blades and turned to see a Park Service helicopter fly low over a stand of pitch pines to the east. They were standing in an open area. Instinctively, Eric hurried beneath the branches of a heavily foliaged oak.

"What's the matter?" she asked, following him.

"Hate those things," he gasped.

"Helicopters must fly over all the time. Wharton State Forest is only about ten miles from here."

"That's what they're called? Helicopters?" Eric said, his hunched shoulders relaxing as the aircraft disappeared.

"We'd better start home," Terry said softly, removing the closeup lens before packing her camera in her shoulderbag. How could a teen-ager of at least normal intelligence possibly be unfamiliar with the word *helicopter*? she wondered. However, she had no immediate need to satisfy her curiosity— not with an entire summer at Warlord's Hill lying ahead.

"She is a Hedricks?" the Old Man said in his rumbling voice, drawing out the words slowly, as if he were savoring the final drops of a bottle of rare wine. "You are absolutely certain?"

"One of the last direct descendants of the *St. Charles* immigrants," Harry Krug said, wishing that he had kept the information to himself longer than four days. But in the Old

Man's presence, he had lacked the courage to hide the truth any longer. "Conrad Webber mailed me photocopies of a newspaper article on her parents' and brother's deaths last year. The clipping arrived in Washington this morning, just as I was leaving for the airport."

Harry Krug had started packing as soon as Peter Uhl, assigned to the morning watch on Roy Hammil, reported that the subject had boarded a shuttle flight to Newark, obviously heading back to Warlord's Hill. Krug had been reluctant to follow, since sending Lew Dorn to Idaho had left the vital Washington base shorthanded, but his orders were firm: Stick with Hammil until his investigation was completed.

Before reading the newspaper story, the Old Man switched the three-way bulb in his desk lamp to the highest position. The unaccustomed brightness cast a harsh, metallic glow over his deepset gray eyes. He finished the article, placed it on the table. "That she should come here," he marveled. "That, out of the thousands of women Roy Hammil might have married, he chose *her*! As if a cosmic power had bent mathematical probability to confirm the rightness of my course!"

Only days ago, Harry Krug had silently cursed what he considered the Old Man's excessive caution. Now he wanted to urge him to be patient, to consider that the success of the June 28 plan was more important than a token act of vengeance. But it would do no good to argue. "Webber and Lew Dorn haven't phoned in a report since Thursday night," he said, hoping to divert the Old Man's attention from Terry Hammil. Actually, Krug wasn't worried about the huntsmen's safety; by now they must be deep' in the mountains of northwestern Idaho, far from telephones.

But the Old Man could not be diverted from his obsession. "What does she look like?"

"One of the firemen in Bremen said she's beautiful. Tall with dark blond hair. Of course, he didn't realize her background."

"It has been years since I actually saw a Jew," the Old Man said, half to himself. "Except for the animals Dr. Zimmerman provides for the Ceremony of Passage. I had forgotten that, especially when young, they often appear no different from other men and women."

"What will you do with her?" Krug asked carefully.

"I'll decide when Dr. Zimmerman returns from Lakewood tomorrow," the Old Man replied. "They were all supposed to be gone by now, Master Huntsman. We were to be living in a world cleansed of racial and moral degenerates. And now one of them has penetrated the sanctuary itself."

The Old Man dimmed his table lamp. Somehow, the fading of the bulb's incandescence from 150 to 50 watts seemed to lower the temperature of the room.

It was less a dream of his own than a flawed memory of someone else's dream, told to him in childhood and immediately forgotten, the way one forgets accounts of other people's dreams. He was surrounded by vague gray shapes that, if it were his dream, he was certain he would have recognized immediately. But it was not his dream, so they never assumed identifiable forms or spoke in identifiable voices. They were like the ghosts of men and women who had been so polite in life that, after death, the best they could manage in the way of haunting was to let their presence be known—but not strongly enough to induce fear. . . .

Roy Hammil was awakened by the sound of quick bootsteps on the stairs. He sat up, momentarily confused. Then he remembered going to the bedroom to unpack his suitcase, lying down to rest for a few minutes.

"Why didn't you let me know you were coming back today?" Terry asked as she rushed through the door. "I wouldn't have gone off the way I did."

He sat up on the edge of the bed, stared at her in wonderment, unable to believe that a week could have made such a change in her appearance. Her skin had taken on a flawless, glowing softness he hadn't seen in more than six months, and the shadows had disappeared from beneath her eyes. The familiar, faded Western blouse and jeans, too loose the last time he had seen her wear them, now fit as perfectly as they had before the funeral in Albuquerque.

"Finished sooner than I thought."

"Anyway, welcome home," she cried, coming to him.

This isn't *home*, Roy Hammil wanted to say, taking her in his arms. However—since, at present, no place else was home either—he remained silent.

⊗ NINE ⊗

"**A**m I really that dull?" Lloyd Bauer asked with a good-humored grimace, glancing at the report on his desk. "No orgies with the girls from the House secretarial pool? Not even a bribe to a Washington cop to avoid a drunk driving charge?"

Roy Hammil had dropped off a summary of his notes at the mansion early Tuesday morning. Less than an hour later, Bauer had telephoned the guest house, summoning him to the ground-floor study. "According to everybody I talked to," Roy said. "*including* a couple of the girls from the House secretarial pool."

"Then I must be that dull." Bauer sighed.

For the first time since taking on this baffling job, Roy found himself growing angry at Lloyd Bauer—the kind of anger that comes from talking to a complex man who patronizingly insists on behaving like a simple man. "Last week you told me I could ask the questions a working reporter might ask," he said. "I assume you meant a reporter covering an actual senatorial campaign."

"Yes."

"Then I can think of only one question that might really count. Who the hell are you?"

"I don't understand."

Roy felt the momentum of the exchange shifting in his

favor. He lit a cigarette, leaned back in his chair. "In the long run, that's the big question that will be asked. Over and over again. Hasn't come up until now because you've run from a district where the Republican nomination practically guarantees election. But in a statewide race, people *will* want to know who you are. Your opponent will make sure of it."

"I never realized I had an identity problem," Bauer said.

"Yesterday morning I picked up a batch of pamphlets and press releases from your last campaign," Roy explained. "Didn't get around to looking at them until after breakfast."

"Routine stuff."

"Extremely routine. My favorite was the direct mail piece with the photo of you, Nora, and the boys lined up on a Sears and Roebuck sofa. I've seen five thousand variations on that flier over the years. Goes into millions of mailboxes every election. It's the one where the candidate touches all the local bases, lists the elementary and high schools he and his wife attended, the PTAs and service clubs they belong to, the hometown charities they support. The whole we're-just-plain-folks bit. Hardly any of that was in your piece. A foreigner, with no knowledge of your family history, would think your life started the first time you ran for public office. There's even less background on Nora."

"You weren't hired to criticize old campaigns, Roy." Bauer's fingers irritably drummed against the leather frame of his desk blotter.

"Next year, if you try for the Senate, it'll be a new campaign. One in which hard questions will be raised."

"We've never emphasized that approach," Bauer admitted grudgingly.

"Why not?"

"Because Nora and I *aren't* just plain folks."

Roy had already learned from his wife that Nora Bauer had grown up at Warlord's Hill, was the daughter of her father-in-law's personal physician, information that hadn't appeared in a single newspaper or magazine piece Roy had read about the congressman. He understood Lloyd's reservations in an age when constituents expected politicians to be superficially commonplace. The circumstances of Lloyd's and Nora's early lives had a sealed-off, elitist quality that a shrewd opponent could exploit, especially among working-class voters.

"You have a point," he conceded. "Still, you've fallen into a basic error. Most people really don't give a damn if a politician is rich or not—as long as he *tries* to offset the image. Doesn't even have to be an effective try. Nelson Rockefeller's I'm-really-a-regular-guy act was so phony it made a hippo's teeth ache, but he won most of his elections."

"First chance I get I'll sign up Nora as a Cub Scout den mother and have myself photographed eating a blintz," Bauer promised sarcastically. "Where do you plan to go from here?"

That Lloyd was bringing their meeting to a close startled Roy. He had not even mentioned the section of the report dealing with his father's private expropriation of millions of dollars in prewar German assets. "I'm not sure yet," he replied. "Incidentally, whatever happened to your Aunt Margarethe?"

"I want to give those pages further study," Bauer said. "You're sure of the facts?"

"The sources were obscure but reliable."

"I should be grateful to you. Without meaning to, you've come up with the answers to questions that have puzzled me all my life. Why my father retired so young, fenced off the estate. Why I was educated at home. Dad always said it was because of my health—I had nearly crippling asthma as a child—but somehow the explanations never quite rang true."

"You didn't know any of this?" Roy asked, managing to conceal his astonishment.

"Did you?"

"I don't live here, Lloyd. And it was before my time."

"Mine, too." Bauer studied Roy for a moment, his expression simultaneously sad and amused. "You find it hard to believe, don't you? That I have so little information about all the sources of my family's fortune?"

"Your father was never publicly accused of pulling a scam," Roy said. "Even the economists I studied only hinted at it."

"Haven't thought about my aunt in years. My father and she had a terrible quarrel, never spoke to each other again."

"A quarrel about what?"

"Is this relevant to your investigation?"

"Probably not."

"But you're asking anyway?"

"Your father and Margarethe van Behncke are public figures," Roy said. "Her husband plotted to assassinate Adolf Hitler. Paul Bauer—to his credit, as far as I'm concerned—cheated the top Nazi industrialists out of a fortune. They're both in the history books—maybe as footnotes or at the bottom of paragraph twelve on page six hundred and eighty-three—but nonetheless they are there. And if you go as far in national politics as the experts think you will, they'll move *out* of the footnotes. It's inevitable. Ask that poor cousin of Jackie Onassis who lived in a decaying house with two or three hundred cats and, all of a sudden, found herself on the front page of the *National Enquirer*."

Lloyd Bauer stood up, moved to a window, and thoughtfully peered out over the mansion's broad south lawn. "After the war, my father tried to get Aunt Margarethe and her son to the States," he said. "For some reason she was forced to remain in Europe for years, but he managed to obtain a visa for the boy. Ironic, really. Poor little Theo survived air raids and exposure and near-starvation. And he died in the place where he had finally found refuge."

"Here at Warlord's Hill?"

Bauer nodded. "He was playing in an abandoned gravel pit, was caught by an earthslide, and broke his neck. One of those freak accidents that no one can possibly foresee. But Aunt Margarethe blamed my father, severed all contacts with the family."

"When did it happen?"

"Around nineteen forty-seven or forty-eight. My father rarely talked about it—or about Margarethe. I suppose he tried occasionally for a reconciliation. He'd hoped that she would settle here, I imagine. My mother died a few months after I was born. Margarethe was his only sister—and Warlord's Hill is a lonely place under *happy* circumstances. . . . Aren't we straying pretty far afield?"

"Your lawyers must know Mrs. von Behncke's present whereabouts."

"Hardly a mystery, Roy. She's lived in Winter Park,

Florida, since the early fifties." Lloyd Bauer suddenly turned to face him, his eyes narrowing with suspicion. "You want to interview her?"

"Yes."

"Why?"

"Because, if you try for the Senate, someone *else* might interview her. You should know in advance what she's likely to say."

"I couldn't have been more than twelve years old when my aunt came home from Germany. I've never even met her. How could anything she say damage me?"

"I'm playing by *your* rules, Lloyd, not mine," Roy said. "So I can't know what I'm supposed to be looking for until I find it. The worst accusation any working reporter had to bring was that your father bought your first election."

Lloyd Bauer's laughter was deep and genuine. "To protect his financial interests?"

"Yes."

"They tell those stories about any politician from a wealthy family. You know that as well as I do."

"I also know that the stories are frequently true."

"Even when the diabolically clever old man who controls the politician's every move *has* no interests?" Lloyd Bauer asked with a mocking smile. "My father is usually awake at this hour. Would you care to meet him?"

The crumbling brick walls, so covered by ivy that they seemed part of the forest, lay just a few hundred feet upstream from the old foundry dam. "All that's left of Bassing Furnace," Eric told Terry Hammil. "It was the biggest ironworks in the Pines, but there were lots of others—whole towns built around forges. Then the high-grade iron strikes in Pennsylvania put them all out of business. Nothing left now but ruins like these."

Since Terry hadn't wanted to go far on Roy's first day back at Warlord's Hill, she had asked Eric to show her the area bordering the main compound. "What's that?" she asked, pointing to a high mound of what looked like reddish-brown, irregularly shaped rocks.

"Bog iron ore," the boy said. "I guess that pile has sat

right there for more than a hundred and fifty years. Only place in the world you find bog iron is the Pines. Rain water soaks through the beds of pine needles on the ground, picks up acid that leaches iron out of the sand. You can see it after a big storm—a green scum on the streams and lakes. Mixes with gravel and sandstone on the banks and when the stuff hardens in the dry season, that's bog iron.''

Terry gazed at her young companion with puzzled eyes. As always, when dealing with the topography and history of the Pine Barrens, he spoke with assurance. But whenever she maneuvered the conversation around to the present, his speech became stumbling and uncertain, as if he knew nothing of the world beyond the estate's gates. "Eric, have you ever been away from the Pines?" she asked impulsively.

That now-familiar, clouded look settled over his fine-bonded features. She could tell that he wanted to lie to her—and knew instinctively that he would not. "No, ma'am," he said in a low voice.

"But what about your education?"

"Already graduated."

"From that little school in town?"

"Yes."

"Haven't you ever *wanted* to leave?"

Eric stared at her without comprehension, as if to say: *Everything I need is here.* And, she thought, that might not be far from the truth. All of the estate workers she had seen were healthy and well fed and seemingly content; the houses in which they lived were solid and perfectly maintained. Less than an hour's drive from Warlord's Hill, other men, women, and children—migratory workers who harvested the crops on most south Jersey farms—were crammed into filthy tarpaper shacks, dressed in ragged hand-me-downs, subsisting on skimpy meals of rice and beans and scrap pork. Many years ago Eric's parents—or, more likely, grandparents—had made a better deal, become a part of Paul Bauer's strange private world, actors contracting for minor roles in a costume drama that never closed.

"Do any of you ever leave?" she asked—and immediately felt foolish, remembering the uncorroded brass plaques on the town's war memorial.

Before she could apologize for her thoughtlessness, Eric said defensively: "Folks come and go all the time. My dad's working outside the wire now. And Wilma's son, Vic, has been off someplace for months."

"I'm sorry, Eric," she said. "I didn't mean to sound condescending. Should we start home? My husband must be about finished with his business."

Eric's dog had wandered off behind the ruins of Bassing Furnace. The boy clapped his hands and the animal instantly reappeared, following them as they started back toward the lake road.

The old man sat by an east window; its fully open drapes afforded a broad view of the pine woods. The late morning sun, pouring through the glass, bathed the room in a soft golden glow.

"This is my father," Lloyd Bauer said.

The instant a stout, gray-haired woman in a nurse's uniform opened the door to the second-floor bedroom, Roy Hammil guessed what lay beyond: The musty smell of death-too-long-delayed had reached his nostrils. Tanks of oxygen and the small refrigerator in the corner and the tubes hanging expectantly from a steel-framed bedside stand soon afforded visual confirmation. The shrunken, pajama-clad figure by the window seemed incidental to the banks of life-support equipment. Small, colorless, and silent, Paul Bauer occupied his wheelchair the way the discarded shell of a lobster occupies the edge of a dinner plate, existing only to define the shape of the living organism that had once filled it.

"I'm sorry, Lloyd," Roy Hammil said when they returned to the hall. "How long has he been that way?"

"Since the third stroke, about a year and a half ago. Sometimes he can raise his right hand or blink, but I'm afraid that's about it."

They went downstairs and were about to re-enter the study when a tall, heavy shouldered man in khaki work clothes came through the front door. Roy was immediately struck by the contrast between the newcomer's powerful outdoorsman build and garments and the pallor of his skin, as if he were a lumberjack who improbably had chosen to work only at night.

"You wanted to see me, Harry?" Lloyd Bauer asked, obviously annoyed that the man had not rung before entering.

"If you can spare a couple of minutes."

"Harry is our Master Huntsman. The title dates back to the days before my father turned the place into a wildlife sanctuary."

"Of course, we still hunt, sir," Harry Krug told Roy. "We have to. With no natural predators, the deer, especially, would overbreed and starve in the winter. But we only kill the weak and the sick. Always been mighty careful about that."

The ambulance from the Golden Era Retirement Center—the only modern vehicle permitted on the roads of Warlord's Hill—had passed through the gates a few minutes before noon. Dr. Roger Zimmerman sat in the rear, beside a stretcher bearing the unconscious body of Mrs. Sophie Braunstein. Choosing the eighty-six-year-old woman for the Ceremony of Passage had troubled Zimmerman. Usually he selected only patients who were hopelessly senile or suffering from physical agony so unbearable that not even the heaviest dose of morphine provided effective relief. Although the sticklike figure on the stretcher was nearing death from liver and kidney deterioration, she was still capable of walking without a cane and her mind functioned with reasonable clarity. However, because of the emergency created by the June 28 plan, he had been forced to compromise with his personal ethics in this case. Besides, he was certain that, if the opportunity were freely offered, Mrs. Braunstein would prefer extinction to the months of increasing pain and enfeeblement that lay ahead if her life followed its natural course.

During the journey from Lakewood, his thoughts had not been primarily on the woman. In a sense, she was already gone, since he had signed her death certificate more than a week ago, his customary procedure with patients chosen for the Ceremony of Passage. It allowed time for previously unknown friends and relatives to appear. If an exhumation were ordered—and in thirty-four years this had never happened—the patient's life would be terminated in such a way that death

119

by natural causes could be faked, the body placed in its already marked space in the home's private cemetery. However, such events were extremely unlikely. The men and women who lived at Golden Era had been picked from the penniless aged; they had willingly traded degradation in filthy welfare hotel rooms or hospital charity wards for the security and comfort of the Lakewood facility. Only two requirements were necessary for admission: Jewish ancestry and the word *none* written in the application space marked *next of kin*.

The safety period after the filing of Mrs. Braunstein's certificate had ended last night. He was making arrangements for her transfer to Warlord's Hill when Harry Krug had unexpectedly turned up at his office. "The Old Man told me you were coming back tomorrow," the Master Huntsman said, going on to explain how he had learned the truth about Terry Hammil's background. "You have to talk him out of killing her—not in the pit, at least. It just won't make sense to our people."

Mrs. Braunstein stirred and raised a quivering left hand. Zimmerman grasped it comfortingly in his own, and she settled back into the sedated sleep in which she had existed for days, hidden in a special, soundproofed room in the retirement home's attic. The mottled, yellowing texture of their joined fingers was disturbingly similar, Dr. Zimmerman thought. Only recently, with a sudden chill, had it struck him that he was already two years older than the youngest person he had delivered to the pit.

The ambulance crossed a slight ridge, descended into the thickly wooded valley that sheltered the Warlord's Hill clinic, passed the clinic itself, and finally halted at the cinderblock annex. It took the driver and attendant only a few minutes to transfer the comatose Mrs. Braunstein to the care of waiting nurses. Dr. Zimmerman's home—a two-story brick colonial—was shielded from the medical buildings by a thick stand of oak. After the ambulance dropped him off, he went into the living room, waiting for the telephone message that would summon him to the shadowed bedroom on the top floor of the mansion. He had never before disputed the Old Man's wishes and dreaded the confrontation that lay ahead.

*   *   *

As he walked down the road from the mansion, Roy saw Terry and a slightly built boy, trailed by a large gray dog, heading toward the plank bridge. Terry noticed him and waved. He returned the wave and quickened his pace, halting abruptly when the dog uttered a threatening growl. However, at a signal from its master, the animal sank to its haunches.

When he was close enough to make out the boy's features, Roy understood, with a deep wrench of pity, why Terry had prevailed upon Nora Bauer to lend her his services as a guide. The move had puzzled him, since he knew that it usually took his wife weeks or months to make new friends. Now he understood. The kid didn't resemble Philip Hedricks facially but his slender frame and pale blond hair and awkward manner was uncannily reminiscent of Terry's dead brother. And he was about the same age Philip had been when Terry left Two Moons Ranch for a college in the East, returning only for brief visits. Last Sunday she had told him how much Warlord's Hill had reminded her of that lost childhood home. Now, in less than a week, she had found a living surrogate for one of the beloved people who had vanished with it.

"You haven't met Eric," Terry said, turning toward the boy. "I'm sorry, but you've never told me your last name."

"Dorn."

"Eric Dorn. My husband, Roy Hammil."

The boy acknowledged the introduction with a shy, twitching shrug. "Be needing me anymore today?" he asked Terry.

"I don't think so."

"Tomorrow?"

Terry glanced inquiringly at Roy.

"I'll be gone most of the day," he said.

"Regular time then?" Eric said.

"Fine."

Roy waited until Eric and the dog were out of earshot before remarking, "Kind of quiet, isn't he?"

"Not on some subjects. Where are you headed tomorrow?"

"The city."

"New York?"

Roy nodded. "Why don't you come along? While I'm working you can shop or visit friends. We'll have dinner, stay over at a hotel."

"Darling, I'm just settling in *here*," she said with a husky laugh. "And I'd get in your way. You'd be right in the middle of an interview and have to break it off to meet me. Used to happen all the time, remember?"

As they walked hand in hand toward the guest house, Roy wondered about the woman he had married. During the years they had lived in Washington and Manhattan apartments, Terry had never expressed nostalgia for Two Moons Ranch. Only after the loss of her entire family had she begun to dwell upon the life she had voluntarily left ten years earlier. The trouble with his speculations was that Roy himself had no personal yardstick against which to measure her emotional reactions. Whatever memories he had of his own parents had long been lost, their personalities merged with the couples who had looked after him in at least a dozen different St. Louis foster homes. "Your father was killed in the war," one of those temporary caretakers had told him, "and your mother just ran off." "They got sick and died," another had informed him curtly. The majority said nothing. After a while it hadn't mattered. Most men were middle-aged before they realized that the past would inevitably betray them; Roy Hammil had known it when he was twelve.

But what in the hell do my hang-ups have to do with Terry? he thought, tightening his grip on her hand. Obviously she had found a kind of peace at Warlord's Hill. When they made love last night, she had received him without the tension that had constricted her body for months. After she fell asleep, he had checked the bathroom cabinet, discovered that the cotton was still in the full bottle of Valium tablets she had brought from New York. That in itself was reason enough to stick out the summer here. Maybe temporary immersion in a simpler time—even an artificially sustained past like Warlord's Hill—might have a kind of healing power if the present was still not quite bearable for her. At the very least, another month or two here could do no harm.

Darkness had fallen, he had eaten his dinner, and still the phone remained silent. The Old Man must already know what I'm going to say, Dr. Zimmerman thought. He had always known, even a half century ago when Zimmerman and Paul

Bauer were undergraduates at Leipzig and the Old Man had been the university's most brillant young philosophy instructor—and, outside the classroom, a leader of the emerging National Socialist party.

Three years before Hitler came to power, the Old Man had recruited Zimmerman and Paul for a Nazi support group. As American citizens they had not been eligible for full membership, were of primary value as contributors of hard foreign currency to the organization's treasury. "Our enemies keep lists and it is better that your names not appear on them," the Old Man had explained. "We will eventually have great need for your services—not here but in the United States." And they *had* been needed later—in ways he had never realized. Paul, the Old Man's confidant, must have been more aware of what was to come in the years ahead. But had even *he* conceived that his son and Zimmerman's daughter would be needed? Eventually, Zimmerman's grandchildren?

This house is too big, he reflected, wishing he were back at his apartment in the Golden Era Retirement Center. It had been too big even when he shared it with Nora and his wife. Fortunate, simpleminded Ann. During the thirty-eight years of their marriage, she had never conceived of Warlord's Hill as anything except a vast country estate, been delighted that the servants were not only unfailingly obedient but white, equally delighted that their daughter shared a private classroom at the mansion with Paul Bauer's son. She chided him occasionally about bringing the oldest and most debilitated Golden Era patients to the clinic annex. "It's so depressing," she often told him. "Why do they have to come here to die?" He always replied: "To spare the other residents emotional pain." Her equally inevitable answer: "What about *my* emotional pain? Always somebody sick next door." Even now, thirteen years after her own death, he wondered why he continued to deeply miss so stupid a woman.

"Are you thinking about Ann?" the Old Man asked.

Startled out of his reverie, Dr. Zimmerman sat upright in his armchair. How long had the Old Man been studying him? he wondered. And why?

"Yes, Joseph, I was," he said.

"I knocked but apparently you did not hear. Do you mind that I let myself in?"

"Of course not." As usual, on the rare occasions that he saw the Old Man in strong light, Dr. Zimmerman marveled at how little he had changed over the years. His once-dark brown hair was now white, and the furrows in his gaunt, angular face were a little deeper—but his body seemed as erect and hard as when they had first met.

The Old Man sat on a small couch across from Zimmerman's armchair. "I was always sorry I never really got to know Ann," he said. "But it was better that she continue to regard me only as Nora's tutor."

"Much better," Zimmerman said.

"Did you bring us a Jew?"

"Yes."

"We will need two."

"Only one huntsman has been prepared for the Ceremony of Passage."

"I have another candidate in mind."

"No one can be brought here immediately without endangering security," Dr. Zimmerman protested.

"There is the Hedricks woman," the Old Man said. "Although I suppose, like Krug, you want to spare her. I could tell from his expression how he really felt about the matter. Now he has recruited you?"

"She's too young."

"That has never prevented anyone from dying."

"Too young for the pit," Dr. Zimmerman said. "We brought the Bremen refugees to Warlord's Hill in nineteen forty-one, when the United States was still neutral. No one outside Germany, in those days, had an inkling that a program of moral purification had begun. The most extreme action advocated by the national Bund was the transportation of Jews and other undesirables to special reserves. A few local factions, like the Bremen group, accepted the idea of euthanasia for racial defectives too old or sick or feeble-minded to perform useful labor. And when you came back to Warlord's Hill after the war, you did not choose to extend these policies."

The Old Man shrugged. "I saw no reason to disturb the

consensus among our people. Not until we were in a position of authority outside the wire."

"Then you *must* see the illogic of using Mrs. Hammil for the Ceremony of Passage. Executing old Jews, only days or weeks from natural death, is a universally accepted ritual. The shooting of a young, healthy woman will provoke questions, doubts. Krug has already been forced to kill three huntsmen who rebelled. Vic Schall will probably be the fourth. Why risk discord in the sanctuary itself just for the sake of a symbolic gesture?"

Anger clouded the Old Man's silver-gray eyes. "The proper manipulation of symbols is the true source of political power."

Zimmerman knew that he had gone too far. In his desperation, he had forgotten that the Old Man had been one of National Socialism's foremost theoreticians, had helped draft the Nuremberg racial laws. His last statement had often been quoted by Hitler himself in speeches at party congresses. Not to destroy one of the last descendants of the Hedricks family—even a defenseless girl—was as unthinkable to the Old Man as refusing to quarantine the world's last smallpox carrier would be to a dedicated physician.

The Old Man rose, stared down at Dr. Zimmerman from his immense height. "Goodnight, Roger," he said at last, striding toward the entrance hall. Zimmerman heard the door softly open and close.

Had he made any impression at all? the shaken doctor wondered. After June 28, according to the original plan, the three outsiders who knew the deepest secret of the sanctuary would be dead. Then most of the huntsmen outside the wire were to be called back. The Ceremony of Passage would be suspended, since only children and a handful of unreliable adult males had not already undergone the ritual. According to the Old Man's scheme, the years of quiet waiting would begin, the prolonged training period when Lloyd and other potential leaders recruited from among the sons of prewar German sympathizers would begin reaching the top levels of state and national government, paving the way for an inevitable Nazi coup.

And already the first stage of the plan was coming apart, changed day by day at the Old Man's whim. Roy Hammil's research had pinpointed more potential candidates for death. And now the Old Man was contemplating the unnecessary slaughter of Hammil's wife. He had not left Warlord's Hill in thirty-two years, isolating himself from the contemporary world by his own wish; could he be losing control of his mental faculties? The possibility had first occurred to Zimmerman when the Old Man had shrugged off the news that one of the three original assassination targets had disappeared, taking Vic Schall with him as a captive. If every other aspect of the June 28 operation succeeded, the danger would not be reduced a single degree as long as John Rawls remained at large.

The AP story, only four paragraphs long, was at the bottom of a column on page fourteen of the *Kansas City Star* second section. THREE SLAIN IN IDAHO WILDERNESS the tiny headline proclaimed. John Rawls silently cursed himself for not having the patience to search further for Vic Schall after he disappeared in the Priest River. A game warden had discovered the still-unidentified bartender's body washed ashore only a few hundred yards downstream from the fishing shack. After finding spent shells from two different rifles, police had combed the area around the shack, turning up the common grave of the two Nazis—also unidentified—and Rawls' Pinto. He had hidden the car deep in the woods.

Rawls had noticed the item while eating dinner at a Howard Johnson's restaurant on Interstate 70. He folded the paper back to the front page, placed it on the unoccupied counter seat to his right, slowly finished his meal of fried clams, and ordered another cup of black coffee. By now, he figured, the Idaho State Police must have identified Vic and traced the Pinto's ownership. He had removed the license plates and scaled them into the river but had lacked the time or proper tools to obscure the engine and chassis serial numbers. The deaths of the thugs in Coeur d'Alene had not been investigated with real enthusiasm, since the cops had probably figured from the evidence that he had killed in self-defense, then panicked and ran. However, Vic had been his friend— and if the corpses in the Priest River grave were muggers, they had sure as hell been operating in unlikely territory. He was now the chief suspect in five murders—and this time the manhunt would be real.

He sipped his coffee while figuring the odds. The sensible move would be to go into hiding again until his pursuers gave up. He had more money than ever before in his life, and could stay underground for years, if need be. But that would only delay the inevitable. He was certain that the names on the papers he had taken from the Nazis were fake; without even their aliases to go by, the police would have a rough time linking them to the rented Cherokee. If Rawls ditched the four-wheel-drive vehicle—used on the trip because both the cops and Vic's comrades had descriptions of the Pinto—he would have to take public transportation or pay cash for another car, drawing unnecessary attention to himself.

No, he decided, I'll continue as planned. But he realized he must limit his route to secondary roads, avoiding highways heavily patrolled by State Police. It would add days to the journey, but he had no choice—especially transporting the three cases of dynamite he had bought the day before in Cheyenne, Wyoming.

⨳ TEN ⨳

When Roy Hammil came through the entrance doors of the East Fifty-seventh Street offices of Huggins and Associates, the receptionist looked at him with astonishment, as if he had been on a leave of absence for two years rather than a week and a half. "Anyone taken over my office yet, Gladys?" he asked.

The girl shook her head. "Mr. Lockwood won't be moving in until tomorrow. But your secretary has been reassigned to Hal Rogow."

"All I need is a chair and a clear desk," he said. He glanced at his watch, saw that it was nine forty-two; Merle Huggins would still be holding the morning staff meeting. If he worked fast, he could accomplish his mission and be gone before Merle realized he had even been in the office, thereby avoiding a prolonged conversation with his garrulous employer.

From the moment he learned the details of the last four decades of Bauer family history, Roy had wondered why Paul Bauer had established the Foundation for Geriatric Research. Here was a man so withdrawn from society that he had created one of America's great wildlife sanctuaries as a source of private pleasure, banning the most highly qualified conservationists from access; a man so distrustful of contemporary civilization that he had gone to bizarre lengths to make sure that his physical surroundings reflected a bygone year in every detail. At the same time he had donated seventy million dollars of his personal fortune to a medical program of wide-reaching significance to the very world he had forsaken. Unless Bauer had hoped the foundation came up with a serum guaranteeing him eternal life, his behavior seemed curiously inconsistent.

Except for frequent mention of the original endowment, Paul Bauer's name seldom appeared in the pamphlets and press releases Roy yanked from the PR company's files. The only extensive material on a familiar name dealt with Dr. Roger Zimmerman, a member of the foundation's governing board and director of the Golden Era Retirement Center, one of many nonprofit facilities sponsored by the foundation. Although the policy was only implied, the elderly indigents who entered the homes served as voluntary test subjects for life-prolonging drugs and techniques developed by Bauer-supported research at major universities.

Roy recalled the ambulance he had seen approaching the gates of Warlord's Hill last week. Dr. Zimmerman obviously had enough pull to get an exemption from the estate's ban on modern automobiles—more than Paul Bauer's son had ever managed.

The sketchy details of Zimmerman's background explained the clout. Terry had already told him that Paul Bauer and the physician were lifelong friends, but not until reading Zimmerman's biography had he realized the closeness that must have existed between the two men. Both had been born to wealthy German-American families on Philadelphia's Main Line. Both had been partially educated in Europe, entering Leipzig University in the late twenties. Later, however, choice of profession had separated their lives—Zimmerman graduating from the University of Pennsylvania medical school; Bauer entering the family firm, taking over full control upon his father's death in 1937. But the personal friendship had remained so strong that, in time, their only children had married.

It's so damned *neat*, Roy thought, almost angrily. Like one of those seamless Victorian novels where a rich boy and girl grow up in neighboring English country houses, have a couple of misunderstandings but finally get married and spend the rest of their lives strolling hand in hand over impeccable green lawns. But no real life is free of loose ends, not even Lloyd Bauer's life. If it were, Roy would not be following this blind trail to an unknown goal.

After learning that Gerald had driven Roy Hammil to Chatsworth that morning, Lloyd Bauer felt the tension start to build within him. Logically, he should be relieved, since it proved that Hammil still had no inkling that the potential threat to Lloyd's political career lay within the fences of Warlord's Hill. What could poor old Aunt Margarethe—or anyone else outside the wire—tell him?

However, the doubts continued to dull his concentration as he sat behind his study desk, fitfully attempting to insert local references into the stock welfare-reform talk he was supposed to deliver that evening at a Rahway Elks Club dinner dance. Stupid to have worked at home, he decided; if he had gone to his district office, Sid Levin could have drafted and polished the routine material in less than twenty minutes; Lloyd had already spent at least an hour and a half on the trivial job, having put down nothing useful. Suppose a few obscure links between the sanctuary and the old Bremen still existed—and Roy Hammil stumbled upon them?

The aggravating noise of a vacuum cleaner intruded on Lloyd's thoughts. He threw down his pencil, slid open the study's double doors, and saw Catherine running the machine along the hall carpet. The voluptuous young maid smiled and turned off the cleaner. The morning was warm, and tiny beads of perspiration stood out on her flawless white skin. He had often wondered why the sanctuary's women never seemed to be touched by the sun. Female house servants were supposed to keep their hair up, but Catherine had always ignored the rules; the thick, rich auburn mass cascaded halfway down her back. It had been nearly two years since he had made love to the girl—or, except for giving casual orders, even spoken to her. He wondered if time had started to loosen the taut youthfulness of her breasts, or subtly thickened the sweeping inner curves of her tiny waist, obscured by her bulky apron.

Nora and the kids had gone down to the lake, probably wouldn't be back until lunch. Another maid was on duty during the day but she would still be upstairs, cleaning the bedrooms. "Come on in, Catherine," he said. She smiled with immediate understanding, brushing past him as she entered the study. He joined her, sliding the double doors closed but not bothering to lock them. No one, not even Nora, was permitted to disturb him when he was working.

Without speaking, Catherine undressed, carefully folding each article before placing it on a chair. Her prim neatness aroused him more than if she had scrambled out of her garments, or let them slip to the floor in a pile. And her gradually exposed body was as ripe and vibrant as he had remembered. The last article she removed was her brassiere—one of those rigidly supporting, rubberized white bras that young women outside the sanctuary had scorned for decades. When it slipped free, her breasts seemed to spring forth, eager for freedom. She flicked a loose strand of dark red hair off her brow and started toward the oversized black leather couch.

"No," Lloyd Bauer said. "The way I like best."

Catherine nodded and went to her hands and knees on the floor. Her breasts hung straight down, curves swaying only inches above the deep carpeting. Lloyd Bauer opened his denim pants and mounted the girl, thrust himself effortlessly into her already enveloping wetness. As an inexperienced young man, he had never quite been sure that the girls of Bremen weren't faking their responses, had wondered why they had not been humiliated by the casual way he made use of their bodies. But, like all the others, Catherine's moans of pleasure were genuine; the writhings of her wide buttocks against his heavy belt buckle unfeigned. She felt honored that Lloyd Bauer had chosen to take her on the office floor. It was a power that he possessed only within the boundaries of Warlord's Hill, a power that the Old Man had given him, one of the few powers that Lloyd would hate to relinquish on the long-anticipated day when he at last banished the Old Man and his followers.

As his thrusts grew deeper and more urgent, Catherine's shoulders and upper arms quivered under the assault. "Let yourself down," he commanded. Softly moaning, she lowered her body toward the floor. He reached around, caught her breasts just before they touched the rough carpet, felt the mounds of soft flesh spread out gratefully over his cushioning hands, her dark, hard nipples nudging his palms. His hands opened and closed around her breasts in unison with his climactic stabs.

Lloyd Bauer rested his sweating right cheek on Catherine's naked back, listening to shuddering breaths rise through her rib cage. His slack lips lay against the pink indentations created by the taut strap of her discarded bra. He gently kissed the temporary welts, like a parent trying to heal a toddler's minor bruise.

The moment Nora and her sons entered the front hall—and she saw the upright vacuum cleaner abandoned opposite the study doors—she realized that Lloyd was with the red-haired maid. It had happened again and again over the years, with many of the sanctuary's young women, but before he had always taken his pleasure in the guest house on the other side of the foundry stream. Of course, that was no longer possible. For the first time in Nora's memory, the "guest house" actually held guests.

"Go get dry," she snapped at Paul and Roger, who clutched sopping towels over their skinny shoulders. A sudden overcast had prompted their early return from the lake. When the boys had started up the stairs toward the Bauers' living quarters, Nora looked at the study doors again, fighting the impulse to fling them open. But she knew that she would not, just as she knew that the girl's role at Warlord's Hill was as rigidly set as her own. From childhood, Catherine must have been taught that Lloyd Bauer was the heir to his father's role as protector and overlord, that she owed him an allegiance so complete that it included unrestricted access to her body—just as Nora had been taught that, one day, she would bear Lloyd's children, would share the unspecified greatness that the Old Man promised lay ahead for both of them.

And what, in the forty-second year of her life, had it come down to—except standing, incapable of action, outside a door while Lloyd fornicated with a bovine maid young enough to be their daughter?

Angry tears scalding her eyes, Nora turned, went to the

vacuum cleaner, removed the loaded inner bag, opened it, and dumped the fuzzy, gray debris in front of the study doors. It was a childish thing to do, but Nora had recently begun to realize that she was still a child, that Lloyd was a child, that her father was a child, that Paul Bauer was a child. Only the Old Man was not a child—and, probably, never had been. She pictured him, a fully formed monster, clawing his way out of his mother's womb, rending her body to scarlet shreds as he emerged.

Muffling her sobs, Nora fled up the stairs.

"My husband?" Catherine asked hesitantly. "Do you know where he is?"

Lloyd Bauer, sitting on the couch, had been watching the maid dress as fastidiously as she had removed her garments half an hour earlier. Her question startled him. "You're married, Catherine?"

She reached behind her back to tie her apron. "For a year and a half," she said. "To Vic Schall, Wilma's son."

"I didn't realize."

"Doesn't matter," Catherine replied with a shrug. "Not with *you*. But he's been gone for months and I'm worried about him. The Master Huntsman just says that he's working outside the wire and will be home soon. Wilma doesn't say much, but I know she worries, too."

Lloyd Bauer struggled to frame an answer, unwilling to admit that, until this moment, he had no idea Wilma had a son. He had known her since childhood but, by the Old Man's edict, he had been forbidden to ask household servants and grounds workers about their personal lives. The tradespeople of Bremen and most of the forestry staff were as much strangers to him as the inhabitants of an isolated village in Mesopotamia. "I'm not familiar with Mr. Krug's work assignments," he said, "but I'll speak to him about your husband at the first opportunity."

She gave him a grateful smile, went to the sliding doors, and hesitated in surprise when she opened them. Lloyd joined her and saw the pile of vacuum-cleaner dirt near the threshold, left the way a witch doctor might curse an enemy by depositing a strangled cat on the doorstep of his hut. He heard the voice of his older son from the next floor and realized that Nora and the boys had come home early.

"Just clean up the mess and take off for the rest of the day," Lloyd said, patting the maid on the shoulder. He suddenly realized that he would never make love to Catherine again—not because his wife, obviously, had discovered his impulsive act, but because by volunteering information about her personal life, Catherine had broken one of the rules that governed day-to-day life at Warlord's Hill. Lloyd hated but understood the necessity of maintaining the wall of ignorance erected between the Bauers and the other men and women of the sanctuary. Nevertheless, the accidental revelation that the Old Man was sending some of his people outside the wire for months at a time worried him. What in God's name could be the purpose?

The vacuum cleaner was purring again when he went upstairs and entered his family's personal apartment, which occupied most of the mansion's second floor. He found Nora, her eyes red and swollen, sitting on the edge of their bed. She looked at him sadly. "In the house, Lloyd?"

"I didn't know it mattered to you," he said. "Never will happen again, I promise. Do you want me to send her back to Bremen?"

"She does her work well enough."

They stared at each other for a long, strained period of silence. As he had many times, Lloyd Bauer thought about the oddness of their marriage. He had never felt physical passion for this awkward, homely woman—and had known since their teens that she was intellectually inferior to him—but they shared a special bond, engendered by the childhood belief that they existed in a world created for them alone. After all, hadn't their parents and the Old Man said so again and again?

"Lloyd, we have to stop coming here so often," she said. "The boys are old enough to notice things—and they're asking questions I can't answer. Or *wouldn't* answer even if I could."

"Soon," he promised. "I'll be able to act soon."

Desperation deepened the lines around her eyes. "Who is the Old Man? Really?"

"Our teacher," Lloyd Bauer said bitterly. "And our fathers' teacher."

"What *else*, Lloyd? You know more than I do. You must!"

"Yes, I suppose I do."

"Then tell *me*. Who is the Old Man?"

On the hundreds of previous occasions Nora had nagged him with the same dangerous questions, he had replied with evasions: *For your own peace of mind, it's better that you know as little as possible. . . . Something terrible happened years ago—involving your father and mine—something that has to be hidden as long as both of them are still alive. . . . The Old Man is a necessary evil. . . .* He almost began the litany again but realized that continuing to deceive Nora might be dangerous. For the first time, outsiders had passed through the gates of Warlord's Hill, and, ironically, one of them had been commissioned to unearth the facts Lloyd Bauer still attempted to conceal from his own wife. Perhaps it *was* time to share his burden with the only other person who could understand the choices he had been forced to make.

Lloyd Bauer was in his second congressional term when, almost by accident, he discovered the Old Man's real identity. A group of constituents, most of them extermination-camp survivors, had asked him to help expedite long-delayed deportation proceedings against Anton Begovnic. A naturalized American citizen, he had been accused of murdering hundreds of Jews and political prisoners while serving as a police official in Nazi-occupied Yugoslavia. It was one of more than a dozen similar, unsettled cases against now-elderly immigrants charged with war-time crimes in their homelands. Although Lloyd knew he had no influence over a purely judicial matter, Sid Levin compiled a file on Begovnic. Among the evidence gathered in an earlier hearing was a faded German propaganda photograph that showed the uniformed collaborator escorting a party of Nazi dignitaries around the labor camp where the atrocities occurred. Towering above the others was the gaunt, weathered man who had been Lloyd Bauer's only teacher from early childhood until his entrance into college. The photo's caption identified him as Joseph Keppler, a Nazi official, but specified no duties or title.

At first, Bauer tried to convince himself that the resemblance was coincidental, even though he had occasionally heard his father refer to the Old Man as Joseph. To Bauer and Nora, their tutor had never had a name; he existed simply as a figure of absolute, unquestionable authority. However, in the following weeks, Lloyd conducted further research on his own, using the Begovnic case as a cover. His legislative position gave him routine access to material in the National Archives, including documents recently declassified under the Freedom of Information Act. Many of the records he studied were yellowing and dry, had not been opened for decades.

He soon realized that the Old Man must be Keppler. Although he found no other photographs, links to Lloyd's father and Dr. Zimmerman became obvious. Keppler had been a philosophy instructor during the years Paul Bauer and Roger Zimmerman studied at Leipzig University. Biographical details were scant. He had spent much of his childhood and adolescence in the United States, where his father taught mathematics at the University of Chicago. After the Keppler family's return to Germany in 1921, Joseph, although still in his late teens, had joined the National Socialist party and became a Nazi organizer in the universities of northern Germany. Following Hitler's rise to power, he wrote three studies scientifically justifying the repression of Jews and other minorities. In 1935, he became assistant supervisor of the *Auslander* movement, a concerted program of propaganda and political action to develop ethnic German populations overseas into potential subversive forces in their adopted nations. Joseph Keppler's special area of interest had been the United States. In 1937, still unknown to American law enforcement agencies, he had returned to the United States as a sales representative for a chemical firm and rented a home in Bremen, New Jersey, a town south of Philadelphia.

Lloyd Bauer had overheard house and field workers speak of the ''old'' Bremen as a lost Eden. Because of the rules against all but the most uncomplicated socialization between the Bauers and the estate staff he had made no further inquiries, assuming that they were referring to the German port city. Although vaguely aware that the workers had a shared background, he had never imagined that their former home was a nondescript working-class community on the White Horse Pike, less than forty miles from Warlord's Hill.

After America entered the Second World War, the Bremen town council had changed the community's Teutonic name to Spring Gardens, which explained why Lloyd had never made the connection after he began traveling widely outside Warlord's Hill. The city fathers had more reason than most for the anti-German name change, he realized as he read on. The Bund had made political inroads into other south Jersey towns with large numbers of first- and second-generation German-Americans—but their domination of Bremen was complete. By 1940, bundists held every municipal office, filled the ranks of the police and fire departments. Name after familiar name leaped from the page—Mayor Maurice Dorn, Councilman Sam Webber, Fire Chief Otto Uhl, Chief of Police Robert Krug . . . Men, three of them now dead, whom he had known as head forester, agricultural field supervisor, fire brigade captain, and Master Huntsman at Warlord's Hill.

In November 1941, the Justice Department and the New Jersey state attorney's office drew up indictments accusing these men and four other Bremen citizens of murder and conspiracy to commit murder. Undercover FBI agents had discovered that the Bremen police force doubled as a highly trained assassination squad that had been responsible for killing at least a dozen Bund opponents and suspected informers within the movement itself.

Although he was not named in the charges, it became evident much later that Joseph Keppler had been the real leader of the Bremen organization, as well as primary liaison between the German government and the national Bund. His activities were revealed in 1945, with the capture of the *Auslander* section's files. When America entered the war, they made clear that Bremen was scheduled to become the headquarters of a coast-to-coast network of Nazi agents and saboteurs. The names of other potential traitors in the grandiose, but never implemented, scheme were not found. However, they reputedly numbered in the thousands.

On the night of November 18, 1941, a team of federal and state agents swept down on Bremen to arrest the eight suspects. The warrants were never served. Somehow warned in advance, the bundists had fled, taking their families with them. The move was so sudden that most of their personal belongings were left behind. Despite the reckless haste of the escape, not one of the fugitives was apprehended or even heard of again. A few weeks later, the Japanese attack on Pearl Harbor made the search for a handful of pro-Nazi fanatics insignificant, although for years the FBI continued to follow up what inevitably turned out to be false leads.

Days after the eight Bremen families disappeared, Joseph Keppler left the country. By February 1942 he had made his way back to Germany and assumed new duties as a deputy chief of operations for *Abwehr*, the intelligence agency supervising the worldwide espionage cells recruited from the *Auslander* societies of the thirties. The last reference to Keppler in the captured Nazi files was a set of orders—dated February 11, 1945—releasing him from *Abwehr* duties for a special assignment, the nature of which was not described. By war's end, Joseph Keppler had vanished as completely as the eight families of Bremen had four years earlier.

And, Lloyd realized, he had found refuge in the same sanctuary.

Lloyd Bauer had felt no sense of shock or outrage over discovering that he had spent his childhood and adolescence surrounded by murderers and their kin; that his father and father-in-law, by sheltering traitors, were themselves indirectly guilty of treason; that the man who had shaped his personality was a disciple of the most evil force of the twentieth century. Instead, he was puzzled.

If they are Nazis, he wondered, why am *I* not a Nazi? Why isn't Nora? The Old Man had us in his power from birth, could do anything with our minds that pleased him. But the reign of National Socialism in Germany had been accorded no more weight in their schooling than the fall of Troy. Politics and history of any kind had been taught with the same detachment brought to mathematics or chemistry. He had been in his second year at Princeton before he realized that men and woman actually felt loyalties to such abstractions as nationality or common culture or religion. The only loyalties Lloyd Bauer knew were to his family and the eternal preservation of a sprawling piece of real estate called Warlord's Hill. The major decisions of his life—all, he believed until now, of his own volition—served those ends, even his entry into politics. With a Bauer in Congress, the Interior Department was less likely to pursue proposals—defeated twice over the years—to condemn the ecologically priceless estate and absorb it into the National Park system.

A week later, without telling Nora of his discoveries, Lloyd Bauer flew north and confronted his father. Paul Bauer, frail but still mentally active, smiled calmly. "I'm surprised that you didn't guess years ago," he said. "Shall we go upstairs and discuss it with the Old Man?"

Lloyd's teacher, sitting in the semidarkness of his bedroom, reacted no more strongly than Paul Bauer. "It is better that you know," he said.

"Why have you allowed this situation to continue?" Lloyd asked, turning to his father before the Old Man could reply. "Why did you and Roger Zimmerman hide those people in the first place?"

"It was our duty," Paul Bauer replied in a tone of unshakable certainty. "And it continues to be our duty."

"Out of the eight accused men only Otto Uhl is still alive. And he's senile. Even if he weren't, why in the name of God would he be put on trial after more than forty years? All of the prosecution witnesses must be either dead or not in much better shape than Otto."

"Your father isn't dead or senile," the Old Man said. "Or Dr. Zimmerman. Or myself."

"What could the government do to *you?* Deport you as an illegal alien? I spent a week studying every available list of unapprehended Nazi war criminals, from the Nuremberg transcripts to Simon Wiesenthal newsletters. The name Joseph Keppler appears *nowhere.*"

Anger flared briefly in the Old Man's gray eyes. "One does not have to be a fugitive from Zionist tyranny in order to pursue truth and justice!"

"You still believe in Nazism?"

"Yes," his father said firmly. "And we have worked for its eventual triumph all our lives. Before the war, I secretly contributed more than three million dollars to the German-

American Bund and other groups sworn to stamp out the Jewish and Marxist conspiracy against Western civilization. I bought Warlord's Hill on Joseph's advice, to provide a secure base for an expanded Bund. During the war, we hid escaped German soldiers from prisoner of war camps and helped them reach South America. Our home served as a safe house for agents trained by Joseph in Germany.''

"Why are you telling me all this *now?*" Lloyd asked.

"To show you that our loyalty to the party was total," the Old Man interjected. "And remains so."

"To what *purpose?*"

"We are the only heirs to the pure, inviolate spirit of the movement," the Old Man said. "Undisciplined, neurotic rabble like the American Nazi Party only degrade the glories of the past. Besides, such groups have been so heavily infiltrated by government informers that they would collapse in days if a genuine political revolution were ever mounted here. That is why maintaining the sanctuary is so vital. Hitler himself, just before the end, stated that the United States was the natural breeding ground for the inevitable revival of National Socialism. When the day of rebirth comes—probably a day when your father and myself are long dead—the sanctuary will provide a nucleus of superbly trained, dedicated warriors, uncorrupted by the spiritual and moral degeneration that swept the world after the collapse of the Reich.''

Preserved like the rare plants and animals in the forests of Warlord's Hill, Lloyd thought. Or like corpses in cryogenic vaults, waiting to be defrosted in some future golden age when science had abolished death?

If Lloyd had not grown up at Warlord's Hill, he would have scoffed at the notion that such a mad subterfuge could be carried on successfully for decades. But he himself had experienced the awesome force of the Old Man's will, had accepted his voice as the source of all knowledge. By the time the heads of the eight families even considered the possibility of re-entering society, they must have been too old and too dependent on Paul Bauer's bounty to make a change. Most of their children—and all of their grandchildren—had never known any other existence. On reflection, their acquiescence was less extraordinary than the willingness of religious sects like the Amish to stubbornly hold on to archaic ways while in day-to-day contact with modern life. And the Nazi doctrines and trappings and the torchlit ceremonies that were still held in the deep woods south of the lake must have constituted the basis of a crude religion for the inhabitants of Bremen, with Paul Bauer as a remote but beneficent god and the Old Man as his high priest.

"When you and Nora were children, we decided the wisest course was to keep you unaware of the sanctuary," the Old Man said. "You would both eventually have to live outside the wire, be exposed to influences from which you could not be fully protected. In time, of course, you'd have been told."

Lloyd Bauer had already decided that temporarily he was powerless to alter this bizarre situation. What would be gained by public revelation except the humiliation of his and Nora's families—and, just as certainly, the destruction of his own political career? And what harm could the Old Man and his followers do as long as the training programs and barbaric rallies were confined to the estate?

The Old Man's deep voice cut into Lloyd's brooding thoughts. "How did you learn my name?"

Lloyd told of the deportation proceedings against Anton Begovnic, how he had chanced upon the photograph.

"I visited a Yugoslavian labor camp in nineteen forty-four," the Old Man mused. "To select workers to build a radio intercept center in the mountains north of Belgrade. But I don't remember anyone named Begovnic. I wonder if he remembers me?"

As the Bauers left the room a few minutes later, Lloyd heard the Old Man pick up the telephone and ask the operator for Harry Krug's extension.

The deportation of Anton Begovnic soon became academic. Four days after Lloyd returned to Washington, a rooftop sniper put a bullet through the aged collaborator's heart while he was sipping iced tea on the back porch of his house in Newburgh, New York. An unsigned letter to the police proudly claimed that the writer, a member of the Jewish Defense League, had pulled the trigger. A JDL spokesman disclaimed responsibility, while praising the killer's motives.

* * *

For the next five years, Lloyd Bauer and the two old men who shared the mansion at Warlord's Hill rarely spoke of the sanctuary, as if that afternoon's chilling revelations had never occurred. But the problem was never far from Lloyd's mind, especially when he and his family were at the estate. On summer nights, when the wind blew from the south, he occasionally heard the faint rumble of drums and knew that the ordinary-looking men and women of the new Bremen had again gathered to perform their hidden rituals. After a series of strokes turned his father into a mindless shell, he knew that the day was fast approaching when, as master of Warlord's Hill, he would face the choice of disbanding the Old Man's cult or, like Paul Bauer, becoming a slave to it.

But now another choice had to be faced, triggered by an offer from the Republican state committee. If he sought next year's nomination for the Senate, Lloyd was assured of full party backing in the primary. To the astonishment of the committee chairman who brought him the news, Lloyd asked for two months in which to make up his mind; a statewide campaign would focus unprecedented media attention on himself—and Warlord's Hill.

He had long been aware that the Old Man's apparent lack of interest in the world outside the wire was fraudulent; Roger Zimmerman kept him fully informed on matters of real importance. The weekend following the political leader's supposedly confidential offer, he and Nora went to Warlord's Hill. Gerald, waiting on the front steps, told Lloyd that the Old Man wished to see him.

Dr. Zimmerman, also waiting in the third floor room, opened a bottle of champagne when Lloyd crossed the threshold. Three glasses were set out on the Old Man's reading table. "Congratulations, my boy," said the smiling physician. "We understand you're to be our new junior senator."

"I haven't given them an answer yet," Lloyd said.

"Why not?" the Old Man asked.

"The reasons should be obvious."

While the champagne remained untouched, the older men repeatedly assured him that no journalist could possibly unearth the sanctuary's existence. Zimmerman—to Lloyd's surprise, since he usually limited himself to supporting the

142

Old Man's remarks—provided the argument that finally swayed him.

"Suppose we test our defenses?" he said. "Engage a reporter to act as a cat's paw—but supplied with no more information than any other newspaperman?"

"And if he *does* learn what's been going on here?" Lloyd asked sardonically.

"Insist on frequent reports. If he finds a strong lead to the sanctuary, you can simply end the investigation. And your candidacy."

Lloyd laughed. "What kind of reporter would make a deal like that? And how could we be certain he'd quit nosing around *after* we paid him off?"

"I know of someone—indirectly employed by the foundation—who would be perfect. And have no motive to continue on his own."

Even as Zimmerman continued his plea, Lloyd Bauer wondered at the Old Man's uncharacteristic silence, beginning to suspect that the whole presentation had been worked out in advance. But, once more, he allowed ambition to undermine caution. Three weeks later, Roy and Terry Hammil were driven through the gates of Warlord's Hill in a 1934 Packard limousine.

Tears filled Nora Bauer's eyes when her husband finished speaking and sat beside her on the edge of their high, walnut-framed nineteenth-century bed. She did not cry because of the emotional impact of his words. Except for the easily memorized cliches necessary for survival in campaigns or at Washington cocktail parties, Nora knew little of politics or history; the Old Man had made certain of that. To her, the Nazis were a faintly mythic group of Europeans who, she gathered, had lost a big war. That her father had been—and still was—a Nazi was equally insignificant. She had felt no love for Roger Zimmerman since the day, when she was five, that he had taken her by the hand and led her for the first time up the staircase to the Bauer mansion's top-floor schoolroom. The room's ceiling was so low that the man who was to be her teacher seemed supernaturally large. She had screamed and cried to be taken home, but her father had departed without a backward glance.

Until the birth of her own children, she had never really loved anyone except the thin, wheezing little boy who often shared that schoolroom with her for the next twelve years. She had watched him grow into a tall, handsome, outwardly commanding figure whose callousness and constant infidelities she forgave because, like herself, he bore no responsibility for his nature. Her tears were for Lloyd, induced by pity and suppressed anger at his failure to acknowledge that he, too, was a puppet, ruled by the Old Man, secure only in this personal kingdom to which he was heir. After more than a week or two in Washington or traveling, her husband's strength visibly drained away, to be replaced by a look of chronic, haunted doubt.

Even as Lloyd spoke, question after question had tumbled through her mind—but she had voiced none of them. He would simply fall back on his usual defense against seeking the truth: refusing to admit that it existed. She could comprehend why the original Bremen fugitives had stayed at Warlord's Hill. But what kept their children and grandchildren inside the wire? The Old Man must have a hold on them, too, perhaps even more crippling than the chains of loyalty, ambition, pride, and fear of disgrace that he had coiled around Lloyd and herself.

"It will be all right in the end," Lloyd promised, clutching her thin hand tightly. "But I can't act *now*. You must understand why."

"Yes," she replied numbly. "You *have* to wait. You can't help it."

And still the silent questions came. Why had the Old Man allowed strangers to use the guest house, perversely violating his strictest rule? Just chatting with Terry Hammil on their morning horseback rides or at lunch—her first prolonged, informal contacts with a woman who had grown up outside the wire—had forced Nora to reexamine aspects of her strange, constricted life that she had always taken for granted. Lloyd's revelations made it even more inconceivable that the Old Man had permitted the girl—and her dangerous knowledge of the real world—access to the estate.

I gave him no choice, Lloyd had announced proudly weeks ago. She realized this was just another self-deception. Roy and Terry Hammil were living at Warlord's Hill because, for reasons of his own, the Old Man wanted them here.

✖ ELEVEN ✖

By late morning, Roy Hammil had finished skimming Huggins and Associates' current files on the Bauer Foundation for Geriatric Research. He had found nothing that might compromise Lloyd. The congressman wasn't even a trustee of the organization, nor had he access to its funds or influence over its policies.

He sighed in frustration, lit a cigarette, leaned back in his desk chair, and pondered his next move. Using syndicate and wire service contacts, he could arrange introductions to Jersey reporters who had covered the local end of Lloyd Bauer's political rise, but he knew that he would just be replaying the Washington interviews. He still felt that the source of Lloyd's fears lay either with the acts of another family member or an event in the congressman's life before he entered politics. The latter possibility would mean researching his background from birth onward—or, under their peculiar agreement, gathering the facts that might be uprooted by a reporter who never had access to Warlord's Hill or its inhabitants. He felt like a runner deliberately placing lead weights around his ankles before a race.

However, to expedite another phase of the investigation, he called Langston Fellows in Alexandria. "I found out that Margarethe von Behncke settled in Winter Park, Florida, after she came to the States," he told the columnist. "Could you do me another favor, Lang?"

"Telephone her and set up an interview?" Fellows guessed with a sigh.

"I gather she's damned near as reclusive as her brother. An old acquaintance like yourself will stand a better chance of getting through. If it helps, assure her nothing she tells me is for publication, that I'm simply doing background research for her nephew's campaign."

"I'll give it a try," Fellows promised.

"Check back with you tomorrow morning," Roy said.

He had hung up the phone before realizing that he was not alone in the office. A broad smile on his puffy, florid face, Merle Huggins had silently entered, waiting in the doorway until the call was completed. "Didn't expect to see you around for a while," the agency president said. "How're you taking to life at Warlord's Hill?"

"I've hardly been there," Roy said, rising.

Huggins' gaze moved to the stacks of file folders on the desk. "Checking out foundation literature?"

"Might be useful when Lloyd makes his pitch to the Social Security crowd," Roy lied. "I hadn't realized it was that big an account."

Huggins shrugged. "Our first client, as a matter of fact."

Knowing that Huggins was capable of pinning down a listener for half an hour of idle conversation, Roy mentioned an imaginary lunch date. "Better get these back where they belong."

He had picked up the stack of folders and was edging toward the door when the other man asked in a casual voice, "Roy, did you know Roger Zimmerman before you came to work here?"

"Never heard of him until a couple of days ago. What made you think I had?"

"Something you said once . . . Probably got it wrong. Have a good lunch."

After Roy Hammil's departure, Merle Huggins returned to his own office, debating whether to inform Dr. Zimmerman that Roy had been poring over foundation material, even though the reason Roy gave for studying all those press releases and pamphlets made perfect sense. What secret motive could he possibly have?

On the other hand, he remembered Zimmerman's words more than three years ago, when he had told Huggins to offer a ridiculously high-paying job to Roy, then Langston Fellows' chief aide. "He is a young man in whose future I take great interest," Zimmerman said, "but under no circumstances must he know that I sponsored him for the position. I don't even want him to work on foundation business. In *any* capacity."

Of course, Huggins didn't question the physician's order, although he felt that glorified courthouse reporters like Hammil were rotten PR prospects. Only a handful of people knew that the agency's initial financing had been a private loan from Paul Bauer, the multimillionaire whom Huggins had never met. Without the continued patronage of the Bauer Foundation, the firm couldn't maintain its present eminence.

"But what if Hammil doesn't want to work for us?" Huggins asked.

"He probably *will* turn you down," Zimmerman replied.

Zimmerman's cryptic prediction proved correct. Then, a few weeks after the refusal, Roy Hammil phoned to say that he had changed his mind. To Huggins' surprise, Roy performed so well in his new profession that Huggins seldom thought about the unusual circumstances under which he had been hired—until Zimmerman indirectly set up Roy's leave of absence to work on Lloyd Bauer's senatorial campaign. Huggins, who had grown to like Roy, had been fleetingly tempted to tell him about his earlier, obviously unknown link to the Bauers. But he had not. Betraying Roger Zimmerman's confidence was a risk he had no desire to take.

Failing to report Roy's sudden interest in the foundation would be another unnecessary risk, Huggins decided.

His secretary put through a call to the Golden Era Retirement Center, learned that Zimmerman had not come in today—to Merle Huggins' relief. In the back of his mind, he had always felt as though he were part of a conspiracy against Roy Hammil, no matter how often he told himself the notion

148

was ridiculous. After going to such trouble to advance Roy's career, Zimmerman and the Bauers could only have his best interest at heart.

The chance encounter with Roy Hammil in the mansion the day before had, in a sense, benefited Harry Krug, although he had initially cursed himself for not using the rear staircase, his usual custom; his features were now known to Hammil, freeing him of the routine duty of trailing the man. He had seen no point in passing on the surveillance mission to others, even if trained huntsmen were available. Since learning that Jim Blum apparently had not told Langston Fellows about the $100,000 bribe, Krug no longer considered Hammil a serious danger to the sanctuary—as long as his research kept him away from the Pine Barrens.

Krug's uncharacteristic optimism evaporated when, just after noon, the guard at the main gate called to say that the eldest Miller son had delivered an urgent taped message, phoned in from the Washington outpost.

Even before he placed the cassette in the player on the Old Man's desk, Krug suspected that the news would be bad. In anticipation, he had driven straight to Dr. Zimmerman's house and insisted the physician accompany him to the mansion. Now Zimmerman sat nervously on the edge of a chair. The face of the Old Man, who was at his usual post by the reading table, remained rigidly expressionless.

The sound of Peter Uhl's voice—subdued, almost stunned— emerged from the machine. The last order Krug had given him before leaving Washington was to scan northwestern newspapers, available at out-of-town newsstands. The source of his message, Uhl declared, was yesterday's *Coeur d'Alene Press*. A front-page story revealed that a body discovered on the bank of the Priest River had been identified as Victor Schall, a bartender at a local club.

"Lew and Conrad found them!" Zimmerman exclaimed with relief.

"Tape's not over yet," Krug grunted.

However, Uhl said, police still had no clues to the identities of two other men buried in a shallow grave nearby. Like Schall, they had been killed by gunfire. Even the physical descriptions, imprecise because of extensive damage to both victims' skulls, were enough to tell the listeners that Lew Dorn and Conrad Webber had been lost.

"Impossible," Zimmerman gasped weakly, his parchment-yellow face growing even sallower.

Krug gestured him to silence as Uhl, after a brief pause, continued to read aloud. A car discovered less than a mile from the grave had been traced to a road worker named John Rawls, already sought for questioning in the slaying of two men in a Coeur d'Alene alleyway. Uhl completed the recording by asking who would replace Lew Dorn as commander of the sanctuary's Washington outpost.

"We have to postpone the June 28 operation," Krug said, switching off the tape player.

"No," said the Old Man.

"Vic Schall was his prisoner for nearly a week," Krug protested. "Do you believe for a minute that Vic didn't tell him about the sanctuary?"

Dr. Zimmerman's throat tightened with fear as he imagined police excavating forty-three empty graves in Lakewood. All of the men of whose deaths they had just learned had been born at the estate clinic, delivered by Zimmerman's own hands; he had even, years ago, treated their slayer. If the sanctuary fell, he would fall.

"Of what use is the information to him?" the Old Man asked. "He is now wanted for *five* murders. Suppose the worst happens and the authorities take him alive. Why would they believe a mass killer, an escapee from a government mental hospital? Warlord's Hill is safe as long as no *sane* man or woman can corroborate his fantastic story."

"Either way, we risk everything," Zimmerman said.

"Proceeding with the plan is the less dangerous course," the Old Man said. "Roger, how much longer can you keep Paul alive? Even using the most advanced drugs and techniques developed by the foundation. Three months?"

"I'm not sure. Who can be sure?"

"A year?"

"Perhaps."

"When Lloyd inherits Warlord's Hill, he will grow bolder and seek to limit our activities. It's inevitable. He knows nothing of the Ceremony of Passage, of what the huntsmen do outside the wire. In time—when he's established in the Senate and realizes that far greater power lies ahead—he will understand his true role. But until this happens we will have to draw back, wait, and rest. The first phase of the plan *must* be completed before Paul dies."

The Master Huntsman only partially understood the exchange between Zimmerman and the Old Man. "What if he doesn't stay in hiding?" Krug asked. "What if he heads back East, tries to take us on by himself?"

"That would be madness," the Old Man snapped, annoyed at Krug's interruption.

"Nevertheless, it's a possibility. And he *is* mad."

"All the more reason for going through with Monday's operation. We can better concentrate on eliminating him after we've disposed of enemies closer at hand."

As he drove through the pines toward Chatsworth, Roy Hammil thought again about the gap between Lloyd Bauer's words and his behavior. He was certain that the congressman spoke the truth last week when he complained of the constrained atmosphere of Warlord's Hill. Nevertheless, Roy had found nothing seriously disturbing about the fact that, as Jack Rudd and other Washington newsmen had told him, Bauer brought his family back to the estate as often as possible. If his father had the force of will to maintain a world of personal fantasy for more than three decades, it wasn't surprising that he could command intense loyalty from his only son.

True reservations had taken root yesterday, though, when he saw Paul Bauer's frail body propped in a wheelchair. Under the circumstances, Lloyd had probably been granted power of attorney to manage his helpless parent's affairs. If so, why had he made no changes in the rules governing day-to-day routine at Warlord's Hill? Even if Paul Bauer regained mental lucidity from time to time, his range of vision was limited by the windows of his bedroom. What had prevented Lloyd from running in an outside telephone line, from ending the frustration of being cut off from his staff whenever he passed through the gates? Why continue the time-consuming routine of switching cars at the Miller house?

The logical answer, of course, was that he felt obligated to honor his father's eccentric wishes as long as Paul Bauer remained technically alive. However, the representative had impressed Roy as essentially pragmatic, unlikely to allow pointless sentiment to interfere with his needs and ambitions. That he continued to maintain all the estate's anachronisms made as little sense as a magician creating complex illusions night after night in an empty theater.

But what the hell does any of that have to do with my job? Roy thought as he saw the squat bungalows of Chatsworth ahead. What did it have to do with Lloyd's paralyzing indecision about running for the Senate? "Outside Congress he doesn't exist," Jack Rudd had said. Roy had begun to wonder if he existed *anywhere*. Every moment he spent with Lloyd Bauer, he had been conscious of the man's curious opaqueness, of the kind of personal control that might mask either inner complexity or a character so simple as to border on the vacuous. He was only certain that Lloyd's personality— and the source of his mysterious fears—had their origins at Warlord's Hill. And by the terms of their deal, he could not question anyone as long as they were inside the fences.

Before leaving New York, Roy had tried to phone ahead to the Miller house to arrange for transportation to Warlord's Hill; the line had been busy. A few minutes after entering Chatsworth, he was glad he hadn't left the parkway to try again.

Earlier in the week, Terry had asked Gerald to drop off three rolls of 35 mm film at the Chatsworth general store. "He put them on special order," she had told Roy that morning, "so could you stop off and see if the prints are in yet?" To his surprise, the bulky envelope was ready. He paid, shoved the packet into his jacket pocket, and was turning to leave when he noticed a stack of thin paperback books on the counter. *"Lost Trails of the Pine Barrens* by Rev. Felix Rodeburg"* the cover proclaimed. He picked up a copy, thumbed through it, and saw immediately that it was a vanity publication, cheaply photo-offset.

"Mr. Rodeburg knows more about the Pines than anybody," the middle-aged woman behind the counter said. "We sell fifteen, twenty copies a year."

152

"Anything on Warlord's Hill?" he asked idly, starting to put the book down.

The woman gave him a puzzled squint, as if she had never heard of the region's largest private estate. "Bassing Furnace," she firmly corrected. "Nobody local *ever* calls it by that new name."

Roy Hammil bought the book, asked: "You know Reverend Rodeburg personally?"

"He's the pastor at Zion Lutheran Church, just west of town on five-thirty-two."

"Thank you," Roy said, glancing at his watch. It was barely two-fifteen, leaving him plenty of time to glean a little unscheduled background material. He had never met an amateur author who wouldn't drop whatever he was doing to discuss his work, even with a stranger.

Before setting out to find Reverend Rodeburg, Roy drove to the Miller house, then knocked on the kitchen door. It was opened by a hunched, immensely fat old woman. "I'm Roy Hammil," he said. "I believe we talked on the phone last week. Could you please arrange for an estate car to pick me up at four o'clock?"

The old woman nodded once and, without speaking, shut the kitchen door.

Located less than two miles outside Chatsworth, the Lutheran church was a spare, freshly painted structure just slightly larger than a local bungalow. Beside it, as if intentionally designed to make the church look more imposing, sat a tiny cottage that served as the parsonage. A yellow bulldozer was parked in the rutted sand driveway; a stocky, gray-haired man in greasy denims stood by the open hood, wrapping rubberized tape around a frayed engine wire. He looked up in surprise when Roy turned the Jaguar into the drive.

"Is the Reverend Rodeburg at home?" Roy asked as he got out of the car.

"Talking to him," the man growled. The Reverend's annoyed expression turned to a smile when he noticed the paperback in Roy's hand. "Come on into the house and have a beer."

* * *

"Collection plates don't yield much in the Pines," Felix Rodeburg said, nodding out the kitchen window at the bulldozer. "I pay for the groceries with that old Cat—pulling stumps, clearing firebreaks for the township, anything handy."

Roy glanced down at the minister's book, on the bare wooden table next to the tall glass of beer Rodeburg had just poured for him. "Did you make much from *Lost Trails?*"

Rodeburg laughed gently. "Not even printing costs, as I'm sure you must know. Just one of those peculiar things backwoods preachers do from time to time. Occasionally, we get tourists who have a few hours to kill on their way back from the beach or the casinos in Atlantic City. They've heard stories about those strange Pineys who've inbred so long they aren't much more than drooling apes, all the crazy old lies. They get lost, naturally—and, if they keep to oiled roads, end up hours later in Chatsworth, scared to death and wondering where they've been. My little book tries to tell them."

"When the lady in the store said you were the local historian, I figured you might be kind enough to answer a few questions."

"About the Pines? Or Warlord's Hill?"

Rodeburg's words startled Roy. He had told the minister that he was temporarily living in the area but had not mentioned the Bauer estate. "A little about both, actually. How did you know we were staying there?"

"That's all people talked about after Sunday service. How you and Mrs. Hammil drove up in a weird foreign car— Jaguars aren't exactly common in the Pines—and the Bauer limousine was waiting for you."

"But no one was around but the chauffeur."

"All outsiders are noticed—and remarked upon. But not with malice or suspicion. We have very little of either." Rodeburg took a deep quaff of beer. "As a makeshift historian, *I* should be questioning *you*. Except for Congressman Bauer, you're the first man I've spoken to in thirty years who's actually been through the gates."

"Why do the people here still call it Bassing Furnace?"

Rodeburg released a tolerant sigh. "Because it *is* Bassing Furnace. During the Revolution, an army officer—probably from New York—took it upon himself to rename the mansion.

The Bassings sensibly restored the original title after Independence. Which it kept until, a century and a half later, a rich outsider bought the land and apparently decided Warlord's Hill sounded more baronial than Bassing Furnace. It was within his rights to do so—and within the rights of everybody else to ignore his foolishness.''

"What's the point?" Roy asked.

"Consistency. You've noticed those two-rutted tracks through the woods? Seem to go no place?"

"Sure."

"Many of them are nearly three hundred years old—and, long ago, they *did* go someplace. To bog iron and glass-making towns that vanished down to the last brick or piece of fieldstone. Still, if I were to ask a friend to meet me noon tomorrow at Hogg's Junction, he'd be there right on time. Hogg's Junction was a village south of here where five tracks intersected. Burned clear to the ground in eighteen sixty-three but any Piney worth his salt knows where it *used* to be. Couple hundred years from now, where Warlord's Hill used to be won't mean much. Where Bassing Furnace used to be probably will. In the Pines, knowing where you're at is more important than knowing where other people want you to be.''

"How are the Bauers regarded?"

"Hardly have contact with them. You see people from the estate coming and going in those old cars once in a while— mostly the men, for some reason—but they never talk to anybody. And the congressman—seems like a smart young fellow—speaks to ladies' groups and such.''

"They employ no one local?"

Rodeburg shook his head. "Not since the first few years. Actually, it was nineteen forty-eight or nine when they really sealed off the place. Until then, they just had ordinary barbed wire, like a farmer uses to keep in stock. Some of the workers Paul Bauer brought in lived outside, came to church, made friends with their neighbors. But after that accident with the children, he bought thousands more acres, enough to put all the workers' houses inside a new fence. The Millers were the only family that stayed put—and they keep to themselves.''

"I heard Paul Bauer's nephew was killed around that time," Roy said, "but no one mentioned *other* kids."

Rodeburg refilled their beer glasses. "Don't recall the details after all these years. A group of children were buried when a gravel pit wall collapsed."

"Did the others die, too?"

Rodeburg shrugged helplessly. "I'd forgotten the accident until we started talking. Except for Bauer's nephew, they were outside kids, here on a summer vacation."

Roy had assumed, based on his research, that the Warlord's Hill fence had been erected because Paul Bauer feared retaliation for swindling Nazi industrialists out of millions. Suppose Bauer suspected that little Theo von Behncke had actually been murdered as the first installment of that retaliation—a sadistic warning of the fate of other family members if Bauer didn't return the confiscated fortune to its true owners. As the son of an anti-Hitler conspirator, the child would have made an especially tempting object of revenge.

For the next hour, Roy pretended to listen to Felix Rodeburg's monologue about the past and present of the Pine Barrens. His thoughts were focused on the approaching weekend. Figuring that Langston Fellows might be able to set up a meeting with Margarethe von Behncke, he had packed a carry-on bag that morning and told Terry that he might be gone for several days. Now he had another reason for delaying his return to Warlord's Hill. A grotesque possibility, compounded of verbal discrepancies and seemingly straightforward facts that, on reflection, didn't quite mesh, had edged into his consciousness. His suspicions were so bizarre and improbable, so potentially damaging to so many lives that he was tempted to ignore the line of investigation. However, Lloyd Bauer had hired him to unearth the truth—with the stated implication that, once unearthed, Lloyd reserved the option of reburying it forever.

Roy was unaware that an antique Packard limousine had slowed down on the road outside—just long enough for Gerald the chauffeur to check the rear license plate on the red Jaguar parked in the parsonage driveway.

Late afternoon shadows were moving over the mansion's east lawn when Harry Krug took Dr. Zimmerman home. For moments the two troubled men sat silently in the open front seats of the 1937 Land Rover that served as Krug's command car. As they had both known all along, the Old Man had triumphed: The June 28 plan would be implemented.

"Do you believe we're doing the right thing?" Zimmerman asked as Krug turned onto the dirt road that led to the medical compound.

"No."

"Then why didn't you speak up?"

"Because, to survive, I must remain loyal to the Old Man," Krug said. "No other loyalty is possible. Same thing must have occurred to you, Dr. Zimmerman, a long time ago."

"He didn't mention Terry Hammil once," Zimmerman murmured, pretending not to notice the Master Huntsman's sarcasm. "I thought I'd gotten through to him. God knows I tried."

"You don't understand the Old Man at all, do you?"

The question confused Zimmerman. "Better than anyone, except Paul. It's been more than fifty years."

"He listened to everything you said, appreciated fully that sending her to the pit would be an error. If it were you or me making the decision, we'd just say to hell with it, let her go, and no harm done. But not the Old Man. He's sitting up there right now, figuring out how to kill her anyway, just because her maiden name is Hedricks."

That afternoon Eric Dorn had guided Terry to a quaking bog—an open marsh so thickly covered with sphagnum moss that, from a distance, it resembled a centuries-cold lava field. The illusion remained until they reached the edge of the marsh and Terry saw the moss moving in a continuous ripple, like loose skin on the back of a nervous lizard.

"Most bogs are still," Eric said, "but every once in a while you run across a quaker. Sphagnum just shifts around all the time. Underground streams do it, the Old Man told us kids. Streams so far down that only wispy stuff like the moss feels the currents at all."

"Your grandfather?"

"Who?"

"The old man you mentioned. Is he your grandfather?"

"No, ma'am," Eric said, his shyly curious gaze moving again to the black vinyl case Terry carried over her shoulder.

For days, Terry had been increasingly disturbed by the fact that a child as bright as Eric Dorn had been deprived of a chance at a decent education, locked into an outdated, servile life because of a rich man's willful selfishness. So, when she had heard Eric's now-familiar knock on the guest house's rear door, she had impulsively hurried upstairs and taken her transistorized TV-radio-cassette player from the bedroom closet.

"Just a toy," she said. "Roy gave it to me for my birthday."

"What kind of toy?"

Terry hesitated. The life-style of the people at Warlord's Hill was none of her damned business! And lending Eric the set could be regarded by his parents as a frivolous attempt to stir discontent. They might not be far from wrong, she thought. Eric and dozens of other estate children had grown up oblivious to the narcotics and racial turmoil and gang violence that were poisoning thousands of other young lives in cities and towns less than two hours' drive from here. But she had sensed in him a deep need to at least glimpse what was occurring outside the closed world of Warlord's Hill.

"A portable TV set, basically," Terry said, sitting on a grassy hummock. She opened the case, removed the gleaming black-and-silver unit, raised the antenna, and flipped the television *on* switch. Eric knelt beside her, staring with fascination as the tiny screen's initial gray blur tightened into a sharp image. The program was a *Mary Tyler Moore Show* rerun. The actress, an indignant expression on her rubber-chipmunk face, glared at Edward Asner, playing her boss in the news room of a Minneapolis TV station.

"Mr. Grant, I don't care what *Ted said on the air,"* Mary Tyler Moore replied to Asner's defensive blustering. *"What you did just now was a terrible, terrible mistake!"*

❊ TWELVE ❊

Harry Krug awoke before dawn and dressed, slipped out of his bedroom and down the hall as silently as if he were tracking prey; stealth had long ago become part of his normal body movements.

As he passed the open door to his thirteen-year-old daughter's bedroom, he glanced inside. The sleeping Elsa was, as usual, grinding her poorly aligned teeth. Twice a year, Dr. Zimmerman brought the retirement center's dentist to the clinic, where he treated the estate workers and their families, doubtless baffled by being confined to the medical compound for the entire visit. But orthodontics and other complicated, time-consuming procedures were out of the question, unfortunately. His child would grow up with crooked teeth, but that was a small price to pay for protecting her, as long as possible, from the corrupting reality of the world beyond the wire. Besides, when the Old Man died and Krug inevitably took his place as the true leader of Warlord's Hill, such injustices would be put right.

Krug went downstairs to the kitchen and ate a hurried breakfast of reheated dinner coffee and stale cinnamon buns. He had slept poorly the night before. Only minutes after entering the house, he had received a phone call from Gerald, disclosing that Roy Hammil had canceled his transportation from Chatsworth. "I was to pick him up at four o'clock," the chauffeur had declared. "On the way in, I passed the Lutheran church and saw his car parked in the driveway. I went on to the Millers' and waited. He showed up at a few minutes past four and said that he wouldn't need me after all. He gave me a note for his wife."

"And?"

"*Been unexpectedly delayed,*" Gerald had read aloud. "*Keep the bed warm. Love, Roy.* What should I do?"

"Reseal the envelope and deliver it," Harry Krug had replied, amused at the chauffeur's anxiety.

The Master Huntsman had his own fears, but Roy Hammil played little part in them, since Terry's continued presence at Warlord's Hill constituted a natural alarm system. As long as Hammil allowed his wife to remain inside the wire, Krug was certain that he was still trapped in the maze of irrelevant facts formulated years ago to deceive any possible investigators into the Bauer family's past. The figure provoking Krug's insomnia had been John Rawls. He had told himself over and over again that the Old Man was right, that Rawls would not reverse his consistent pattern of fury followed by blind flight. Nevertheless, Krug had often faced quarry that, goaded beyond endurance, would wheel for a suicidal charge against his weapon. And, by destroying Vic Schall, Conrad Webber, and Lew Dorn, Rawls now must realize that his pursuers were not invincible, that they bled and died like other men.

If Harry Krug had the power, he would have canceled the June 28 plan and immediately assigned every huntsman outside the wire to the search for Rawls. But until next Tuesday his only recourse was to stiffen security within the sanctuary. He usually left the supervision of guard changes to a deputy but, this morning, he decided to handle the routine task himself, in case discipline had weakened since his last inspection.

The sun still had not risen when Krug crossed Elm Street to the police station. The morning shift of firetower guards, lounging by a waiting truck, snapped to attention when they recognized his heavy, lined face, the color of weathered granite in the gray predawn light. "I'm coming along today," he told the driver, clambering into the passenger side of the truck cab.

Ordinarily, a shift change required three trucks but, with so many huntsmen outside the wire, Krug had been forced to alter the policy of staffing all the firetowers, concentrating his men on the outer perimeter. From either the air or ground level, the structures looked innocuous, their overhanging roofs hiding the fact that the guards were armed with high-powered rifles. The towers had been carefully situated so that every inch of cleared ground around the fence could be bracketed in a lethal crossfire should attack come.

Bouncing along the narrow forest road—the sanctuary's key route left intentionally unpaved in order to merge more fully with the thick woods on either side—the truck took more than an hour to reach all of the manned towers. Intersecting tracks, even more obscure, led to essential installations: the cement-walled arsenal and indoor rifle and pistol range; the kennels where dozens of attack and tracking dogs paced nervously in their runs, waiting for their masters to take them on patrol; the region of dense thickets and gullies where huntsmen honed their martial skills in grueling, endless exercises; the turnoff to the heart of the sanctuary, the pit where the Old Man conducted the community's most sacred rituals.

Krug was gratified to see that each guard waited until his relief reached the observation platform before beginning his own descent, assuring that surveillance of the fence remained unbroken even for a few seconds. From every tower, he carefully scanned visible stretches of wire with binoculars, assuring himself that the steel mesh remained intact. Nevertheless, he planned to order a continuous ground patrol of the perimeter as soon as they returned to Bremen. At the third tower, the lights spaced thirty feet apart on the fence flicked off, plunging areas near tall trees into nearly nocturnal shadow; he made a mental note to reset the timer at the main gate.

It was past eight A.M. when the truck braked at the last post. Krug was surprised to see Eric Dorn descend the log-railed stairs. The boy's fine-boned face was pale with fatigue. When Eric reached the ground, Krug gestured him a few yards down the road, out of earshot of the men in the truck. "What were you doing up there last night?" he snapped.

"My shift, Master Huntsman," Eric replied.

161

"Your orders were to keep Mrs. Hammil from wandering into places where she shouldn't go. Orders from the Old Man himself."

"I can do both," Eric said defensively.

"Not your fault," Krug said in a gentler tone, reminding himself that he would soon have to tell Eric Dorn that his father had perished on a mission outside the wire. "Leaving you on the guard roster was my oversight. Nevertheless, the Old Man's instructions cannot be disregarded."

On the drive back to Bremen, Harry Krug pondered the wisdom of allowing Eric to spend so much time in Terry Hammil's company. From the boy's reports, he had gathered that the woman's sole interests were exploring and photographing the preserve's plants and wildlife. But the possibility always remained that, through random remarks, she might subtly undermine Eric's faith in the Old Man's teachings. I'm worrying about nothing, he thought as the truck descended the mild grade into town. The Hammils will soon be gone forever from Warlord's Hill.

It was nearly nine o'clock when the firetower guards disembarked from the truck in front of the Bremen police station and fanned out toward the tree-shaded town's silent side streets.

Instead of entering his house, Eric Dorn went to the backyard utility shed. For three years, ever since he had stumbled upon a secret way to get past the fence without being seen by the tower guards, he had fought the tantalizing urge to explore the vast, dangerous country beyond the boundaries of Warlord's Hill. And now that Terry Hammil had given him the means to do it, what he had found frightened him.

He took Terry's electronic entertainment unit from its hiding place on a high shelf, set it on the floor, and inserted the earphone as she had shown him. With a mixture of eagerness and fearful uncertainty, he switched on the television screen and saw that the picture had grown dimmer; Terry had told him that the batteries lasted only a few hours if used to power the TV. He impatiently switched from channel to channel, seeking a news program. Instead, all he found was a show where furry puppets lugged around huge alphabet letters;

162

another where excited, strangely costumed women tried to guess the price of goods for prizes; a cartoon he had seen at least a dozen times in the Bremen movie house, the one in which Popeye crams Bluto into a length of three-inch steel pipe and then twirls him like a baton. But no further information on the baffling film he had watched just before reporting for firetower duty.

"Eric, come on and eat your breakfast," his mother called from the kitchen window. "What are you doing back there, anyway?"

He hurriedly returned the set to the shelf and masked it by shifting a row of rusty paint cans. The need to learn the truth could not be put aside so easily. But who could he ask? By accepting the television set from Mrs. Hammil, he had already violated one of the sanctuary's strictest rules. Prior to undergoing the Ceremony of Passage, huntsmen were forbidden to seek knowledge of the world outside the wire. If he told anyone in the community about the disturbing film, he would lose forever the opportunity to join the elite force.

I must put it out of my mind, he thought. To do otherwise would be to face the horrifying possibility that the Master Huntsman and the Old Man and his own father had not always told the truth.

The previous day, after giving Gerald the note for Terry, Roy Hammil had driven to the office of the *Burlington County Courier*. The Reverend Rodeburg had told him it was the region's longest established weekly newspaper. However, the plant, located in a small coastal town, had just closed for the day when he arrived. Rather than go through the time-wasting routine of entering and leaving Warlord's Hill, he had checked into a motel.

The next morning, he quickly found what he wanted in the paper's bound volumes of yellowing back issues. On the morning of August 30, 1948, a front-page story revealed, a group of estate reforestation workers heard screams of fear and pain, followed them to an abandoned gravel pit, and discovered that four children had been caught in an earthslide; two of them were fully buried when the workers reached the scene. The victims were rushed to the estate clinic, where Dr.

Roger Zimmerman failed to revive Theo von Behncke, the four-year-old nephew of Paul Bauer. His neck broken, the boy had died instantly.

The surviving children—two brothers and an older sister—were Manhattan residents who had been spending part of the summer with a local farmer, Julius Eberhardt, under the sponsorship of the *New York Herald-Tribune* Fresh Air Fund. The reporter, obviously working from a police report, gave their home address as 527 West Thirty-first Street. Rosemary Cilento, 13, and her brother Vincent, 11, suffered only minor bruises and scratches. But Edward Cilento, 12, was in critical condition wih multiple broken bones and a suspected skull fracture. Following emergency treatment at the clinic, the semi-comatose boy was transferred to a hospital in Lakewood, remaining under Zimmerman's care.

In statements given to a New Jersey State Police sergeant, Rosemary and Vincent said the children had been digging a cave in the pit wall when the earth overhead gave way. Later that day, they returned home with their father, summoned immediately from New York. A brief follow-up piece in the next issue stated that private funeral services for Theo von Behncke had been conducted at Warlord's Hill, where he had been interred in the family cemetery.

At least he could dismiss wild speculations about ex-Nazi assassins, Roy thought as he closed the dusty volume. They would hardly have spared three witnesses. Theo seemingly had died in the kind of random playtime accident that claimed the lives of kids every day. Nevertheless, the most puzzling mystery remained unsolved. Why, immediately after Theo's death, had Paul Bauer established a security system so complete that Warlord's Hill had been virtually cut off from the outside world for more than thirty years? Maybe no link existed between the two events, but the timing seemed more than coincidental.

He went back to his motel, called Langston Fellows. "No luck yet," the columnist told him. "Margarethe von Behncke was out yesterday. I left a message but she hasn't returned the call."

"Do you think she will?"

"No way of telling. Try me again this afternoon."

Roy detected strain in the old columnist's voice. "Something the matter, Lang."

"Sirens again. They've been having trouble in that project across the way. A gang of whites came in and beat a couple of teen-agers half to death last night. The night before a building burned down—obviously arson. A woman died."

"A little early in the season," Roy said wryly, "even for Washington."

"Sometimes I'm glad I'm a cripple. Keeps me indoors."

Roy's next call was to Leo Garvey, a retired *Daily News* police reporter who had moonlighted as the column's New York legman. After going to work for Huggins and Associates, Roy had occasionally hired him for research projects. "I'm trying to locate three people," he said, "and with hardly anything to go on."

"Might not be as tough as you think," Garvey said when Roy had given him the names, 1948 ages, and last known address of the Cilento children. "That's the old Hell's Kitchen area—still heavily Italian. And Italians move only after earthquakes and major fires. Even if these people left, they probably have relatives in the area. You in a hurry for this, Roy?"

"One hell of a hurry."

"Then I'll get right on it. Number where I can reach you?"

"I'll be on the road most of the day." He glanced at his watch. "I'll call you again at four, okay?"

"Fine. The youngest kid's name was *Vincent* Cilento?"

"Yes. Why?"

"I remember a middle-ranking Mafioso named Vincent Cilento. Haven't heard anything about him for years, though. Could that be your guy?"

"For all I know," Roy said, "he could be a leading candidate for the next Supreme Court vacancy."

"I just wondered. Cilento isn't that common an Italian name, at least around New York."

After hanging up, Roy recalled the dozens of times he had scoffed at reporters who "knew" when they were about to crack a story. "A sure sign that they've swallowed a pack of lies," Langston Fellows had remarked many years before. "The only thing you can trust, without quadruple-checked documentation, is your own doubt." Nevertheless, Roy had a gut feeling that he was days or even hours away from discovering the source of Lloyd Bauer's fears.

The day's plan had been for Eric to guide Terry Hammil to a dwarf forest. Areas of fully mature pitch pines and oaks that reached a maximum height of five feet were unique to the Pine Barrens. Botanists and soil experts, after decades of study, had failed to satisfactorily explain their formation.

However, the boy didn't show up at the guest house until midafternoon, too late to start out on the long horseback ride to the freak woodland. "I'm sorry, ma'am," he said when she answered his knock on the kitchen screen door. "Forgot until I got home yesterday that I was on night firewatch. I told my mother to wake me up in a couple of hours but she let me sleep straight through the morning."

"Your regular duties have to come first," she said. "Did you walk all the way from town?"

"Yes, ma'am."

"Then sit down and I'll fetch you something cool to drink." She opened the screen door to admit him.

"Mrs. Schall around?" he said hesitantly.

"Who?" she asked, then realized he must mean Wilma; at last, another estate worker servant's family name had been discovered. "She went to the mansion to visit her daughter-in-law."

The boy sat at the kitchen table and looked up at her shyly as she set a glass of milk before him. "Could I keep the machine until tomorrow?"

"Of course." She wondered what his reaction had been to the miniature TV. Everything, no matter how silly and banal, must have fascinated him. She tried to remember the current Friday evening programs, could not. Since the death of her parents and brother, she had rarely turned on a set.

"Didn't try it until late," he said. "Right before I went on watch. I saw the newsreel at ten o'clock—but a lot of things didn't make sense. One part in particular."

"Perhaps I can explain."

He took a sip of milk. "What do Jews call their church?"

"A temple."

"There was a temple in a place called Bloomington. Right across the street was an old store . . . with a big swastika flag in the front window. . . . Whole crowd of Jews—more than a couple hundred—were running around like crazy. They threw rocks, smashed in the window glass, and tried to attack the men in uniform standing outside the store."

Terry recalled a recent news story about the American Nazi Party's plan to set up a headquarters opposite one of the major synagogues in Bloomington, Indiana. Like dozens of similar incidents in recent years, their obvious goal had been to goad the congregation and supporters to violence and gain national publicity for their movement. Apparently, the stratagem had produced the desired results. She explained the background to Eric, but the bafflement on his smooth face grew more intense.

"I figured most of that out by myself," he said. "What I didn't understand was why the *police* acted the way they did. They protected the men in Nazi uniforms and drove back the Jews with their clubs. It didn't make sense."

"I know how you feel," Terry said softly. "I've heard all the arguments about how even animals like the Nazis have the right to speak freely, that even statements of blind hatred are protected by the First Amendment. But emotionally I can't accept the fact that they're allowed to walk around loose."

Eric Dorn rose, staring at her with wild, almost haunted confusion. "They *should* be in jail!" he cried, almost pleadingly. "Or executed! Why weren't they?"

Terry stepped backward, as if physically thrown off balance by the boy's unexpected reaction. Dorn was a German name. Was it possible that relatives—grandparents, perhaps—had been victims of Nazism during the Second World War? If so, they must have died at least thirty years before Eric's birth, leaving his tortured fervor still unexplained.

Before she could ask him, his trembling right elbow knocked over his glass; milk ran down the zinc tabletop, dribbling to the floor. Terry hurried to the sink, picked up a dishcloth, turned to wipe up the milk, and heard the screen door slam shut. She saw Eric striding toward the trees, the gray dog, as always, at his heels. In seconds, both figures were out of sight.

I was wrong to give him the TV set, Terry thought guiltily. Eventually, Eric's idealistic illusions would be shattered—but the process shouldn't have been started by an outsider.

Roy Hammil reached Princeton just before noon and went to the university library, where he examined class yearbooks for the period in which Lloyd Bauer had been an undergraduate. Even in Lloyd's senior year, the frail figure in the photographs bore little resemblance to the man Roy had met two weeks earlier. Lloyd had mentioned that, as a child, he had been a victim of crippling asthma. Nevertheless, Roy was startled by the contrast.

He continued his research in the files of the *Daily Princetonian*. References to Lloyd were infrequent. Strangely, for a man who had developed into a prominent politician, he had never run for student office, had not even joined a fraternity. At what point and how, Roy wondered, had the shy, physically weak scholar taken on a new personality, even a new body?

At four, Roy went to a bar and put through his scheduled call to Leo Garvey. "Only took an hour or two to pick up leads," Garvey said smugly. "Rosemary Cilento left the neighborhood last year, when she divorced an Eighth Avenue butcher named Daniel Morelli. Went to live with a married daughter in Port Jefferson, out in Suffolk County. Daughter's address is Twelve Barbara Place."

"And the other two?"

"Couldn't locate anyone who remembered a brother named Edward. Or even hearing Rosemary talk about him. I guess the ex-husband would know, but he's out of town, won't be back until late tomorrow night. I could follow it up after the weekend."

"Probably not necessary," Roy said, wishing he had continued to search the *Burlington County Courier* for later references to the child. Considering the extent of his injuries, he might have died weeks or even months after the accident.

"Younger brother *is* Vinnie Cilento, the mob guy I told you about. He's been up in Attica more than eight years. On narcotics and second-degree murder raps. A big heroin buy got out of hand, and Vinnie gunned down another hood who was short-weighting the goods. Want me to dig up the details?''

"Not unless it happened when he was eleven," Roy said. "Chances are I can learn all I need to know from the sister. Only have one question to ask, as a matter of fact. But if she *can't* answer it, I'd like you to try to set up a meeting with Vincent Cilento."

"Won't be in prison, though," Leo Garvey said. "Vinnie is getting out on parole June twenty-eighth, day after tomorrow."

Roy's next call—to Langston Fellows—was equally productive. "All arranged," the ex-columnist said. "Margarethe von Behncke has agreed to see you tomorrow. That doesn't give you much time to get down there, but I wouldn't postpone the interview. She sounded *very* hesitant."

Once again circumstances would force Roy Hammil to spend a night away from Warlord's Hill—and his wife. He called in a message to Chatsworth, glad for the first time that he was unable to speak directly to Terry. If he had heard her soft, slightly husky voice on the other end of the line, he might have revealed his true feelings about the place she had come to love and he had disliked at first sight. *After this weekend,* he would have said, *if I'm right about what's bugging Lloyd Bauer, we'll be living in the present again. Nineteen thirty-nine wasn't that great a year, anyway.*

The sun was setting when Harry Krug, driving his Land Rover along the main road, passed Lloyd Bauer's oncoming Cord convertible. He waved but, as usual, Lloyd ignored him. Nora sat beside the congressman in the front seat; their two squirming boys were in the rear. "Lloyd has a speech on Sunday and meetings in North Jersey next week," the Old Man had told Krug yesterday. "I'll suggest that he take his family with him. Better if they are away from here until the operation is over."

As if a trained dog like Lloyd Bauer would dare disobey one of the Old Man's "suggestions," Krug thought with contempt. He looked forward to the day when Paul Bauer and the Old Man were dead and he was summoned to Lloyd's office to be told that he was discharged as Master Huntsman.

How would Lloyd react to the news that his fortune and prominence and political power meant nothing, that he was actually the servant of the people of the sanctuary, not their ruler? Again, like a trained dog, he guessed.

Krug had been summoned to the mansion for a meeting on the disposition of forces during Monday's operation. The instant he entered the Old Man's top floor room, he knew that the plan had been changed yet again. Mounted on the wall were two charts, bearing the names of enemies marked for execution and the huntsmen assigned to the killings. Three potential victims were on the first chart, the plan that would be carried out if Roy Hammil's investigation failed. The second chart, based on the faint possibility of Hammil's success, was more than twice as long—and now another name had been added.

"Why *him?*" Krug asked.

"Roy Hammil spoke to Reverend Rodeburg for hours yesterday," the Old Man said calmly. "After which, without explanation, Hammil canceled his return to Warlord's Hill. Obviously Rodeburg gave him the information that provoked the change in plan."

Hammil has talked to dozens of people, Harry Krug wanted to shout. We can't kill *all* of them—even if we knew who they were.

Before Krug could speak, Dr. Zimmerman, slumped as usual in a corner chair, said quickly, "Don't fret so, Harry. The second list won't be used. Hammil phoned in a message for his wife late this afternoon. He said he was flying to Florida tonight."

"Margarethe von Behncke," Krug guessed with a sigh of relief. "But that still leaves Monday. Suppose he knows about the Cilentos and tries to find them?"

Dr. Zimmerman smiled confidently. "Not once has Hammil failed to get a daily message to Terry. When he phones the Miller house tomorrow, he will be told she is ill, that he should return as soon as possible. This afternoon I gave Wilma a powder to slip into her food. By tomorrow she'll develop the symptoms of moderately severe flu. High fever, vomiting, physical weakness, cold sweats. A condition serious enough to keep Hammil close to home for two or three days. On Wednesday, Lloyd will come back and ask for a report on the investigation, then announce that he's satisfied with the results. He'll say that from now on he wants Hammil to work strictly on campaign publicity. Toward the end of the week, the plumbing in the guest house will fail disastrously, flood both floors. The Hammils will be offered the use, again rent free, of the Sutton Place apartment the foundation maintains for out-of-town gerontologists. They will leave Warlord's Hill and, in a month or so, Lloyd will arrange for Hammil to return to his regular position at Huggins and Associates.''

"*Is* that how it will be?" Harry Krug asked the Old Man, remembering the look of hungry expectancy on his gaunt face when told of Terry Hammil's accursed family history.

"God willing," said the Old Man, his sunken, silver-gray eyes fixed on the longer execution list.

More than three hundred miles from Warlord's Hill, John Rawls was also studying a list. It contained just two names and addresses: *Wayne L. Rhue, 127 Tollhouse Drive, Bethesda, Md.* and *Lyle Stallings, 13 Barbara Place, Port Jefferson, NY.*

Rawls had neared a crossroads—the intersection of the Pennsylvania Turnpike and Interstate 70 South. After days of using backcountry routes, traveling only during hours when State Police patrols were at their lightest, he had yielded to impatience and taken a major highway. Since a series of killings in rural Idaho was unlikely to be covered by eastern newspapers and TV, the risk seemed minimal.

But now, parked in a turnpike rest area, he had to decide which of the probably fictitious identities he should check out first. Considering that the Nazi who shot himself had carried more papers, the Washington area seemed the better bet. On the other hand, Port Jefferson was a small town on Long Island, closer to his eventual goal—the dark, nameless forest that had spawned Rawls' pursuers.

His mind made up, he headed back into traffic. Minutes later he left the parkway at Exit 12, turning onto I-70. If he drove straight through, he would be in Washington by late evening.

❊ THIRTEEN ❊

Early the following afternoon, Margarethe von Behncke received Roy Hammil on the camellia-bordered rear terrace of her home in Winter Park, a wealthy retirement community in central Florida. In view of her tragic personal history, he had expected to encounter an embittered crone. However, as she approached, he was instantly reminded of Langston Fellows' description of the young woman he had met in the mid-thirties—tall, ash-blonde, elegant. Except for her hair, now fine and white, and the inevitable lines of age, the adjectives held true. Her resemblance to her nephew was striking; she possessed the same sharply defined, theatrically beautiful features.

"I suppose you know that I didn't really want to see you," she said when he had introduced himself. Her voice carried an undertone of strength, the voice of someone who, having survived hell, feared nothing on earth. "I'm repaying a debt to Langston, one he didn't remember until I mentioned it on the phone. In nineteen forty-eight, he wrote a column urging the government to restore my citizenship. At the time the State Department wouldn't issue me even a tourist visa."

"Why not?"

Margaret von Behncke shrugged. "Simple enough. As the American-born wife of a Wehrmacht general, I was considered a traitor."

"Even though your husband was a leader of the anti-Nazi movement?"

"You're too young to remember that chaotic time, Mr. Hammil. Immediately after the war, anyone who claimed to have secretly worked against Hitler was regarded as a self-serving liar by the Occupation authorities. Ewald Löser, a director of the Krupp munitions works, risked his life for years slowing production schedules, changing specifications to insure that thousands of Wehrmacht artillery pieces would break down after a few firings. And he was convicted at Nuremberg, spent years in Spandau prison before the Allied high commissioner was convinced of the truth. But surely you haven't come all this way to hear me ramble on about the past?"

"That's exactly why I've come," Roy said.

She led him to a patio table, where an elderly black houseman served canapés and two vodkas and tonic. "What can I possibly tell you about my nephew?" she asked. "I've never met him."

"I'm trying to get a handle on what formed his personality and attitudes, his view of the world."

"Not *what* but *whom*," Margarethe von Behncke said. "From the moment of Lloyd's birth, I'm sure my brother's primary aim in life was to create a being in his own image—obsessed with power, capable of any ruthless act in order to gain his ends. Even as a child, he frightened me with his need to dominate everyone about him."

"That description hardly fits Lloyd."

"Really? What *is* he like?"

Roy thought for a moment. "Charming, intelligent, cautious, suprisingly indecisive."

"Perhaps," she replied. "But if so it would be despite Paul's best efforts. He could have had only one reason to shut himself and the boy inside that estate—to make certain no 'dangerous' foreign influences affected his son's development."

"For what purpose?"

"I have no idea. I've only seen Paul a few times since I was in my late teens. Our mother was German and, when my parents divorced in thirty-two, she took me back to Europe with her. Paul rarely visited us, even when he studied at

173

Leipzig. As you may have gathered, I didn't particularly like him."

"Yet you sent your son to live with Paul Bauer after the war."

Margarethe von Behncke's facial muscles tightened and her clear blue eyes grew cold. "Yes."

"I'm sorry," Roy said hastily. "I didn't realize that—"

"I might still be sensitive about something that happened such a long time ago?" She smiled with ironic sadness. "To a woman who has outlived all her children, there is no such thing as a long time ago. It always happened yesterday. But you needn't apologize. To everyone except myself, it *was* a long time ago. That, if Theo had survived, he would be a man of your age is emotionally inconceivable to me, even though my mind tells me it must be true."

Margarethe von Behncke took a long sip from her drink before speaking again, her voice fully controlled. "I had no choice, in nineteen forty-five, about his future. We were living in the cellar of a bombed-out laundry. Theo was more than two years old but, because of malnutrition and disease, he remained the size of a large infant. He had never walked a step. I had tuberculosis. And we were alone. The Americans hated us because I was the widow of a notorious Nazi. The Germans hated us because I was the widow of a man who tried to assassinate Hitler. My father left me a trust fund and dividend checks had been piling up in a New York bank for years, but, without approval from the Occupation government, I couldn't touch the money. I was a wealthy woman who, because of a vengeful bureaucracy, was unable to feed her own baby. That left Paul.

"His agents reached us a few days after I sent him a cablegram. I was admitted to a sanitorium in Switzerland, and Theo was flown to America, where he supposedly would be safe. I'll never forget the man who took him from me—a tall, thin man with a long, creased face and strange gray eyes. I thought I'd join Theo in a few months, but the disease had progressed further than I'd known—and I wouldn't have been able to get a visa anyway. By the time I left the sanitorium and the State Department changed its mind, Theo was dead."

174

"And afterward you refused to have further contact with your brother?"

Margarethe von Behncke glanced at him with astonishment. "Who in the world told you that?"

"Lloyd."

"It would be just like Paul to leave him with that impression," she sighed. "In the beginning I *was* bitter, but eventually I accepted the fact that he wasn't responsible for the accident. In nineteen fifty-one, I wrote, said that I wanted to see Theo's grave. The reply came from Paul's lawyer, giving me permission to visit Warlord's Hill whenever I pleased. However, because of the estate's security system, several days' advance notice would be required."

"I'm familiar with the security system," Roy commented wryly. "Did you go?"

"The next weekend—for the first and last time."

"Then you *have* met Lloyd? At least as a child."

She shook her head. "I met no one except servants. After I saw Theo's tombstone, I asked the chauffeur to take me to the mansion, expecting my brother to be waiting. The chauffeur said that Paul and my nephew would be away until the following week but that the staff had prepared a room if I cared to stay overnight. Naturally, I did *not* care to. I never went back again."

The reaction of anger and humiliation Paul Bauer must have anticipated, Roy thought. Another piece of the puzzle had fallen into place.

"How is my brother, by the way?"

Roy described the shrunken, mindless, wheelchair-bound form on the second floor of the mansion.

"That he's still alive at all is miraculous," she said with a note of sympathy Roy had not expected. "In nineteen forty-four, he underwent surgery for prostate cancer. At that time survival from such an operation, beyond a few months, was practically unheard of. In the sixties, he lost a lung and most of his stomach. And, knowing Paul, I'm sure he's been arrogant enough to will his organ-free body for medical research."

Roy Hammil sensed the lingering hurt behind the old woman's grim, strained humor. But Margarethe von Behncke could not know how cruelly her brother had betrayed her. One more interview—with whichever Cilento he managed to contact first—remained on his schedule. However, he was certain of what the answer to his single question would be. When he had it, he would present the evidence to Lloyd Bauer and ask him to authorize the legal procedure that would confirm his suppositions beyond doubt. Lloyd himself would have to decide whether or not to tell Margarethe von Behncke that her son was still alive.

Lloyd and Nora Bauer spent so little time in their New Jersey residence—a modest brick house in his congressional district, north of the Pine Barrens—that a faint mustiness always hung about the interior. As a result of the humid air that had settled in last night, the odor was stronger than usual.

By the time they returned from church—obligatory whenever they spent a weekend at their official home—the sky over the small town was the scabrous, moldy gray of rotting canvas. A strong east wind gave further evidence that a storm was moving in off the ocean. Nora was glad that the weather had turned bad. Roger and Paul, as usual, were complaining about being taken away from Warlord's Hill. At least now she could point out that they couldn't have swum or played in the woods anyway, not that the news would mollify them.

That evening Lloyd was to explain a new farmlands preservation bill to a conference of environmental groups at Rutgers University. He didn't maintain a study in this seldom-used house, working, instead, at a desk in a corner of the master bedroom. Nora silently entered and, for a few seconds, watched him read over his notes, penciling corrections.

"Lloyd, how does the Old Man keep all those people in Bremen?" she asked. "Why don't any of them just pack up and leave? Surely at least a few must have wanted to over the years. What are they afraid of?"

He glanced up in annoyance. "Lupe might hear you."

"She doesn't know enough English to understand us." The Bauers' Puerto Rican maid worked only here and at their house in Chevy Chase.

"You can't be sure."

"Yes I can. I've spent six years trying to stop her from

176

washing permanent press clothes in hot water. How *does* he keep them there? It can't be by force. The huntsmen wouldn't stop their parents and brothers and sisters from moving."

"I don't know," Lloyd admitted, irritably tossing down his pencil. "What's the difference?"

"The Nazis in Germany—didn't they kill Jews?"

"Millions of them. Everyone knows that."

"I didn't know," she said quietly. "Not how many, anyway. Until I drove to the public library yesterday and looked it up. I'd never been in a library before. Terry Hammil is Jewish. She mentioned it, quite casually, on our last ride."

Angry, Lloyd Bauer rose from behind the desk. *"Real* Nazis—in Germany—killed Jews! Not a bunch of pathetic halfwits dressing up and parading in the woods—probably when the moon is full! And no one at Warlord's Hill gives a damn about Roy Hammil's wife. How could they dare harm her even if they wanted to? Dozens of people, including you and me and her husband, must know she's living at the estate."

"The Old Man is a *real* Nazi," Nora persisted. "You told me yourself he worked for Hitler and people like that."

"She is in no danger," Lloyd snapped, going into the bathroom and slamming the door.

Although she realized he was probably right, doubts continued to race through Nora's mind. She stared at the bathroom door, heard a faucet running full force, and knew that Lloyd was repeatedly washing his face with a cold, sopping cloth, something he did only in moments of great stress. He would remain in the bathroom until she departed.

She went downstairs, sat on a sofa in the ordinary living room they maintained for visiting constituents, and clasped her thin, trembling fingers together. Why *would* they harm Terry, she wondered nervously, if, as Lloyd claimed, all they want is to keep outsiders from learning about the past? But it couldn't be that simple. If it were, why did the men continue to wear swastika armbands and brownshirt uniforms, hold secret rallies? Why, even within the vast boundaries of Warlord's Hill, did they flaunt what they wanted to conceal?

Suppose Terry—now alone at Warlord's Hill, given to solitary explorations of the forest—stumbled upon evidence of what the Old Man and Nora's father and the people of Bremen really were? Would they dare let her leave? Why, since Nora was supposed to help divert Terry, had she and the children suddenly been sent away from Warlord's Hill? Lloyd had claimed that the trip "home" had been his idea—but, as usual, he had mentioned the move after visiting the Old Man's quarters.

A more personal question began to nag at Nora Bauer's mind. Even if she discovered for certain that Terry's life was in peril, would Nora have the courage and will to act on the knowledge, destroy her own family for the sake of a near-stranger?

Probably not, she realized with a shudder of self-loathing.

That morning Terry Hammil had overslept, awaking just before noon with a queasy swirl in the pit of her stomach. Even getting out of bed and pulling on a robe required enormous effort. The pale, drawn reflection in the bathroom mirror confirmed the obvious: She had caught a bug.

She went into the hall, called down to Wilma, and returned to bed, soon heard footsteps on the stairs. However, instead of the stout housekeeper, a thin, narrow-faced woman entered the room. "I'm Mae," the stranger said. "Wilma wasn't feeling too good when she got up, asked me to take over for her today. You don't look too good either, Mrs. Hammil."

"I'm not too good either," Terry agreed.

"You want me to leave a message for Dr. Zimmerman? Called the clinic earlier about Wilma but the nurse said he was in Lakewood, might not be back until tonight."

"I'll be fine."

"Fetch you tea and toast then, something easy to get down?"

Terry managed to eat the light meal, then threw it up in the bathroom minutes later. Trembling, she again slid under the bedcovers, feeling perspiration erupt from every pore in her body. But I felt so well last night, she thought. Usually, the day before a bout of flu, she became listless and irritable. This affliction had struck with the speed of a venomous snake.

The sweating abruptly stopped and she fell into a deep,

fever-induced sleep. She dreamed about her brother, Philip. He was sitting on the termite-eaten front steps of the abandoned bungalow she had chanced upon in the woods south of the lake. While she watched from the center of the weed-choked road, he rose and slowly walked to her, reached out, took her hand. His fingers were unexpectedly cold and moist, like the webbed talons of a lizard. She tried to pull away, but the talons tightened.

Terry sat up with a sharp cry, saw that real fingers—thin, old, discolored fingers—were clutching her hand. She raised her gaze and looked into the watery eyes of Nora Bauer's father, seated on a chair by the side of the bed. "Just taking your pulse, Mrs. Hammil," he said soothingly.

She sank back on her pillow. "You should have wakened me first," she gasped.

His fingertips again sought her inner wrist, eyes turning toward the pocket watch in his left hand. "This is an old-fashioned procedure, but then I'm an old-fashioned M.D. It's expected at Warlord's Hill."

Dr. Zimmerman went through the motions of a routine examination—asked Terry to sit up while he checked her lungs with a stethoscope, took her temperature, announced that she had a slight fever. "Nothing serious enough to require a stay at the clinic," he said, shutting his medical bag. "If it helps any, you're not alone. Wilma is down with the same virus."

"Must have brought it with me from the city."

"Or *we* gave it to you." Dr. Zimmerman patted her shoulder. "Hardly matters, in any event. You'll be miserable for two or three days, and then it'll be over. I'll leave medication with Mae. She'll take good care of you."

Terry suddenly realized that, although all the shutters were open, the room was shadowed beyond the circle of light cast by her night table lamp. "What time is it?"

"A little past three in the afternoon," he replied. "Clouding outside. I imagine we'll have rain before long."

"Could you ask Nora to call me if she gets a chance?"

Dr. Zimmerman stood up. "She and Lloyd and the kids have gone away for a few days. Why did you want to speak to her?"

"Why not? We're friends."

"Of course," Dr. Zimmerman said. Somehow, he had never thought of his daughter having friends—just a father and a husband and children.

"And I think, without meaning to, I hurt her feelings last week. I'd like to apologize."

Dr. Zimmerman halted in the doorway, glanced back at the young, lovely woman in the four-poster bed, and finally understood why making his mock diagnosis had been so unaccountably disturbing. For the first time, he was faced with the prospect of aiding in the execution of a human being whom he did not pity.

"Good-bye, Mrs. Hammil," Dr. Zimmerman said, shutting the door after him.

He drove his wood-framed Buick station wagon to the mansion and parked in the drive behind Harry Krug's Land Rover. The Master Huntsman slouched in the front seat, his wary gaze fixed on the sky to the east, now so dark that the distant, black-green pines were barely visible against the horizon.

"House call over?" Krug asked.

"Yes."

"Prepare for a busy day, doctor. I just took Lew Dorn's wife and son up to the Old Man. Wilma and Catherine and Conrad Webber's mother were already waiting."

"He's telling then *now*!" Dr. Zimmerman gasped in disbelief, suddenly understanding why he had been ordered to inform Terry Hammil that her housekeeper also had been stricken by a viral infection. *"Why?"*

"I have no idea," Krug replied with an embittered shrug. "When was the last time you gave the Old Man a physical examination?"

"More than three years ago. I bring it up occasionally, but he always refuses."

"That doesn't bother you? In a man of his age?"

"What are you implying?" Zimmerman snapped. The note of irritated suspicion in his voice was feigned, since he himself had begun to wonder if time had eroded the Old Man's judgment. Revealing the deaths of Vic Schall, Lew

180

Dorn, and Conrad Webber seemed a senseless act. Why further enflame the people of Bremen on the very eve of the June 28 operation?

"I don't want to talk about it here," Krug said. "I'll come to your house this evening, after you've comforted the survivors."

Dr. Zimmerman nodded, retrieved his medical bag from the station wagon, and hurried up the mansion's front steps.

Krug again stared with mixed feelings at the ever-darkening clouds. After a spring with unusually little rain, the pines were so dry that, walking through the forest, he often heard blisters of resin-laden sap explode on their trunks. A rainstorm would lessen the danger of fire, a threat that had not greatly troubled him as long as all the watchtowers were in use. But, with most of the huntsmen outside the wire, less than half the structures were occupied full-time. On the other hand, a prolonged storm might interfere with tomorrow's action.

He glanced at his watch, knowing that he had only minutes to wait. "They were on a mission of vital importance," the Old Man's somber voice would be intoning right about now, "fell into a trap set by the political police, fought to the death rather than risk capture, and, under torture, reveal the location of the sanctuary." He had heard the speech before, spoken to the wives, parents, and children of huntsmen tracked down and slain by Harry Krug himself after they had attempted to escape into the world outside the wire.

A scream of horror and grief penetrated the house's thick masonry walls; he was almost certain that it came from the throat of Vic's young wife. An instant later, as if generated by Catherine's cry, a massive gust of wind, damp with sea air, slammed against Krug's face, bending the tops of the trees on the mansion lawn.

Before leaving his Winter Park motel, at a few minutes past six P.M., Roy Hammil attempted to call the Miller house to send word to Terry that he would be back at Warlord's Hill that night. For a few seconds he heard a busy signal and was about to hang up when a recorded voice informed him that, due to a power failure, the number he had tried to reach was temporarily inoperative. He made a second call, to the National Weather Service number for southern New Jersey; another taped voice predicted that the storm attacking the coast would generate gale-force winds at least until the early-morning hours.

He went to McCoy Airport where he was told by a smiling girl at the check-in counter that flights into John F. Kennedy International Airport were on time. The day before, after his abrupt decision to interview Margarethe von Behncke as soon as possible, he had discovered that no reservations were available out of Newark, had been forced to depart from JFK.

As he boarded the DC-10 in Florida, he uncomfortably recalled a *sari*-clad check-in-counter girl who, many years ago, had cheerfully dispatched him into the heart of the worst cyclone in the history of Bangladesh.

By nightfall, the winds had gathered such strength that even Krug's massive-framed Land Rover, heading toward the medical compound, shuddered under the impact of the gusts. Rain had begun to fall—but not the steady downpour that the Master Huntsman hoped would bring relief to the tinder-dry forests. Instead, pulpy, widely spaced drops descended, like globs of hot wax falling from a gigantic, tilted candle. They splattered on the Land Rover's hood and canvas top in an unnervingly irregular fashion. In the distance, a thin line of lightning stabbed earthward with the casual force of a straight razor slashing through a curtain of black cheesecloth.

However, the weather was not Harry Krug's primary concern. Just before leaving Bremen, he had received a phone call from the main gate, where one of the Miller boys had driven to report that the winds had toppled power lines into Chatsworth, knocking out both electricity and telephone service. The system at Warlord's Hill, operating off the estate's own generators, had not been affected.

"We've lost track of Roy Hammil," Krug growled when Dr. Zimmerman admitted him into his house, going on to tell about the power failure. "If he did try to contact his wife, he couldn't have gotten through. And suppose the town phones are still out tomorrow? How can I run the operation if I can't reach my people?"

Unaccustomed to self-doubt from the normally steel-nerved Krug, Dr. Zimmerman led him into the living room and poured a stiff Scotch on the rocks. The doctor placed the glass in the Master Huntsman's tense hand and urged him to sit down. "A few hours' delay won't make much difference," he said. "I'm sure none of the huntsmen would act on his own."

Krug sank into a leather armchair, took a deep swallow of whiskey. "I'm not going to do it," he said. "I've been thinking it over for days. Implementing the second plan would be insanity."

"What if Roy Hammil finds the Cilentos? Unlikely but—"

"Then *Hammil* has to be executed. But not the others on the list. The more people we kill, the greater the risk of failure—and the greater the risk that some son of a bitch we never heard of suspects it hasn't all been a string of random, unconnected deaths. The Old Man sits in his room, dreaming up foolproof schemes that, no matter what, can never go wrong. In the real world, that's not how things work."

"Hammil's wife?"

Krug shook his head in disgust. "The biggest mistake of all. If we have to kill him, you know the setup. He'll finally reach the Millers by phone, be told that Mrs. Hammil is seriously ill. He'll head straight for Warlord's Hill, so worried that he will drive recklessly, lose control of his car at a turn, and crash into a tree east of Chatsworth. Absolutely believable—but not if his wife dies the same day."

"*I* would believe it," Dr. Zimmerman said. "A little over six months ago, her mother, father, and brother died in a car crash. As a result, she's been under psychiatric treatment for acute depression. What more logical trigger for suicide than the shock of learning her husband had died in the same kind of accident?"

Angry now, Harry Krug lunged out of the chair. "A suicide that would happen *here*, focus attention on *us*. How much more 'logical,' for the safety of the sanctuary, if she were instead treated with all the kindness you and the Bauers can muster, left Warlord's Hill convinced of your friendship? That's the way it was supposed to happen before I told the Old Man that she was a Hedricks."

"On Friday you said our only possible loyalty is to the Old Man."

Krug corrected him. "I said that to *survive* we must remain loyal to the Old Man. His words and actions since then have convinced me that he's now a threat to our survival."

"If you fail to carry out his orders, how will you explain later?"

"By telling him the truth—that he is no longer competent to make major decisions. It would help if you backed me up."

Dr. Zimmerman contemplated the possible results of such formerly unthinkable disobedience. How, after all, could the Old Man retaliate? Krug controlled the sanctuary's military force. Financial activities outside the wire—the management of the millions of dollars, concealed in the complex network of Bauer Foundation bank accounts and stock portfolios, that would finance the Old Man's plan for establishing a neo-Nazi regime in America—were in the hands of Dr. Zimmerman himself. Without his cooperation, the movement would be cut off from its major source of funds. The Old Man's only true power, Dr. Zimmerman realized, was the force of his will, the awe he engendered in his followers.

"I'm not sure," he said slowly.

"I am," Krug replied in a near-snarl. "The sanctuary must be protected! Our children—and ourselves—must be protected. Perhaps, in time, everything the Old Man has foreseen will come true. Lloyd might well become a force in national politics, maybe even president, guiding the country toward the kind of system we want. *If* the economy collapses, as the Old Man predicts. *If* white Americans sicken of having their lives rules by Jews and disguised communists, of watching helplessly while a degenerate government taxes them into poverty to feed the unproductive and subhuman."

"It *will* happen," Dr. Zimmerman insisted.

"Maybe," Krug said. Anger had so hardened the rough-hewn lines of his grayish white face that, to Dr. Zimmerman, he looked almost like a statue of himself. "But until the day of victory arrives, the sanctuary is the only safe world for the people of Bremen. It's a tiny world but a world over which I have a measure of control, where my daughter can grow up without fear of being raped and murdered by drug-crazed savages. And—for you and me and everyone else who has taken part in the Ceremony of Passage—the sole alternative to spending the rest of our lives in prison. Just as it was supposed to be.''

''I don't understand,'' Dr. Zimmerman stammered.

''Do you believe for a moment that I don't know the real reason a new fence was put up in nineteen forty-eight?'' Krug scoffed. ''The real reason why you bring those mummified kikes here to be slaughtered?''

Dr. Zimmerman's narrow shoulders hunched under the force of Krug's scorn. *A rebellion will come,* the Old Man had prophesied decades ago to the physician and Paul Bauer. *The heads of the eight families will begin dying off and their younger relatives will grow curious about what lies outside the wire. The acts of my father or my uncle are not my responsibility, they will tell themselves. We must make certain— now—that it does become their responsibility. Nothing welds together the members of a community like sharing the same guilts—and the same fears of retribution. We realized that in Germany even before they set up the camps.*

''Will you support me if I'm forced to violate his orders?'' Harry Krug asked again.

Dr. Zimmerman was about to give an affirmative reply, then hesitated. What if Krug is wrong about the Old Man losing control? he suddenly thought. Suppose, despite evidence of one irrational act after another, he knows *exactly* what he is doing?

The wind was buffeting the walls of the guest house so hard that Mae, the substitute housekeeper, did not hear the knock on the outside kitchen door. She had prepared a tray holding a pitcher of ice water, a glass, and the three pills Dr. Zimmerman had specified as Mrs. Hammil's evening medication.

She had just picked up the tray when the unlocked door opened, enveloping her in a current of cool, damp air. Although, at first, she couldn't distinguish the face of the tall figure in the doorway, she felt no fear; in the more than forty years she had lived here, no crime more serious than an

185

occasional petty theft had disturbed the tranquility of Warlord's Hill.

The figure advanced into the light and she recognized the Old Man, the wide brim of a rain hat pulled low over his deepset eyes. "You are bringing Mrs. Hammil her medicine?" he asked.

"Yes, sir," she murmured shyly; she had never before spoken to him.

A huge hand reached out, scooped up two of the pills, leaving just the orange-and-white capsule on the tray. "Only the sedative will be necessary," the Old Man said. "When you're certain she is asleep, go to the mansion. Gerald will be waiting to drive you home."

Although Dr. Zimmerman had told her to make certain Terry took all of her medication—and not to leave the guest house under any circumstances—Mae did not speak as the Old Man went back into the windlashed blackness. Who would be foolish enough to question the wisdom of even his most inexplicable decisions?

Shortly after midnight, along with other disgruntled travelers, Roy Hammil checked into a Ramada Inn near Boston's Logan International Airport. After maintaining a holding pattern over JFK for nearly an hour, the DC-10's captain had proclaimed that, since continuing strong winds made landing impossible, all flights were being diverted to fields outside the storm area. As soon as Roy entered his hotel room, he again tried to telephone Chatsworth, only to discover that the lines were still down.

God does not want Terry to know where the hell I am, he decided ruefully.

❈ FOURTEEN ❈

The next morning, Terry Hammil was awakened by the faint but insistent ringing of the downstairs telephone.

Why doesn't Wilma answer it? she wondered groggily, struggling out of a sleep so deep that she had been unaware of the winds that had battered the guest house nearly until dawn. Then she remembered that Wilma had also fallen ill and gone home. The other woman, then? Terry couldn't immediately recall the substitute's name. In any case, she was obviously either deaf or away from the house.

Terry got out of bed, and, to her amazement, realized that she wasn't sick anymore, except for mild fatigue. All of her other symptoms—nausea, fever, muscular weakness—had disappeared. Maybe old-fashioned doctors are the best after all, she thought.

She padded downstairs on bare feet; all of the shutters were still closed, steeping the interior of the house in heavy shadow. She switched on a table lamp before picking up the phone.

"Mrs. Hammil?" asked a deep, faintly accented male voice.

"Yes."

"I am the Dorn family's spiritual adviser. Have you been informed of the death?"

"Whose death?" she gasped, shocked out of her drowsiness.

"Young Eric's father."

"How? When?"

"Poor Lew had taken a temporary job down in Cape May, working on a commercial fishing boat. It sank with all hands four days ago, far out at sea, but we weren't informed until the night before last. Apparently, the authorities had difficulty tracking down his home address. A memorial service will be held at ten o'clock this morning at the church in Bremen."

"Bremen?"

"The town where the estate workers live. Do you feel well enough to attend? Eric told me how close you two have become."

"Of course I'll be there," she said. "Can I lend some kind of help *now?*"

"Everything is in good hands," the man said. "A car will pick you up at nine forty-five."

Although the room was warm, Terry felt chilled as she hung up the phone. She hurried to the large front window and threw open the shutters to admit the early-morning light. Except for a scattering of fallen tree branches on the lawn, few signs remained of last night's storm. I was wrong to encourage Eric's curiosity about the outside world, she decided. Perhaps—for these simple, isolated people—only tragedy lay beyond the forests of Warlord's Hill.

Unlike Terry, the Master Huntsman had again slept badly.

His relief that the storm had passed before dawn turned to disappointment when, shortly after seven-thirty, he reached the Miller house and learned that the telephones were still out of commission. For the next hour, he paced the cheaply linoleumed kitchen floor while old, grizzled Dick Miller repeatedly attempted to get a dial tone on one of the three lines that had been installed in the house years ago, in anticipation of this day. Only Dick's fat, ancient mother, sewing a patchwork quilt in the corner, remained calm.

"It will only be a little while more," Grandma Miller assured them. "If you can't trust New Jersey Bell, who can you trust?"

The words had barely left her wrinkled lips when one of the phones rang. Harry Krug rushed to pick it up. "No one

188

met him at the prison," said the huntsman on the other end of the line. "He's taking a bus."

"Nail him at the first opportunity."

"I told you everything would be all right," Grandma Miller said smugly.

With anticipation, Vincent Cilento dropped a dime in the lock of a cubicle in the Attica bus station's men's room. Most cons, when predicting their first actions after release, talked about hugging their kids or screwing or finding a piece of ground so open that they could see for miles in every direction. Vincent's ambition had been to once again use a toilet with a seat on it, behind a closed, locked door. He would work on other satisfactions when he reached the city. He had often wondered why the liberal jerks who wrote articles on prison reform never mentioned that a maximum-security cell was really a small john with cots crammed against the wall. Odors were seldom mentioned.

A thin, balding man, Cilento lowered his pants and settled his narrow buttocks on the toilet seat. At least he wouldn't have any money troubles when he got back home, he thought. Not if the gray-faced man had kept his word. After the death of Vincent's father in 1974, the monthly envelope containing a single thousand-dollar bill had failed to turn up in the mail for the first time in twenty-six years. The sender hadn't known, then, that the fatally ill Angelo Cilento had told his son Vincent the name of the multimillionaire who had authorized what he called "my pension." A few days after Vincent sent a warning letter to Paul Bauer, the gray-faced man had appeared at his West Side apartment with the envelope, which thereafter came by mail. He never saw the man again but, following Vincent's murder conviction, he received an unsigned note in jail. *Payments will continue*, the scrawled words read. *A bankbook will be delivered to you—or anyone you designate—on completion of your sentence*.

The crazy part was that Vincent Cilento had no idea why Paul Bauer had paid the exorbitant blackmail over such a long period. What could Vincent know that might possibly be a danger to him, especially after all this time? So a bunch of south Jersey hicks used to dress up like Nazis and march around a hole in the ground. Hell, that wasn't a crime even in 1948. The bastard who beat up Eddie after he and the blond kid fell over the edge of the pit could have been busted, of course—but who in their right mind would pay thousands year after year to hush up a long-forgotten assault?

His bowels had just started to move when Vincent heard metal scrape against metal overhead. He looked up and saw the twin muzzles of a sawed-off shotgun tilt over a cubicle wall, aimed down at a 45-degree angle. The barrels discharged, and loads of 16-gauge shot plowed into his chest and stomach with such devastating impact that his jacknifed body was driven into the toilet bowl. Oddly, in the last second of his life, he felt no pain from the massive wound but cried out in revulsion when his naked buttocks contacted the cold water. His upended legs gave a spastic kick, and coins fell from his pants pockets, rolling out over the white tile floor.

"It's begun," Harry Krug said to the Millers when he received the telephoned report from Vincent Cilento's assassin.

Krug then called Ralph Webber, Conrad's younger brother, in Port Jefferson. He had reservations about Ralph, since this was his first mission outside the wire. However, the cover identities of "Lyle and Alex Stallings"—two unmarried brothers sharing a small rented house—had been set up so perfectly that, when Conrad was sent to Idaho with Lew Dorn, Krug had no choice except to let Ralph carry on alone.

"Do it as quickly as possible," he told the young huntsman. "Vincent's death might make the twelve o'clock news. Even if she doesn't see it, friends or relatives might start phoning or coming over. Getting to her through forty or fifty hysterical wops might not be all that easy."

Krug hung up, swerved his gaze toward the telephone nearest his right hand, the number Roy Hammil would dial in order to send a message to his wife or order a car from the estate. All huntsmen in the field had strict instructions to use the other two lines, so that the vital call wouldn't be accidentally blocked.

Where the hell *is* he? Krug wondered.

* * *

After less than four hours' sleep at the Ramada Inn, Roy Hammil had returned to Logan Airport, taken the first available flight to JFK, and landed a little before eight o'clock. He had called Chatsworth from a pay phone, got the same recorded message he had heard in Florida yesterday.

He didn't seriously fear for Terry's safety: According to the paper, the storm had caused no injuries, except as the result of automobile accidents. I'm already on Long Island, he thought, glancing at the piece of lined notepaper on which he had written Rosemary Morelli's Port Jefferson address. He could drive out, interview the woman, and be back at Warlord's Hill by the early afternoon.

Twelve Barbara Place proved to be a small, cheaply constructed but well-maintained ranch house at the circular end of a short cul-de-sac; beyond it lay a patch of scrubby woods. As Roy started up the flagstone walk, he heard a baby crying inside the house.

The woman who answered his ring was in her late forties but her features curiously mingled qualities both younger and older: smooth, unlined olive skin; long, carelessly groomed hair, gone completely gray; clear, youthful black eyes; narrow shoulders hunched beneath a faded print housecoat.

"Mrs. Morelli?" he asked.

She nodded.

"My name is Roy Hammil," he said, taking out his wallet and showing her his old syndicate press card, his thumb positioned to hide the long-passed expiration date. "We're doing an in-depth series on Congressman Lloyd Bauer."

"Who?" she asked, glancing over her shoulder. The baby was crying louder.

"He'll probably be the New Jersey Republican candidate for the Senate next year."

"You're in the wrong state," she said. "Anyway, I wouldn't have heard of him. I don't pay attention to politics."

"My questions aren't political."

The baby's cry turned into a shriek. "My granddaughter hates her playpen," Rosemary Morelli said, backing into the house and shutting the door.

A moment later, when the crying stopped, she again appeared. "Okay, what's it about?" she asked impatiently.

Since the woman obviously wasn't going to invite him in, Roy struck fast: "In nineteen forty-eight, you and your brothers and a boy who lived on the Bauer estate were trapped in an earthslide. The boy from the estate was killed."

"He *died*?"

"You didn't know?"

"We just saw the men carry him off." Her surprise gave way to indignation. "Why would you want to bring up a thing like that? After all these years?"

In a few seconds, Roy realized, the door would be slammed in his face. "The boy you saw carried off," he snapped in the near-bullying tone that usually provoked an automatic, truthful response. "How old was he?"

"About Vinnie's age," she murmured—and then anger again hardened her face. "You get the hell out of here!"

As Roy had anticipated, she slammed the door in his face.

Ralph Webber, peering from a bedroom window of the house next door, watched Roy drive off. The ball of fear in his stomach growing even harder, he hurried downstairs and dialed his assigned telephone number with a quivering forefinger. "It's Ralph Webber," he said when he heard the Master Huntsman's voice.

"You've finished?"

"No." Ralph went on to describe the stranger's arrival, just as he was preparing to fulfill his mission. "He was one of the men in the photos you showed me and Conrad the last time we were in the sanctuary, the guys you said to be on the watch for. The younger of the two. He drove a dark red Jaguar."

"How long did they talk?"

"Only a couple of minutes. They she got kind of angry and shut the door on him. Like Conrad, when those Jehovah's Witness people keep turning up on weekends. What should I do now?"

"What you were sent to do," Harry Krug said, hanging up.

Ralph Webber checked to make sure that none of the neighbors were on the street. The building's position, near the end of the cul-de-sac, made it impossible for anyone except the occupants of Mrs. Morelli's house to see his rear yard from inside their homes. With sweating hands, he tied hard knots in a nylon scarf to fashion a garrote.

What if the man in the picture comes back? he thought suddenly. I'd better wait a little while, be sure she's alone. Oh, God, I wish Conrad were here.

Another quarter hour and Rosemary Morelli's dangerous secret, unknown even to herself, will have died with her, Harry Krug brooded.

In less than two minutes of conversation with a reluctant subject, Roy Hammil could not have discovered what had truly happened that night so many years ago. Nevertheless, how had he been drawn to investigate the Cilentos in the first place? Nothing on public record linked Lloyd Bauer in any way with the incident in the pit. Was it possible that Hammil himself had begun to remember the past?

Harry wrote a penciled message on the pad next to the telephones and then ripped off and folded the top sheet. "I want one of your sons to take this to the main gate," he told Dick Miller, who had already moved to his side.

The message would activate the standby team trained to execute Roy Hammil. And that, Krug told himself, would be the end of it. Except for John Rawls, the other earmarked targets would be spared.

What could the Old Man—who, Harry Krug now fully believed, was sinking into senile fantasy—do to block his decision?

At exactly nine forty-five, the silver Packard limousine halted in front of the guest house. Terry Hammil, equally punctual, was waiting on the porch. Gerald got out and opened a rear door.

Since Terry had brought only summer clothes to Warlord's Hill, she lacked a really suitable dress for a memorial service. She had settled on a simple, pale gray frock. Worn with only a single strand of pearls as decoration, the outfit at least verged on the somber.

"Thank you, Gerald," she murmured as she entered the car.

"You're welcome, ma'am," the chauffeur said, closing the door after her.

They drove across the foundry dam, passing the stables; no horses roamed the pastures. Considering the amount of debris produced by the storm, she had expected clean-up crews to be at work, but the lawns and fields were deserted. Of course, she realized, all of the workers must be going to the service for Lew Dorn.

"You must have known Eric's father," she said.

"Yes, ma'am."

"Why was he working off the estate?"

"Some of us do, occasionally. When circumstances make it necessary."

The limousine drove past the huge gray mansion, which seemed as lifeless as the fields and outbuildings. But it really couldn't be, she thought; even if most of the staff were attending the service, the helpless Paul Bauer and his nurse would still be inside. Roy had told her of the elder Bauer's condition on his last night at Warlord's Hill.

When they reached the forest, Terry saw that storm damage had been greater than she at first believed. Large trees had been uprooted by the wind. Several had obviously fallen across the road, been cut-up and hauled to the shoulders earlier that morning. But the earth already looked dry, indicating a surprisingly light rainfall. How could I have slept through it all? she wondered.

"I didn't realize you had a minister here," she remarked, "until he called to tell me about the memorial service."

A church bell began to ring. Although Terry knew Bremen was still miles away, the tolling sounded startlingly loud amid the morning stillness of the pine woods.

After Roy Hammil's departure, Rosemary Morelli attempted again to confine her eight-month-old granddaughter to the playpen—and, again, Gina's furious cries compelled her to put the baby back on the carpeted living room floor.

Rosemary sank down on a couch and watched Gina try to pull herself onto the seat of a straight-backed chair, only to fall repeatedly. Like everybody with Cilento blood, she thought in a burst of self-pity. Even the family's single windfall—the

194

thousands paid to her father for concealing the truth about what had happened to his children—contributed to the disintegration of their lives.

The reporter's questions had brought that night back with crushing immediacy. Rosemary was thirteen again, looking on helplessly while her brother Eddie and the blond boy fell together into the quarry. She had grabbed the six-year-old boy's hand, tugged him after her as she and Vincent fled toward the trees, already hearing booted feet digging into the pit walls. Black, shapeless forms quickly encircled the three children.

By the time the uniformed men dragged them down a steep roadway into the pit, the vicious beating of Rosemary's brother had ended. Blood gushed from his mouth and scalp, he lay unconscious at the jackbooted feet of a young, strongly built man with a face so pale that, even by torchlight, his skin seemed almost gray. Shrieking, Rosemary tried to rush to Eddie's side, but powerful hands closed on her shoulders from behind. Vinnie, a few feet away, whimpered in fear. The six year old, eyes wide but uncomprehending, still had not uttered a word. Past a cluster of brownshirted figures, she could see the blond boy who led them here. Like Eddie, he seemed to be unconscious, lying cradled in the arms of a slender middle-aged man. Another man, wearing ordinary clothes, knelt beside them and opened a medical bag.

The gray-faced youth swerved his vengeful gaze toward the prisoners. "Kill them!" he shouted.

A threatening murmur went through the crowd. Rosemary felt her captor's thick hands rise from her shoulders to the base of her neck and had started to scream when a deep, rumbling voice declared:

"No!"

The hands on her neck loosened at the approach of the tall, gaunt man who had stood before the altar. "Does anyone know who they are?" he asked, peering down at the children.

A man in the rear ranks stepped forward. Rosemary was startled to recognize Mr. Eberhardt, the farmer who had been taking care of them. "The older ones are the Fresh Air Fund trash staying at my place," he said in a strained voice. "We've been looking after the little kid, too."

The tall man turned to the physician. "Are you free to examine the other boy?"

"Yes," the physician said wearily. He picked up his black bag and gave the gray-faced youth a glance of disgust. "Just what do you think you accomplished, Harry?"

"That little bastard pushed him over the edge. I saw it."

"They fell together," the physician said angrily, easing back Eddie's right eyelid with his thumb. "He's in shock. Send someone to the clinic for an ambulance."

The physician took off his jacket, draped it over Eddie, and asked other men to provide warming garments until blankets could be obtained.

Frightened, baffled by their captors' alternating cruelty and concern, Rosemary allowed herself to be maneuvered like a stringless puppet. The next few hours were a series of blurred, disconnected events. She and Vinnie, separated from the tiny boy, being driven through the dark woods in the back of the biggest car she had ever seen . . . Entering a huge house with gleaming paneled walls . . . Led upstairs to a bedroom, where a kindly faced woman in a white apron brought them cookies and hot chocolate . . . Resisting sleep, finally drifting off, lying side by side on a broad bed . . . Later, she thought again and again of the enormous size of everything they encountered, like the giant's castle in "Jack and the Beanstalk."

Early the next morning, they were shaken awake in a manner so familiar that, at first, Rosemary thought she was back in her family's cramped flat and had dreamed the previous night's horrifying events. But it proved to be the same big room and the same big bed. However, the calloused hand that had roused her and Vinnie belonged to their father, peering at them with eyes both loving and—already—sodden with guilt.

"They brought me from the city," he said with his heavy Italian accent. "First you will have breakfast and then the police will come. This is what you will tell the police . . ."

"It isn't true!" Vinnie shouted when they had heard the lies they were supposed to repeat. "None of it!"

Angelo Cilento slapped his son across the face. "This is what you will tell the police," he said to the sobbing child, going over the same false story. "I have been to the hospital.

196

Your brother will be all right. The *dottore* told me this and I believe him."

"They were Nazis, Papa," Rosemary muttered sullenly. "The kid from the woods didn't believe it, either. 'They're bad people, murderers,' I said to him, and then he went crazy and hit me. Eddie grabbed him and—"

"This is what you will tell the police," Angelo Cilento said, slapping his daughter across the face.

And in the end, of course, that *was* what Rosemary and Vincent Cilento told the men in the blue State Troopers' tunics. That afternoon, a silver limousine took the silent children and their equally silent father home to West Thirty-first Street. Almost immediately, the Cilento family's life became easier. Angelo continued at his job as a garbage truck driver but now they had meat with all their meals and Rosemary was confirmed in a white silk dress with real pearls sewn on the bodice and, fulfilling their mother's greatest wish, Vincent was enrolled in a good parochial school.

Months later, Eddie, walking with the aid of canes, came home to a freshly painted and refurnished apartment. By that time, Rosemary and Vincent almost believed the lies their father had forced them to tell. At first she feared that Eddie would ask questions about what had happened to them after he was beaten into unconsciousness. But he never did and Rosemary guessed why: In all this time, only their father had visited the hospital in Lakewood. She never knew what had happened on those visits, but the suppressed rage in her brother's eyes told her far more effectively than words.

"Oh, baby, shut up," Rosemary Morelli snapped when her granddaughter started crying in frustration. She lunged off the sofa, picked up the soft, diapered body, and deposited it on the sought-after chair. Within seconds, Gina had lowered herself off the other side, crawled under the glass-topped coffee table, and stared up at the round bottom of a white plastic vase filled with paper chrysanthemums.

Rosemary went back to the couch, wondering how her and her brothers' lives would have turned out if their father hadn't taken the payoff. Not much different in my case, she decided.

She'd have probably married Danny Morelli, the butcher's son, or someone pretty much like him.

But what about Vincent? Until that summer he had been the "smart kid" in the family, the one who never got into trouble. Four years later, after violating his third Juvenile Court probation for breaking and entering, he was sent to Elmira Reformatory. Maybe, if the father he had loved so deeply hadn't shown him that *anything*—even a child's trust—could be sacrificed for money, his miserable life might have turned out differently.

Or Eddie? Until that summer, he had feared no one and hated no one, always spoke the truth even if it earned him a punch in the mouth from a bigger schoolmate. After he came home from New Jersey, they had all been apprehensive that he might never walk again unaided, despite treatments at an East Side orthopedic clinic that a garbage truck driver couldn't possibly afford. Eddie had faithfully done his required exercises hours each day, his face contorted with agony. By the morning of his eighteenth birthday, he was walking normally. And that same morning, he had packed a suitcase and strode out of the apartment without a word to any of them, never to return.

Rosemary was astonished, after decades of consciously blocking these memories, at how totally she was able to recall what had happened, even to remember names that had not crossed her mind for years. The little, quiet boy had been Roy Hammil—the same name, she realized, given by the reporter! But that couldn't *be*, she told herself. I must have mixed things up somehow!

She was jolted out of her confusion by a light knocking on the back door. Going to the kitchen, she saw Alex Stallings through the screened upper half of the aluminum door. "Hi, Mrs. Morelli," her open-faced young neighbor said. "Could you lend me a couple of slices of bread until I get to the store later? Got bologna but no bread."

"Come on in," Rosemary said, grateful for the interruption. "I don't know how you and Lyle stay so healthy the way you eat. Is he home yet?"

"Still in Pennsylvania visiting Mom."

Rosemary turned her back to him, opened the breadbox,

heard the creak of the back door hinges. "White or rye?" she asked an instant before he looped the garrote around her throat and rammed his left knee into the small of her back.

Why, with such a slight woman, had it taken so long? Ralph Webber wondered, staring at the body on the kitchen floor, his ashen face covered with sweat. Four times he had loosened the garrote, expecting Mrs. Morelli to crumple, but always another rattling gasp had emerged from her bruised throat and he had tightened it again, twisting frantically. Not at all the way the old Jewess had died at Ralph's Ceremony of Passage—silently, almost with gratitude.

Shaking, he struggled to remember what he was to do next. *The police will question you,* the Master Huntsman had warned. *Just say you were asleep, saw and heard nothing. They might even suspect you but only for the first few hours. Maybe less if someone in the family mentions her maiden name.*

Ralph crammed the knotted scarf in his pants pocket and was about to leave when the baby crawled into the kitchen, headed toward her grandmother's motionless form. The child's mother worked in a nearby dry cleaning shop and often came home for lunch. Even if she did, Ralph thought, Gina would be alone in the house for at least a couple of hours; she might accidentally hurt herself. He plucked up the infant with his damp hands, took her into the living room, and deposited her in the playpen.

He had reached his own home when Gina started to cry fiercely. The sound drove him to his bedroom, on the far side of the house. Even there, he could hear the screaming.

Driving toward the Southern State Parkway, Roy Hammil wondered how Lloyd Bauer would react to the news he would bring. It would depend, he supposed, on the depth and nature of the congressman's own suspicions.

Roy saw a phone booth ahead, in front of a corner drugstore. He parked and entered the booth, intending to try to reach the Miller house again. Then it occurred to him that Lloyd Bauer might not be at Warlord's Hill. As a precaution, he dialed the congressman's office and got Sidney Levin, who told him

Lloyd was spending the week at his district residence and did not plan to come in today. He gave Roy the phone number.

The second call was answered by Lloyd Bauer himself. "I have to see you immediately," Roy said. "I've turned up some information it's vital for you to know."

"You can't tell me over the phone?" Lloyd asked after an uncertain pause.

"Too complicated for that." He looked at his watch, saw that it was three minutes before ten. "Suppose I come to your house at two this afternoon? The drive shouldn't take anywhere near that long, but I'm not familiar with the area."

"All right."

No point in calling Chatsworth, he thought after hanging up, since he couldn't specify a time for meeting the limousine. Relief swept over him as he resumed his journey. Even if his theory proved wrong, he had a hunch Lloyd would terminate the assignment as soon as he heard what Roy had to say. After meeting Rosemary Morelli, he had experienced an overwhelming desire to get Terry away from Warlord's Hill.

The limousine entered Bremen, purring up the main street. The town seemed even less inhabited than on Terry's earlier visit. At least, then, she had heard distant phonograph music and had dimly glimpsed a barber and the shapes of men inside the firehouse. But now the barber shop window was shuttered and the firehouse doors were closed. The bell had ceased its mournful tolling while they were still on the forest road.

"They must have started already," she remarked to the chauffeur, noticing that the church's front steps were as empty of people as the rest of the town.

Gerald halted the limousine in front of the church. Not waiting for him to get out and open her door, Terry left the car and hurried up the steps. The minister's deep voice reverberated from the shadowed interior but she could not make out the meaning of the words. She halted briefly on the threshold, smoothed the already wrinkling skirt of her gray dress, took a deep breath, and slipped inside, hoping to find a seat in a rear pew.

"And now," the voice roared, "they have poisoned the sanctuary itself!"

Coming in from sunlight, Terry's vision was initially blurred. The first object she clearly discerned was the church altar, draped with a scarlet banner that framed a white-ringed black swastika. An immensely tall, gaunt old man in a brownshirt uniform stood in the pulpit, his long right arm pointing down the aisle toward her. At first she thought she must be the victim of a perverted joke—then, as the people seated in the pews rose in unison and turned toward her, she knew that this grotesque horror was *real!*

The men wore khaki uniforms and swastika armbands; the women, black dresses. Massed hatred struck her with physical impact, the way a desert wind felt when you emerged from an over-air-conditioned building. Familiar faces had been transformed: Wilma, her plump features mingling grief and unspeakable loathing; Jake, the stable boy, his normally slack face taut with blood lust; Wilma's placidly beautiful daughter-in-law, her full lips now a jagged, resentful scar; Eric, looking years older in his vile uniform, his red-brimmed eyes stunned with sorrow.

For the briefest of instants, Terry felt an absurd impulse to murmur "Excuse me" and then quietly depart. When the men and women began moving out of the pews toward her, she turned and ran. Behind her, Catherine uttered a crazed, malevolent shriek.

Terry burst out of the church, hearing feet pounding up the aisle in pursuit. The limousine had departed, its place taken by a parked ambulance with open rear doors. Standing beside it was Dr. Zimmerman. Because he wore normal clothes—and had been so sympathetic yesterday—she almost started to him for help. Then she realized he, too, must be a Nazi—he and Lloyd and Nora and everyone else at Warlord's Hill.

She cut away from the ambulance and ran toward the nearest side street, afraid to look back. Within seconds, the first pair of hands—Catherine Schall's—clutched at her shoulders. She tumbled to the rough pavement, felt the upper half of her dress rip away, and managed to kick Catherine off and rise once more before half a dozen black-garbed women again pushed her to the ground, tearing at her delicate skin with their nails and teeth, like crows competing for the flesh of a dead rabbit.

"What have I done to you?" Terry cried. "What have I done?"

The smothering pressure on her helpless body suddenly eased. Eric had left the crowd of male onlookers and was yanking the women off her, pushing them away. Her hands trying to cover her exposed breasts, Terry sat up, sobbing her gratitude—just before the boy's fist struck the side of her head. It wasn't a hard punch—his fingers weren't fully closed—but it stunned her more than a blow from a club. Her naked shoulders slumping, she lowered her head and let her tawny hair spill over her scratched, bleeding face.

Dr. Zimmerman approached her, holding a hypodermic needle in his right hand.

✖ FIFTEEN ✖

"**I** had no idea what was going to happen," Dr. Zimmerman told Harry Krug. "Last night, after you left my house, I called the Old Man, said that I was too exhausted to attend the memorial service. He said nothing. Then this morning I was awakened by the ambulance driver on call and told that a woman had been badly injured in Bremen. I sat up front with him on the drive and, when I realized that he was slowing down just outside town, I asked him why. 'The Old Man's orders were to arrive at exactly three minutes after ten,' he said."

They stood beside Zimmerman's Buick station wagon, outside the Miller house. A few minutes earlier, Ralph Webber had confirmed his kill. Krug's relief that the inexperienced huntsman had fulfilled his mission had vanished at the sight of the old physician's sallow, stricken face in the kitchen doorway. "We had better go outside," Krug had said, not wanting the Millers to overhear.

Dr. Zimmerman took a deep, ragged breath before describing the scene that had awaited him at the church less than an hour ago.

"Is Hammil's wife alive?"

Dr. Zimmerman nodded. "I knocked her out with sodium pentothal, took her to the clinic."

"The clinic?" Krug said. "Or the place where you store the old Jews?"

"I *couldn't* put her in the main building. It isn't secure. And she won't sleep forever."

Krug started toward the Miller house. "I told you he'd find a way to get her into the pit without risking the community's disapproval. I can almost hear him whipping them into a frenzy over what was supposed to have happened to Lew and Conrad and Vic. Gearing back a little to tell how a woman embodying pure Jewish evil had secretly crept into their midst. Without really explaining how, blaming her for the deaths. Then she comes through the door at the instant he's worked them to the highest pitch. It couldn't fail."

Dr. Zimmerman grabbed at Krug's shoulder, halting him. "What should I do now?"

"Prepare what's left of her for the Ceremony of Passage. He's beaten us."

Krug pulled free of Dr. Zimmerman's grasp, strode back into the house, and sat at the kitchen table. The Old Man had forced him to proceed with all phases of the operation's alternate plan. Terry's "suicide," on the heels of her husband's fatal "accident," would inevitably create suspicions in the minds of two people Hammil had contacted during his investigation.

The Master Huntsman reached for a telephone, wondering if the orders he was about to transmit actually would achieve permanent peace for the sanctuary. Suppose other breaches in security had occurred, threats from sources neither he nor the Old Man even imagined?

The hill-ringed inland town where the Bauers maintained their official residence had experienced the storm only as light rain and moderately strong winds. For the first time in weeks, Lloyd had shared Nora's bed. She knew that he was probably feeling guilty over being caught with the red-haired maid, but that didn't matter; the joy of having him move inside her again, the even greater pleasure of drifting off to sleep with his lips sucking her left nipple had wiped out her resentment.

Lloyd's manner yesterday had been distracted and brusque. Today he seemed more relaxed than he had in weeks—until just before ten, when he took a phone call that revived his dark mood. "Roy Hammil will be here at two," he said, coming back to the dining room, where they were eating a late breakfast. "Says he has important information for me."

"Lloyd, why would the Old Man deliberately hire an outsider to see if *other* outsiders might learn about the sanctuary?" she asked hesitantly. "I didn't put that very well but you must know what I mean."

"I already told you," he snapped. "If the danger of potential exposure starts to look serious, I'll turn down the nomination for the Senate."

"That doesn't make sense when you think about it. If the Old Man is trying to protect you, wouldn't it be simpler if the men of Bremen burned those stupid uniforms, lived like any ordinary group of farmers and forestry workers? If no one has learned about them in more than forty years, why would the risk be greater now?"

Lloyd drained his coffee and, leaving most of his breakfast on its plate, rose from the table. "The Old Man has his reasons."

"But shouldn't *you* know what they are?"

Nora expected him to stalk off, as he usually did when she put too much pressure on him. However, he remained in the room. "Won't matter," he said flatly. "I have no idea what Roy wants to tell me but, whether it's earth-shattering news or silly gossip, I'm sending him back to the PR business."

"I think that's best."

"By the way," he added, a shade too casually, "did you tell anyone at Warlord's Hill that Terry is Jewish? Even your father?"

"No."

"Don't. Better to eliminate any unnecessary strain while they're still living inside the wire."

So he was lying yesterday, Nora thought in dismay. Lloyd isn't any more sure than I am about Terry's safety.

Terry regained consciousness with her mind utterly clear, as if less than a second had passed since the hypodermic needle had plunged into her arm. Terror still coursed through her body, and she could still feel Eric's blow and the rending nails and teeth of the women of Bremen. That she was now in a narrow hospital bed in a gray-walled room seemed an act of evil magic.

She sat up, releasing the scream that had been rising in her throat at the instant the drug took hold.

The only response to her piercing cry was the soft, slow slapping of too-large bedroom slippers. A thin, sad-eyed old woman in an ill-fitting black wig appeared in the doorway. "You're too young to be in this place," the old woman said, "but I guess it's better than no company at all."

"Where are we?" Terry gasped.

"Damned if I know," the old woman replied with a shrug. She wore a shapeless white cotton nightgown, exactly like the garment Terry now found herself in. "I figure they're going to kill us, though, don't you?"

The resignation in the old woman's voice somehow calmed Terry. "I'm not sure."

"I think they killed Mr. Feld. He was just being led out of a room in the Golden Era attic when they brought me upstairs. I was kind of surprised. Dr. Zimmerman told us a couple of weeks before that Mr. Feld was dead. Pneumonia. But there he was, big as life. Then, when they moved me here, I found some of his things—his pipe and his wife's picture—in a wastebasket. But no Mr. Feld." She paused in her ramblings, carefully adjusted her wig with both thick-veined hands. "For a while, I couldn't figure out why Dr. Zimmerman would want to kill Mr. Feld and me. I never hurt anybody and I don't think he did. So I decided it must be because we're Jews. You ever hurt anybody?"

"No."

"You a Jew?"

"Yes."

"Got to be it then."

"But that's insane!"

"Always was," said the old woman, shambling off again in her worn slippers. "I lost two sisters at Auschwitz, and I bet they never figured it out either."

Unpleasantly aware of the odor of iodine, Terry looked down at her exposed arms, saw yellowish-brown stains covering dozens of superficial cuts. Small bandages covered three

206

larger wounds on her right leg and shoulders. She got up and went into the hall, just as the old woman turned into her own room. At the end of the hall lay a heavy, steel-sheathed door. She ran to it, twisted the knob, and discovered that it was locked.

Terry choked back the urge to release another scream or pound on the door with her fists. She went to her room, peered through the heavy steel mesh covering the single window, saw the familiar twisted pines in the distance, and realized she must still be on the Bauer estate. What, in that first moment of fear inside the church, seemed impossible was not only possible but irrefutable. The old woman was right, they were going to die here—simply because they were Jews.

Terry thought about the portrait of Raphael Hedricks that had hung above the big fireplace at Two Moons Ranch, of the slightly smug, triumphant smile on her ancestor's lips. In the mountains of New Mexico, he had established a refuge for his family, so remote from the barbarians who had persecuted them for centuries that his descendants had come to regard their own religion as an almost whimsical link to a bygone time. Poor Raphael hadn't known that the barbarians might one day create refuges of their own.

She suddenly wished that she had finished her letter to Leah Golding.

How long could the baby keep crying? Ralph Webber wondered, peering out his bedroom window while waiting for Mrs. Morelli's daughter to come home for lunch.

Even before he telephoned the Master Huntsman, more than an hour ago, Gina's shrieks had become frenzied. He and Conrad were under strict orders never to call the Miller house from their home phone. He had already, unthinkingly, violated the rule once—after recognizing the man from the photograph—and had not wanted to do it again. But how could he have left the house, driven to a payphone, and returned while the crying continued? Suppose a neighbor observed him and later undermined his story about being asleep all morning? Anyway, the Master Huntsman will never know, he had told himself. And he said no one would suspect me.

He was about to leave the window when Mrs. Halvorsen, the middle-aged woman who lived on the opposite side of the circle, came out on the front steps and stared with anxious uncertainty at Mrs. Morelli's house. She must be wondering why no one has stopped the kid from crying, Ralph thought. After a few seconds, Mrs. Halvorsen half-turned, as if to go back inside. Then, changing her mind, she walked quickly across the circle and rang Mrs. Morelli's doorbell.

Ralph threw back the covers on his bed, rumpled the sheets, and punched an indentation in the pillow. Soon the police would be here, so everything had to look right.

He had already changed into pajamas when he remembered the garrote in his pants pocket. He broke a fingernail in his frantic efforts to unfasten the knots. Even when the last one came loose, clusters of telltale wrinkles remained in the material.

He rushed to the kitchen, put up the ironing board, and plugged in the steam iron. The nylon scarf was flawlessly smooth when he heard the first siren. Gina had stopped crying. He folded the scarf neatly, ran back to his bedroom, placed it in the proper drawer, and again went to the window. By now four police cars had squealed to a halt in front of Mrs. Morelli's house. Mrs. Halvorsen, holding the now-silent Gina in her arms, stood on the front lawn, excitedly talking to a stocky man in a dark suit.

No one will believe I slept through all this, Ralph decided uneasily. More than a dozen other neighbors had already gathered on the street, moving back as an ambulance pulled to the curb behind the police cars. Ralph donned khaki work clothes and went down to join them. As he approached the rapidly growing group of onlookers, Mrs. Morelli's daughter swung her Dodge Aspen into the driveway. Tears streaming down her cheeks, she ran into the house.

"Who would do such a terrible thing?" the elderly man from the corner asked his wife. "She never hurt anybody."

What *had* Mrs. Morelli done to endanger the sanctuary? Ralph wondered vaguely. He had once asked his older brother, but Conrad's only reply had been a glance of disdain, probably meant to conceal the fact that he didn't know either. Conrad had always hated to confess ignorance.

Last night's storm—and the Reverend Felix Rodeburg's part-time occupation—had made his execution child's play. The team of huntsmen had found him on a back road, using his old bulldozer to push fallen tree limbs and other debris to the sandy shoulders. Probably before the day was over, his body would be discovered at the bottom of the muddy hill. Everyone would assume he had lost control of the machine on the steep grade and been thrown out of the driver's seat just as the big Cat overturned, crushing him beneath its immense weight.

However, word of yet another successful kill did not relieve the Master Huntsman's belief that they were taking too many risks. None of this would be necessary if, eight years ago, Vincent Cilento hadn't unwittingly saved his own life by murdering another drug dealer.

The Old Man and Paul had thought that Angelo Cilento's death would put an end to a quarter-century of blackmail payments. Angered by the letter from the immigrant's younger son, they decided to settle the Cilento problem once and for all. Lloyd had just started his first term in the House and would most likely become increasingly prominent in the years ahead, stirring even stronger greed in Vincent.

Krug had delivered the first payment to the hoodlum in person in order to familiarize himself with Vincent's current appearance and the layout of his home. Unfortunately, the day before his execution was to be carried out, Vincent Cilento was arrested for murder and held without bail right through trial and sentencing. His death, then, had to be postponed until he completed his prison term. Late in May, after eight years in Attica, the parole board granted his freedom; the release date was June 28.

The fact that, after his conviction, Vincent didn't ask that the monthly payments go to his sister showed that Rosemary Morelli must be unaware of the continued extortion. However, because of her potentially dangerous memories, she would have to die, as would Edward, the other brother. As a precaution, huntsmen had kept track of him over the years as, constantly changing his name, he wandered from one laborer's job to another, finally enlisted in the army and rose to the rank of master sergeant during three tours of duty in Vietnam. He received a Silver Star and a Medal of Honor nomination before a jungle ambush left him so severely wounded that he was given a medical discharge.

Later he was arrested for nearly beating a man to death in a Charleston, South Carolina, bar. The victim's only provocation, witnesses testified, had been to declare that "Hitler went crazy later on, but he started out with the right idea." To avoid jail, he signed himself into a VA mental hospital and was diagnosed a paranoid-schizophrenic; in less than six months he escaped. The police failed to pick up his trail; the Master Huntsman did not.

Repeatedly, Krug begged for permission to assassinate Eddie Cilento, arguing that, since he had not made contact with his family since the mid-fifties, they might never learn what happened. "No, we'll just continue to watch him," the Old Man replied. "Italians have peculiar loyalties. If Vincent should connect his brother's death with us—while still in prison, where we can't touch him—he might expose the sanctuary. It's much better that they all go at the same time."

All very sensible, Harry Krug thought, staring at the silent phones on the Millers' kitchen table. Except that they now had lost contact not only with Eddie Cilento but with a fifth child who had spied on the ceremony in the pit.

Before the erection of the new fence, Paul Bauer had sought to maintain the illusion that Warlord's Hill was simply another rich man's sprawling country estate. The eight fugitive families from the old Bremen lived deep in the forest, but other former bundists of unquestionable loyalty were settled after the war in houses outside the estate's formal boundaries. One of these buffer tracts was a small farm, operated by Julius Eberhardt and his wife, Mary, a distant cousin of the Uhls. For several summers, as part of their effort to make the area look respectably commonplace, Paul Bauer had permitted Eberhardt to take in slum children on vacations sponsored by the *New York Herald-Tribune* Fresh Air Fund. However, Roy Hammil—the six-year-old boy—was an unexpected personal guest, the son of Mary Eberhardt's high school best friend. The woman's husband, a Camden shipyard welder out of work since spring, had found a job in St. Louis, and the wife had asked Mary to keep the boy until she rented an apartment in their new home.

Much of this information was given to Krug by his father on the morning after the tragedy in the pit. "The Old Man has put it all together," said the then-Master Huntsman, gulping down black coffee. He and Gerald had just returned from New York with the Cilentos' father. "Mary Eberhardt went to bed early, as she often does when Julius is at a rally. The children must have sneaked off into the woods when they were sure she was asleep. Eberhardt swore neither he nor his wife had any idea they had made friends with a kid from the estate."

"And now?" Krug asked.

His father shrugged. "I don't think the Old Man will have trouble dealing with Cilento. He looks mean, stupid, and greedy. And the Hammil boy is too young to understand—or remember for long—what really happened. Julius has already taken him home and put him to bed. Dr. Zimmerman doesn't even plan to tell the cops that he was with the others when the accident happened. But the Old Man thinks it would be wise to occasionally check on him in the future."

And so the ongoing bribery of Angelo Cilento was begun. Two weeks later, Roy Hammil's father drove east to pick up his son and returned immediately with him to the Midwest. Soon Paul Bauer extended the size of the preserve to take in the Eberhardt farm and hundreds of additional acres. The Eberhardts, given the option of remaining behind the new fence or taking over another Bauer-owned farm in north Jersey, chose the latter, living on the same land until their deaths. On Bauer's orders, their original farm was never again worked; the house gradually became a weathered shell, virtually swallowed up by the encroaching forest.

A telephone rang, jolting Harry Krug out of his contemplation of the past. He momentarily hoped that it was the line left clear for Roy Hammil. Instead it proved to be the center phone, over which Peter Uhl delivered a report from Washington: "The police patrols have been cut back, Master Huntsman. We're ready to go."

Harry Krug flinched at the enthusiasm in Uhl's voice. It reminded him too much of his own youth, when, trying to impress the Old Man, he had stomped Eddie Cilento and urged the other men to attack Rosemary and Vincent. Many years were to pass before he learned that only fools and madmen killed with enthusiasm.

"When I give the word," Krug said, wishing that Lew Dorn was still alive and commanding the Washington force. But maybe their run of luck would continue. After all, Peter Uhl had been operating outside the wire two years longer than Ralph Webber—and, even lacking his older brother's guidance, Ralph had completed his assignment.

The Old Man had often mentioned that the Zionist cabal secretly controlling the FBI had also infiltrated thousands of agents into state and municipal police forces; their actual duties were to ferret out local level members of underground resistance forces like the huntsmen. The instant the stocky man opened his wallet to display a shield—and introduced himself as Detective Sergeant Nathan Weiss of the Suffolk County Police Department—Ralph Webber was on his guard.

He asked the plainclothesman inside, but Weiss said that he preferred remaining on the doorstep. Maybe I haven't been singled out, Ralph thought, noting that another detective was ringing Mrs. Halvorsen's doorbell. The body of Mrs. Morelli still had not been removed to the waiting ambulance. He wondered what they were possibly doing with it.

"I just have a few questions," Weiss said, going on to take down Ralph's name, address, and occupation—night attendant at an Exxon station on the Smithtown-Port Jefferson Bypass. "Do you live here alone?"

Ralph shook his head. "With my brother, Lyle, but he's upstate visiting our folks."

"How long have you resided at this address?"

"About eight months."

"Did you see or hear anything unusual this morning, especially in the vicinity of the Gianturco house?"

Ralph looked at the detective without comprehension—then remembered that the place next door must be owned by Mrs. Morelli's daughter and son-in-law, whose name he had never known. "I always thought of it as Mrs. Morelli's house," he said at last. "Hardly ever spoke to anyone else in the family."

"You were friendly with her, then?"

"Oh, sure. Working nights like I do—and her stuck taking care of the baby—we talked a lot of afternoons. Somebody murdered her?"

"We think so."

"Mrs. Halvorsen was talking out front. She said Mrs. Morelli's face was blue when she found her on the kitchen floor."

"Yes, I believe it was."

"I didn't hear anything before the sirens started. Get off work at eight, eat something, and hit the sack."

"Not even the baby crying?"

"Gina carries on a lot. I'm used to it."

Sergeant Nathan Weiss regretted that he had not accepted the offer to come inside. The thin, tow-haired youth's replies carried a frightened undertone. However, Weiss was too experienced to regard this as a necessary indication of guilt. Any man alone in a house when a woman next door is murdered knew damned well that the cops would routinely zero in on him. From the position of Rosemary Morelli's body and the state of her clothing, it seemed unlikely that she had been raped. Nevertheless, Weiss wished he already had a complete medical examiner's report.

"We'll probably be getting back to you, Mr. Stallings." The detective had started to turn away when he noticed the newly dried blood on the young man's right index finger; the nail had been torn halfway to the quick. He gestured at the injury. "When did that happen?"

Ralph had been nervously rubbing his upper left arm when the unexpected question was thrust at him. He peered down at the broken fingernail. "This morning. Meant to put on a Band-Aid but, with all the excitement, I forgot."

"How did you break it?"

"Shut a cabinet door on my hand. Why?"

Nathan Weiss was about to press on with further questions when a plainclothesman called to him from the front steps of the Gianturco house. "Nate, could you come over a minute? It's important."

Reluctantly, Weiss joined his colleague. "I've been taking statements from the Gianturcos," the plainclothesman said. "You heard about that Mafioso who got blown away in a toilet right after he was paroled from Attica? Happened a few hours ago."

Weiss nodded.

"Mrs. Morelli was his sister."

Weiss sighed with immediate understanding. The medical officer now completing his preliminary examination of the body had said that the pattern of bruises on Mrs. Morelli's neck indicated the use of a garrote, a traditional weapon of Mob hit men—and, like any veteran cop, Weiss did not share the naive popular notion that the Mafia never sought retribution on the relatives of offending members, especially their women.

"You were sure talking to the guy next door a long time," the plainclothesman said.

"Acted funny."

"Never can tell, Nate. Suppose . . ."

"What professional killer would be dumb enough to live on the same block with his victim for eight months, letting the whole neighborhood see what he looked like?" Weiss scoffed. He glanced back at Alex Stallings, who had remained in the open doorway, again taking in his fair, straight features and fine yellow hair. "Besides, a Mafia hit man would be Italian. That kid is one hundred percent kraut."

For more than an hour, Terry Hammil had sat trembling on the hospital bed, knees drawn up behind her clasped arms and pressed to her forehead. Increasingly grotesque possibilities had flooded her thoughts.

Did other places like this, fenced-in bastions of Nazism fronted by people like the Bauers, exist all over the country? Had another set of monsters in New Mexico murdered her parents and Philip, disguising the crime as an auto accident? Were the victims only Jews like herself, members of historic families? That couldn't be, she realized, since the old woman's accent and manner marked her as ghetto-bred. So it must be *all* Jews!

She heard the steel-sheathed door open, leaped off the bed, and ran into the hall just in time to see a nurse and a tall, burly man in a white tunic push a wheeled table inside.

"Why have you put me in here?" she cried. "Who are you?"

Ignoring her, the pair departed. A few seconds later, the old woman emerged from her room, carrying a straight-backed chair, which she placed at the table.

"Lunch," she announced.

Terry laughed bitterly. "I'm afraid I don't have much appetite."

"Well, then, fetch a chair and talk awhile. By the way, I'm Mrs. Sophie Braunstein."

The old woman's eerie composure again calmed her. She brought a chair to the table, which was covered by a fine linen cloth and held two bone-China bowls filled with a rich-looking beef stew; a plate of warm, freshly sliced bread; plastic pitchers filled with ice water and red wine. But the only eating utensil at each place setting was a soup spoon.

"At the Golden Era, they put a vase of fresh flowers on each table before every meal," Mrs. Braunstein remarked nostalgically. "Dr. Zimmerman always seemed so kind and thoughtful. Goes to show, you can't tell by appearances."

"No," Terry said, recalling the last time she had spoken to Eric Dorn. *They should be in jail!* he had said of the Nazis he had seen on television. *Or executed!* How had they taught a child to lie with such diabolical, shameless skill?

"What's *your* name?" Mrs. Braunstein asked, biting off a small chunk of bread, chewing carefully.

"Terry Hammil."

"Doesn't sound Jewish."

"My husband isn't."

"The *Terry,* I meant."

"It's really Teresa."

"Sounds even funnier."

"I suppose it does. We were a funny kind of Jew."

"What happened to your husband?"

This was a question Terry had intentionally tried to force out of her mind since her imprisonment began; too many horrors had already been faced. Dr. Zimmerman and the Nazis in the church would not have dared reveal themselves if they thought Roy could later expose them—and never before in their marriage had he been gone this long without attempting to contact her.

"I think they've killed him," she said, tears filling her eyes as she at last gave voice to the probability she had struggled so hard to suppress.

Mrs. Braunstein reached out, stroked the back of Terry's hand with her bony fingertips. "Guess we're on our own then."

I will not die here, Terry Hammil told herself in a surge of anger. But the old woman was right. To survive she would have to draw upon her own strengths and guile. If Roy were dead—and everyone at Warlord's Hill was a member of this demented conspiracy—no possible source of outside help remained.

By two o'clock, it was all over. Mrs. Morelli's blanket-covered body had been taken away in the ambulance half an hour earlier. Shortly afterward, the Gianturcos placed two suitcases in the trunk of the Aspen, strapped Gina into an infant's car seat, and drove off. Probably to stay with her husband's family, Ralph Webber figured. Mrs. Morelli had once remarked to him that her in-laws lived in Syosset. Then the last police car departed—and, within minutes, the last of the gawking onlookers, many unknown to Ralph, who had gathered on the street.

Barbara Place was back to normal.

Everything had happened exactly the way the Master Huntsman said it would, Ralph thought with relief. The Jewish cop clearly *had* suspected him but changed his mind only minutes later. Now all Ralph had to do was wait for Conrad. Their orders were to stay in the house, continue their regular routine until the next rent fell due, then quietly return to the sanctuary.

His torn fingernail had started to hurt. He glanced down at the sensitive, red flesh, deciding the injury might get infected if he didn't tend to it. He went upstairs to the bathroom, squirted Bactine on the fingertip, and covered it with a Band-

Aid. The fatigue he had pretended that morning had become genuine. Feeling an overpowering need to sleep, he slouched into his room—and discovered a stranger sitting on the edge of the bed.

"Why did you murder my sister?" asked John Rawls.

✖ SIXTEEN ✖

"**Y**ou're Theo von Behncke," Roy Hammil said. "The real Lloyd Bauer died in nineteen forty-eight."

"And you are out of your fucking mind!" his companion gasped, face draining of color.

A few minutes earlier, Lloyd Bauer had admitted him into the house. The rest of the family had been banished upstairs during the meeting. "What have you to tell me?" Bauer had asked as soon as they entered the living room. Roy had decided to give him the truth head-on.

He was startled by the congressman's reaction. "I thought you knew," he said. "Or at least had strong suspicions."

"What possible evidence could support such an idiotic theory?" Bauer asked, sinking into a chair, clutching its arms with both hands.

"Three other children were involved in the accident. I tracked down one of them, Rosemary Morelli, this morning. She said the boy who died was the same age as her brother Vincent. About eleven."

"That's *all!*" Lloyd scoffed. "What if, after so many years, she simply remembered wrong?"

"Lloyd, if you want, we can end this conversation right now," Roy said. "Naturally, you have my word that I'll never repeat what I've told you to anyone. I just did the job you hired me to do, under the rules you laid down."

Bauer loosened his grip on the chair arms. "I'll hear the rest."

"What do you remember of Theo?"

"What is there to remember? He was four or five when he died."

"And you were ten?"

"Yes."

"Then you must have lived with him more than two years, were probably there the day of the accident. If a family tragedy like that occurred when I was ten, I'd sure as hell remember it. *And* my cousin."

Confusion touched Lloyd Bauer's face. "I *do* remember."

"*Personally* remember—or, when you were a small child, remember being told about him?"

A first, faint trace of fear joined the confusion.

Roy continued, "The real reason Paul Bauer lived in total seclusion and put up those damned fences was to seal you off from society, control your life right down to distorting your sense of time. Easy to do in a private world without newspapers or television or calendars or *any* indication of change. What was to prevent him from convincing you that you were older than your actual years? To a little kid, numbers don't have real meaning. If there are eight candles on the cake, then he figures he's eight. Paul Bauer's sister was the only real threat in the early years, and he handled that by insulting her so cruelly that she never came back to Warlord's Hill."

The blood had returned to Lloyd Bauer's face, but tiny beads of sweat now dotted his upper lip. "*Why?* What would he have to gain?"

"A son instead of a nephew, a descendant who shared his own blood," Roy guessed. "According to Margarethe von Behncke, he was a dominating man with dynastic ambitions. And after prostate surgery, other natural children were impossible. If he settled for naming Theo his heir, the boy could have been claimed eventually by his mother, might develop in ways he disapproved. You were the only future he had, Lloyd."

"It still comes down to one woman's word."

"Your college yearbook pictures convinced me I was on the right track. According to the records, you were nearly twenty when you entered, a fairly advanced age for a freshman. Yet you looked fifteen—because you *were* fifteen."

Lloyd Bauer stood up, his fists knotted against the sides of his legs. "I already told you I was a sickly kid. Asthma, a freak calcium deficiency, one illness after another. Dr. Zimmerman wouldn't allow me to enter college earlier."

"Fortunately for Paul Bauer, you had a first-rate mind but he didn't dare let you leave Warlord's Hill until you were physically mature enough to pass for a boy in his late teens. And your childhood troubles were caused by war-time exposure and near-starvation. Your mother told me that at two you still hadn't walked."

"My mother died in nineteen thirty-nine," Lloyd Bauer insisted. At the same time, he nervously recalled his first year at Princeton, the sense of inferiority that had nagged at him, classmates' sarcastic remarks about his high-pitched voice and physical weakness. Roy Hammil's claim couldn't possibly be true, he told himself. But doubt had been planted.

"I can hardly ask my father about this nonsense. He doesn't hear or speak."

"Dr. Zimmerman looks healthy enough, and he had to be in on it, beginning with the falsification of the death certificate. If he won't admit anything, you can exhume the body of the boy who died. Positive identification isn't necessary. If the bones are those of a ten-year-old then you *have* to be Theo van Behncke."

"We're driving to Warlord's Hill," Lloyd Bauer snapped. "Right now. Just give me a minute to tell Nora."

Briefly left alone in the living room, Roy pondered Lloyd Bauer's reaction to his words. Obviously, he had not feigned his shock at the revelations—which left Roy with a disquieting question of his own. If Lloyd had never doubted his parentage, what in the hell *had* he feared Roy might expose?

As he entered the main hall of the cinderblock annex, followed by the hulking attendant, Dr. Roger Zimmerman dreaded his encounter with Terry, anticipating hysteria. Instead he found her sitting on her bed, hands clasped loosely in her lap, her usually clear green eyes clouded with despair. "Why am I here?" she asked plaintively.

He patted her shoulder. "You recall going into the church for the memorial service?"

Terry nodded dazedly.

"I'd just turned onto Elm Street in the ambulance when you entered. A precaution. Lew Dorn's wife hasn't been well. A moment later you ran out, crying in a frenzy, tearing at your clothes. It took half a dozen of the townspeople to hold you down while I prepared a sedative."

She shook her head in disbelief. "I saw Nazis . . . But that couldn't be . . . Not here . . ."

"The foresters wear their uniforms to funerals and other ceremonies," he said soothingly. "You've been very ill, and the light inside the church is poor. You just got confused."

As he rambled on in his unctuous attempt to convince her she had been hallucinating, Terry felt hatred and contempt. He actually *wants* to believe his lies, she realized, because life is easier for him if he believes them. That was why the midday meal had been so well prepared, in china bowls, served on a linen tablecloth. So that Roger Zimmerman could tell himself later that he had done everything in his power to make his prisoners comfortable. She fought the urge to give way to anger, to drop her numb mask. But if this fussy little monster and his helpers could be convinced that she was almost catatonic, they might not guard her as closely, increasing her chances of escape.

She sat motionless and obedient while he changed her bandages. "Nothing that required stitches, thank goodness," he said. "You won't have scars."

"What is this place?" she asked, gazing vacantly at the soundproofed ceiling.

"An annex to the clinic," he said, daubing fresh iodine on a deep scratch in the left side of her neck. "Occasionally I bring patients from the Golden Era Center here. Old people who lose control, create problems for the others. A change of scene tends to calm them. Like Mrs. Braunstein. You've met her?"

Terry nodded again. "She talks a lot but none of it makes much sense. Where is my husband?"

"We're still trying to reach him."

"Can't I go back to the guest house? I'm all right now."

"Not immediately, I'm afraid," Dr. Zimmerman said. "You'll be far better looked after here. And I don't claim to be an expert on emotional disorders."

"Please let me go home," she begged.

"I can't assume the responsibility, Mrs. Hammil. My daughter told me how your family died, how seriously you were affected by the tragedy."

Your daughter told you *nothing*, Terry wanted to shriek. Because *I* didn't tell Nora!

After Dr. Zimmerman's departure, Mrs. Braunstein came to Terry's room. "Hid next door and listened," she sniffled. "I do *too* make sense. Don't I?"

Terry put a comforting arm around the old woman's spare shoulders. "I wanted him to believe we weren't getting along."

"You lie real good," Mrs. Braunstein said admiringly. "But Dr. Zimmerman is awful hard to fool."

However, as he walked back to his home, Roger Zimmerman felt no suspicions, only greater relief. Mrs. Hammil's passivity would make tomorrow night less harrowing for him. Even so, he inwardly cringed at the duty of preparing so young and vital a woman for the Ceremony of Passage.

At last he had a name and a place, John Rawls exulted as he drove the dust-covered Cherokee toward the Verrazano Narrows Bridge to Staten Island. Warlord's Hill, the private estate of a family called the Bauers . . . Near a town called Chatsworth . . . From the moment he saw the fear in the little Nazi's eyes, he had known that the man would talk—and, unlike Vic Schall, tell the truth. The son of a bitch had actually looked surprised when Rawls continued to hit him.

As Rawls had anticipated, the trip to the Washington area had been a waste of time. He arrived late Saturday night, checked into a motel. The next morning he went to Bethesda, found no one named "Wayne L. Rhue" in the telephone book. However, 127 Tollhouse Drive proved to be an actual address. For the rest of the day, he staked out the silent, seemingly unoccupied suburban house. Just before dark, a station wagon pulled into the driveway. His first glimpse of the car's occupants—a young black couple with three little girls, all wearing bathing suits—destroyed hope that they

222

might be linked to the Nazi he had killed in Idaho. To make certain that they lived in the house, Rawls waited until the father unlocked the front door. Then he drove off.

He still had "Rhue's" private investigator's ID and VISA card as possible leads. However, without official standing, he couldn't get access to the credit firm's customer address files. Since it was Sunday, the detective agency offices were closed. Anyway, a phone call asking for "Wayne L. Rhue" could be made just as easily from New York. In the unlikely event that the agency acknowledged employing a man by that name, he could pursue the lead later.

At dawn he started north. He reached Port Jefferson by afternoon and repeated his Bethesda routine. But this time the phone book carried the listing STALLINGS, L., 13 BARBARA PL. He located the street, a small cul-de-sac, on a Suffolk County map, parked the Cherokee several blocks away, continued on foot, and eventually found himself part of a crowd gathered behind a police barricade at 12 Barbara Place. Within seconds, the hushed conversation of the other onlookers told him that a woman named Rosemary Morelli had been murdered inside the ranch-style house.

More than two decades had gone by since Rawls had last thought of himself as Eddie Cilento; it was a name from a self-banished past. But in the early years of his exile, he had occasionally telephoned childhood friends, asking about his brother and sister. One of these widely spaced calls revealed that Rosemary had married Danny Morelli, the son of the neighborhood butcher.

Rawls waited with the others until the body was wheeled out on a stretcher, even though he knew that the woman's face would be covered. When the ambulance drove off, his flat black eyes moved toward the house next door.

The Nazis watched Rosemary, too, he thought, his rage still too great to permit grief. From as close as they could get, the way they watched me. She may even have regarded her slayer as a friend, the way Rawls had regarded Vic. He had already spotted one of the occupants of 13 Barbara Place—a thin, blond-haired man in his early twenties. Several times he came out the front door, joined the spectators, and spoke with neighbors before retreating inside. He probably would keep up this show of concern until the police left.

Rawls walked away from the crowd, turned a corner, silently moved through the patch of scrubby woods behind the cul-de-sac's circle, came up on the rear of 13 Barbara Place, and discovered that the kitchen door was unlocked. He entered and crept upstairs. The first bedroom he checked was neatly made up, probably having belonged to the late "Lyle Stallings." The second had been recently occupied. He sat on the edge of the rumpled bed and waited.

Rawls' first thought after beating the Nazi to death was to drive to New York, find Vinnie, and warn him that his life was in danger. Even before he reached the Long Island Expressway, he learned that he was too late. He had turned the Cherokee's radio to a news station, hoping to get additional details on Rosemary's murder. Instead, he heard a report of the assassination, only hours ago, of a paroled convict named Vincent Cilento. Gritting his teeth, he had turned south toward the Verrazano Bridge.

Why had it never occurred to him that the Nazis would also keep track of his brother and sister, Rawls wondered guiltily as he left the Staten Island end of the bridge, cutting toward an exit ramp sign that read: GOETHALS BRIDGE—NEW JERSEY. He already knew the answer. All along, he had counted Rosemary and Vinnie among the persecutors, along with the father, who, out of greed, had denied his own son's passionate desire for justice. With a shudder of revulsion, he recalled the endless months he had lain in a nameless hospital, his shattered legs in traction, his shaved head heavily bandaged after the operation to remove bone splinters from his fractured skull, his broken ribs imprisoned in a body cast. Three times a week his father had come, demanded over and over again that he swear by the Holy Virgin that he had been hurt in an earthslide. Months later—although his injuries were healed, he was still confined to the hospital—he broke down and, tears of resentment in his eyes, said, "Yes, Papa, I promise."

"Then we will go home," Angelo Cilento replied.

His brain injury had left him with only spotty, blurred

memories of where he and his brother and sister had been when they saw the Nazis. The few times he tried to ask Rosemary or Vinnie, they turned away from him. So, suppressing his anger, he worked on rebuilding his body, waiting for the day when he was strong enough to walk out the door of the apartment that had been furnished and decorated with money earned by his pain, to shed the life and even the name he had come to hate.

Everything worked out until, one fetid afternoon in the jungles north of Nha Trang, a round from a Communist light machine gun tore into his thighs, breaking the bones of both legs in virtually the same, permanently weakened areas that the gray-faced Nazi had smashed more than twenty years earlier. He was taken out by chopper, eventually evacuated to the States, where months of hospitalization began. Later, a doctor told him that amputation had barely been avoided. "I'm going to find the bastards who did this to me," Rawls told him. "Might be rather difficult to track down specific Vietcong, Sergeant," the doctor replied with an uneasy laugh. "That's not who I'm talking about," Rawls replied. But, as it turned out, he hadn't found the Nazis. The Nazis had found him.

Realizing that he was driving too fast, Rawls eased up on the gas pedal, edging into the Staten Island Expressway's slow lane. This close to his goal, he couldn't risk a speeding ticket—and a possible search of the Cherokee's cargo area, where the dynamite was concealed. GOETHALS BRIDGE—1 MILE, a sign proclaimed.

Rosemary and Vinnie were victims, too, he thought bitterly. Their bodies had been whole, but they must have felt the same fears he had, the same conflict between family loyalty and the truth. They must have made the same promise Rawls finally had been forced to utter and, like him, been haunted by it for the rest of their lives. Even his father had been a victim, in a way. For the first time he could picture Angelo Cilento—weary, barely literate even in his native Italian—faced with the deal the Nazis must have offered. If the kids keep their mouths shut, we'll never have to worry about money again, he must have figured. That's the way the real world works. Later they'll thank me.

225

Goethals Bridge—an old, narrow girdered structure—appeared ahead. On the other side lay New Jersey—and John Rawls' final confrontation with his unseen enemy.

It was nearly three-thirty when Roy Hammil braked the Jaguar at the entrance to Warlord's Hill. The armed guard came out of his shack and gazed suspiciously at the contemporary car, like an aborigine getting his first view of an airplane. Only after recognizing Lloyd Bauer did he swing open the gates.

After leaving the congressman's home, Roy had automatically headed for Chatsworth, expecting that the ritual switch to a pre-1940 auto would be carried out. However, Lloyd had surprised him by declaring: "I know a faster way to the estate. It's about time I stopped that nonsense anyway." Except for giving Roy directions to back roads through the Pine Barrens, these were the only words his preoccupied passenger had spoken during the trip.

"How do I get to Dr. Zimmerman's clinic?" Roy asked, assuming that Lloyd intended to question the physician.

"Just drop me off at the mansion. Someone else I want to talk to first."

Who? Roy wondered. Except for servants and the motionless form of Paul Bauer, the sprawling house must be unoccupied. But after destroying Lloyd's faith in his own past, he felt he had no right to probe further. His distasteful job was done.

When he halted in front of the mansion, Lloyd hurried from the car and bounded up the front steps without a backward glance. Roy drove on to the guest house, called out for Terry, and received no reply. Probably tracking through the woods with that kid again, he decided, carrying his small suitcase to the bedroom. He unpacked, accumulating a pile of soiled garments for the bathroom laundry hamper. At the bottom of the bag lay the thick packet of Terry's developed photographs, forgotten since he picked them up in Chatsworth last week.

Roy took the packet downstairs, made himself a Scotch and water, sat on the living room couch, and idly studied the prints. For the most part, they were closeups of rare plants.

The single exception was a shot of an unpainted, disintegrating bungalow with a tilted RFD mailbox in front of it. He riffled past and then—not quite knowing why—returned to the shot of the house, imagining its walls painted a fresh yellow and the shingled roof restored, the fields beyond the structure filled with rows of tall corn.

I've seen the place before, he thought. But that was impossible. Except for the area around the mansion and the main road to the gates, he had traveled nowhere at Warlord's Hill, hadn't visited the Pine Barrens until he accepted the assignment from Lloyd Bauer. He sipped his drink, stared at the picture of the house for another few seconds, then tossed the stack of prints on the coffee table.

Roy Hammil had always done his best to resist attacks of déjà vu.

✳ SEVENTEEN ✳

"So Hammil put some of it together," the Old Man said. "That's not important."

"I *am* Theo von Behncke?" Lloyd Bauer asked in a stunned voice.

"You *were* Theo. That's not important either. Where is Roy Hammil now?"

"He went on to the guest house."

"I'm afraid his wife won't be there to greet him. She's in the clinic."

A few moments earlier, Lloyd had burst into the top-floor room, discovered the Old Man half-dozing in an armchair, a German translation of *Dombey and Son* on his lap. At the sound of the opening door, the Old Man had regained full awareness, his silver-gray eyes flaring to brilliant life. He smiled with tolerance when Lloyd had repeated Roy's words.

"Why did you and my father do it?" Lloyd said.

"For much the reason Hammil surmised," the Old Man said. "Paul's loyalties to the party were always mixed with a sort of quasi-royalism. He never actually came out with it but, even when he was my student at Leipzig, I sensed that his true ambition was to establish himself as the leader of a Nazi-dominated America. It might have happened. He was able, courageous, the single largest contributor to the Bund. And remember, if we had won, the most powerful non-

Germans in today's Europe would be named Mosley, Laval, Quisling."

"But the war was *over*!"

"Just the first phase. As I told you earlier, the sanctuary exists as a spiritual center and training ground. However, it is only part of the movement Paul and I established. Everyone believes that he cheated the major German industrialists out of millions as a protest against their so-called war crimes. Actually, the funds were channeled into a long-term plan of political action. Dozens of men your age and younger, the sons of clandestine American supporters of National Socialism, were raised from childhood under an educational plan conceived by myself, owe their careers to our guidance and financial sponsorship. Many of them are now entering the upper echelons of political life at both state and federal levels. They don't know the names of most other members of the movement and will not until the time comes to rally around a truly commanding figure. He was—in Paul's dream, at least—to be Lloyd Bauer."

The Old Man told him of the night the two struggling boys plummeted into the pit during a torch-lit rally, how Dr. Zimmerman discovered the fall had fatally broken young Lloyd's neck. Only hours later, when they were back in the mansion, did the Old Man suggest to the grief-stricken Bauer that they bury the child as Theo von Behncke and replace him with the sickly four-year-old boy who, since arriving in America, had been confined to the estate clinic.

"It seemed the logical way to insure the movement's future," the Old Man said. "Paul was our primary source of funds and, without a descendant to carry out his personal goals, his interest might have waned, perhaps vanished. Naming Theo heir to the Bauer fortune, as Hammil pointed out, would have achieved nothing if Paul's sister regained custody. We needed total control over the child's development. Besides, the son of a *Wehrmacht* general who helped plan an assassination attempt against Adolf Hitler would prove an unacceptable leader to many. Personally, I despise that sins-of-the-fathers business— except, of course, among the genetically corrupt races. The fact that Hitler himself failed to execute the plotters' families shows that he shared my view.

"The problem of the Cilento children remained. If we were to convince Margarethe and the rest of the world that Theo was dead, we had to attract as little attention as possible, pass it off as a commonplace childhood accident. The simultaneous death or disappearance of four other children—three of whom had been sponsored on their vacation here by one of the country's most powerful newspapers—would accomplish exactly the opposite. So we paid off the Cilento family. The remaining child at first seemed to present a problem. He was only six, and his parents had already moved to the Midwest. Within a few years, both had died—the father in an industrial accident, the mother of a heart condition. He should have disappeared into the great mass of American *untermenschen*. Instead he became a successful Washington journalist."

"Roy Hammil?" Lloyd sighed.

The Old Man nodded. "In the beginning, when you were a junior congressman, Hammil didn't present a threat. However, as your prestige grew, it was inevitable that your paths would cross. Publicity on your background—including life here at Warlord's Hill—was certain to become more prevalent and detailed. Much safer if he were no longer a journalist when it happened. A change to public relations was easily arranged. And then when you expressed fears about running for the Senate, I conceived of a *real* use for Hammil—to assure you and myself that none of the sanctuary's secrets could be discovered by a reporter."

"And if he *did* discover them?" Lloyd Bauer asked tensely, already guessing the answer.

"Eight years ago I decided that any outsider who witnessed what happened in the pit that night, even if the knowledge was buried in his subconscious, must die. Due to unforeseen circumstances, the executions had to be postponed."

"Until when?"

"The process has already begun. Vincent Cilento and his sister were disposed of today, along with the local man who put Hammil on their trail."

"Why are you revealing all this?"

"I wouldn't be if you hadn't learned that you were born Theo von Behncke," the Old Man said. "You'd have accepted the death of Roy Hammil in a car crash, the suicide of his despondent wife, everything else. In your heart, you'd be suspicious of the circumstances, but your nature and training would never permit you to acknowledge it, even to yourself. But such convenient self-deception is no longer possible, Lloyd. The time has come for your Ceremony of Passage.''

At the Miller house, Harry Krug had managed to get down a cold ham sandwich, his first meal since a predawn breakfast. Soon he would have to make a decision on postponing the Alexandria kill. As was the case with the Reverend Rodeburg, executing Langston Fellows—solely on the chance that Roy Hammil had revealed dangerous information to his former colleague—struck Krug as an unnecessary risk, even if carried out in such a manner that a link to the sanctuary could never be established. To proceed while Hammil himself was still alive would be sheer folly.

Where is he? Krug wondered angrily, staring at the silent telepone. According to Ralph Webber, Hammil had spoken to Rosemary Morelli nearly seven hours ago. Why had he failed to return to Warlord's Hill? Even if he had heard by now of the "gangland slayings" of Vincent Cilento and his sister, he had no reason to connect the acts with the Bauer family.

Unless, Harry Krug thought, Hammil had recognized Rosemary Morelli and remembered the pit. Impossible, he decided. The woman, in her late forties, could bear little resemblance to the thirteen year old of that summer, especially to someone who had last glimpsed her when he was six.

Nevertheless, Krug remained near the phone, wishing he had access to a newspaper or radio. Although the Millers resided outside the sanctuary, they obeyed the rules that governed the lives of those within the wire. *They're the perfect family to run a message center,* Krug's father had remarked after the new fence was erected. *Totally loyal, totally without curiosity, almost retarded.*

Krug heard the roar of a motorcycle and knew one of Dick's sons must be bringing a message from the gate. The boy hurried into the kitchen, then handed the Master Huntsman a folded slip of paper. The note reported that Roy Hammil and Lloyd had arrived together at Warlord's Hill in the former's Jaguar. Too relieved to ask himself why Lloyd had chosen to bypass the regular system, he decided a reply wasn't necessary; the Old Man would make certain Hammil never left the estate again.

He called Peter Uhl in Washington, told him to proceed with the plan, went to the refrigerator, and took out a beer. Grandma Miller beamed, "I can tell the worst is over," she said. *"Whatever* it is you boys are doing."

Lloyd Bauer—at last aware of the incredible depth of the Old Man's madness—slumped in a chair listening to his tutor calmly describe long-past and still-pending acts of savagery. He had already told of the dozens of dying Jews who, over the years, had been sacrificed in the Ceremony of Passage, binding young huntsmen to the sanctuary with ties of blood.

"Terry Hammil will join them," he said. "As a Hedricks, she is a living symbol of centuries of corruption and must not be permitted to breed. By tomorrow night, most of the huntsmen will be back inside the wire. Her death will immortalize for them the moment that the sanctuary became fully secure. Then a period of moral strengthening will begin, while they wait for the day when they will help forge a new order of society."

Lloyd Bauer rose from the chair. "I've heard enough."

"Stay a moment longer," the Old Man said. "Are you aware of what will happen to you if you expose the sanctuary? Do not bother to lie. I know that you are considering such a rash action. And I could do nothing to prevent it, since your authority here is far greater than my own. To the people of Bremen you are a messiah, daily risking your life in a hostile world to free them from the ever-present threat of execution or imprisonment."

"A threat that doesn't exist," Lloyd replied with angry sarcasm. "Or wouldn't exist except for your barbaric rituals."

"Be that as it may, the sanctuary is the real source of your strength. Instilling in you the psychic need for total power over others was the keystone of your education, a far more potent shaper of character than any ideology I could have taught you. If the sanctuary falls—and the truth about your birth is disclosed—even the mild power of an American political leader will be lost to you. As a German national, you

232

would be stripped of your present office and barred from holding others. The stigma of what we have done here would remain on your family for generations, even if you personally escape official vengeance. The power of great wealth would be taken away. Paul's will stipulates that, if he is predeceased by his only son, the entire Bauer fortune passes to the foundation. You need the sanctuary, Lloyd, the way a vampire requires blood."

"I've already thought of all that," Lloyd said. He left the deeply shadowed room.

Minutes later, a grim-faced Lloyd Bauer started toward the medical compound in a Hudson Terraplane convertible, pushing the 1936 car to its top speed.

When the hands on the living room clock passed five-thirty, Roy Hammil began to worry. Although sunset was still at least two hours away, he knew that Terry—even guided by the boy—preferred to be back at the guest house by five. "I got really lost last week," she had told him. "In places where pine and oak grow together, it's dark by four in the afternoon."

Besides, he thought, Wilma should already have started dinner. He had not been concerned earlier about the housekeeper's absence, assuming she was visiting her daughter-in-law. Between meals, she usually had few duties.

He went to her room off the kitchen, knocked. When no one answered, he entered and saw that the top of the chest of drawers no longer held the comb and brush set, the silver-framed photograph of her son. He checked the closet, only to discover it had been cleaned out.

What in the hell is going on? he wondered. He quickly walked back through the kitchen, intending to call Lloyd Bauer. Waiting in the living room were Gerald and two younger men, both carrying semiautomatic rifles.

"We've come for you, sir," the gray-uniformed chauffeur said.

"How long have you been lying to the Old Man?" Lloyd Bauer asked Dr. Zimmerman. "Ten years? Twenty?"

They sat in the living room of Zimmerman's residence, where Lloyd had pressed the physician for specific facts on the neo-Nazi conspiracy the Old Man had described. Who were the legislators and government officers controlled by the group? What front organizations had been set up to distribute funds, handle accounting procedures, enforce discipline? Zimmerman's replies had been halting and evasive; often he had seemed on the verge of tears.

"I lost control of it all, Lloyd," he confessed at last. "In the beginning, right through the fifties, your father kept contact with the people who worked with us during the war. We set up political education programs for their children, put the brightest male students through college. Some of them *are* prominent now—but they've probably forgotten, if they ever knew, who helped them get started. And when Paul's health failed completely and I had to take over his work besides running the clinic and the foundation and—"

"Enough," Lloyd said scornfully, recalling the Old Man's comment about "convenient self-deception." All of Warlord's Hill was a convenient self-deception. "What you're saying is that the great movement consists of a pack of frightened, brainwashed thugs who've spent most of their lives hiding in the woods. You've murdered dozens of innocent people to sustain an illusion."

"To protect *you*, Lloyd. That was why the Old Man started the Ceremony of Passage. A few of the older huntsmen know who really died in the pit that night. Harry Krug taunts me with it sometimes. If any of them felt sufficiently free of pressure to try living outside the wire, the truth would have left with them. And I only selected Jews who were in great pain, on the verge of natural death. I made certain that they felt nothing at the end, didn't even realize what was happening to them."

Lloyd Bauer went to a broad window overlooking the medical compound's lawn, stared at the mass of tall oaks that blocked off all view of the cinderblock annex. "Were the Cilentos on the verge of natural death?" he asked. "Are Terry Hammil and her husband on the verge of natural death?"

"No, Lloyd." He's going to betray us, Zimmerman thought, his stomach muscles tightening with fear.

"I'm leaving Warlord's Hill immediately," Lloyd Bauer said, a cold hardness in his voice that Zimmerman had never before heard. "You and the Old Man and that animal Krug do what you have to do—one last time. But when I come back here the day after tomorrow, you're to admit a new patient to your private madhouse."

"Who?"

"The Old Man. I'm locking him up until the day he dies."

Dr. Zimmerman's jaw fell in astonishment. "You *can't!*"

"Oh, yes, I can," Lloyd said with a bitter laugh. "He told me so himself about an hour ago."

After Lloyd's departure, Dr. Zimmerman poured a straight whiskey with shaking hands, recalling a statement the Old Man had made to him years before: *Lloyd is one of us, without yet realizing it. But until he becomes strong enough to defy me, he himself will not comprehend the reserves of ruthless will and ambition I have instilled in him since childhood.*

Even unknowingly approaching his own downfall, Dr. Zimmerman reflected, the Old Man had been right.

John Rawls suddenly realized that someone else was threading his way through the dense forest—but on the other side of the barbed-wire-topped fence. He threw himself flat, thumbing back the safety on his Sturm-Ruger .44-magnum carbine.

Locating Warlord's Hill had been simple. He had found a description and a map in a guide book called *Lost Trails of the Pine Barrens,* sold to him by a woman in the Chatsworth general store; inexplicably, tears appeared in her eyes when she handed him the paperback. After setting up a vantage spot on a slight rise west of the estate's gates, Rawls had realized that sneaking into the place would be much more difficult than he had thought, due to a network of unobtrusive watch towers inside the fence. He had studied them through binoculars, observing that, although widely spaced, each structure provided an unobstructed sightline of a vast stretch of fence—and, equally frustrating, of the other towers. He could easily pick off an individual guard but not without alerting sentries on either side. Finally, he had moved off through the woods, hoping to locate a blind spot farther along the perimeter where he could cut through the wire. After the first hour, his hopes began to fade. Then he had caught his first, fleeting glimpse of the figure on the other side of the fence.

He doesn't know I'm here, Rawls decided when the vague form continued to move on a course roughly parallel to his own. Otherwise, he'd have gone to ground, too. Rawls rose, proceeded in a wary crouch, wondering why someone inside the estate would, like himself, be keeping to deep woods and thickets. Twice the figure detoured to avoid crossing patches of open space, proving that he sought to dodge the eyes of the tower guards. Rawls wished that he could get close enough to see who he was dealing with, but it was impossible without entering the cleared strips bordering the fence.

Rawls abruptly lost sight of him. Either the man had noticed him and taken cover or had turned away from the wire. He detected a faint rasping sound, like the claws of an animal digging into the earth. Puzzled, he sank to his haunches, patiently watching and listening. The noises ceased, but only minutes later he heard someone hurrying through the woods— now on Rawls' side of the fence.

He followed, caught up with his quarry in a copse of birch trees, ordered him to clasp his hands behind his neck and turn around—and found himself peering into the frightened hazel eyes of a slightly built boy in his mid-teens.

That morning, sitting beside his weeping mother in Bremen church, Eric Dorn finally saw clearly that the sanctuary was a fraud.

Spies are among us, the Old Man thundered from the pulpit. A descendant of one of the original corrupters has passed through the wire and sent out information that led to the murders of Victor Schall and Conrad Webber and Eric's father! Dazed by grief, Eric paid little attention to the Old Man's rhetoric—until he went on to tell how the demonic enemy had used grace and beauty and false innocence to mask their treachery. He's talking about Mrs. Hammil, Eric thought. She and her husband are the only strangers at Warlord's Hill.

He continued to listen, clutching his mother's hand tighter, surrounded by the approving, increasingly angry mutterings of the other mourners. The Old Man's words make no sense, he wanted to shout. If the Zionists already suspect we're here, why would they send in spies? They'd simply break down the gates and slaughter us all. Unless, as the film he had seen on Terry's miniature TV set indicated, everything Eric had been taught since childhood was a lie.

"And now they have poisoned the sanctuary itself!" the Old Man proclaimed, his right arm lashing upward to point an accusing finger at the church entrance.

Eric turned with the others, saw Terry Hammil standing in the rear aisle, her face white, eyes wide with shock and fear. She turned and ran, instantly pursued by the crowd.

Outside, Eric watched the women bear the struggling girl to the roadway, tearing at her flimsy gray dress; her necklace broke and pearls ricocheted off the pavement like hailstones. Knowing that they might rip Terry to pieces, he ran to the knot of clawing, shrieking women, pulled them off her—and suddenly realized that the onlookers must regard his act as treason. Sickened at what he had to do, he struck Terry in the face. The crowd shouted its approval.

After Dr. Zimmerman took Terry away in the ambulance, Eric was summoned into the church and told by the Old Man that tomorrow night he would undergo the Ceremony of Passage—and have the privilege of personally avenging his father's death.

He'll make me execute her, the boy told himself as he walked his mother back home. Although only huntsmen who had already performed the ceremony were permitted to attend the ritual, Eric had heard older friends boast of how coolly they had fired a bullet into the despised victim's skull. He had often wondered if he would have the courage to squeeze the trigger, even knowing that the target was less than human. But none of the things he had been told about Jews since he was in kindergarten applied to Mrs. Hammil. She was quiet, gentle, invariably kind. Even if he had not seen the newsreel of outsider police protecting men in the same uniform he now wore, Eric wouldn't have believed that she was part of a worldwide plot to exterminate people like himself and his family.

But if the Jews and the Communists *aren't* after us, he

237

thought in a burst of anguished doubt, who *did* kill my father and Conrad Webber and Vic Schall?

Late that afternoon—alone in his bedroom, his uniform hung in the closet—Eric Dorn at last decided irrevocably that he did not believe the Old Man. To refuse to kill Terry Hammil would just bring him disgrace in the eyes of the people; another young huntsman would perform the ceremony, and Terry would die anyway. He must find help for her on the other side of the wire.

Eric Dorn's curiosity about the world beyond Warlord's Hill had reached its peak two summers earlier, on the first clear morning after days of heavy rain. In his restless, solitary wandering, he had often passed the weed-filled bed of a drained artificial lake near the southwest fence. Except for the disintegrating remains of a small cement dam—marked with the incomprehensible symbol WPA 1937-38—little remained to indicate the original purpose of the depression in the forest floor.

Drawn by the sound of sluggishly running water, Eric went to the dam and looked into a narrow, open shaft at its base. It went down only four or five feet; at the bottom lay the opening of a wide pipe; accumulated rainwater was gurgling through it. Obviously the main source of the lake's drainage, the pipe must have been filled with earth and rocks at the same time its water source was blocked. Over the years, rains like those of the past week had cut a new channel through the displaced fill. But his most remarkable discovery came when he climbed out of the shaft, got his bearings—and realized the pipe must extend below the nearby fence.

Even knowing the dangers that lay in wait outside for any member of the eight families driven into hiding by Jewish murderers so long ago, Eric felt an irresistible temptation to venture into the unknown forest. What harm could there be in looking around just a little bit?

For more than a week, he returned to the spot every day to dig debris out of the pipe until it was clear enough for him to crawl through on his hands and knees. The other end, about forty feet past the fence, opened on to a hillside, right above a narrow creek; the brush around the pipe mouth was so heavy that anyone passing a few feet away would be unlikely to notice it.

On his first—and only—journey to foreign territory, fear drove him back inside the wire. He had walked a few hundred yards into the woods on the other side, then halted in consternation. Where am I going? he wondered nervously. Although the terrain was the same in every way as the Warlord's Hill woods, the trails ahead would be completely strange to him. Suppose he got lost, was unable to find the pipe again? His only recourse would be to go to the sanctuary gates, thereby bringing dishonor on his mother and father. He ran back to the pipe, scuttled through it, and carefully resealed the entrance with rocks.

In the years since, Eric Dorn thought repeatedly about another exploration—but never actually tried until the day of Terry Hammil's capture. After making certain that his exhausted mother was asleep in her bedroom, he slipped away from Bremen, raced to the drained lake, removed the debris, and crawled through the pipe. He had no clear plan about what to do next, no idea whether the nearest alien town was five miles away or fifty. All he knew was that he had to stop the Old Man from murdering Terry Hammil.

Only minutes after entering the unfamiliar forest, he heard a snarled command to halt, turned, expecting to see a sanctuary guard, and instead encountered a stranger with wiry black hair and a dark, seamed face. He wore a heavily laden knapsack and held a sniperscope-mounted carbine aimed at Eric's midsection.

"Who are you, kid?" the man asked. "And how the hell did you get through that fence?"

Ever since Dr. Zimmerman's visit to the annex, Terry Hammil had roamed from room to room, testing the steel mesh window screens, searching drawers and under beds in the hope of finding a forgotten medical instrument, any object that might be used as a tool or weapon. Each stark chamber was exactly like the last—antiseptically clean, containing only essential furnishings.

"Young people always figure there's a way out of things,"

239

Sophie Braunstein sighed as she watched Terry check the last room. "Hardly ever is, though."

"Oh, shut up!" Terry snapped; instantly, she was ashamed of the outburst. "I'm sorry, Sophie."

"That's okay. Place like this gets to you."

Terry heard the hall door open; the nurse and the brawny attendant must be wheeling in dinner. "Go on," she whispered. "I'll be along in a minute."

She waited until the door slammed closed again before joining Mrs. Braunstein at the table. Dinner proved to be another single-dish meal—a noodle-and-chopped-veal casserole, again served in bone-China bowls. Sitting down across from Mrs. Braunstein, Terry suddenly perceived a possible flaw in the security. If Mrs. Braunstein was right—and Dr. Zimmerman had told the truth earlier—until now the building had held only old, infirm prisoners. Their jailers must be accustomed to minor accidents.

Terry, not touching her own meal or even sipping water, sat quietly until Mrs. Braunstein finished eating. Then she rose, walked around the table, picked up the other woman's bowl, and dashed it to the cement floor. It broke into more than a dozen fragments. She bent quickly, retrieving a large, triangular shard.

"Why'd you do that?" Mrs. Braunstein asked in astonishment.

"Don't tell them I came to the table."

"But *I'll* get blamed."

"*Please* don't tell them!" Terry begged.

Terry ran to her room, hid the fragment under the mattress of her bed, lay down, and waited, staring at the ceiling, struggling to control her too-rapid breathing. A few minutes later, the steel-sheathed hall door clanged open and a female voice chided: "Clumsy old thing! That came from Dr. Zimmerman's own kitchen! I ought to make you clean it up yourself."

Terry heard quick, irritated footsteps. A nurse appeared in the doorway, studied her coolly. "Don't want to eat yet?"

"No, thank you," Terry murmured.

"Going to be awfully hungry by morning."

"I'm fine."

"Suit yourself."

When the overhead hall lights dimmed, Terry got out of bed, retrieved the fragment of China. She knelt by the cinderblock outer wall, began gently honing the longer sides of the triangle against the rough surface.

Braunstein's snores were echoing through the annex by the time the delicate tip of the China fragment reached stiletto sharpness.

※ EIGHTEEN ※

"What happened, Lloyd?" Nora Bauer asked anxiously when, more than an hour after Lupe had cleared away the dinner dishes, her husband returned home. "Why did you and Roy Hammil go rushing off like that? Has he learned about the sanctuary?"

Lloyd Bauer laughed bitterly. "Doesn't have an inkling. His research took a different turn."

"I don't understand."

"Better that you don't," he said. "And this time I'm not letting you beat me down with questions. One thing I've learned today is that some bodies *have* to stay buried."

Nora had never seen such a look of determination on Lloyd's face—or, beneath it, such desperate unhappiness. But she knew it would be pointless to press him further, sensing that he had made an irrevocable decision. "Did Roy stay at Warlord's Hill?"

Lloyd nodded.

"You saw Terry?"

"No. He just dropped me at the mansion and went on."

"You fired him?"

"I told you I didn't want to talk about it," Lloyd said, heading for the stairs.

Nora stared after him, a chill enveloping her body. His tone, the careful way he spaced his words, even his facial expression had suddenly reminded her of the Old Man. There could be only one explanation for the metamorphosis. Her husband had gone beyond ignoring the existence of the evil at Warlord's Hill and was now a participant in it.

I should have moved to a hotel, Langston Fellows thought nervously as he gazed out the window of his study on the top floor of the Alexandria town house. Until earlier in the evening, peace apparently had been restored to the public housing project across the street. Then, just after eight o'clock, he heard fire truck sirens; another blaze had broken out in a project building. Gangs of teen-agers gathered, screaming obscenities at the firemen, so hampering their work that a police riot force moved in, making dozens of arrests. Minutes after the fire was extinguished, gunshots erupted at the other end of the project; according to a later radio news report, white youths had fired on a group of blacks from a moving car, critically wounding three of them.

Could bust wide open tonight, the old columnist brooded as he went back to his desk, unsuccessfully trying to proofread a newly typed section of his memoirs. No one had any idea what had provoked the violence. The area had been calm for years, and no outbreaks had occurred in the inner city ghettoes across the Potomac. Even hot weather couldn't be blamed, since so far the summer had been unusually cool.

Fellows, abandoning his distracted attempt at work, decided to go to bed. During earlier periods of racial strife, the Alexandria police had cordoned off the row of expensive town houses from their disintegrating neighbors; he assumed they would do so again. He edged his frail legs out from behind the desk, pulled himself erect on his walker, carefully made his way onto the steel inner balcony overlooking the five open floors of library shelves, and grunted with effort as he swung the walker in a right turn. He blinked in surprise when he saw two young white men—dressed in conservative suits and ties—positioned between himself and the elevator.

"Who are you?" he gasped. "What do you want?"

They approached with calm purposefulness. Each taking one of Fellows' thin arms, they effortlessly flung him over the balcony rail, his hands still clutching the walker. The wail of police sirens drowned out his thin scream as he plummeted.

Except for the first, terrible instant of impact, Langston Fellows felt no pain after his body slammed to the library floor. How can I be alive? he wondered as he lay there, flopped on his back. Then he realized that the walker—now a mass of twisted, flattened steel tubing—had hit the floor beneath him, absorbing much of the shock. He tried to sit up but discovered he could move nothing below his neck.

Helpless, he watched in horror as his assailants, still on the highest walkway, began yanking armloads of books from the shelves, pitching them over the rail. Heavy hardcovers rained around him like falling rocks, crashing into his numb, blood-soaked body. At last a boxed, two-volume edition of *The Speeches of Justice William O. Douglas* hit him full in the face and consciousness ended.

"I figured that's what a pack of crazy, illiterate niggers *would* do," Peter Uhl said over the phone. "After we left the house, we tossed gasoline bottle bombs over a couple of garden walls in the row. The police will never figure anybody would go to all that trouble to kill just one old guy."

"It was *my* plan, Pete," the Master Huntsman reminded him. Except for the books, he added mentally, resolving to keep an eye on Uhl after he and his companions closed up the Washington outpost and came back to the sanctuary. Krug had learned long ago that sadists usually proved untrustworthy.

But at last the June 28 operation was over, Krug thought as he hung up the phone. Except for John Rawls. He had already decided that the Old Man had been right: The former Eddie Cilento had once again gone into deep hiding. If he had learned the location of the sanctuary from Vic Schall and headed back East, he would have arrived days ago and already launched the suicidal attack Krug had feared. Now he could be tracked down by skilled huntsmen released from other duties, unhampered by the necessity of delaying Rawls' execution.

Grandma Miller had gone to bed hours earlier, but her son remained in the kitchen. "Want to sack out here, Master Huntsman?" Dick Miller asked. "We got plenty of room."

"Thank you," Harry Krug replied, "but it's time to head home."

As he anticipated, the Old Man was waiting for him in the mansion. Krug gave his report and asked what had been done with Roy Hammil.

"He is under guard in the basement," the Old Man said, going on to describe that afternoon's confrontation with Lloyd Bauer. "Later, Dr. Zimmerman called, said that Lloyd had visited him briefly. He told Roger that we should do whatever was necessary, and then he left the estate. He said he would return on Wednesday."

At first, Harry Krug felt elated. For years he had worried about how Lloyd Bauer would react if he prematurely learned the entire truth about the sanctuary and his own ancestry. By departing from Warlord's Hill before the executions of Langston Fellows, the Hammils, and the last of the old Jews, he had implicitly condoned the actions. And then Krug understood the cause of the disquiet in the Old Man's voice. Lloyd had given his fateful decision to Roger, not the Old Man himself. It was a gesture of contempt.

"We can't keep Hammil downstairs forever," Krug said carefully.

"His unexpected arrival with Lloyd complicates matters," the Old Man said. "Obviously, staging an automobile accident is impossible now. It would be best if he simply vanishes. When inquiries are made, one of Lloyd's assistants will say that Hammil finished his assignment, packed up, and drove away with his wife, planning to go back to New York. Their disappearance will become one of those unsolved mysteries the popular press features for a few days."

"Then why is he still alive?"

"Because I will need him on Wednesday."

Harry Krug knew instantly that the Old Man was making an overwhelming error. The day after next, Lloyd Bauer would come back to Warlord's Hill, confident that the slaughter would be over. Instead the Old Man would tell him that one execution remained, demand that he take part, if only as an observer. Until Lloyd has blood on his own hands or at least has seen it flow, the Old Man must have reasoned, he cannot be a true member of the movement—not yet under-

245

standing that, by revealing the last of his secrets, the Old Man had made himself as dispensable as the worn-out Jews in Dr. Zimmerman's clinic. His power was gone, like that of a great juggler afflicted, overnight, with crippling arthritis.

"If you don't mind, I think I'll go on to Bremen," Harry Krug murmured. "It's been a rough day."

However, Krug's work had not ended. Entering his home, he was greeted by his wife, who told him that Lila Dorn had left a few minutes earlier. "She's worried sick. Eric went off into the woods before dinnertime and hasn't come back."

Dr. Zimmerman had told Krug how the grief-wracked boy had struck down Terry Hammil in front of the church, then had been chosen by the Old Man to execute the woman in the following night's Ceremony of Passage. The kid has always been a little strange, Krug thought, a loner who made few friends among the other children of Bremen. Suppose the responsibility of the ceremony, right on the heels of his father's death, had caused his mind to snap?

Krug hurried to the Dorn house, knocked on the front door. It was opened by Eric Dorn himself, his face as slack with fatigue as Krug imagined his own must be. "You didn't have to concern yourself, Master Huntsman," the boy said. "I got back home while my mother was over at your place."

"Where were you today?"

"In the pines, thinking about my dad. Always think clearest out there."

"If you don't feel well enough to perform the ceremony tomorrow, I'll speak to the Old Man," Krug said. "I realize how hard it is to execute people you've actually grown to know, even after they've betrayed you."

Eric Dorn's jaw tightened with determination. "No, Master Huntsman," he said. "I *must* be the one who kills Mrs. Hammil!"

That night Harry Krug slept soundly for the first time in weeks—but in the forest south of Bremen, John Rawls continued his labors.

Half a dozen times he made the round trip to the patch of woods where he had hidden the Cherokee, returned with a knapsack-load of dynamite, and hauled it after him through

246

the narrow drainage tunnel. Pale light was on the horizon when the last batch had been moved beneath the fence, hidden in a cache camouflaged by brush and tree branches blown down in Sunday night's storm.

And then he rested briefly, his back against the trunk of an oak tree, his finger coiled around the trigger of the carbine lying across his knees. He again recalled the previous night's encounter with Eric Dorn, his growing realization that the boy was telling the truth.

"Where is a town?" Eric had asked when Rawls gave him permission to lower his arms. "I have to find a town."

"What for?"

"A woman—a friend of mine—is in terrible danger!"

"From the Nazis?"

The boy looked startled by the calm question. "Are you a policeman?"

John Rawls smiled ironically. "No. But I can do you a hell of a lot more good—if you level with me."

The words poured out in an anguished torrent. All Rawls clearly understood was that tomorrow night his enemies intended to murder a woman named Terry Hammil as part of some ritual, and that this boy had been chosen as her executioner. "They want me to kill her in the pit," Eric said in a throttled near-whisper.

"Take me there," John Rawls asked.

"But I have to talk to the police."

"If you do, she won't stand a chance." Rawls gestured in the direction of the unseen fence. "Those people over there are rich and powerful. You're a backwoods kid nobody ever heard of. You know what'll happen when you tell the cops that story?"

Eric shook his head.

"They'll slam you in a mental ward for observation, contact the Bauers, and report everything you said. Then the Nazis will murder your friend right away, bury her so deep in the woods Jesus Christ himself couldn't find her."

"But if *you* went with me—"

"Happen even faster. I'm *already* supposed to be crazy. All the help you're going to get is from me. There isn't anybody

247

else. . . . Show me the way through the fence, how to find the pit."

The boy hesitated for a few seconds—then nodded agreement.

Eric led him through the drain pipe, along rutted trails to a sandy road; except for unusually heavy tire tracks, it looked no different from the scraped-dirt routes on the other side of the fence. "This road links up with everything," the boy explained. "Places like the kennels and the arsenal that you can't drive to on oiled roads."

Rawls immediately understood. The Vietcong had used a similar system back in the late sixties, cutting wide, obvious trails through the jungle to deceive pursuers, actually moving vital supplies on a tree-shrouded network of parallel foot paths. It was while reconnoitering such a path that Rawls had taken a machine gun slug through the legs.

The sun had almost set when they reached the pit. In tormented memories, Rawls had pictured it as a huge amphitheater gouged out of the earth, capable of holding thousands. In reality the excavation was barely wide enough to accommodate a hundred men standing elbow to elbow. Only maintenance of the embanked roadway slanting down the northern wall contradicted its look of abandonment.

"Now we'll go back to the lake," Rawls said, "but this time I'll lead the way. If I make a wrong turn, wait a while before telling me. I've learned a lot from wrong turns."

Rawls noticed the surprised respect in Eric's eyes as he retraced their course through the forest without a single error. He doesn't know I've been a hunted animal most of my life, Rawls thought. During the trek, Rawls asked Eric dozens of questions about the inhabitants and physical layout of Warlord's Hill. What were the main buildings and their locations? Who usually lived or worked in them? Where was Terry Hammil being held? At what hour would the ritual in the pit begin? What exactly would happen tomorrow night, minute by minute?

"Gerald explained the ceremony to me," Eric said. "At ten o'clock, the huntsmen will begin the rally. Half an hour later, Terry and the other one will be delivered to the top of the pit ramp in an ambulance."

"Someone *else* is supposed to die?"

"An old female Jew. Until now it's always been old

Jews," Eric said. "The Old Man will call out the names of the candidates for the Ceremony of Passage—me and Jake Uhl. We'll go up the ramp to the ambulance, along with a couple of other huntsmen, to carry the sacrifice if she can't walk. Dr. Zimmerman always drugs them, I understand. Then, at the Old Man's order, Jake and the female Jew will go back down the ramp and the Jew will be told to kneel. Jake will take the pistol offered by the Master Huntsman and . . . do it. Then I am supposed to repeat the ritual with Mrs. Hammil."

"Uh-huh," Rawls grunted. The boy had sounded as though he were reciting the program for a school fraternity initiation.

Darkness had fallen when John Rawls and Eric got back to the drained lake. And now Rawls faced a crucial decision. Could he risk releasing this scared, confused kid, trusting him to remain silent? On the other hand, if Eric didn't return home tonight, search parties would be sent out. If he was not found, tomorrow night's rally would probably be canceled, depriving Rawls of the opportunity to wipe out most of the enemy with one blow.

"You *will* get her away from here?" Eric asked—and the throbbing anxiety in his voice made up Rawls' mind for him. "You promise?"

"Tomorrow, do whatever they tell you to do. I'll handle the rest."

"How did you learn about the sanctuary? No one from outside is supposed to know. *Who are you?*"

"I'm a guy like you," Rawls replied. "A guy who's been fed more lies than he can stomach."

Of course, Rawls' own words had been lies. If possible, he would save the Hammil woman. But his real aim was to trap the Nazis in the pit—the gray-skinned man and the tall, gaunt leader and all the faceless fanatics who had pursued him for years, murdered his brother and sister—to destroy them with a single movement of his hand.

The morning light was now strong enough for Rawls to find his way. He filled his knapsack with dynamite sticks, started off through a thick ground mist. Several trips would be necessary to transfer the entire cache of explosives—but by early afternoon the pit would be prepared.

Terry Hammil had occasionally wondered if she could kill another human being. She was no stranger to the physical process of death. Growing up in the mountains of northern New Mexico, she had hunted quail, deer, and other game from childhood, had three times looked on while her father fired bullets into the brains of critically injured saddle horses.

But I won't think about horses or birds or deer, she decided, touching the sharpened China shard hidden in the pocket of her blue hospital bathrobe. I'll think about snakes. During the summer months, their father had paid Terry and Philip a fifty-cent bounty on each rattlesnake they killed near the house. When the narrow mountain streams dried up, the reptiles were often driven to seek water in irrigation ditches or the Hedricks' swimming pool. In July and August she and her brother had risen at first light, donned heavy gloves and high leather boots, and hunted the snakes with softball bats. Sometimes they managed to club half a dozen before breakfast. Killing snakes had been easy.

That morning Terry had eaten breakfast, her first meal since her imprisonment began. The serving procedure had varied slightly from the day before. Only the muscular male attendant appeared, pushing in the wheeled table, then leaving the women to eat alone. Half an hour later, he came back and removed the table. The movements of the jailer were bored and perfunctory. Why not, Terry asked herself, if he was used to dealing with aged, helpless men and women? What problem had he encountered that couldn't be solved with a shouted threat or a slap in the face or a brutal two-handed shove against a pair of frail shoulders?

Lunch was brought at exactly twelve-thirty. The meal—spaghetti with meat sauce and a lettuce and cucumber salad—was served on plastic dishes. Dr. Zimmerman must have resented the broken bowl. Despite the tension that had turned the inside of her mouth dry, she forced herself to eat most of the spaghetti. She would need nourishment to sustain her in the critical hours ahead.

Sophie Braunstein had emptied her plate and was pushing her chair away from the table when Terry whispered, "No."

"I'm done."

"Stay here until he comes for the table."

"Why?"

"Just do it. Please!"

"You don't have to get mad," Mrs. Braunstein said reproachfully, picking up the last slice of bread, peeling off the crust with her narrow fingers. "Never liked rye bread, but it's better with peanut butter than whole wheat. I keep asking, but they never serve peanut butter here."

Terry's grip tightened on the China shard as she waited for the sound of footsteps approaching the steel-sheathed door.

Only a few hundred yards away, Nora Bauer had finally learned the full, revolting truth about Warlord's Hill.

"There was no way I could stop the rituals once they got going," her father pleaded with a helpless wave of his right hand. "The patients would all have died in days or weeks, anyway. And, if you look at the big picture, I've done far more good than harm. The foundation's medical breakthroughs, cumulatively, have added tens of thousands of years to the life spans of the elderly."

Nora got up, hurried to the bathroom off the kitchen, and clutched the edges of the sink until the shudders stopped coursing through her body. She wiped her clammy face with a towel and returned to the living room on legs that still threatened to collapse under her. "How long has Lloyd known?" she asked in a weak voice.

"Since yesterday afternoon," Dr. Zimmerman replied. "And tonight's ceremony will be the last. I can live the rest of my years in peace—and the futures of you and your husband and the children will be secure."

That morning, Lloyd Bauer had left their district home before breakfast, telling Nora he would not be back until late evening. He and Sid Levin would spend the entire day working on a speech he was to give next week to the state VFW convention in Asbury Park; afterward, he had to drive to Short Hills for dinner with a group of influential north Jersey businessmen, potential supporters of his Senate candidacy.

For the first time in her life, Nora had started reading the morning newspaper delivered to the house. Lloyd had been gone less than half an hour when Lupe brought it in from the porch. A front page headline proclaimed: RETIRED COLUMNIST LANGSTON FELLOWS SLAIN IN RACIAL CLASH. Terry had spoken of how close she and her husband had been to his former employer. Nora realized that Roy and Terry, sealed off at Warlord's Hill, had no way of learning what had happened. She telephoned the Miller house and told that silly, mumbling old woman to send a messenger to the estate. "Just tell the Hammils to call me as soon as possible," Nora instructed. "And emphasize that the matter is very, very urgent."

When neither Hammil had contacted her by ten o'clock, Nora phoned Lloyd's office and was told by Sid Levin that her husband had left without explanation a few minutes after coming to work. She read and reread the newspaper article on the bizarre murder. It couldn't possibly be connected with Lloyd's strange, guilty manner last night, she told herself, nonetheless disturbed by the coincidence. Where *had* Lloyd gone this morning—and why hadn't the Hammils tried to reach her? Peculiar as they were, the Millers had never failed to deliver a message to Warlord's Hill. After all, that was the only function they had.

Finally she told Lupe to watch the boys and drove to the estate in the old Hudson that Lloyd had parked in the driveway. That had been another surprise; she had never known him to take one of his father's antique autos beyond Chatsworth.

Nora reached Warlord's Hill shortly before noon and drove straight to the guest house. When no one answered her knock, she entered and looked around. Like Roy Hammil the day before, she discovered that the housekeeper's room had been cleaned out. Puzzled, she went upstairs to the master bedroom. It also held only basic furnishings—and the closets were empty.

Her first thought was that whatever Roy told Lloyd had so angered her husband that he had ordered the couple to leave the estate immediately. But, if that were true, why had he kept the news from Nora? She had *wanted* Terry away from Warlord's Hill.

Now deeply worried, she drove to the estate's main garage, planning to turn over the Hudson to Gerald—and, as she approached the building, she saw the Hammils' burgundy

Jaguar just inside the converted barn's open double doors. How could the Hammils have left without their car? Perhaps they had moved to the mansion for some reason, Nora thought—but that made no sense either. The Old Man would never chance having Roy learn of his presence in the house. Only one person might possibly tell her the truth, she decided, driving toward the medical compound.

Dr. Zimmerman, his sallow face drawn, cringed when he opened the front door of his house and saw his daughter. "You're not supposed to be here!" he cried. "Not until tomorrow!"

"Lloyd told me everything, Daddy," Nora lied.

"Even about the Ceremony of Passage?"

"Yes."

"He shouldn't have," Zimmerman said, his shoulders slumping as he stepped back to let Nora through the door. "Why spread the pain to you?"

For nearly twenty minutes, Roger Zimmerman explained to his daughter how he had been forced for years to participate in acts he abhorred. Even more frightening to Nora than the facts themselves was that her father expected her to understand and forgive, as if he were apologizing for forgetting her sixteenth birthday.

"What has the Old Man done with Terry's husband?" Nora finally asked, desperate to maintain control.

"I don't know. Haven't spoken to him since yesterday."

They must have already killed him, Nora Bauer thought. She took a deep breath and said, "We're going to take Terry away from here. In the station wagon. You'll drive and I'll sit up front with you. If she crouches down on the floor in back, the gate guard won't notice her. They always just wave you through."

Zimmerman rose from his chair and stared at his daughter as if she had gone mad. "We *can't!*"

"Why not? No one except the Old Man has the power to question anything you do here."

"But it would mean the destruction of all of us. You, Lloyd, even the children. All of us. I've already explained that after tonight the executions will end."

"I want them to end *before* tonight, Daddy. If you won't help, I'll drive straight to the nearest State Police headquarters and tell them everything you've told me."

Zimmerman sank back into the chair. "Lloyd was informed yesterday that Langston Fellows would die. He let the order stand. You know what that means?"

She nodded. "That my husband is now a murderer, too. I don't want to become a murderer. It's that simple, Daddy. The only way you can stop me from telling is to kill me or lock me up forever."

Zimmerman was defeated. "All right, I'll drive you out," he muttered harshly. "Terry Hammil is in the annex, just past the oak trees."

Terry heard footsteps beyond the door, took the five-inch China shard from her pocket, and held it under the table, amid her robe's lower folds. She forced herself to concentrate on memories of the tall old man standing before the swastika banner, of the hatred in his voice as he denounced her, of the women of Bremen tearing at her body and Eric's fist smashing into her forehead. How dare they! she thought in fresh rage. How dare they! She clutched the fragment so hard that her fingers ached.

"Aren't finished yet?" the attendant asked irritably as he came through the door. He was a tall, fleshy-faced man in his late twenties.

"I want to leave now," Terry said in the dazed voice she had assumed all through her imprisonment. "I won't move until you tell Dr. Zimmerman to let me out."

The attendant pushed the table away, grabbed Terry beneath the left arm, and started to yank her erect. As she rose—her gaze fixed on the ring of fat beneath his chin—she thrust her right arm upward with all her strength, plunged the shard into his throat. She encountered astonishingly little resistance to the blow, no more than that offered by stiff bread dough to the blade of a table knife.

His expression more puzzled than pained, the attendant released Terry and stepped back, hair-thin lines of blood trickling from his nostrils and the corners of his mouth. He raised his hand to the piece of China embedded in his throat, gripped the rounded end of the shard with his fingertips, and wiggled it delicately, like a child testing a loose baby tooth. Then he pulled it free. A scarlet torrent gushed out of the wound, running down his starched white tunic. His lifeless body crumpled to the cement floor.

"Didn't figure you were going to do *that!*" Mrs. Braunstein said.

"Be quiet," Terry whispered. To her surprise, she felt nothing after killing the man; clubbing rattlesnakes had induced more guilt.

She slipped through the open door, entered a short corridor, and realized the building must be L-shaped. Down the corridor lay a small room with a table and chair and a single lamp but no medical equipment. Obviously a nurse had been kept on duty only until Dr. Zimmerman was satisfied that Terry had accepted her fate.

"Come on," Terry urged Mrs. Braunstein when she returned to the main hallway. "We have to get away."

"Where will we go?" the old woman asked. "Nothing out there but woods."

"I've been all through the pines. I know lots of places to hide!" She tugged lightly at Mrs. Braunstein's hand. "Hurry!"

The old woman shook her head. "Terry, every fifty feet I'd have to stop and rest for ten minutes. You send somebody back for me when you get out, okay?"

Terry looked at Mrs. Braunstein's thin, withered body and reluctantly agreed that the old woman was right. She reached out and stroked her hair, forgetting that it was a black nylon wig. "Good-bye, Sophie," she said, tears in her eyes.

"Stop yakking and get away from this dump."

Nora and Dr. Zimmerman had just stepped onto the path to the annex when they saw a slim figure in a blue bathrobe hurry out the building's only exterior door, dash across a short stretch of lawn, and disappear into the pine forest.

"It's Terry!" Nora gasped.

They entered the annex and discovered the body of the attendant. Mrs. Braunstein sat a few feet away, munching on the slice of bread she had decrusted earlier. She nodded vaguely toward the attendant and said, "Girl must have gone crazy, huh?"

❊ NINETEEN ❊

"**I**'m leaving now," Nora Bauer told her father outside the annex.

She had briefly considered trying to catch up with the fleeing Terry Hammil, but realized it would be impossible. In the few weeks Terry had spent at Warlord's Hill, she had learned more about the forest than Nora had in a lifetime. Her only recourse was to go to the police and hope they acted before Terry could be killed or recaptured by the huntsmen.

They reached the driveway in front of Dr. Zimmerman's house. "Good-bye, Daddy," Nora said, getting behind the wheel of the Hudson convertible.

The old physician nodded once, shambled toward the clinic next door, didn't look back as Nora drove off.

Minutes after fleeing into the woods, Terry Hammil encountered a rutted track that led south. She turned onto it, hoping to find the abandoned house she had discovered weeks ago. The decayed structure would provide shelter for the night, and she had noticed thick patches of huckleberries growing nearby. She reproached herself for refusing to eat the day before.

But I'm out of that place, she thought with a shudder.

If only she had proper clothes. The robe and nightgown impeded her movements, and the thin rubber soles of her slippers probably wouldn't last a day. She decided to carry the slippers when she was walking on sections of sandy track, to wear them only to cross rough terrain.

She rounded a bend in the trail, saw a cleared area ahead—and, in the middle of it, a fire watch tower. Unaware that only the towers on the perimeter were currently manned, she scurried for cover amid the trees. She knew the chief danger of leaving the pathways: the possibility of entering a stretch of woods so dense that she would be unable to approximate her position by the sun, and become hopelessly lost. But, to her relief, she soon found the track she had followed earlier.

Terry went on deeper into the forest, hoping that the slain attendant's body would not be discovered until dinnertime, depriving her pursuers of a fresh trail.

"Leaving already, ma'am?" the guard asked when Nora Bauer braked the Hudson at the estate gates.

"Yes," Nora replied, trembling with relief. Until this moment, she had been afraid that her father would change his mind. He hasn't betrayed me, she thought. *Finally*, he hasn't betrayed me.

The guard started toward the gates, but halted when the telephone rang in his shack. He hurried back inside, emerging seconds later to say: "The Old Man wants you at the clinic, Mrs. Bauer."

In the end he couldn't do it, having chosen the sanctuary over his own daughter. Nora considered ordering the guard to let her through, but knew he would not obey. She had never truly been the mistress of Warlord's Hill. Like her husband and father, she was just another of the Old Man's servants.

The silver limousine was parked in front of the clinic when she returned. Gerald stood beside it. "He's in your father's office," the chauffeur said as he opened the door of the Hudson. "Lucky one of the nurses noticed you driving off."

Nora entered the building, found the Old Man waiting by the open office door. She had expected him to be rigid with anger; instead, his manner was somber.

"Did they tell you what has happened?" he asked.

Nora shook her head, brushed past him into the office, and saw Roger Zimmerman slumped face down on his desk. His right hand lay next to an empty, overturned pill bottle. For the first time, he really acted like my father, Nora thought in anguish. And he had to atone for it by taking his own life.

She heard hard, rapid footsteps, the Master Huntsman's shout to the Old Man: "Mrs. Hammil is gone! She killed Max Holst!"

Now the anger Nora had anticipated finally touched the Old Man's furrowed face. "Why did you come here today, Nora?" he asked.

In midafternoon, Terry Hammil heard dogs baying distantly, knew that the huntsmen had picked up her trail. She repressed a panicked urge to run. Her only chance was to find one of the dozens of shallow streams that ran through the forest, to keep to the water until the animals lost her scent.

The barking had grown louder when she spotted a line of white cedars, remembered Eric telling her that the trees marked brooks, even underground currents that occasionally break to the surface. Again she left the pathway, staying among the cedars, heading east. Her slippers were already so worn that she could feel the pressure of small stones through the soles.

Less than half an hour later, she discovered a fast-running stream, waded into the current, and walked along the gravelly bed until the brook resumed a course below ground. Exhausted, her legs numb from the chill waters, she fell to the earth, sucking air into her aching lungs. She could no longer hear the dogs.

Terry forced herself to her feet and staggered on. To where? she asked herself. She had no weapons; and even if she reached the fence, she had no way of breaking through the heavy chain link.

For three hours after organizing the hunt, Harry Krug remained at his headquarters in Bremen, waiting for word of Terry Hammil's capture. That she had remained at large this long was incredible. Every available man had been thrown into the search, and apparently she had been free less than thirty minutes before the escape was discovered. So far he had received a single, frustrating report. Hounds, given the scent of the dress torn off her body the day before, had picked up a trail south of the clinic but had lost it again.

Krug at last yielded to his curiosity and returned to the clinic, arriving just in time to see an ambulance with Golden Era Retirement Center markings leave the drive. The Old Man was watching it depart.

"You have found her?" he asked eagerly when Krug pulled up in the Land Rover.

"Won't be long now," Krug promised, nodding quizzically at the ambulance.

"Tomorrow poor Roger will be found in his Lakewood apartment," the Old Man explained. "Everything will be as it was. He'll be bent over a desk with an empty bottle of Lidocaine in front of him. But it will not have happened *here*."

"And Mrs. Bauer?" He had left before the Old Man completed his interrogation of Nora.

"She insists she came to tell the Hammils of Langston Fellows' death and discovered they were no longer at the guest house. She went to ask her father about them but he knew nothing. So she decided to go back home, speak to Lloyd."

"You believe her?"

The Old Man smiled indulgently. "Roger must have told her the truth, and she intended to inform the authorities. Because of a sentimental failure of will, he could not bring himself to stop her, choosing death instead. It will be all right when Lloyd comes back. Nora could defy her father, even myself, in her timid way. But from early childhood she was conditioned to obey Lloyd in all things. I made certain she literally had no other object to love, not even a doll or a pet. One of the keys to power, Master Huntsman, is the elimination of choices."

"I know," Harry Krüg said, recalling how his own choices had been systematically eliminated over the years. "Where is she now?"

"Still in the clinic. She grew hysterical—or feigned it in order to stop my questioning. Either way, it gave me an excuse to order a strong sedative for her. She'll sleep for hours."

However, the problems presented by Nora Bauer and her father's suicide were not uppermost in the Old Man's thoughts, Krug soon realized. "You are certain you will have the Hedricks girl back by tonight?"

"We're sweeping the area where she's hiding. She can't last more than an hour or two longer."

"I don't want to postpone the Ceremony of Passage. In a way, it is fortunate that she killed Max Holst. It shows our people how even the most innocent-seeming Jew harbors vast reserves of cunning and treachery."

The pines suddenly thinned out, and Terry found herself on the edge of one of the broad meadows that dotted the estate. Rather than chance being caught in the open, she began to circle around through the trees—until she heard a familiar, whirring flutter and saw a helicopter approaching from the northeast, probably on its way to the fire station at Wharton State Forest.

Deciding on a desperate gamble, Terry ran into the meadow, shouting and waving her arms to get the pilot's attention. She sobbed when the helicopter abruptly changed course, beyond the trees. "Damn it! Damn it!" she screamed, her hands tightening into futile fists.

She heard the dogs again—coming from the area she had just left. The nearest cover was a mass of thickly clustered pines. She raised the skirt of her nightgown with both hands and fled toward the trees after kicking off the now-tattered slippers, crying out as clumps of sharp-edged meadow grass tore at her feet.

Terry sensed that something was wrong. The distance between herself and the trees was lessening at an incredibly fast rate. She was almost to the pines before she realized that none of them was more than five feet high; she had stumbled on one of the dwarf forests Eric had promised to show her.

She darted a frantic glance over her shoulder, saw rifle-bearing men, holding dogs on strained leashes, come out of the normal-sized trees on the other side of the meadow. She flung herself flat on the ground, crawled deeper into the strange, stunted woods. But she knew it was too late, that they must already have seen her.

I have killed a man, she thought, suffered hours of pain—
and gained nothing.

Unlike Terry, John Rawls had learned from Eric Dorn that
most of the fire towers were temporarily unstaffed. He now
stood on a sixty-foot-high observation platform, watching
through binoculars as the Nazis closed in on the girl.

Hours earlier, when he first heard the far-off baying of
hounds, he had thought that Eric had reported his presence
after all, and he started toward the drainpipe that ran under
the fence. Then he hesitated. The boy undoubtedly would
have described him to his superiors, who would immediately
have guessed his identity and known he was armed. Dogs
were only used to hunt animals—or defenseless human beings.

Rawls cautiously moved toward the interior of the estate,
twice climbing watch towers in the hope of glimpsing his
enemies or their quarry. The second tower overlooked the
meadow across which Terry had fled. He focused his binoculars on her just before she began running toward the dwarf
forest. Young, blonde, pretty, she must be the prisoner chosen to die in the pit tonight. Somehow she had escaped.

He studied Terry's delicate features—twisted with fear and
despair—as the Nazis dragged her out of the miniature trees.
He had intended to let the Ceremony of Passage almost reach
completion before springing the trap, taking the chance on
rescuing her and the nameless old lady at the last minute. But
that was when "Terry Hammil" was an abstraction, not flesh
and blood.

How could he free them before the ceremony, Rawls
brooded, without wrecking his own plan?

Harry Krug was at the dinner table with his wife and thirteen-
year-old daughter when the front doorbell rang. He answered
it and was told by Jake the stablehand, Peter Uhl's younger
brother, that Terry Hammil had been recaptured. Krug nodded his approval and went back to the meal. But his steak
now tasted inedibly dry; he pushed the plate away.

Like Dr. Zimmerman, Krug had decided the time had come
for escape—but not through suicide. He had discovered years
ago that the army of secret supporters claimed by the Old

Man was nonexistent, that the sanctuary existed solely for the sake of its own survival, like an animal so voracious that it spends all its waking hours eating just to stay alive. Now, because of the Old Man's obsession with sacrificing Terry Hammil in the pit, survival was seriously threatened for the first time. Even if Zimmerman's death and the disappearance of the Hammils provoked only routine investigations—and if Lloyd Bauer succeeded in silencing his rebellious wife—public and official attention would be focused on Warlord's Hill, breaching the wall of anonymity that, far more than the fence, had been their greatest protection.

During the years he had dispersed funds to huntsmen operating beyond the wire, Krug had diverted nearly a quarter of a million dollars to a dozen bank accounts, under as many names, insurance against the day he might have to flee with his family. He had no fear of being tracked down, as he himself had stalked and slain earlier defectors. Only his friend Lew Dorn had possessed the skills to replace Krug as Master Huntsman—and John Rawls had ended that danger.

"Why are you so quiet, Papa?" his daughter asked, a nervous smile revealing the crooked, overlapping front teeth that she usually attempted to hide.

"Just tired, Elsa," he said quietly. "By the way, I think that pretty soon now we'll be able to get those teeth fixed."

"It was the craziest thing," Mrs. Braunstein chattered. "Dr. Zimmerman and this lady looked around for a minute and walked out. Didn't even shut the door. Was almost two o'clock before a nurse came in and all hell broke loose."

Minutes earlier, the exhausted Terry Hammil had been returned to the annex by her captors. A grim-faced nurse and the stocky attendant who had driven Dr. Zimmerman to the church were waiting for her. She had numbly obeyed the nurse's order to shower and change into a clean nightgown and robe. Terry now lay in bed, barely aware of the old woman's words.

"Why would Dr. Zimmerman not tell, do you figure?" Mrs. Braunstein mused.

"I don't know."

"How come they didn't shoot you?"

"I don't know that either. Sophie, can I rest now? We'll talk later."

"Oh, sure. You missed dinner."

"Doesn't matter."

The last sound Terry heard before falling into deep sleep was the melancholy slap of Mrs. Braunstein's loose slippers on the floor. Then, what seemed only seconds later, she was startled awake by a jab of pain, looked down to see the nurse withdrawing a hypodermic needle from her left forearm. The room was shrouded in darkness. "After the trouble you caused, you don't deserve the shot," the woman said. "But the Master Huntsman insisted."

They're going to kill us now, Terry realized with a surge of horror. She scrambled out of bed, ran into the hall. Mrs. Braunstein—breathing harshly, wig askew—lay semiconscious on a wheeled stretcher by the main door. Another stretcher, unoccupied, waited beside it. Already, Terry could feel the effects of the injection, a spreading numbness in her hands and feet.

"Larry, I need help with this bitch!" the nurse shouted.

A short, powerfully built man with bristly black hair and dark, fierce eyes came through the door. Terry backed away, staring at the semiautomatic carbine in his thick hands. To her astonishment, she heard a frightened whimper behind her. The man calmly walked past Terry and went up to the nurse, who was cowering against the wall.

"I don't know what you gave them," he growled, "but if you don't take a dose of it yourself, I'll blow your head off."

Terry, her vision blurred, started to lose her balance, felt a supporting arm around her shoulders, realized that it belonged to Nora Bauer.

All evening John Rawls had been haunted by the look of terror on Terry Hammil's face as the Nazis pushed her across the meadow. He knew that she and the other prisoner would probably die, along with the disillusioned boy who had guided him yesterday, if he fulfilled his decades-old dream of striking down his enemies while they were gathered in the pit. His heedlessness had already cost the lives of his brother and sister. Reluctantly, he chose to scrap his cherished plan, free

Terry and the old woman, and lead them out through the drain pipe.

Rescuing the two women from the lightly guarded medical compound did not prove as uncomplicated a task as expected. Not wanting to leave anyone behind to give an alarm, he decided to clear out the main clinic before approaching the annex. He had waited until nine-thirty to make his move, certain by then that most of the sanctuary's men would be on their way to the pit.

The single nurse on duty was easily overpowered. After binding and gagging her with adhesive tape and knotted surgical gauze, he proceeded from room to room, beginning to think the building was empty of patients. Then he discovered a locked door, picked it. The only occupant, lying fully clothed on the bed, was a thin, sallow-skinned woman with frightened eyes.

"You're from outside?" she cried. "You've come to help us?"

He nodded, dumbfounded at discovering a third prisoner. Why hadn't Eric mentioned her?

Minutes later, it was all over. An ambulance, waiting to convey Terry Hammil and the old woman to the pit, was parked in front of the annex, it's white-jacketed driver lounging against a front bumper. Rawls came up on the man from behind, bashed in his skull with the stock of the carbine, used the same method to kill a second unwary attendant, sitting in a small room just off the entranceway. "Larry, I need help with this bitch!" a woman's angry voice called from an adjoining corridor.

After forcing the nurse to inject herself with the powerful sedative used on the prisoners, Rawls went over to the wizened, almost fleshless old woman on the stretcher, stared down at her, suddenly conceived a way to carry out his original mission after all.

"Take off her clothes and wrap her in a blanket," he told Nora.

"Why?"

"Just do it! Mrs. Hammil's stuff is probably too big." Behind them, the nurse slipped to the floor, a thin line of saliva trickling down her chin.

After they had placed Terry and Mrs. Braunstein in the back of the ambulance, Rawls donned the driver's jacket, dashed back into the annex, returned carrying the nurse, slung her in beside the other unconscious women. Incongruously, he wore a large, strapped purse over his shoulder.

The news, delivered by Nora as they drove off, that Terry Hammil's husband was being held in the basement of the Bauer mansion, did not disturb Rawls. He had planned to stop there anyway. The building contained something he needed.

Without removing his gaze from the road, he slipped the purse off his shoulder and thrust it toward Nora. "I found this in the front room. Must belong to the nurse. See if there's any cosmetics."

The baffled Nora fished out a lipstick and a compact. "Will these do?" she asked nervously.

"Just fine," Rawls said with a deep, anticipatory laugh.

"I admire concentration," Langston Fellows had remarked shortly after hiring Roy, "but sometimes you overdo it. People who zero in too intensely on small mysteries often overlook the big ones."

Lang had been right, Roy thought ruefully. From the moment he guessed the secret of Lloyd Bauer's real parentage, he had focused his attention on proving his case, self-censoring all apparently irrelevant facts. But this time he would lack the chance to go back for additional research. Although no threats had been made, he knew he was going to die in this shadowed basement—and never even learn why.

Handcuffed to a water pipe, he sat on the floor across from a young estate worker cradling a rifle over his knees. "What have you done with my wife?" he said. He had asked the same question of the other guards without receiving a reply. This man, scarcely out of his teens, had come on duty for the first time half an hour ago.

"Mister, *I* don't know."

"Is she alive? Can't you tell me *that*?"

"From what I hear she is—but I don't hear much."

"I have to use the bathroom."

"Only when two of us are watching you," the guard said,

just as they heard the inside basement door open. "Guess you're in luck, though. Somebody coming."

He rose from his folding chair, craned his neck to see who was descending the stairs—and took a slug in the abdomen that drove him ten feet backward before he collapsed. The assailant—a short, dark-skinned man wearing a white jacket—lowered his carbine, searched the guard's pockets. He found the handcuff key, freed Roy, and gestured him toward the stairs.

"Got to move fast," he barked. "Your wife and the others are waiting at the garage."

"Who the hell are you?" Roy asked.

"No time to talk." Rawls picked up the guard's rifle, shoved it into Roy's hands.

A 1937 GM ambulance was parked in front of the estate garage. Terry, clad in a bathrobe, was sprawled on the ground next to the open rear doors. Roy rushed to his wife, saw with relief that she was alive but, apparently, in a drugged stupor. A tiny old woman wrapped in a drab hospital blanket lay beside her. Except for a few white wisps, the woman was hairless.

Nora emerged from the garage. "I didn't know what they really were until today, Roy," she cried. "My father, the Old Man, all of them. *I just didn't know!*"

Rawls waved her to silence. "I'm leaving now. Nobody around here is alive—or at least moving—so you shouldn't be bothered for a while. Don't do *anything* until ten thirty-five. Might get me killed. And don't figure you can drive up to the gate, shoot the guard, and let yourselves out. Riflemen have the place bracketed from the watch towers. Got all that?"

Roy nodded.

"If I fuck up tonight and you're stuck here, try to contact a kid named Eric Dorn. He's the one who got me through the fence." Rawls climbed into the cab of the ambulance. "Good luck."

Roy and Nora watched him drive up the hill to the mansion and halt by the front door. "Why did he go back?" Nora asked anxiously.

"We'll figure it out later," Roy said, handing her the rifle. As he picked up Terry, a glint of recognition appeared in her clouded green eyes; she threw her right arm around his neck, squeezing weakly. He carried her into the garage and eased her into the back seat of the Jaguar before returning outside for the old woman. If they had to get away fast, he wanted her and his wife ready to move.

When the old woman had joined Terry in the rear of the Jaguar, Roy retrieved the rifle and partially closed the garage's double doors, leaving them sufficiently ajar to provide an unobstructed view of the road. He glanced at his watch, saw that it was six minutes past ten. Whatever business the dark man had in the mansion, he must have finished. The ambulance passed the garage, turning south.

"This is an embarrassing question for a Pulitzer-winning reporter to ask," Roy said to Nora Bauer, "but could you give me *some* idea what is going on?"

His attempt at humor turned ash-dry in his mouth when he heard Nora's answer.

Minutes after the ambulance reached the estate's secret main road, John Rawls heard the drums. The rally had started.

Soon he could hear the singing—sometimes soft but more often harsh and strident—exactly as it had sounded the night he and Rosemary and Vinnie and the small boy his sister had befriended followed the fifth child through the woods, not knowing that the course of their lives would soon be changed. Rawls tried to banish the memory, to concentrate on the work at hand. He had explored the area on foot that morning, but darkness obscured the landmarks he had noted.

Then the ambulance's headlights revealed the turnoff to the pit. He looked at his watch, saw that it was ten twenty-seven. He and his human cargo would be on time.

In a freshly pressed uniform, boots gleaming, Harry Krug stood at attention in front of the massed huntsmen. Everyone except Ralph Webber, whose orders required him to remain in Port Jefferson, had made it back inside the wire. Peter Uhl was in the first rank, beside his initiate brother, the muscles in his throat swelling as he joined in singing the old Bund anthem.

When the song ended, the Old Man—standing before the white altar—began his ritual speech of welcome to the two candidates for the Ceremony of Passage. Krug paid no heed to the familiar words. Instead he recalled what the sanctuary's leader had told him while they were waiting to descend into the pit and join the formation.

"My authority will end tomorrow," the Old Man had said calmly. "Lloyd will look on while you execute Roy Hammil. He will finally be compelled to share full responsibility for our acts. However, I will never be forgiven for tricking him. He may permit me to spend what little is left of my life alone with my books. Or he may order you to kill me after you shoot Hammil. If so, obey without question."

Krug had been too startled to utter a protest.

"He will make you destroy your uniforms and banners," the Old Man had continued fatalistically, "all other physical links to the movement. This will not matter. The sanctuary itself will go on because he cannot survive without it. One day—when he acknowledges the truth about his destiny and his nature, the nature *I* gave him—the huntsmen will be needed again."

Greeted by the inevitable roar, the Old Man had started down the embanked roadway, Harry Krug striding four steps behind.

As the Old Man spoke to the huntsmen, Krug's thoughts dwelled on his earlier words. It had never occurred to him that the Old Man seriously believed Lloyd Bauer had the capability—or the desire—to one day form an effective National Socialist movement in America. But, of course, the Old Man *had* to believe he could, with the same fervor that had compelled him to endanger the sanctuary rather than spare Terry Hammil. Not to believe in Lloyd, *not* to kill a descendant of the first Jewish corruptors of the New World would render his life meaningless. "One of the keys to power is the elimination of choices," the Old Man had told Krug that afternoon—failing to understand that, when he sealed himself inside Warlord's Hill decades earlier, he had eliminated his own.

"Huntsmen Uhl and Dorn, step forward and prepare to

take your place among the sanctuary's chosen,'' the Old Man cried.

The words jolted Krug out of his introspection. He saw the clinic ambulance halt at the top of the steeply graded roadway into the pit. The butchery was about to begin.

✖ TWENTY ✖

Everything was almost as Rawls remembered—the torches upheld at arm's length, the rows of drummers and flag-bearers, the scarlet swastika banner topped by a steel eagle with outstretched wings. From the rim of the pit, the gaunt, towering leader looked no older than he had when Rawls was a child. However, the gray-faced man's position in front of the ranks showed that he had risen greatly in status over the years.

Rawls opened the rear doors of the ambulance and began easing out the first stretcher. On it lay an emaciated figure in a nightgown and hospital robe, a cheap, badly fitted black wig on its head. He awkwardly lowered the stretcher to the ground, unfastening the elastic straps around the figure's chest and bony legs. A nurse or another male attendant must usually accompany the driver on these missions, Rawls figured. But the rim was so shadowed, when contrasted with the pool of torchlight below, that the change in procedure probably would not be noticed.

Eric Dorn and another young huntsman stepped out of the ranks, saluted the leader, and walked side by side toward the loose-earthed roadway. Two other Nazis fell in behind them. Rawls backed toward the open right-hand door of the ambulance's cab, where the shadows were deepest and he was within easy reach of the carbine. He heard four pairs of booted feet lock-step up the graded embankment.

The dark man had failed, Eric thought in sick despair as he, Jake Uhl, and the escort climbed rapidly toward the waiting ambulance. He wondered if he could actually kill Terry Hammil. But what choice had he now? He should have summoned the police, not trusted a stranger whose motives for penetrating the sanctuary he did not even know.

He and Jake reached the rim, where they again came to attention. The two escorts bent over the frail figure on the stretcher, unsuccessfully trying to make it stand erect. "The old Jewess won't know what's happening," Jake whispered to Eric in obvious relief. Eric barely heard him, staring at the victim's wrinkled, dead-eyed face. The sunken cheeks were heavily powdered and rouged; the withered mouth covered with a thick smear of lipstick.

Realizing that the sacrifice could not possibly walk, the escorts raised it by the armpits and dragged it down the embankment, its dangling feet cutting a narrow double trail in the earth. Jake Uhl swallowed hard, then followed them.

Like the others, Eric had paid little attention to the ambulance driver, who stood beyond the dim light cast by the massed torches, invisible except for his white jacket. Now he stepped far enough out of the shadows for Eric to see his face.

"Wait until they reach the bottom," the dark man ordered. "Then get away from here fast."

Eric turned, peered into the back of the ambulance, and recognized the unconscious figure strapped to the other stretcher—Ruth Bestwick, one of Dr. Zimmerman's nurses. He glanced back toward the dark man, realizing that he had already vanished into the night. Too confused to consider alternatives, Eric dashed toward the trees.

All eyes in the pit were trained on the sticklike, bathrobe-clad body lying face down before the white altar.

"Are you prepared for the Ceremony of Passage?" Harry Krug asked the pale, sweating Jake Uhl, his fingers touching the butt of his holstered automatic pistol.

"Yes, Master Huntsman," Jake Uhl said in a low voice.

Krug stared down at the motionless form at Jake Uhl's feet, realizing how important Dr. Zimmerman had been to the ceremony. Somehow, through persuasion and the judicious use of drugs, he always had managed to create the illusion that the man or woman chosen for death actually desired extinction. The scrawny figure before them seemed already dead—until it uttered a faintly audible gasp and raised its face out of the dirt. The cheap nylon wig fell off, revealing fine, neatly barbered white hair.

The Old Man gave a half-strangled cry. Like Harry Krug, he had immediately recognized the stroke-ravaged features of Paul Bauer.

Only Rawls could have done this, the Master Huntsman thought—and realized what was going to happen.

"Get out of here!" he shouted to the gathered huntsmen. "Any way you can!"

Even as he ran up the embanked roadway, Harry Krug knew from the baffled silence behind him that the warning had not registered. He darted a frantic glance back. A few men had belatedly followed him toward the roadway, and a handful from the rear ranks were climbing the pit walls. But the formation remained basically intact. Not even the Old Man understood the danger. He had knelt, raised Paul Bauer to a sitting position, and peered at his rouged face with stunned incomprehension.

Harry Krug reached the top of the roadway and had already passed the ambulance when the charges planted in the pit's floors and walls exploded. The force of the blast lifted him clear off the ground.

Minutes earlier, after whispering his terse warning to Eric Dorn, John Rawls had run to the dense thicket where he had concealed his equipment, fastened the wires to the terminals on the detonator box, pushed the plunger, and felt the earth shudder beneath him. As he expected, the explosion was a mighty subterranean growl; he had planted the dynamite as deeply as possible, given the brief time to work. The muffled report—and the gritty cloud of erupting earth that obscured the stars—told him that he had placed the charges well.

273

He yanked extra ammo clips from his knapsack, crammed them into his pockets, and cautiously moved toward the pit. If any of the bastards were alive, they'd be yelling soon.

But he heard nothing except the slow, steady sifting of dislodged soil into the pit. The cloud had settled to a fine, stinging mist when he reached what used to be the top of the roadway. The ambulance, the ground beneath it undermined, now lay on its roof far below, invisible except for its wheel, jutting out of the tons of loose dirt that now covered the pit bottom.

Rawls had anticipated an exultant rush if his trap worked. Instead, he felt drained of emotion. He spotted a man clawing his way out of the earthslide like a frenzied mole, raised the carbine, and shot the Nazi between the eyes. The man sank out of sight, rejoining his comrades in their mass grave. He waited for other survivors to appear, soon realized that none would.

He knew that he had stayed too long. The watch tower guards must have heard the blast and would already be sending a party to investigate. He had started to turn away from the pit when he heard Eric Dorn scream, "No! No more! Not any more!"

Rawls completed the turn and whipped the carbine into firing position—an instant too late. The gray-faced man, standing less than ten feet away, squeezed off two pistol shots. The slugs hit Rawls' chest so close together that he felt a single crushing blow. Instinctively, his finger tightened around the semiautomatic carbine's trigger, squeezing until the magazine was empty. The gray-faced man fell, not to move again.

John Rawls managed to stay erect long enough to stagger toward his enemy's lifeless body. It had ended the way he had always wanted it to end—with the tormentor from his childhood at Rawls' feet, not the other way around. The triumph would be brief, he knew, but better than none at all.

He sank to the earth, leaned back against a pine trunk, and tasted the blood starting to rise in his mouth. He was only faintly aware of Eric's presence. A moment earlier, the boy had ventured out of his hiding place, reaching the pit just in time to see the Master Huntsman move up behind Rawls. His involuntary cry had been a howl of revulsion, not a warning.

"You promised to help Mrs. Hammil," he said, his voice quivering as he knelt beside Rawls. "Not to do *this*."

"They killed *me*," Rawls murmured weakly. "More than thirty years ago. . . . They'd have killed you, too, finally. . . . One way or the other. . . ."

"Who *are* you?" Eric asked.

Doesn't matter, Rawls started to say—and then abruptly recognized that it did matter, had always mattered. He tried to speak, but before the words emerged, the blood gathering in his chest cavity finally flooded his lungs.

Realizing that the man was dead, Eric Dorn stood up, tore off his swastika armband, and slowly walked into the forest.

"What was that?" Nora Bauer had asked nervously when they heard a distant rumble.

"No way to tell," Roy said. It was ten thirty-two. Three more minutes and he would be free to carry out the only course of action likely to save their lives. "Those damned trees insulate sound like cotton batting."

For more than half an hour, he had silently stood guard at the garage door, thinking over Nora Bauer's revelations. Weeks earlier, he had wanted to tell Terry that holding on to a bygone time could be dangerous, that the past could betray you. It hadn't occurred to him that the unremembered past might be even more perilous. Langston Fellows, Felix Rodeburg—God knows how many others—were dead because of a childhood ordeal he had blocked so thoroughly that it might never emerge.

He waited until ten thirty-five, then left the doors. He picked up an empty ten-gallon fuel can he had spotted in a corner. Hurrying outside to the gas pump in front of the building, he filled the can, flung it into the front seat of a Model A Ford. As with all the other cars, the keys were in the ignition. Obviously, in a world as controlled as Warlord's Hill, no one had cause to fear thieves.

Handing the rifle to Nora, he said, "If anyone but me comes in, shoot them."

"I'm not sure I could."

"Not much choice if we're going to get out of here," He

hesitated. "Nora, you're Lloyd's wife. Those lunatics won't dare harm you. Go up to the house, sit this out."

"Until today, I spent my whole life sitting things out," she replied.

He had opened the garage doors and already warmed up the Ford's antique but perfectly maintained motor when Terry left the Jaguar, clutching its roof for support. Roy rushed to his wife, took her in his arms. "Just rest now, honey," he said. "Give the stuff a little more time to wear off."

"Where are you going?" she asked.

He told her.

"Burn it!" she cried out ferociously, clutched him to her. "Burn all of it!"

Roy drove to the edge of the thick woods north of the main compound. At first, pouring gasoline over masses of pine needles embedded on the forest floor, he feared that Sunday night's rain might have dampened the ground to such an extent that the fire would die as soon as the fuel was consumed. But seconds after he ignited the needles with his cigarette lighter, he was confronted with an inferno. The wind, stronger than half an hour earlier, pushed the crackling flames northward. Dry, resin-laden pine branches burst like strings of firecrackers.

By the time he drove off in the Jaguar with Terry, Nora, and the still-unconscious old lady, the northern horizon was awash with orange light. He found a dirt track off the lakeside road and parked deep in the trees.

Roy and the younger women left the car to stare at the spreading conflagration. If Nora was right, most of the men at Warlord's Hill were now miles away from the Bremen fire station and would never be able to extinguish the blaze without help. You don't destroy an illusion playing by the magician's rules, Roy had decided while they were hiding in the estate garage. You destroy it with reality.

Three Forest Service helicopters fluttered out of the night, circling the burning area again and again. Minutes later they heard fire sirens from the direction of the gates, followed by gunshots. The ambushed firemen would immediately turn back, radio for help from the State Police, Roy Hammil realized. The standard procedure for saving a burning ghetto that didn't want to be saved would follow in due course.

"I'm naked and bald!" Mrs. Braunstein wailed from the back of the Jaguar.

The old woman's cry of offended dignity banished the last traces of the drug clouding Terry Hammil's mind. She hurried back to the car. "It will be all right soon, Sophie," Terry said. "Just a little while longer."

Mrs. Braunstein nodded, pulled the blanket closer around her spare shoulders, and went back to sleep.

"Lloyd and I will make it up to her," Nora Bauer said softly. "We didn't know, Terry. We really didn't."

You didn't, Roy thought grimly—but Lloyd did. At least since yesterday afternoon. But he would deal with the problem of Lloyd Bauer later.

Within half an hour, gunfire again sounded, accompanied by the shrill cry of police car sirens. The invasion of Warlord's Hill had begun.

Even after sirens sounded deep within the estate, Roy insisted that they remain in hiding and kept his rifle ready. After losing the battle at the gate, the huntsmen would probably fall back to organize a second defense line. He was unaware that only a handful of perimeter guards remained alive to make a stand.

By two A.M. the forest was silent except for the roar of aircraft dropping water and chemicals on the fire. Roy drove the women back to the main compound. The floodlit grounds looked like a battle zone. Platoons of state troopers in riot gear stood around with shotguns and automatic weapons, like nervous replacements waiting to be sent into combat.

Sidney Levin, Lloyd Bauer's aide, was talking to a State Police captain on the mansion's front steps. He broke off the conversation when he saw Roy and Nora Bauer emerge from the Jaguar. Levin rushed over. "Nora, you're okay!" he cried out in relief. "What in God's name has happened?"

"Where is Lloyd?" Roy asked.

"Last I saw of him he was on his way to a dinner in Short Hills," said the baffled Levin. "When I heard on the news about the fire and the shooting, I called the house. Lupe said he had never come home, that Nora had gone to Warlord's Hill. All I could think to do was to head here and hope Lloyd had done the same thing."

The State Police captain caught up with Levin. "You're Representative Bauer's wife?" he asked Nora.

"Yes," she replied in a low voice. "I'll answer your questions in a minute, after I get my friends into the house. We have a sick old lady here."

Terry, who had already left the Jaguar, barely heard Nora's words. Her attention had been drawn to a group of civilians—the women, children, and old people of Bremen—huddled together on the south lawn. Holding the lapels of her robe closer to her body, she approached them. Wilma recognized her, whimpered in terror, and tried to hide behind Catherine, who usually flawless white skin was streaked with soot. A teen-aged girl with crooked, protruding front teeth shrieked and threw herself into the arms of a woman who had to be her mother. Many of the others covered their faces, as if Terry's gaze might cast a fatal spell on them.

One of the young troopers guarding the group glanced quizzically at Terry. "Lady, what's the matter with these folks? Why won't they talk?"

"They're afraid of you. Of everybody."

"We had to drag them out of their houses, even though the fire was bearing right down on the town. Some of them got away from us, ran into the flames. Never saw them again." The trooper shook his head. "Jesus, what did they think we were going to do? Throw them into a concentration camp?"

"Probably," Terry said, going back to the car.

The sun was starting to rise when they reached the pit.

For most of the early morning, Roy Hammil had sat by Terry's bedside in the mansion. Mrs. Braunstein had been flown by helicopter to a hospital in Hammonton, but his wife had refused to accompany her. "I won't let them see me leave," she had said of the people of Bremen, an angry determination in her voice that he had never before heard. "They'd think I was running away. We'll go the same way we came."

She had finally drifted off to sleep just after four-thirty. He had released his grip on her hand and gone downstairs to the living room, where he learned that a State Police patrol had found Eric Dorn wandering aimlessly along a dirt road. "The kid looked like he was half in shock," the captain said. "He said all the other men are dead, killed in some kind of explosion. We're going to check it out at first light."

"I'd like to come with you."

At first, standing on the rim of the pit, the scene seemed peaceful. To a passerby, it would have looked like any other quarry whose walls had eroded and collapsed over the years—the exposed wheels of the overturned ambulance merely an abandoned piece of equipment. But as the light grew stronger, the truth was revealed. Parts of dismembered human bodies became visible on the surrounding ground or lodged in the branches of pines like grisly Christmas tree decorations.

Sidney Levin, his face ashen, stood beside Roy. "That's where they murdered the old Jews," he said hoarsely. "Nora told us everything while you were upstairs. But I can't believe Lloyd was part of anything like that."

"Not until he absolutely had to be," Roy replied, suddenly guessing where Lloyd Bauer had gone. He imagined the congressman learning last night about the still-unexplained carnage at Warlord's Hill, realizing that the sanctuary would be exposed, seizing an opportunity to escape personal implication.

"Couple more bodies over here," the State Police captain shouted. "Can you identify them, Mr. Hammil?"

The first corpse lay sprawled on its back. "The estate's Master Huntsman," Roy said. "Harry something."

A few feet away, their rescuer of the night before was slumped in a seated position against a tree, black eyes staring emptily toward the pit.

"And him?" the captain asked.

The words came unbidden, from a spontaneous fusion of long-repressed images and recent knowledge. "His name is Eddie Cilento."

Roy Hammil had finally remembered.

The following morning, Lloyd Bauer entered the living room of Margarethe von Behncke's home in Winter Park, Florida—and realized instantly that she had been warned of his unannounced visit. Her eyes cold and remote, she sat stiffly on an eighteenth-century couch.

"Go back to Warlord's Hill," she said, surprised that, even from newspaper photos, she had never noticed that he had her long-dead husband's eyes and jaw. "You aren't welcome here."

"Who told you I was coming?"

"Roy Hammil called. He said you'd *have* to come, that it was the only way you could show the world that you weren't part of my brother's crimes. But I won't allow you to use me."

"You know that you have two grandsons?"

Margarethe von Behncke nodded. "I hope that one day your wife will bring them to visit me."

"You don't understand," Lloyd Bauer said—and the anguish in his voice was genuine. *"They never gave me a choice!"*

"I would have accepted that if you'd called me on Monday, as soon as you learned who you really were. Instead you abandoned four innocent people to the beasts. Roy Hammil said he doubts you'll even be charged, that no one can legally prove you knew what would happen to the Hammils and Langston Fellows and the old woman if you failed to contact the police. But I'll take no part in making your escape from justice easier."

"I had no choice even then," Lloyd Bauer said bitterly.

After the houseman showed Lloyd out, Margarethe von Behncke allowed the trembling she had suppressed to finally take over her body. She managed to push herself to a front window and watched her son drive off, probably on his way to the airport—and, eventually, to join the other refugees at Warlord's Hill.

Grief returned, a deeper, more profound grief than she had felt the first time Theo was lost to her.

At a few minutes past noon, Terry Hammil said good-bye to Nora Bauer on the mansion steps. "I'm sorry," the congressman's wife said, reaching out to gently touch the other woman's bruised face. "I've already said that, haven't I? Too often?"

"What will you do now?" Terry asked.

"Look after Lloyd and the children, go on pretending he's really not what I know him to be."

"You'll *stay* with him?"

An ironic smile touched Nora's thin lips. "I have to. I realize you don't understand."

"I *can't* understand," Terry admitted.

"Actually, things may grow better now. We'll leave this awful place, Lloyd will resign from Congress and . . . well, they'll be better." Nora hesitated, her smile returning. "I'm not sure I believe it either."

It was Terry's second farewell that day. Earlier, while Roy was off the estate making a phone call, a state trooper had brought Eric Dorn to the mansion. Until permanent shelter could be found, the survivors of Bremen had been quartered in estate outbuildings. After thanking the boy for helping to save their lives, Terry had gripped both his hands. "I once saw my whole world crumble, Eric," said Terry. "And, until yesterday, I wasn't sure I could survive the loss. Roy and I will do everything in our power to make sure you survive yours." He hadn't replied, but his limp fingers had tightened slightly around her own.

"Time to shove off," Roy called from the drive, where he had just finished cramming suitcases into the Jaguar's trunk. The Hammils' luggage and other possessions had been found a few hours earlier, neatly stacked next to the estate incinerator.

"Where will we go, Roy?" Terry asked as they drove away from the mansion. Except for a black, hazy cloud over the now-contained fire, the sky was clear.

"A motel for the first few days," he said. "It's not really over yet, honey. There'll be more statements to sign, inquests, hopefully Grand Jury testimony on a conspiracy to commit murder charge against Lloyd Bauer."

"He's already been destroyed. I saw it in Nora's eyes," Terry said quietly. "Could we stop in Chatsworth for a second? I have a letter to mail—to Leah Golding."

They drove through the broken gates of Warlord's Hill, past clamoring TV film crews and newspaper reporters herded behind a State Police barricade. Within minutes the Hammils were enclosed by the deep stillness of the Pine Barrens.

About the Author

George Fox is a screenwriter and the author of two novels. He lives in southern California with his wife and daughter.